Amish Knit &

Stitch Circle

COMPLETE SERIES

Smicksburg Tales 4

Karen Anna Vogel

Lamb Books

Contact the author on Facebook at:
www.facebook.com/VogelReaders
Learn more the author at: www.karenannavogel.com
Visit her blog, Amish Crossings, at
www.karenannavogel.blogspot.com

Dedication

To Tim, my husband of thirty-four years, for his patience, support, encouragement and help with storylines.

You are my leaning post

Maggie (MJ) a reader so inspirational she made her way into this novel

.

TABLE OF CONTENTS

How Pennsylvania Dutch overflows into

Western Pennsylvanian slang.

"To be" or not to be, that is the question. Folks in Western PA, along with local Amish do not use "to be". It's not "The car needs *to be* washed." We simply say, "The car needs washed." This is only one example. This book is full of similar "grammar errors" but tries to be authentic to how people talk in our "neck of the woods."

Amish – English Dictionary

Ach – oh
Ausband – Amish Song book or hymnal
Boppli – baby
Bruder – brother
Daed - dad
Danki – thank you
Dawdyhaus – grandparent's house
Furhoodled – Mixed up in the head
Gmay - community
Gut – good
Jah - yes
Kapp- cap; Amish women's head covering
Kinner – children
Nee- no
Mamm – mom
Oma – grandma
Opa –grandfather
Ordnung – order; set of unwritten rules
Wunderbar – wonderful
Yinz – "You all" or "you two". Only spoken in Western Pennsylvania, simply called *Pittsburghese*.

EPISODE 1

A Knot

Granny shielded her eyes from the blaring sun. Was it ten o'clock already? She arched her back and soon Jeb was by her side, hand on her shoulder, massaging the knots.

"*Danki*, Jeb. All this planting makes me realize how old I am."

"Deborah, I'm older, *jah*?"

She took a handkerchief from her apron and wiped her forehead. "Mighty hot for May."

"End of May, almost June. And you're still tuckered out from Colleen's wedding."

Granny couldn't help but smile when thinking of Colleen standing beside Hezekiah's wheelchair as they exchanged vows. But he was walking now, a miracle of sorts it seemed. But his speech was impaired. "Jeb, who's helping Hezekiah plant?"

"Many hands make light work." He took off his straw hat and fanned himself with it. "Several men told me they'd be going over to help."

"All Amish?"

"*Jah*, all Amish. Who else?"

1

Granny fidgeted with the hand spade. "Are any single?"

"Deborah…no matchmaking. It's the *gut* Lord's job."

Poking him in the side with her elbow, she laughed. "*Jah*, I know. But Lottie needs a husband. I told her I'd help."

A groan from deep within Jeb seemed to echo off the hillside. "Who do you have in mind?"

"Well, Lottie's a bookworm and sewer, although she talks a mile a minute. So, deep down she's reserved. I can't say what kind of man she needs. But she's from Millersburg and like us, more progressive in our thinking."

"We still cut our own ice for the iceboxes. Folks in Troutville think we're backwards."

Buggy wheels grinding on the gravel driveway and a baby crying made Granny's heart leap. She turned to see Fannie and Mona with baby Anna. Granny waved vigorously, her arms aching to hold the *wee* little girl.

Mona brought the horse to a stop.

"*Mamm*, you did *gut*," Fannie said.

"*Jah*, you're fears of driving are vanishing?" Jeb asked Mona.

Mona glanced over at her daughter and then a warm, deep smile lightened her face. "Fannie makes me drive while she holds Anna. But my agoraphobia, or whatever that evil dread was that kept me cooped up, is getting better."

Fannie handed Granny little Anna and got out of the buggy. "*Mamm* needs to recondition her mind, like I did." She pointed to her *mamm*. "God has not given you a spirit of fear but of peace, love and a sound mind."

Mona chewed her lower lip and nodded. "I'm trying."

"We're doing more than 'try,' *jah*? Tell them our news."

Granny, puzzled, looked up at Jeb to see if he knew about any news. He shrugged his shoulders and appeared as baffled as she was. There was no change in Mona's life, her biggest leap out of her mundane existence was to attend knitting circle. And how much she learned from knitting and reading classics, especially *Black Beauty*, her childhood abuse coming to her memory. What ugly emotions surfaced in Fannie when she realized her *mamm* wasn't at all like Mrs. March in *Little Women*, or Marilla in *Anne of Green Gables*. But like a poison extracted out of a body, they'd released their bitterness and were now building a whole new foundation to their relationship.

"We're going on a trip to New York," Mona said in a monotone. "Visiting Ella."

Fannie put one hand on her heart. "I've missed Ella something fierce and she invited us to stay at their farm in East Otto for as long as we like. Her *boppli's* due next month and we want to help."

Jeb scratched his head. "How about Freeman?" Jeb interrupted. "Who'll care for his cows?"

"Freeman will. He's not going."

Jeb planted clenched fists on his hips and Granny shot a prayer up for him to calm down.

"Who's driving you? A man I hope."

Fannie glanced at her *mamm*, at Granny and then met Jeb's turquoise eyes. "We're taking the train. Just *Mamm* and me and Anna."

Jeb clucked his tongue. "By yourselves with no men? And such a small group. It's not safe."

Fear was evident on Mona's face. "*See Fannie*. It's not safe. My fears aren't *furhoodled*."

"*Jah*, they are," Granny blurted. "Lots of Amish ride the train." She nestled Anna in one arm and grabbed Jeb's hand, giving it a knowing squeeze that meant, *please hush up.* "Fears need to be met and conquered. What if Moses stayed on Mount Sinai when God said to go into Egypt and free my people out of slavery?

Jeb started to speak but Granny nudged him with her hip. "Fear's a torment, the Good Book says, and Mona, I think what you're doing is brave and *gut*."

Another groan from Jeb increased the rising tension. "Anyone from Troutville on that train ride?"

"Maybe," Fannie said. "Not sure. Why?"

"They have cell phones now, of all things. Use them for business only but I say it's wrong. Have to admit, though, it'd come in handy if you had an emergency."

Fannie gawked. "Cell phones? With pictures?"

"I hope not," Granny said. "It's wise to ban *any* phone unless hooked into a phone shanty with a cord ever since..." she stopped short, not wanting to bring up the past. The incident about Luke looking at girly pictures when working for the English, almost losing Ruth in the mix. Granny's heart tightened just thinking about what happened two years ago. She looked up at the cotton-like clouds against a blue sky. *Danki, Lord that you intervened and saved poor Luke from the lust of the eye and flesh. And bless him as he and Ruth raise a new boppli with Down Syndrome.*

"Granny, you alright?" Fannie asked, eyes wide. "Let me take Anna."

Pulling the *boppli* closer, Granny objected. "I'm fine. Just deep in thought."

"About knitting circle?" Fannie shifted. "*Mamm* and I won't be able to come for a month or so. All the packing and getting things ready and all."

"They won't know we're gone," Mona said with a surprising lilt in her voice. "That Lottie will keep the chatter going non-stop."

Granny, shocked that humor peeked out of Mona's usual serious nature, laughed all the more. "*Jah*, she can talk a tail-end off a horse."

"A what?" Jeb squinted at Granny like she was off in the head.

"It's a line from *Anne of Green Gables*," Fannie offered. "And it fits Lottie perfectly."

~*~

Suzy watched animated Marge bobble around her little yarn shop, not able to make her yarn choice for a summer scarf. "You'd look good in pink. It's anti-aging," Suzy chirped.

"Anti-aging? I'm in my thirties… not fifties," Marge flashed a teasing grin. "I think I'll go for black, since I can still wear it without looking dead."

Suzy readjusted her black necklace. "Fifty-something isn't old, and black is timeless."

Marge turned and smirked. "And I'm crocheting this scarf."

"I surrender. Even though I know knitting is more…sophisticated than crocheting. Have it your way."

Marge grabbed light pink yarn and plopped herself in the chair near Suzy's desk. "I'm as sophisticated as they get, living in the *dawdyhaus* again…"

"But this time you have electricity, so what's the problem?"

"Oh, no problem, really. It's just that Joe wants farm animals again, and we all know how that turned out last time."

"You can't name animals like pets."

"Tell Joe that."

"You're glad to be living in Smicksburg again, right? I mean, you and Joe have some settling in to do, but you don't regret taking on your new job."

"Heavens, no," Marge quipped. "The farmhouse is freshly painted and electric and plumbing is in."

Suzy still was amazed at all the changes that took place in their little town, all due to women knitting and reading classic books. The need to care for orphans, or foster kids with no chance of returning to their parents, had the town in a buzz. Some afraid the boys would be hooligans, others thinking of adoption for the first time. "You have an important job, Marge, being like a house mom to the boys –"

"Only three. It's easy." Marge stared at the pink yarn on the desk. "I don't know why I'm so emotional."

"Tired from the wedding maybe? Want some tea?"

"I sure would. Something that calms the nerves, caffeine-free."

Suzy got up to enter the back room where she had a table set up for tea. She and Colleen had started their 'Jane Austen Teas' and she missed the girl sorely. But Colleen had a new husband who was recovering from a horrible accident and she was needed at home. Before Suzy made it to the back Dutch door, the bell at the front of the store jingled and she heard Janice entering, looking rather stoic. "What's wrong?"

"What? Nothing's wrong." Janice said hello to Marge and then started to peruse the bargain basket of yarn. "No, I'm fine. How are you two?"

Suzy knew her pastor's wife well. When Janice said everything was 'just fine' with no smile, she was upset. "Spill the beans, Janice."

"What beans?" Janice asked, intensely eyeing yarn.

"Ya, Janice," Marge said. "You look pale."

Janice rolled her eyes. "Now that's a new one. How can a woman of color look pale?"

Suzy put a hand up. "I know my colors and your shade has changed. You're lighter, trust me."

Janice mumbled something Suzy couldn't make out.

"Say what?" Suzy asked.

"It's Wednesday. You'll find out tonight at Bible Study. And bring a fan so you don't faint."

Marge looked back at Suzy, confusion written on her face and mouthed out the words *'fan'* and *'faint.'* Her eyes begged Suzy to ask Janice what was wrong. Obviously, Janice was hiding something.

"Want some tea in the back room?

"Not in a *Jane Austeny* mood," Janice snapped and then buried her face in the navy blue yarn she was holding. Her thin body shook as she sobbed.

Suzy had seen these meltdowns before....in herself. Janice had only a few, so this was serious. She ran around the desk and put a hand on Janice's shoulder. "Are you sick?"

"Sick of being a pastor's wife," Janice growled, her lips quivering. "Sometimes the sacrifice is too much."

Suzy told her the yarn she was holding was free, and took her hand and led her back to the tea room. Marge followed, close on Janice's heels.

Suzy put the tea kettle on. "I say you need chamomile for the nerves. What on earth is wrong?"

"I'm a pastor's wife and I'm not supposed to be telling anyone, another cross I bear. *Confidentiality.*"

"But it's being announced at church tonight, so we'll know anyhow," Marge reasoned. "We can pray for you..."

Janice sat erect and took a cleansing breath. "Jerry, as you know, got his doctorate and can now teach at a college... down South. An interim pastor will take over until we get back."

"What?" Suzy cried. "You're moving? Jerry said he was settled in Smicksburg. He feels called to preach in rural areas, right?"

Janice snarled. "Well, once the Baptist board heard about our firm plans for the boy's home, they felt that maybe someone young could relate. A thirty year old young man, to be precise."

"But that's age discrimination." Suzy took a seat, feeling like her legs might give out. "And we have an independent Baptist church."

"But Jerry's in a huge ministerial and he said there's safety in a multitude of counsels."

"Look at Jeb Weaver!" Marge cried. "He's in his seventies and the kids flock to him for advice."

"The Amish respect the elderly, not putting them out to pasture," Janice raised a shaking fist. "As I age, I want to be Amish."

Suzy heard the tea whistle, the most soothing sound on the planet. *Help Janice, Lord*, she prayed as she poured hot water into three teacups and slipped in bags of chamomile tea. They *all* needed it now. Handing a cup to each woman, Suzy took a seat. "So, this is temporary if the pastor is an interim, right? He's a fill-in, so no one's being hired, right?"

Janice nodded. "Jerry wants to take some summer classes, help assist in a few, and see if he fits in, if there's that peace that God said will lead us."

"And this young kid will run the church all summer?" Marge asked. "What about Arbor Creek and the boys?"

"He'll help with the boys and we all know what flashy ideas a young pastor has," Janice snapped. "I say give me that old time religion, it's good enough for me. He'll probably have a rock band for worship, a smoke machine and disco ball hung in the church."

Marge stifled a laugh. "Disco ball? Janice, if I was a gambling woman, I'd bet that the folks of Smicksburg don't want this new modern worship, even though I like it myself."

"What are you saying?" Suzy asked. "That our hymns aren't good enough? Ginny plays the guitar to upbeat music."

Marge took a sip of tea. "We use overhead projectors and felt boards in Sunday school. Sometimes change is good."

Janice's featured softened. "You know what, Marge, you're right. Maybe some fresh eyes on the church would be good." Her teacup shook in her hand. "But what if Jerry likes teaching and doesn't miss Smicksburg?"

"I'm going to pray he hates teaching," Suzy said, and then covered her mouth, shocking herself that she said that out loud.

Janice's eyes misted. "I'm glad you said that."

"Why?"

"It's nice to be needed… missed." Tears spilled down her cheeks. "I'm going to miss this little town."

Suzy pursed her lips, forbidding tears to fall. "Fears of yesterday and regrets of tomorrow are twin thieves, robbing us of today… or something like that. An Amish proverb I like. We'll take this one day at a time." She grabbed Janice and Marge's hands. "Let's pray God gives us all strength."

"Pray for Granny, too. I won't be at her summer knitting circle and she lives for that thing."

The little bell on the door jingled again and soon Lottie skipped into the back room, her light mint green dress, white apron and vivid blue eyes making her look like a Victorian doll, Suzy thought. "Well, you look as fresh as spring," Suzy teased.

Karen Anna Vogel

Lottie was beaming, nodding at Janice and then Marge. "I was over at the Sampler and met the most interesting person," she said, her cheeks crimson now. "He's new in town, just like me."

"Is he Amish?" Suzy asked, afraid of what she'd hear.

"No. He just moved here. Really loves the small town feel, but said he felt even better after meeting me."

Janice cleared her throat loudly. "Sounds like a pick-up line. What's his name?"

"Phil. I forget his last name." Lottie suddenly appeared to be startled, like a deer in headlights, having given out too much information. "It's just nice to meet someone who's new in town and likes books as much as me. He's over at Serenity Book Nook now." She scurried over to the clipboard and scanned Suzy's 'to do' list. After a few seconds, she said good-bye to Janice and Marge and went to work in the front room.

Suzy shot one eyebrow up. "She met a good-looking *Englisher*. Hope she has better sense."

"If Granny has her way, Lottie will be married to a good Amish man of fortune, in need of a wife," Marge giggled. She quickly put a hand up. "I'm sorry. Quotes from all those books we read all winter keep popping up as I speak."

Suzy heard what Marge said and gave a polite smile, but Lottie was an awfully pretty girl. A strawberry blonde with deep blue eyes, and a complexion like a model in a Dove soap commercial. Coming from Ohio, and a more liberal settlement, would she be too open-minded, letting an *Englisher* into her affections?

~*~

Maryann flung off excess water from a tea towel and hung it up to dry on her clothes line. She took a deep breath, taking in the smells of late May, especially the lilacs. Michael, her dear husband, had dug a full grown bush off the Smith's property before they lost it to the bank. The family sold all their shrubbery, exclaiming that the state didn't own trees, flowers and bushes... *yet.*

She tucked a brown wisp of hair back into her white prayer *kapp.* She was still in love after having a brood of *kinner.* And she was glad to be alive, having battled breast cancer a year and a half ago. *Michael dug up that bush late winter, in March, when I was at my lowest.* How did she miss the connection? Most likely he'd gotten the idea from Jeb Weaver who planted roses for Granny thirty-some years ago after her miscarriage. Now, Granny had red roses climbing up her wraparound porch, Jeb having a green thumb to separate the root balls and transplanting them, erecting more trellis as he went along.

I'll make Michael's favorite meal tonight, she decided.

"*Mamm,* do you have a minute?"

Becca, her oldest at sixteen, had been asking that question all morning. She handed Becca a dripping towel. "Sure, I have time. Planting time is always so busy, laundry gets backed up."

Becca flung water from the towel. "*Mamm,* it's important. May take more than a minute."

"*Jah,* I have time to have a real talk," Maryann said, her heart twisting since Becca usually had a cheerful disposition and her tone screamed that she was anxious about something.

"*Mamm,* what do you think of Gilbert?"

Maryann aptly attached two clothespins to the line and reached down to get her glass of ice water. *This was going to be a talk to remember.* Feeling perspiration form on her upper lip, she took a swig. "I think Gilbert's a nice boy."

"*Man. Mamm*, he's a *man*. And I'm sixteen and a woman. We've known each other since birth and know we're the ones for each other."

Maryann couldn't help but gawk at her daughter. "Marriage? You're too young."

"You married *Daed* young."

"Not sixteen, for sure and certain."

"For courting, which will lead to marriage…"

"Did he ask you to court?" Maryann wanted to freeze time, life being too liquid, always moving like a roaring river. *Becca was twelve not long ago.*

Becca took her *mamm's* hand. "I'm not that little brown-eyed girl anymore."

"You still have brown eyes."

"But my vision's changed. I see from a woman's eyes now."

Maryann embraced her daughter and held her a little too tightly. "I understand. You have feelings and it's natural to want to wed someday, but take it slow." She pulled Becca away and held her at arm's length. "And watch his behavior. Right is right, no getting around it. White lies don't exist and how he reacts is the real Gilbert."

Becca's eyes were two orbs, fixed in place, until they rocketed up.

"Don't roll your eyes like the English," Maryann chastened.

"*Mamm*, have you heard something through the grapevine that Gilbert tells lies?"

"*Nee*, just saying don't make any excuses for poor behavior, is all. When you think you're in love, you tend to see what you want to see… and ignore bad qualities."

1. Becca's eyes softened. "Do you like Gilbert?"
2. "I do. *Jah*, I do. Maybe too much."
3. "How so?"

"If you were courting one of the Yoder boys in Trader City, we'd be inspecting him and testing his character to no end. But Gilbert's like my son."

Becca shivered animatedly. "That's an odd thought," she said with a laugh.

Maryann joined in, adding that she changed Gilbert's diapers right alongside her when she babysat.

"I'm glad we talked," Becca said. "I feel better."

"We haven't talked more than a few minutes."

"Well, it was weighing heavy on me, keeping secrets."

"Secrets?"

"Gilbert took me home from a Singing twice."

Maryann winced. She'd imagined that when Becca came home from her first Singing, they'd talk all about it, a new tighter bond forming. But it appeared that bonds were loosening as her *kinner* aged and emptiness filled her.

She gulped the lump in her throat. "Has anyone milked the goats yet?"

"What?"

"With planting and all, your *daed* in the fields, you best check."

Becca tilted her head. "*Mamm,* you all right?"

Maryann quickly nodded and Becca headed towards the goat pens. When out of sight, Maryann let the tears freely flow. Why she was crying, she didn't even know. But Granny said tears cleansed a body and soul.

~*~

Lizzie grabbed the platter of cold cuts off the counter and placed them on the table. How nice it was being a part of the Weaver family over the past year. Memories of her wedding swirled in her mind. She gazed at Roman, her sweetheart since a teen, and though many obstacles and heartaches fractured their love, they came together again, in their thirties.

Blonde haired and blue eyed Jenny, now eight, stomped away from her last Memorial Day Weekend, insisting she plant the garden with her *oma*. Now they had a real bond, since Jenny opened her dear heart to a new *mamm*. The twins, Millie and Tillie, hadn't remembered their *mamm*, and had instantly vied for Lizzie's attention, their chestnut colored eyes always accepting, and for that, Lizzie was grateful. *Accepting chestnut eyes, just like Romans...*

Jenny was the image of Abigail, Roman's first wife. She'd given him three daughters, and for that reason Lizzie felt inadequate, comparing herself to Abigail at times. Lizzie knew Roman loved her, telling her she was 'the apple of his eye,' but she was obviously infertile and why she felt shame, she didn't know.

"*Oma*, are you going to take pies over to the boys, too?" Jenny asked Granny.

"*Jah*, for sure. But they eat more, so maybe will have to make twice as many."

"Boys can eat like the pigs," Millie said, chuckling.

Roman lifted a finger in her direction, the signal to hush her mouth. Words not uplifting were not spoken around the table.

"Deborah," Jeb said evenly. "You make pies for the girls at Forget-Me-Not Manor. Isn't that enough?"

"Come again?" Granny prodded.

"*Ach*, you know how I want you to slow down a bit. And some of those boys are men, being sixteen. I read the papers."

"And?" Granny inquired, one eyebrow up.

"Some can be mean. Maybe they're in foster homes because they didn't honor their parents."

Lizzie didn't want to argue with her father-in-law, but had to speak up. "*Daed*, the boys were screened, *jah*? They were abused, not unruly. They need our love and protection."

Jeb pulled at his long gray beard and sipped some homemade root beer. "Well, time will tell. I see an attitude in Charles I don't like."

"Charles?" Lizzie gasped. "He's so tenderhearted."

"Really? Seems lazy to me."

Granny swatted Jeb's arm. "He's finding his footing. Jonas is over there now visiting him."

Jeb cocked his head back, looking dumbfounded. "How'd Jonas get there? In his wheelchair?"

"I drove him over, *Daed*," Roman said. "Charles is the best thing for Jonas. He's a *gut* boy."

"*Man*, I'd say," Jeb said, and then waved his hand in the air in surrender.

Lizzie squeezed Roman's hand and nestled a little closer to him on the bench. She'd only told Marge her desires about Charles. Her *daed*, Jonas, was like a grandfather. Couldn't Roman be like a *daed* in time? Not for the work around the farm and rocker shop, but a hunting and fishing partner. Someone Roman could do his 'man cave' things with, as Marge put it. *Ach*, they could fish at Jeb's fishing hole or even go down to Keystone Lake. "Of course," she said.

4. "Of course what?" Tillie asked with a shy smile.

5. "*Ach*, speaking out loud. Sorry."

6. "Tell us," Granny insisted.

"How about the boy's fish at Keystone Lake? There's a place to rent boats."

"You'll have to ask Jerry and Janice," Granny advised. "The English sue, from what Janice was telling me. So, everything they do with those boys increase their costs, due to insurance payments."

"How sad," Lizzie said. "But if one of the boys got hurt, who would sue, since they have no kin?"

Jeb groaned. "The English can complicate something as simple as a fishing trip. What if a boy would drown? The state would come in and investigate and maybe try to shut Arbor Creek down. It's very sad."

"What if Charles was adopted into an Amish family?" As soon as Lizzie said this, she chided herself. It would open a can of worms, questions that could unlock her secret wish to adopt Charles. She looked around the table, Jeb's fork suspended in mid-air, frozen. Lizzie felt heat rise into her cheeks. *Jah, Lizzie, you're becoming as rash in your speech as your English friend Marge. Need to hold your tongue.*

~*~

Jonas wanted to stand up and applaud the God who put these three boys into his life, but his knee braces, due to MS, made it painful, so he just remained in his chair that faced the boys. Memories of him having Amish camp with the Baptist church last summer lifted his mood higher. To think that the English would pay to ask a 'real' Amish person questions. *Jah*, the Amish were such a curiosity to the world, since they never adopted the modern lifestyle, which seemed to spell sadness and stress on all the boys' faced in front of him.

"Charles, can you pass out the hoagies Lizzie made?"

Charles, now standing tall, still dressed in lots of black, but not in an eerie Gothic way. No, Charles was taken from his abusive home after running away from it, hitchhiking up to Smicksburg. How shocked Jonas was that the letters they'd exchanged had affected Charles to the point of realizing he deserved to be treated like a human being.

Jonas stiffly placed a napkin on his lap and took a sandwich from Charles. "*Danki.*"

"Need help?" Charles leaned down and whispered in his ear.

"I'm right as rain. No problems at all."

After a few bites, Jonas eyed each boy, noticing hollowness in their eyes. Were they in shock to be in foster care or were they depressed? "I see you've all met?"

The oldest one, being sixteen, slightly nodded. "Yep. Live in the same house."

Jonas squinted at the toad-haired boy. "I'm getting old. What's your name again?"

"Denny. Denny Boles."

Jonas nodded and looked at the other boy, brown curly hair. "And you are?"

"Brian. Brain Adams."

He put his head down sheepishly and Jonas shot a prayer up to comfort this boy, the youngest at twelve. "So, how do you like living out in the sticks?"

"The sticks?" Denny challenged with a chortle.

"The country," Jonas added. "Some call it the sticks and I say the more land a man has around him, the better. But since you boys all came from the city, I wonder what you think of Smicksburg."

"Boring," Denny exclaimed. "I've heard of cow tipping, and I believe it now."

"What?" Jonas didn't know if Denny was being obstinate or just needed someone to listen.

"*Cow tipping.* I saw it on TV. Kids in the country being so bored they go tip a cow over."

"Well, can't say I've heard of such a thing. Cows are gentle creatures, unless you take the shortcut over to the Weaver farm."

"Why?" Brian asked.

Jonas knew the Weaver's lone cow was as gentle as their sheep, but needed to abide by Jeb's rule: *the boys can't use the path to my house.* "Well, that cow can charge. Best stay off the path to the Weavers. Jeb doesn't want anyone to upset Old Bull."

"*Old Bull?*" Brian blurted. "Is it a bull then? Will it charge at anything red?"

Jonas saw the mirth in Charles eyes, the boy knowing Old Bull. "Well, it's his name, *jah?*"

"Does it have big horns?" Denny asked, eyes wide.

"Just stay off the path and you'll be safe, is all I'm saying." Jonas said, guilt starting to creep in. "He's a docile creature, really, unless provoked."

"What's docile mean?" Brian asked.

"Tame and gentle-like." Jonas shifted in his chair. "Now, what would be some things you boys would like to do up here in the sticks?"

"Ride horses," Charles said. "I want to drive an Amish buggy into town."

Jonas winked. "I think I know that, you having mentioned it a hundred times. How about you Brian? You like horses, too?"

"Never been on one."

"Me neither," Denny added. "Riding a horse would be cool."

"What do you like to do, Jonas?" Charles asked. "We can learn stuff from you."

"He's crippled," Denny said wryly.

Charles darted up, wheeling a fist over Denny's head. "Shut up."

"What's wrong with you, *Charlotte?* You don't scare me."

"You should be," Charles huffed, "and stop calling me Charlotte."

"Whatever. Chill out."

Charles lowered his fist, to Jonas' relief. "I've known Charles since last summer. We were pen pals."

At that, Denny started to chuckled until he doubled over, making Charles turn completely red in the face.

"What's so funny?" Jonas asked, bewildered.

"Pansy boy wrote you letters, like a girl?"

"Like a man," Jonas shouted, surprising himself. "And he got his stepdad some help in the bargain." He pointed a crooked finger at Denny. "What makes you such a man?"

Denny shrugged his shoulders. "I work out and have muscles. People look up to me, since I'm tall, too. And they fear me."

Jonas shook his head. "That's a bully in my book."

Denny looked like he was just punched in the face. He lowered his head and mumbled something.

"What did you say?" Jonas prodded.

"Nothing."

"Well," Jonas said, "let's get back to what you boys would like to do this summer. How about fishing in Weaver's fishing hole. It's stocked with fish." Jonas leaned forward as if relaying top secret information. "Jeb needs to stalk his own pond because he can't catch a fish on the lake to save his life."

"What lake?" Brian was quick to ask.

"Keystone Lake. Mighty deep and miles long. Not far from here."

"Can we go?" Brian asked, eyes filled with wonder.

Jonas scrunched his lips to one side. He knew he'd have to ask the Baptist first, due to all kinds of red tape. "I'll do my best to make it happen."

Denny remained silent but his countenance became calmer and more respectful. Jonas wondered if he'd embarrassed the boy, but had to call out, and then make a report to give to the Baptists, any unbecoming behavior. Jonas knew how Charles felt, being bullied due to his own small stature, and deep down believed he got defensive. And having a visible handicap had always made fodder for jokes and snide remarks among the English. Jonas hardly left the small town of Smicksburg due to it, he had to admit.

Lord, why am I being so overly circumspect? Have you brought these boys into my life to help me?

~*~

Marge's heart lifted as she made her way into the white clapboard church that night. Memories flooded her as she remembered Joe being so resistant last summer to step foot into a church. As she followed him into their regular pew, she marveled that last summer, he went from atheist to believer. So much good had happened with Jerry as their pastor and Janice as the ever-giving pastor's wife. *How could Jerry think of leaving?*

A young man sat in the front row and as people tended to mingle before Jerry started teaching, she felt his awkwardness and went up a few rows to greet him. "Are you a visitor?"

A dazzling smile brightened up his handsome face. "I'm Phil Darby, the visiting pastor.

Marge gazed, dumbstruck as this man shook her hand. His last name was *Darby*? Sounded like Darcy and he was everything she imagined Jane Austen's Mr. Darcy to be: *drop dead gorgeous with puppy dog eyes like Collin Firth*....only with blond hair.

"And your name is?" he asked, expectantly.

"M-Marge. Nice to meet you. Janice told me all about you," she blurted.

His shaggy brows shot up. "Does anyone else know about me coming? Jerry suspected no one knew."

"Well, ah, well, we knitting ladies talk," Marge struggled to say. "Janice is a *wunderbar gut* friend."

"A wonder bar… what?"

Marge pursed her lips. "Oops. I live among the Amish. My best friend Lizzie is Amish, and so I talk like her sometimes." She was panting now. "Have you met any of the Amish? Go to the Country Junction and you'll be sure to meet some."

"Welcome. Everyone take their seats," Jerry boomed in his normal loud voice.

Marge did a little curtsey and shook Phil's hand and ran back to sit by Joe.

Joe stared through her. "Marge, do you still love me?"

"What?" she whispered.

"You're so flustered; you acted like a schoolgirl around that man. Who is he?"

Marge took her notepad and started to fan her face. "The new pastor I was telling you about."

"You were flirting," he said, leaning closer to her. "I'm hurt."

Marge's eyes bugged out. "*Flirt?* Oh, honey, no. I was flustered. I didn't know that…"

"What?"

"We had Mr. Darcy as a new pastor. I mean Darby. Darby, not Mr. Darcy like Collin Firth."

To Marge's shock, Joe started to laugh. "How many times have you put that movie on? I know I'm not a 'Mr. Darcy' Hollywood type."

Marge slid her arm through Joe's. "He's not my type anyhow." She leaned her head on his shoulder, thankful that she had a soul mate who knew her through and through, accepting her many quirks.

~*~

After the service, young single women hovered around Phil Darby like bees around a hive. Suzy pulled Marge by the hand, clearly annoyed. "Looks like Casanova's come to Smicksburg."

Marge nodded. "All these women vying for his attention, as if he were Mr. Darcy, not Darby."

"What?" Suzy asked, her head shaking.

"His name is Darby. Sounds like Darcy."

"I didn't notice," Suzy said, pulling Marge further, into a corner. Suzy's heart was about to break, Jerry making the announcement about leaving for a 'spell,' not saying it was just for the summer, and that 'young blood' was what Arbor Creek needed made Suzy feel nauseated. Why did *young* always mean *wise* in the English culture? The Amish saw so many things in reverse.

She handed Marge a clipboard. "Ginny's taking on lots of Janice's jobs and now I'm in charge of visiting shut-ins. Pick a name."

"How often do I have to visit?"

"Only once a week, and they're all local." Suzy grabbed the clipboard back and read out loud: "*MJ. Wants to meet an Amish woman to learn how to bake.* I think you should visit this woman along with Granny."

"Why Granny? How about Lizzie? I'd kill two birds with one stone. Visit a shut-in and see my best friend."

Suzy tapped the clipboard with a pen. "Well, I guess you could ask Lizzie, but is she as good a baker as Granny?"

Marge shook her head. "No one bakes like Granny. I'll ask her, but she's, you know, getting pretty old."

"Only seventy-one and has more energy than me," Suzy quipped. Laughter erupted from Phil Darby and again, Suzy felt blood rush to her face. "Honestly, I don't know what to make of that man. Seems like a show-off."

"I think he's fine," Marge said. "I mean fine as in okay for the church, not fine as in the drop dead gorgeous kind of fine."

Suzy narrowed her eyes, feeling like a hawk wanting to pounce on prey. "If Jerry leaves for good, I am too."

"What?"

"I'm not going to have someone who's only thirty, wet behind the ears, be my pastor. I need someone seasoned... like Jerry."

Marge huffed. "Getting set in your ways. Change can be good. And he seems like someone from a different era, really. Like a Jimmy Stewart, Bing Crosby type of guy."

"A movie star. *Exactly*. He's charming enough." Suzy held her middle and shivered, even though it was a warm May night. "And I'm not afraid of change."

"Crochet then," Marge challenged.

"No, I don't like the look of it. Too lacey."

Marge snapped her fingers. "See, you're stuck in your ways. Some crochet patterns have a tight weave; it looks like a cable knit."

Suzy held up a hand. "I knit—"

"Do you ladies need a ride home?" Phil Darby interrupted. "It's starting to rain."

"My husband drove. We live three miles away," Marge said hastily.

"I can walk," Suzy said, evenly.

Phil pat Suzy's shoulder. "It's not a problem."

"I have an umbrella and I walk a lot."

Phil shifted nervously, but a smile continued to beam from his face. "I'm going to need help knowing what really needs done in this church. Jerry and Janice suggested I talk to you. I don't want to let them down."

Suzy studied Phil's face. Did she see humility and a servant's heart? "Sure, we can help," she found herself saying.

~*~

The next morning, Granny found herself in Marge's red sports car, headed over to help a shut-in. Jeb's words of admonition ran through her mind. *You bite off more than you can chew. You have knitting circle this afternoon.* Yes, she did, but she made shortcake last night when the misty rain cooled the house, and Lizzie and the girls picked bowls of strawberries from their patch. *My grandkinner hulled and sliced a bucket-full; bless their hearts,* Granny thought. Jeb was just over-protective of her, or else he meant it when he called her an 'old woman.'

They pulled into a yellow Cape Cod style house. "Looks like the Three Bears live here," Marge exclaimed. "So cozy."

"Three bears?" Granny asked. "If three bears live around here, you'd see signs. Bark scratched off trees –"

"Granny, it's a book about talking bears. And their house is charming."

Talking bears. How ridiculous, Granny thought. "So, tell me, why is this lady a shut in?"

"Oh, we don't ask unless they tell us. We just visit."

"Then how do you know how to help them?"

"Most shut-ins are lonely. We give them friendship, no strings attached."

Granny sighed. "So, the English need friends. That's sad."

"Granny, not everyone lives in a cloistered community like the Amish, having the same friends since childhood. I'm thirty-something and just found my best friend in Lizzie."

Granny nodded, agreeing to disagree with Marge. She knew the Amish ways were better than the English, finding it pitiful how there was no safety net, not even for children, hence the need for foster homes. The Amish took in each other's *kinner*, not strangers.

The two walked up the cobble-stone walkway to the house, and Marge kept chattering on about the window boxes, charming white picket fence, just like something out of a fairytale.

When Marge knocked on the door, a tall man, middle-aged with grayish-white hair, extended a hand, shaking hands with them with a firm grip. "So nice to meet you, and MJ is thrilled. She already wants to make you pins."

Granny pointed to the safety pins that took the place of buttons on her dress. "I have enough pins, I'm thinking."

The man laughed robustly. "Well, these pins are a little different. Come on into the kitchen. MJ's having her coffee. I'm Andy, by the way."

As they followed him through the small living room into the kitchen, a woman with brown, chin-length hair and hazel eyes motioned for them to take a seat around her table. Her eyes lingered on Granny and then she exclaimed, "So you're my baking teacher!"

Granny nodded, unable to hide her delight. "I love to teach women how to bake pies, but I learned how to make fondant last winter."

"Fondant," MJ said wistfully. "I've seen the most gorgeous cakes on television done in fondant. Looks elegant." MJ turned to Marge. "I'm sorry to fall all over an Amish woman and ignore you. Now, what's your name?"

"Marge," she said and then motioned to Granny. "This is Deborah Weaver, but we all call her Granny."

"You're Granny? The woman with the knitting circle?"

"*Jah*. Are you surprised I knit?"

"No, surprised you knit with Amish and English. And I hear you make pies for Forget-Me-Not Manor." She clasped her hands. "It was a secret prayer of sorts, to have you come."

"How so?"

MJ's eyes misted. "Well, I heard you're as kind as they come, and seeing so few people, I don't have time for negativity."

Andy pulled up a chair next to Marge. "Honey, go ahead and tell them why you're homebound."

MJ took a deep breath. "I have Short Bowel Syndrome. I only have an inch of small intestine, so I spend three days a week getting hydrated."

"Through a drip IV?" Marge asked. "I'm a nurse..."

At this, MJ appeared to have courage to go into more detail. "You see, I had growths, polyps, in my large intestine. They were removed, but it seemed like two more grew where one was removed. My intestines became deformed, so long story short, about ten years ago, they removed my colon and intestines." She lowered her head. "I have to wear a bag."

Andy put an arm around her. "We're high school sweethearts and nothing can make me love this woman less. She has a hard time talking about wearing a bag."

MJ leaned her head on Andy's shoulder. "I've lost most friends, them not being able to handle my condition, but Andy took his wedding vows seriously. In sickness and in health..."

Granny's heart was stirred to see a couple appear to grow through adversity. "MJ, seems like you have what most women lack: a husband who cherishes you, *jah*?"

"Yes, and I'm grateful."

"Would you like to come to knitting circle today?" Granny asked. "Would be *wunderbar gut* for you."

"I have hydration therapy all day and my pain levels get so high, sometimes I just need my bed and pain killers."

"Not even for a few hours a week?" Granny prodded.

"Well, once a month, maybe. Right now, I'm going through a bad spell. My pain meds aren't doing the trick, but I have my pins to take my mind off the pain."

Andy gingerly got up and soon returned with a clear plastic container. He opened it up on the table revealing yarn in all colors, crocheting hooks, plastic canvas and miniature books.

Granny picked up a pin. "How nice. Who's this for?"

"One of my authors. I read a lot, being hooked to a machine so much, and I make pins for my favorite authors. Things in their books Andy finds miniatures for. This author likes to knit, like you, so Andy found a miniature ball of yarn and knitting needles. When my pain gets unbearable, I make more pins. Making others happy brings lots of joy to my life."

"And you should see the list of authors who write to MJ." A look of pride overcame Andy's face. "Some are New York Times best-selling authors."

Granny assumed that was a big deal, selling lots of books in New York. "Give and it shall be given unto you, pressed down and shaken over, *jah*?"

Andy nodded. "Lots of TV preachers use that as a ploy to give to their ministry, but from what I've learned from MJ, it's giving love and time that really changes people's lives."

"Andy, you're embarrassing me," MJ chided. "I make these pins to keep sane."

"And she crochets dresses for author's kids or grandchildren. Or, potholders and whatnot."

"Only authors?" Marge asked.

"No," MJ said. "I have lots of friends on Facebook who read a lot, being bookworms like me, and I make things for them."

"Sent out sixty-four packages last week," Andy boasted.

Granny came to visit a shut-in, expecting to be drained emotionally when she left. But this MJ was so inspirational, she wondered why *she* wasn't more of a giving person. Maybe she could embroider handkerchiefs and put them in the mail as gifts. Granny was just in awe over the love between two people who gave a whole new meaning to unconditional love.

~*~

Becca flashed a bright smile and waved to her *mamm* as she drove the buggy onto the road. Was it her imagination, but did her mamm look careworn? Her regular check-ups to the oncologist always brought good reports: cancer-free.

Becca snapped the rein to make the horse trot. *Lord, help my mamm. She's acting too anxious lately. And too weepy.* She inhaled, taking in the scents of lilacs mixed with damp earth, the smell of planting season. Flowers popping up, showing their faces again, and vegetable seeds being buried to provide food for the winter. How she relished the rhythm of life. But truth be told, she feared the sudden changes courting brought on. *Thoughts of marriage.* Knowing so many English girls, their only big concern was making good grades in high school to get into college, not marriage.

Becca guided the horse onto another back road as she made her way to Fannie and Melvin's dry goods store. As much as she tried to keep admiring spring in all its glory, her mind wandered to Gilbert. How could she tell him they couldn't get married anytime soon? He was two years older, and at eighteen, he felt he was a man. He also would inherit his parent's farm and could marry younger, *'like his daed did when he was eighteen.'*

A breeze cooled her face as heat rose into her cheeks, setting them on fire. Becca loved the Amish way of life, but as a woman, she had plans. *A bucket list*, her English friends called it. Things you do before you die. And one thing she'd dropped into her bucket was taking a train trip to Pinecraft, Florida, the Amish and Mennonite vacation town. Never having seen the ocean, she asked pen pals who'd been to Pinecraft to send her post cards, and the more she got, the more she desired to go. And this was just one thing on her bucket list. Taking a correspondence course to learn about herbal medicine was another one. Her *mamm's* illness was greatly aided by all kinds of tinctures, pills, and whatever the herbalist had in her bag. Even the cancer doctors said she recovered faster due to alternative medicine.

Becca shook her head to stop thinking such nonsense. She was Amish and should be collecting things for her hope chest, not clutter her mind with English fancy things. When the dry goods store came into view, she pulled in and jumped out of the buggy to tie her horse. Shopping was always fun, especially if Fanny was manning the store.

"Now what's your name, sweet thing?" a deep, raspy male voice asked.

Becca spun around to see a man, she assumed a teenager, about her age, sitting on the steps leading to the store. His light blonde hair lifted with a breeze and then settled down around his handsome face again. She didn't want to reply to his question, knowing some English were mighty big flirts. But she held his gaze, wondering where he came from. "Hello. Are you new in town?"

He sprang to his feet, revealing a tall, muscular frame. "The names Denny. Moved her a few weeks back. I live at Arbor Creek, the home for misfit toys.

*Toys? Misfit*s? It was evident he was embarrassed that he was in foster care. "My name's Becca. Anything I can do to make you feel more at home at the Baptist…home?"

"Home for misfits. Go ahead and say it."

"I didn't know what it was called. I'm sorry."

Denny raised a hand. "No, I'm sorry. It's called Arbor Creek. Why? I have no clue. There is a creek out back, but that's about it."

"And you live near Granny and Jeb Weaver, right?"

He rubbed on his stomach. "Granny should be on TV. Makes the best pies ever."

"I know. I think it's Granny's sweetness that makes the pies all the more special."

He arched his back and swatted a pesky fly. "Some people have all the luck. So she's your grandma?

"*Nee*, we just all call her Granny. It seemed to stick." She searched his blue eyes, now downcast. "Do you miss your grandma or something?"

"Never met her. Never met any aunts of uncles neither. My parents kept to themselves."

Becca wondered if he was intentionally withheld the love of relatives. Would they have stepped in and reported child abuse if he'd known them? Such pain in his eyes now, she wanted to embrace him, and the thought petrified her.

She took a deep breath. "Many people who move to Smicksburg are *Englishers* looking for a family and finds friends that become like one. Maybe the Lord led you here for a reason…"

"The Lord? Lead me? What do you mean?"

"You know," Becca continued. "God. Maybe he saw your loneliness and saw fit to bring you here."

Denny avoided eye contact and kicked a nearby stone. "I don't think the man upstairs cares much about me."

"He does…"

He shrugged and kicked another stone. "Whatever."

Compassion gripped Becca's heart, and without much thought asked, "Want to come over to our house for dinner sometime? I have seven brothers and sisters and you'd find out we can be crazy, too."

Denny met her gaze, as if he didn't hear her right. "Seriously?"

"*Jah. Mamm* says there's always room for more at our house, one more dish to wash doesn't make any difference when there's already a sink full."

He scratched his chin. "I have to ask permission to go anywhere. They think I might run away. Joe, the guy who runs Arbor Creek, is 'watching' me now."

"You wouldn't run away, would you?" Becca asked.

Denny winked. "Not since I met you."

Becca, stunned at his boldness, put her head down, knowing she was starting to blush.

"I'm sorry. I was the class flirt back home but the more I see Amish people, I see how stupid I am. I talk to fill in…space."

"Space?" Becca asked, meeting his eyes now.

"You Amish don't say anything unless you mean it. At first I thought it was rude to wait so long for someone to answer a question, but now I see they…can't explain it."

"Measure our words since words have power. We try to guard our mouths from idle chatter."

Denny's eyes mellowed. "I'm learning that. My counselor said I was verbally abused. I thought abuse was just being beat up or something, but words hurt."

Joe exited the store with three large paper bags, and Denny rushed to grab two off of him. "Thanks. Hi there, Becca."

"Hi Joe. So glad you and Marge moved back to Smicksburg."

"As long as I have electricity, I'm fine. Marge and I kind of went off the deep end last summer...living off the grid. Not for us."

"Joe," Becca forced herself to speak. "Can Denny come over to our place for dinner sometime?"

Joe gave Denny a wry look. "He knows the rules. No leaving Arbor Creek unassisted until his trial period's up."

"Can Becca come visit us then?" Denny asked, cracking a knuckle.

Becca had been warned by her *mamm* about getting too close to an English guy, but she felt her motives were pure; she wanted to help Denny feel like he was part of a community.

"I suppose she can. Any good at math, Becca?"

"I like math," Becca offered.

"Okay. How about you visit and tutor Denny in Math?"

"It's algebra," Denny warned. "I hear the Amish only go to eighth grade."

"I learned algebra in fifth grade," Becca said, a little too defensively. "All you do is put in letters instead of numbers."

Denny smirked. "I'm sure it wasn't high school algebra."

"We used Ray's Arithmetic in school and it said it went up to high school."

"Maybe high school level on *Little House on the Prairie*."

Joe burst into laughter. "Denny, you're going to find lots of surprises up here in *Amishland*." He turned to

Becca. "You'd make a great tutor. Think you can get him up to par this summer?"

Becca warily met Denny's deep blue eyes again. "Do you want my help?"

He nodded. "I'm pretty far behind in math, being a stupid moron, as my mom said."

Stupid moron? Words do hurt, Becca thought as she saw shame write a cruel mark across Denny's face. "You just need some encouragement."

~*~

Jeb handed Granny a bouquet of lilacs, and planted a kiss on her cheek. "For you, Love."

It never ceased to amaze Granny that after decades of marriage, love could still deepen and grow. "*Danki*, Jebediah."

"Jebediah? What's wrong?"

"Nothing at all. Why?"

"You never call me Jebediah."

Granny slipped her arm through his and led him out on the wrap around porch, to their swing. "I've been reminiscing about when we first met. I called you Jebediah then…"

Jeb clucked his tongue. "Reading Jane Austen again? She sure brings out the romance in you."

"*Nee*, our anniversary does" Granny bit her lip as soon as she said this. Jeb was a fine man, but he forgot the anniversaries. *But their fiftieth year?*

He pulled her close. "It's been fifty years this month."

"Month's almost over…" Again, Granny felt like a pouting child, but out came the words.

"How do you know I don't have a surprise up my sleeve?"

"I wash your laundry, that's why. Only thing on your sleeves lately smells like fish."

"Deborah, your dander is up over nothing at all. I have a plan."

You're making a plan, she thought. Knowing self-pity was selfish and being thankful was the key to happiness, she took his hand and kissed it, then pat it fondly. "You're all the present I need. I'm nervous about something."

"And that is…"

"Lottie. Since she moved in with Colleen and Hezekiah, she barely comes out of the house. She'll never find a husband this summer."

Jeb chuckled. "You and your matchmaking. Most likely, Lottie's helping with Hezekiah. Their close cousins and from what I know, she tends to him a lot, giving Colleen time to care for her bees."

"When Lottie serves men their lunch after the church service, she's as red as beets. Think she's just shy?"

"*Hot.* She's hot laboring over us menfolk. *Nee*, she's a talker for sure, not a shy bone in her." Jeb kissed her head. "Stop that fretting. Are you nervous about the knitting circle?"

"Why would I be?"

"You don't like to sew."

"I've sewn enough shirts, trousers, and quilts in my lifetime to clothe a whole Amish settlement." She cringed. "Danki for getting my quilting frame out of the storage shed, but I'm not happy to see it." Granny looked out the back field, admiring the black and white speckled sheep Jeb bought her last year. "*Nee*, I love to knit and spin but have precious little time to do it."

"You knit most days."

"Haven't spun in a while. Now, a day of spinning would be a real treat." She put the lilacs up to her nose and inhaled the pungent fragrance.

Jeb took the bouquet. "I'll divide these into mason jars and put them throughout the house." He motioned towards their long driveway. Jack, their black Lab, running to meet the red car. "Looks like Marge is here already."

Granny squeezed Jeb's middle. "*Danki.* What would I do without you?"

He pinched her cheek playfully. "Without me, you'd have less clothes to stitch up and socks to darn."

"Don't tease, old man." Love gripped her heart. What would she do without Jeb? Their wedding fifty years ago seemed like yesterday for some reason. Was it the scent of spring, or the fact that five decades had been spent with the same man and she loved him even stronger?

~*~

Granny set her shortcake, cut into squares, beside the silver bowl full of sliced strawberries that sat on her kitchen table; the women could add the strawberries to the top, if they liked, or simply have plain shortcake. Granny usually favored plain old shortcake, no topping necessary, but when strawberries were in season, the fresh fruit, along with a sprinkle of sugar, was a treat indeed.

The fellowship and laughter of the knitting circle friends in the living room warmed Granny's heart, but when Lottie's voice rose above them all, she cringed. Why did the girl chatter up a storm, monopolizing the conversation? *Lord, give me grace to deal with that Lottie. She baffles me, but then again, I've only known her for a few weeks. Give me patience...*

When Granny entered the living room, Lottie laughing in a high pitch about something said, she noticed Suzy's countenance was fallen, as was Marge's. Granny took a seat on the bench in-between them, seeing ample room. "How are my English friends?"

"Tired," Marge said, almost in a whisper.

Tired of Lottie talking, Granny wondered. And Suzy wasn't in charge of this circle and she suspected this was upsetting her. She leaned towards Suzy and said softly. "Knitting is much better, *jah*?"

Suzy nodded and then whispered in Granny's ear. "We English buy clothes. Fabric is expensive."

"We're making a quilt, not clothes."

Suzy sighed. "I know. Maybe I'm getting set in my ways."

"Trying new things keeps us young," Granny encouraged.

Lottie stood up, displaying large white cotton squares. "Welcome to the sewing circle. As your teacher, we'll learn how to not only make a quilt, but embroider."

Marge groaned. "Embroidery?"

"*Jah*," Lottie said, undaunted. "I have iron-on transfers of kittens and dogs. I thought we could make *boppli* quilts for Fannie and Ruth."

Ruth put a hand over her heart. "Danki. Little Debbie will come to treasure her own quilt."

"Do you have bird transfers?" Granny asked. "Ruth's an avid bird watcher."

"*Ach*, Granny," Ruth said, "any animal is fine."

"I do have bird patterns," Lottie said. "You can use satin stitch to fill in their colors, making them look more life-like. What's your favorite bird?"

"Finches," Ruth chirped. "They get along, unlike cardinals and blue jays." Ruth put a finger to her cheek. "Wait, bluebirds are my favorite. Luke made bluebird boxes for *Mamm* last year and now we have bluebirds everywhere."

"I'll bring all the bird patterns I have over to your place this week so you can pick out what you want," Lottie offered. "I don't know a bluebird from a canary."

Granny was touched that Lottie was so obliging and her speech tender, not so brash. Was this the real Lottie?

Maryann spoke up. "I've always loved embroidery. So relaxing and if we're doing this quilt in squares, I can take my little embroidery hoop out on the porch and enjoy my lilacs." She glanced at Granny. "Sure smells like lilacs in here, but no windows are open yet."

"Jeb put small bunches in jelly jars throughout the house. Didn't you see any?"

"*Nee*," Maryann said.

"Jeb did that for you?" Lottie asked. "How sweet."

"Jeb's the nicest man east of the Mississippi," Marge added. "And he treats Granny like Mr. Darcy would Elizabeth Bennet."

Granny put a firm hand on Marge's knee. "We're not discussing literature at this circle."

"Sorry," Marge said, hurt in her voice.

"*Ach*, I'm the sorry one. I'm embarrassed at all the praise folks give to my marriage. Most people are as happily married as we are."

"Not so," Suzy said. "Now Dave and I, we're two peas in a pod, but the stories women tell me at the shop. Women open up over knitting. No better therapy than knitting."

"Crocheting calms me," Marge said. "I'm crocheting afghans for the boys at Arbor Creek."

Suzy huffed. "Why is it every time I praise knitting, you have to praise crocheting?" She leaned over at Marge, wanting an answer.

"They both mean knot or tie in some way," Lottie said.

"What?" Suzy and Marge said in unison.

"Crochet is French for hook, so hooks are used in crocheting. Knitting comes from the Dutch word, *knutten,* meaning to knot something. Embroidery just means to use a needle to embellish something, so it's all the same craft, right?"

Silence. Granny dared to look around the room, and yes, she saw bewilderment on each face. "Where'd you learn all that?" Granny asked.

"I'm a bookworm, as you know. And learning word origins can be like a game."

Marge and Suzy sat still, until Marge started to shake, and then Suzy soon followed suit. Soon they were roaring with laughter.

"What's so funny?" Lottie asked. "Don't you two like to read?"

Maryann put a hand up. "They're not laughing at you. Marge crochets and Suzy knits. I think they just got a revelation of how foolish their debate has gotten."

Hallelujah, Granny thought. The constant jabber between Marge and Suzy about which was better, or which came first, was foreign to Granny's thinking. This *joking* the *English* practiced was not the *gut* kind but the kind that created tension and competition, and she did not appreciate it.

Lottie passed out the twelve inch white squares along with paper transfers. "Pick the one you like and we'll iron on the pattern using Granny's iron."

Marge's brows furrowed. "Iron. There's no electricity here."

"I have a propane iron," Granny quipped. "If you didn't lose your patience last summer, I could have taught you how to live off the grind."

"Off the grid, Granny. Not grind. And I can't live without electricity. We already talked about that."

"*Jah*, we did. Just think television robs you of time."

"We only watch an hour a day," Marge defended.

Suzy leaned towards Granny. "With Janice gone, it's us two English against all the Amish. We're outnumbered."

"You can invite an *Englisher* friend."

"That's not the point," Suzy explained. "We've always agreed to disagree? Live in Christian love, the tie that binds?"

"We could ask Missy, though," Marge suggested.

"She's too busy with her tea shop," Suzy said, wringing her hands.

Granny felt a nudge in her heart. Was it her, Lord? Was she causing discord, division, pitting Amish ways against English? "I'm sorry, Marge. My pride, thinking the Amish way was best, just made its way out of me."

Lizzie came in the side door, face flushed. "Sorry I'm so late. Was taking a nature walk with the girls."

"Homeschooling in summer?" Suzy asked.

Lizzie beamed. "We're doing bugs, one of Jenny's favorites. Better to study them in warm weather. I love homeschooling so much, I think I'll teach Tillie and Millie next year."

Maryann almost dropped all the transfer papers on the floor. "What's wrong with our Amish schools? All my kids go."

Lizzie stood up tall and regained composure. "I've been gobbling up books on homeschooling and it's just too much for me to explain, but I see the benefit."

"Seems like a lack of discipline to me, not making the kids wait their turn, sit still, be with other kinner," Maryann continued.

Granny, exhausted, stood up. "Anyone want some meadow tea? Cools a body down." She eyed Maryann and then Lizzie, who soon became silent.

Granny excused herself, saying she needed to tell Jeb something. She made her way into their bedroom and went over to her basket of yarn and hugged it.

"What's wrong, love?"

"Yarn. It calms me down."

"And you need calmed down because…"

"I don't know, Jeb. Seems like all the women want to do is bicker lately. Maybe my knitting circle days are finished. I wanted to bring women together, but all they're doing is badgering each other over such *lecherlich* things."

Jeb, who was in a rocker, along with Bea, their little dog, was reading his Bible, pulled at his beard, looking deep in thought "Maybe they're tired from putting gardens in. Marge is getting used to a new job, too, caring for those boys. But, Deborah, you've been quarrelsome yourself all day. Ever since Fannie came over…"

"I have not. I made the noon meal and visited an English shut-in cheerfully."

"Well, if you ask me, you're seeing in others what you have in yourself."

Granny wanted to stomp and rant. She came in here to calm down, only to be chastened by Jeb? "What is in me, Jeb? Tell me since you know me better than I know myself."

"See, there it is. An off the cuff remark to hide what's inside. And, jah, I'll tell you, old woman. You miss Fannie. She's bonding with her real mamm, and that's *gut*. She's also visiting Ella, someone you still miss, and the letter from Nathan today made you feel…"

Granny was truly stunned at Jeb's wisdom. Of course. Each new knitting circle she had was accompanied with changes, and some change was painful. Girls came and moved on, some physically and some emotionally. Fannie didn't need her in the way she had in the past. She looked into Jeb's tender eyes. "You're right. Change. It's painful. And sometimes, I put up a wall around me, guard my heart, because if I get close, I can get hurt."

"They need you, love."

Granny's chin quivered. "One minute I'm trying to marry off Lottie, the next minute she gets under my skin. I suppose I'm afraid to get to know her."

"She's hiding, and you like transparency. Lottie's shy but tries to hide it. But my advice is, keep an eye on Ruth. She's been heavy on my heart when in prayer. She looks tired. As quiet as a mouse when she came in. Having a kinner with Down Syndrome can't be easy."

"*Ach*, I agree. She' hardly spoken a word." She put her yarn back, feeling renewed by her husband. "Danki, Jebediah Weaver. Faithful are the wounds of a friend. Proverbs 27:6."

"You're welcome Deborah Byler Weaver. He who finds a wife finds a *gut* thing, Proverbs 18:22."

Granny grinned and then pecked his cheek. "Pray for me."

"Jah, I will. Now, better get out there or they'll think something's going on in here."

Deborah's jaw dropped, and then she covered her mouth to hide a shy smile. "Old man!"

She took a deep breath and exited the door, returning to the circle.

"How's Jeb?" Ruth asked.

"Fine," Granny said evenly. "Why do you ask?"

A bewildered look spread across Ruth's face. "Just wondering."

Granny stared at Ruth. She really did look so tired, dark lines under her eyes. Or was it something else? "Is Little Debbie being a handful?"

Ruth forced a smile. "*Nee*, my mamm helps a lot. It's her that I'm worried about. She's been looking pale."

"Does she have a spring cold? Or maybe allergies?"

"Maybe, but I think it's asking a lot to have her watch Debbie so much, and me coming to circle. I'm feeling pretty guilty."

"Don't do that. Knitting helps refresh you, making you more productive in the long run."

Ruth held up a blue outline of a cat, and then puppy. "I think I'll do one of these. No need to do birds. What do you think?"

"I agree. I'm partial to dogs, as you know."

Granny ambled over to get two glasses of meadow tea, giving Ruth a glass and sitting next to her. Yes, Ruth needed her. She took a sip of meadow tea, the spearmint from her own garden permeating her senses. She began to thank God for all the women who would be attending her summer circle. There was a reason they were here, and it exhausted her to try to figure everything out, so she just tried to enjoy herself.

Ruth handed the transfer paper to her and she picked the first puppy picture she saw. A mother dog licking the head of her puppies. That's what she was, she supposed, an older woman who could help this little circle of friends.

"Can we read and discuss books again?" Marge asked, looking around the circle.

"We Amish are too busy to read much in the summer," Maryann said bluntly.

"Wait a minute now, Maryann. There's one book we read all year long, jah?"

"Jah, the Bible. The book that came alive when fighting cancer." She turned to Ruth, "And the fellowship of good friends."

"Well, how about we read Psalms and discuss them. They're really songs," Suzy suggested. "Very short and uplifting. I read five a day, and get all one-hundred fifty done each month. It really helps me get my emotions out. So comforting, I just feel like I'm fixed inside after reading them. Kind of a ragdoll that got patched up."

Granny's eyes misted. "So we can knit and stitch and feel stitched up though fellowship, *jah*?"

"Sounds *wunderbar gut* to me," Marge said in a heavy Pennsylvania Dutch accent that left the women smiling, and soon peace descended onto the group.

Danki, Lord. It's your Word that binds us, no matter our differences, Granny thought.

~*~

Later that night, as Granny sat on her wraparound porch, a shawl covering her shoulders, she closed her eyes and soaked in the sound of the peeper frogs. Having a pond and small creek on their property gave the little critters a comfortable place to sing the praises of summer. She felt like a six year old again, as old as the twins, Millie and Tillie. *Bless my grandkinner, Lord, for helping with the planting and picking all those strawberries so cheerfully. Bless Lizzie for being such a gut mamm to the girls.*

Lizzie. Did she want to adopt because she feared being infertile? And if she was past her prime, being in her mid-thirties, was that the answer? She had such a knack with children so maybe she was the answer to Charles' prayers; to have a *mamm* who loved him and would protect him from an abusive father. Roman would be such a *gut daed* to a boy, too. And he wanted a boy...

Feeling heaviness in her heart, and knowing her Lord wanted to help carry her burdens, she bowed her head and prayed:

Lord,

You have opened my eyes up today. First of all, I think Lizzie's hurting more than she lets on. I'm thankful she's willing to homeschool the girls, but is there a vacuum in her heart that will only be filled with you first, and then maybe adopting Charles? Is it Your love in her wanting to help that young man? If so, Lord, have your way with Roman, my stubborn son. Nudge his heart because he's a gut man and wants to do your will. But he's slow to change, maybe because he's had so much over the past several years. Help Roman and Lizzie have the same desire to adopt, or take it away from Lizzie.

And Lord, I keep thinking of MJ and Andy, such fine Englishers. As I teach MJ to bake, I pray it will bless her, taking her mind off of her pain. Danki for her husband, Andy, and his loving care of his wife. He could give lessons to a few Amish men I know...

Now, Lord, Lottie is a bundle of energy and I must confess, she gets on my nerves. What's bothering her? Her cousin, Hezekiah, is he not doing well? Is she hiding something about his condition? When I visit, he's almost back to normal, his speech still a little impaired, but understandable. I cast Hezekiah and Colleen, my honey girl I miss at circle, on You...

Change Lord is something I'm losing patience with. It gets harder with age. Fannie not being here, not needing me as much, hurts more than I thought. Ella being away up in New York, having a boppli I'll barely know, pains me as well. My knitting circle has brought such joy and healing. Help me to be like You, loving in a sacrificial way, expecting nothing in return. With the years I have left, make me a blessing, Lord.

In Jesus name,
Amen

Dear Readers,
Thank you for visiting Granny and her girls. Early summer in Western Pennsylvania means strawberry

festivals. Most Amish are "puttin' up" strawberry preserves and enjoying strawberry shortcake. Last May, the women at Granny's circle had Angel Food Cake (*Amish Friends Knitting Circle: Episode 1~Planting Time*) but strawberries, of course, are put on shortcake with sprinkles of sugar on top as well. But like Granny said, shortcake is *gut* plain, inexpensive and nice to have on hand for visitors. I leave you with this recipe and we'll meet again in a few weeks when *Amish Knit & Stitch, Episode 2 ~ Unraveled* is released.

Shortcake

1 c. flour
1 tsp. baking powder
Pinch of salt (¼ tsp.)
2 eggs
1 c. sugar
2 T butter
½ c. hot milk
1 tsp. vanilla

Combine flour, baking powder and salt and set aside. Beat eggs for 3 minutes, or until a lemon color evenly throughout. Slowly add sugar to egg mixture and beat 5 minutes. Fold dry mixture into the egg mixture. Add butter to hot milk. Stir into batter, along with vanilla. Blend well. Pour into a lightly greased 8x8 square pan. Bake in a 350 degree oven until golden brown and a toothpick inserted is clean, approximately 10 minutes.

EPISODE 2:

Unraveled

"What did you say?" Granny asked, absentmindedly.

"I know we shouldn't be questioning the Lord's ways, but Ruth needs her *mamm*."

"*Jah*, they were best friends. A heart attack, with no signs? Was Claire under too much stress caring for her *grandkinner*?"

"Doc said it can be in the genes. Claire's *mamm* died young of the same thing."

Granny's heart sunk into her feet. "So the same can happen to Ruth?"

Jeb sipped his morning coffee. "Ruth needs to be monitored by a doc. She'll be seeing Dr. Pal when he's in Smicksburg on Wednesdays. Nice man."

"*Jah*, and foreigners sometimes have mountain wisdom, concerning herbs and whatnot.

"He's from India but an American now. Don't go making him feel out of place when you see him."

Granny frowned as she scooped scrambled eggs onto Jeb's plate. "When I see him?"

"*Jah*, when we see him. He's as kind as they come, and I made an appointment for both of us to get our tickers checked." Jeb pat his chest. "My heart flutters at times."

"Mine races," Granny said, "when you change my doctor without me knowing about it."

"He's local and no need to pay for a driver to Indiana." He took her hand as she sat next to him. "You didn't ask me about my fluttering heart condition."

"Are you sick?"

"Heart-sick, as your Jane Austen would put it."

"She doesn't say that. How sappy. Jeb, what's wrong?" Granny noticed Jeb's forehead was red. Was he really sick? She put a hand up to see if he was hot, but he wasn't. "Okay, tell me about your fluttering heart."

Jeb jumped up, opened the pantry door and grabbed an envelope hidden under a canister. "Happy belated fiftieth anniversary," he said, voice filled with love. "You'll never guess."

"Money for more sheep?"

"*Nee,* much better."

Granny stared at the white envelope. On it was written, *For 50 years of marital bliss.* She bit her lower lip, not knowing if Jeb was teasing or meant it. They'd had their rough patches like any couple. She gazed into Jeb's eyes. "Should I open it now?"

"*Nee,* wait until winter."

"Winter?" Granny asked. "Jeb that makes no sense."

"*Jah,* it does. Can you wait?"

She shook her head. "Course not."

"Open it, then."

Granny ripped the letter open and held up a white paper with print on it. She noticed Amtrak, thanking them for their train ticket purchase for November, Destination, Montana. Two round trip tickets paid for and the dates appeared to be for November 1-10. The price was blotted out by a black marker. Tears stung her eyes. "Jeb, this must cost a fortune."

"And you deserve it, love. The one who still makes my heart flutter." He got up and scooped her into his arms. "We're going to Eliza's wedding. Imagine that."

Granny pursed her lips, joy filling her. Jeb knew she missed Nathan and Lavina something fierce. She locked her arms around his neck and pulled him in to kiss him. That old feeling she had when first loving Jeb, that feeling of coming home, being so comfortable in his arms, overwhelmed her. What did she do to get such a fine husband? Even Jane Austen herself couldn't have written such a sweet love story that she herself was living.

~*~

After Jeb and Granny cleared off the table and dishes were done, Granny pulled the letter from Fannie she'd wanted to take time to relish. She opened the letter to read:

Dear Granny,

I'm so upset. Ruth's mom is dead from a heart attack? I feel wretched being here and not in Smicksburg. I'm on vacation while Ruth's in mourning. Ella can't stop crying. Claire was like a mamm to her and to die at such a young age. Don't know her exact age, but she's not much older than Suzy, Janice and Maryann, right? I mean, my mamm's in her forties.

All the beauty of East Otto has vanished and I'm in the pits of despair. Do not laugh that I'm talking like Anne of Green Gables, but I just can't describe it any better. Well, my mamm said it first, to be honest. She said, "This is a pretty kettle of fish, too, no one to help Ruth raise a baby with Down Syndrome."

And Granny, I don't think Ella likes it up here. She said it's so cold in winter, milk can freeze before it hits the bucket. I think she was joking. She doesn't like all the dairy farming that's for sure, but won't speak up to Zach about it. Secretly, she's fighting bitterness towards him. She told me this in confidence and I won't tell a soul except you. But then again, Ella's so big and pregnant, maybe it's her fatigue talking? What do you think? No boppli born yet and so that could be adding to her irritation.

Ella hinted about coming down to seeing Ruth later this summer, since we missed the funeral last week. But really, Granny, I wish they'd move back to Smicksburg. They can barely get away from here due to their huge farm. No kin around to help. I say Ruth needs Ella and she needs to move back home.

Baby Anna is fine. Mom's driving the buggy out by herself. She made herself memory cards, all the verses in the Bible about overcoming fear and anxiety. I see a real change. Granny, what would our lives be without you?

Much love,

Fannie

A warmth surrounded Granny's soul. Her girls needed her after all. Lord, help Ella through this miraculous pregnancy. Being barren for so long, accepting it, and moving on to adopt the twins, she showed lots of maturity for a twenty-seven year old. Give her strength to adjust to East Otto, and if it's your will they move back home, put it in Zach's heart.

~*~

Lottie took the lacey peach-colored scarf, and Suzy being in the back room out of sight, flung it around her neck. Being Amish, she could never wear such a fancy scarf, with sequins of all things. She gazed into an antique mirror and sighed. Why did she have reddish colored hair? The scarf only accentuated the ever spreading freckles on her face. She was German, so shouldn't she have blonde hair? Her cousin, Hezekiah, didn't have red hair, not even a smidgen.

You're adopted. The teasing on the playground resounded in her mind. *Peter always stuck up for me, saying I wasn't adopted and being a bookworm was a good thing.* Lottie ran her fingers through the fringe on the scarf. Peter, her fiancé, loved her since sixth grade, he admitted. He asked her for a buggy ride at sixteen and they were ready to publish their engagement. She knew him, trusted him, but he ran off to live with a woman? It still seemed like a nightmare and she'd wake-up back in Millersburg and Peter would come over to help at her *daed's* woodshop.

The screen door squeaked and she turned to see Phil Darby. Lottie unwound the scarf off her neck as her mouth went dry.

"Hello, there. The scarf looked nice," Phil said, pushing shaggy blond bangs to one side. "I'm looking for something in that color."

His voice was so mellow and inviting somehow Lottie's heart stopped banging against her ribcage. Why was she so in a panic when talking to men? *Because men can pull out your heart and stomp on it?* Lottie didn't want to chit chat with this man, so came to the point. "Do you want to buy yarn?"

He flashed a broad smile, accenting dimples on both cheeks. "I want to buy something already made. Something a woman would like."

Lottie knew Phil Darby, who some called Mr. Darcy, the perfect man in Jane Austen's *Pride and Prejudice*, was the talk of the little town of Smicksburg. Well, among single women, but here he was, buying a scarf for a lady. *He's probably engaged like most men his age.*

He came closer, observing her. "Is everything alright? Too hot in here?"

"*Ach, nee.* Not at all. Why?"

"You're flushed."

Blushing again, as usual. "Well, maybe it is hot in here. Suzy usually has the air conditioning on, but today she wanted to air things out."

Suzy came in from the back room, humming as she knit. "Did I hear Mr. Darcy's voice out here?"

Now Phil's cheeks grew crimson as he grinned. "You women need to stop calling me that. It's ridiculous."

"Well, I don't think it is. I see the line of single women, in want of a husband, taking their turn after church. Are you dating anyone yet?"

Phil cocked his head forward. "What? I've only been here for a month."

Lottie boldly spoke up. "He has a girl back home."

"Really?" Phil and Suzy asked in unison, and then laughed.

"What makes you say that, Lottie?" Phil wanted to know.

"The scarf. You wanted a scarf for a lady…"

"….My mom."

Silence. Lottie gazed towards Suzy who was smiling. *A rather wry smile.* Did she think she was flirting with Phil? No, she was not like the other girls in town, flocking to their new pastor.

"So, Suzy, what are you making?" Phil asked, shattering the awkwardness.

"A prayer shawl for MJ. She's the most giving person I know, next to Granny, and I decided to use some of my best alpaca. The woman's so inspirational."

"How so?" Phil asked.

"Well, she's very ill, but keeps making pins, crocheted baby outfits, dolls, and all kinds of things for her friends on Facebook. It's her only life now, being homebound, but her husband is the most faithful caregiver. Treats her like he just fell in love."

Phil's countenance darkened. "So, they can give lots of advice about...care giving?"

"He's busy with MJ but I'm sure he'd talk to you. It's only a few miles away. Why not visit?"

Phil fumbled for words and raked his fingers through his hair.

Lottie wanted to take his hand; the lost look on his face came so sudden-like. He was carrying some kind of pain. "I'll go with you," Lottie found herself saying.

Phil's brows shot up. "Really?"

"Well, I, ah, wanted to meet MJ, too, and it being two miles away..."

"You can take your buggy, Lottie, another time." Suzy said evenly.

"No, no, I can take her," Phil insisted. "How about this afternoon I come pick you up here?"

"I won't be here since I only work mornings." She grabbed a piece of paper off of Suzy's desk, feeling Suzy's eyes heavy upon her. She scribbled down her new address. "I'm living with my cousin and his new wife. Helping take care of him."

Phil looked up pensively and then snapped his fingers. "Hezekiah. The one who's recovering from a coma."

"*Jah*, and doing pretty *gut*. His speech is understandable, he's walking and can feed himself."

"That's great," Phil said. "I'd like to meet him. How about I come over around two?"

Lottie's heart felt light for some odd reason. "Two is fine."

Phil placed both hands on her shoulders. "I'll take this scarf. You modeled it beautifully."

Suzy let out a sigh that Lottie feared could be heard across the street. She'd warned her to not get friendly with the English...but Phil was so sweet.

~*~

Becca knocked on the front door of Arbor Creek, and it made her feel quite formal. The Amish used side doors, sometimes not even knocking. But she was here on business: tutoring Denny in math. She clenched her little brown *Ray's Arithmetic* books closer. Denny may laugh at such outdated books they used, written centuries ago but used in one-room schoolhouses longer than any textbook. *And harder than college math*, she'd heard.

The hunter green door flung open and Denny bowed, motioning with one hand to enter. "Come in, my lady."

What? I'm not his lady. Becca froze in place, too stunned to move.

"I'm kidding," Denny snickered. "You Amish are so serious."

Becca wanted to roll her eyes, but didn't. Her *mamm* had admonished that it was a bad habit. "Are you ready for your lesson?" she asked, entering the living room off to the left of the wide staircase that split the front of the house into two large areas. The tan wraparound couch that nearly took up the room would mean she'd have to sit next to Denny. "Can we study at the kitchen table?"

"Marge is in there baking, so we better not bother her. I just lounge on the couch when studying."

"How will we write?"

Denny grabbed a large textbook. "Here, you can write on this." He knocked on the book. "Portable desk, like you Amish have, *jah?*"

Becca pursed her lips, trying not to laugh. "What's wrong with lap desks? And your Amish accent sounds horrible. You don't pronounce the *j* so much."

"*Ach*, well, you need to teach me the Dutch, too?"

Laughter rumbled from within Becca. "Stop that. And why should I care if you can speak Dutch?"

He plopped himself down on the overstuffed couch and pat the seat next to him. "I'm converting."

Becca slowly sat next to him, but left a good two feet of room. "Converting?"

"I want to be Amish."

Becca rolled her eyes. "Just talk to Marge and Joe. They tried living off the grid and hated it. And you have no idea what it means to be Amish. It's more than wearing plain clothes and driving a horse and buggy."

Denny scooted closer to her. "Enlighten me."

Backing away, Becca blurted, "You're such a flirt, Denny Boles. Now, I'm here to teach you math and nothing else. Anyhow, a man would teach you Amish ways. Ask Jonas."

"I have been," Denny said, suddenly looking forlorn.

Becca knew she needed to watch her tongue around Denny, words having crushed his spirit in the past. "I'm sorry. I'm not used to boys being so…cozy with me."

"Cozy? What do you mean?"

"Well, I don't see my boyfriend except on Sundays, after a Singing."

"You have a boyfriend? I didn't know that."

"It's a secret. We court in secret-like. But only on Sundays. Gilbert's like a family member and he comes over often. I see him more…"

"If he's like family, wouldn't that be like dating your brother?"

"Not at all," Becca said. "And lots of Amish marry their childhood sweethearts."

At this Greg's eyes became as big as two round cookies. "Childhood sweethearts? That's just weird."

Becca straightened. "It's our way. Still want to be Amish?"

Denny chewed on his lower lip. "I feel like I belong here. It's nice."

Becca noticed that Denny looked younger, less careworn over the past few weeks. Fishing at Keystone Lake and Jeb's fishing hole, being around men who were mentoring him from the Baptist Church, was literally taking burdens off his back. "I know Jonas and Jeb really like spending time with you. Maybe you'll get adopted."

Denny cracked his knuckles. "It'll have to happen over the next two years. When I'm eighteen, I'm on my own. No more foster homes."

"Homes? You've been in more than one?"

"Five. When you get old, you're not so cute anymore. So, they pass you on." He shook his head. "Well, the caseworker said I acted up too much." Denny beat his chest and anger registered on his face. "I get mad, but who wouldn't? Jonas told me I deserved better."

Becca felt like melting into the couch, dissolving into nothing. As much as she felt smothered by her *mamm* at times, she was grateful to have a stable home. "I'm sorry, Denny. And Jonas is right. You need to talk to him more."

"He's old. I want a friend my age. The guys here are as messed up as me."

~*~

Ruth wept as she laid prostrate over the creeping myrtle groundcover she and her *mamm* had planted in the patch of woods on the side of their property. She was a little girl, her *mamm's* shadow, and like the little seedlings they'd dug in and covered with earth, so now was her best friend. *From dust we were formed and to the dust we return. Oh, Mamm, how can I go on without you?"*

"Why, Lord?" She sobbed, choking on tears. "She was so strong." Sobs wracked her body until she felt limp and could cry no more. She thought back to last summer. She and Luke were finally enjoying a good marriage, thanks to her parents. Her *daed* took Luke under his wing after they reunited, giving them the *dawdyhaus* next to them to watch over, like the Heavenly Father did. Was it all too much?

Was it Luke's abuse and immoral behavior that made her *mamm's* hair gray? Her eyes shot open. Of course. How could she have missed it? In her own suffering, she didn't see her *mamm's* grief. Being a parent to two *kinner* now, it pained her deeper than any human emotion to see them hurt.

She heard branches breaking and shot up. The stray dog that bit her years ago in these woods always made her on edge. But it was Luke. Somehow, she wished it was a stray dog. Anger like she hadn't felt in over a year ran through her veins.

"Honey, I've been looking everywhere for you."

"I want to be left alone," she said in measured tones. "I'm praying."

"You're crying."

She closed her eyes and counted to ten, like Suzy always said to do. She took a cleansing breath and then met Luke's blue eyes. Yes, they were the mellow, loving eyes that won her, but she knew the cruel, sinister eyes that had spooked her *mamm* many times. Anxiety disorder, the doctors had said, and medicine helped. Made him a new man, really, but Luke's behavior two years ago was an enormous upheaval to her parents, obviously leaving casualties. How could she ever forgive him?

He came and sat next to her, putting an arm around her shoulders. "I'm here for you if you want to talk."

She swallowed hard. "Nothing will bring *Mamm* back. Anyhow, it was words that killed her."

"Words?"

She clenched her fists, shook her head rapidly and screamed, "You killed her! Words kill and you killed my *mamm*."

Luke grabbed her and she tried to break free, but without success. Before she knew it, he was carrying her towards the phone shanty. He was calling Jeb, he kept saying.

~*~

"Can I help?" Angelina asked, dark-brown eyes wide, a basket hanging off one arm.

Luke wanted to scream at this neighbor who lived down the road. *What does it look like? I have a screaming woman flung over my shoulders.* "Ruth misses her *mamm*. Can't stop crying."

"Why are you holding her like… *pazzo?* Angelina asked evenly.

"What's that?"

"*Pazzo?* Italian for the crazy."

Luke felt anger deep within. Did she remember how they'd separated because of his abuse? Did she think he was being cruel? He let Ruth down but held her by the middle as she tried to run into the house.

"Luke, the *kinner* need me!"

The kinner! Alone in the house. He released her as she ran towards the house, her prayer *kapp* coming loose and hanging by ribbons down her back.

Angelina tucked gray hair under her paisley bandana, and then put two hands on her broad hips. "You were watching the *bambino?*"

Luke assumed that meant *boppli.* "*Jah*, but was out checking on Ruth…"

"And you have the *bambino* and the boy in the house by themselves?"

Luke threw up his hands. "It was only a few minutes, into the woods. Ruth's in bad shape."

"Maybe she need the time alone." Angelina said in broken Italian, and then held up her basket. "Homemade bread, comfort food."

Luke nodded his head in thanks. "You were friends with Claire, *jah*?"

"She like a *sorella*."

"Sorella?"

"The one you live with in the family? A girl?"

Luke stared at the grass. Feeling as tired as an overworked mule, he didn't have time to try to translate.

"*Sister, the sister.* I mean the sister. Yes?"

"Claire was like a sister?"

"*Si*, I mean, yes. She help my English."

Luke was discovering how Ruth's dear *mamm* did many good works in secret, visiting many who needed a friend. She'd always quoted from the Bible, "*When you do this to the least of these, you do it unto Me.*"

"Claire was a *santo*...saint, and I'm going to repay."

"Repay? Do you owe her money?"

Angelina's eyes misted and her chin started to shake. "When we moved from the Italy, sometimes we lacked the money. My children they work and live in California, send money, and we live like the old country, off the land. But Claire would leave cash in an envelope in our mailbox, for a treat. She think I no see, but I do." Her chin quivered. "We visit often, at my place. We have no car..."

Luke felt his mind was split, half of it inside with Ruth, the other getting a headache trying to understand this Italian woman. "Do you want to come in and give Ruth the bread yourself?"

"I come to help with the *bambino*," She wagged a finger. "Never let two little ones in the house by themselves."

Luke had Debbie in a playpen and Micah was sleeping on the couch. *What could happen?*

Angelina clucked her tongue. "I forgot the thistle seed. Ruth love the birds and now, they will calm her. Tomorrow. I will bring it. Tomorrow."

Tomorrow? Was she coming over often? Why? They had Amish friends and family to help get through this valley of sorrow.

"Yes, it summer, and I walk. Only two mile."

"But you're…"

"Old? Yes, I am. But in Italy we walk more than here and my legs are strong. Now, let's go in and help Ruth."

~*~

Phil Darby saw Lottie swinging on a tire hung from a massive oak tree in the front yard. *She's carefree deep down,* he thought. He pulled into the gravel driveway and once again, was taken by the simplicity of Amish homes. White clapboard with white curtains tied to one side, gray painted porches with plenty of potted red geraniums lined up along the edges.

Lottie waved when she saw him, not at all embarrassed that she was just playing like a kid. *How refreshing,* he thought.

She ran up to the car, barefooted. "You're a little early."

He looked at his watch. "It's one-thirty," he said, awkwardly. "I couldn't wait to meet Hezekiah and Colleen."

"*Ach*, well, follow me."

Was it his imagination, or did Lottie seem disappointed. Did she think this was a date, going to see MJ and Andy? Was he leading her on? Lottie was a beauty, for sure, but she was Amish. He wanted to be her friend, like he was getting to be friends with Suzy. And Smicksburg was a town from the past, a place where people talked to their neighbors and kids played outside, so why not befriend everyone? He caught himself hoping that Jerry and Janice would stay in the South so he could be the permanent pastor.

Lottie ran up on the porch and Phil put the car in park. She was talking to someone through the front screen door and Phil wondered if it was a bad time to call. "I shouldn't have come so early."

"It's alright. Just letting Colleen know you're here." She fidgeted with her prayer *kapp* ribbons that hung down freely, not tied. "She made a pie for you and it's not done."

A beautiful woman with honey colored hair to match her eyes came out on the porch. "I'm Colleen. So nice to meet you, Phil."

Since most people called him Pastor Phil, he was relieved at the informal address. "Nice to meet you, Colleen. You have such a nice place. It smells…sweet."

"The previous owners were avid gardeners, lots of flower beds and bushes. And then there's all the fruit trees out back. Actually, Hezekiah's out in the orchard. Let's take a little walk."

Phil studied Colleen. "You don't have a German accent like the other Amish."

"Oh, I was English and converted."

"For Hezekiah?"

She smiled. "For myself. I love the Amish lifestyle."

Phil shook his head in disbelief. "Don't you miss anything? Modern conveniences? Cell phones? Music?"

"Well, the music part was the hardest, to be honest. When we give something up, it's always hard at first, but you get used to it." She brushed flour off her apron. "I sure learned how to cook and bake, though, and learned from Granny what a trifle is."

"A trifle. Something that takes up our time and isn't really important."

"Yes," Colleen said. "I thought it was a candy at first. A truffle." She laughed.

Phil noticed that Lottie was lagging far behind. "Are we going too fast?"

"*Nee.* Just tired from working in the yarn shop. I'm heading back to the house. Meet me on the porch when you're ready to go see MJ."

Her tone had pain etched into it. Was he being rude, paying attention to Colleen?

~*~

Lottie went back to the house, furious with herself that she couldn't stop staring at Phil Darby. *He's gorgeous on the inside and out.* She should be paying attention to the single Amish men Granny was introducing her to at *Gmay*, not go on a ride alone with Phil. But if she said no to going over to MJ's, she'd look fickle as a schoolgirl. *But why did she care?* But Phil sure was asking Colleen a lot of questions about her conversion. Was he taken with the People? Did he want to turn Amish?

As a chubby, orange, tabby cat approached her, Lottie scooped him up. She stroked his fur that stuck out like dandelion petals. *Okay, Mr. Whiskers. I won't neglect to rub your tummy.*

Neglect. Peter had run across the back pasture to the family farmhouse to sneak a kiss from time to time, but when he met that English woman, he started to neglect her. It was a few months before he broke things off, revealing he was living with her. And soon after, Hezekiah's near fatal accident on his way to Millersburg.

She bowed her head as she continued to pet the cat. Lord, when anxiety fills me, you calm me. Help me now. Life can change abruptly, but you never do. You're the Rock of Ages, as the hymn goes. And I need you more than ever. Help me.

~*~

Granny cupped Ruth's head down to her shoulder as tears and sobs gushed. *Lord, help Ruth bear this pain, this loss.* She took her hand and led her to the cushioned bench in the living room. Jeb and Luke talked in hushed tones in the kitchen.

"Who's watching the *kinner*?" Granny asked Ruth as she stroked her back.

Ruth sat up, trying to collect herself. "Angelina. Upstairs."

"Angelina? Not Amish, *jah*?"

"*Nee*, a friend of *Mamm's*. Don't know her very well." Tears poured from Ruth as she tried to talk. "*Mamm*. She did *gut* works…in private-like."

Why were they letting someone they barely knew watch Micah and Debbie? The door opened and slammed and a louder voice was heard. More sobbing. It was Jacob, Ruth's *daed*.

Lord, bring comfort to this house. Give your strength to Ruth and Jacob. To all of us. We're just all in shock that a healthy woman in her fifties was taken. We're not questioning Your ways, we just don't understand.

Slow footsteps clomping down the steps and a short, stout woman entering the room took Granny back. Who was this?

"I see the expression. I am Angelina, and I take care of the bambinos." She collapsed in an Amish rocker and put her stubby legs on the wooden foot stool. "They asleep for the nap now."

"I'm Deborah Weaver," Granny offered. "Do you live in the house next door?"

"No, I live near Dayton. I walk."

"Walk? Four miles?"

"No, the two miles. But I walk a lot in the summer. Claire, she help me in the cold weather, so I here to help pay back her kindness."

Granny's heart swelled with sorrow. Claire was a woman of few words, but full of good works. Obviously this woman was poor, not having a car, so Claire took her places in a buggy or hired a driver.

"We walk in Italy all the time. Americans, they no exercise."

So outspoken, Granny thought. "Do you walk a lot?"

"*Si*, and I no young."

Granny guessed the woman was her age so didn't want to ask.

"I'm eighty-one. My husband, he eighty-three. But Tony, he sick a lot now and we have the house for sale. Need to go live with children in California."

Granny felt Ruth breathing evenly again, but continued to hold her limp hand and pat it. "What made you settle in Dayton area if your *kinner* are out in California?"

Angelina's eyes mellowed, as if thinking back in time. "We came from Italy, but some of my children no get into the United States. This was ten year ago. They live in Canada and we can visit more easily. But now, we must choose where to live, getting older. It's warm in California for Tony's arthritis."

Granny thought of her sons in Ohio and Montana and how she had to fill her life with others who became like family. Obviously Claire replaced Angelina's own *kinner*, filling a void in the woman's life. "So, do you knit?"

"I crochet. I want to crochet an afghan for all my grandchildren before I die. I make fourteen already."

"That's *wunderbar gut*," Granny said with feeling. "Have you ever tried to spin wool?"

Angelina shook her head. "Not since I come to America. When I was young I did the spinning."

If Claire helped this woman, she'd continue, Granny thought. "Would you like to come to the knitting circle at my house? We're doing embroidery, crocheting, and all kinds of things."

Angelina slowly shook her head. "I need to help this family, and then my husband. No time."

Granny didn't want to start a quarrel with this thoughtful woman, but surely she knew the Amish took care of their own. "My husband, Jeb, is in the kitchen now making plans to help Ruth and Luke. Our *Gmay*, or church, as the English say, help each other."

Angelina leaned her head back on the rocker and closed her eyes. "No, I help here. I pay back Claire for the kindness."

~*~

Lottie sat near Phil on a loveseat across from MJ and her husband, Andy. Being so near Phil made her feel desires, long buried. She was sixteen and out in a courting buggy…with Peter…Her *mamm* had told her that she intimidated him, talking about classic books, herbal medicine, or the Bible. *Uppity*, her *mamm* had called her, making Peter run. But Phil asked her all kinds of questions about gardening on the way over, and she let her knowledge flow freely and he absorbed it. *Why?*

"So, you two were high school sweethearts," Phil marveled. "And married for thirty years. Wow, that's what I call success."

"I call it love," Andy quipped. "And glue."

"Glue?" Phil asked.

"God. He's the glue that holds our marriage together. We used to go to two different churches, but same God."

"Really?" Lottie asked, ears perked up.

"I'm Catholic," MJ said. "Andy was raised Protestant. I couldn't expect Andy to change for me. And I wasn't just a little bit Catholic, I was a Eucharistic minister."

"A woman?" Lottie gasped.

"Well, not a real minister, like the priest, but someone who takes communion to shut-ins. Andy can't take Holy Communion unless he converts, and he doesn't want to. There's a few things we disagree on."

Andy chuckled. "MJ can take communion in *my* church, since we're not so strict."

MJ's lips became a straight line and Lottie didn't know if she was annoyed or there was a secret joke between them.

"Now, we have church here. God's everywhere, right?" Andy asked.

MJ nodded. "We have a small circle of friends who we gather with. Very small. Only four of us, but where two or three are gathered in Christ's name, there he is in the midst of them."

"I love that verse," Phil quipped. "And it's so true. But we're not to forsake getting together in the assembly of believers."

"I agree," Andy said, "but MJ barely gets out so we have our own assembly here, in this living room." He put a hand up. "Please, don't judge."

"Judge?" Phil asked. "Judge what?"

MJ sighed, giving a knowing look to Andy "Some Christians think we're just not right with God since we don't go to a 'real' church. You wouldn't believe the things so-called Christians have said to us…"

"Such as…" Lottie prodded.

"Oh, you know. If I had the faith I'd be healed, and we could make it to church. If I didn't fret and get stressed out, I'd feel better. I say, 'hello, I have one inch of an intestine and…well, I'm too embarrassed to talk about the bag, so I just decide to put them on my prayer list."

"Turning the cheek, loving your enemies?" Phil asked.

"People really don't know what it's like to be chronically ill. I say, "Father forgive them, they just really don't know. When I crochet or do needlework, I pray for them so bitterness doesn't set in."

Phil sighed. "Being a pastor, I understand a little bit. When I give a sermon, most times one person likes to enlighten me afterwards, as to what I needed to 'add' so it could have been a *great* sermon. That sticks me right here." He jabbed at his heart as with a knife. "King David, who wrote most of the Psalms, which are really songs, got discouraged. When his house was destroyed and his men left him, it says He encouraged himself in the Lord…I do that with my guitar. Sing worship songs and it lifts me."

Andy clapped his hands. "You're a real preacher boy."

Phil grinned. "Not a boy. But the older folks in the church treat me like one."

"And it discourages you?" MJ asked, dark circles starting to form under her eyes.

"Well, yes it does. I'm thirty." He groaned. "I'm sorry for talking about myself when I came here to encourage you."

Andy kept glancing over at MJ. "You have. Getting company is always a real treat. But sorry I have to cut this short. MJ needs hooked up to her IV for hydration therapy."

Phil darted up. "Oh, don't let us hold you up."

MJ wagged a finger at Andy. "Wait. I need to get their birthdays on my calendar."

"I'll get them. We need to hook you up." He pinched the back of her hand. "You're getting dehydrated."

MJ took in a deep breath and slowly exhaled. "I'm in the middle of a good book right now, so I'll be thankful I have time to read it." She winked at Andy and then met Lottie's eyes. "Do you read novels about the Amish?"

"*Jah*, I do. Some are *gut*, some not so *gut*."

MJ pointed to a massive bookcase that almost lined the entire wall. "I've read all of those. Take your pick."

Lottie's mouth gaped open. "Really? You've read them all?"

"Yes. Take a few, but some are signed by the authors so be extra careful with those."

Lottie knelt down to eye the books better and picked out seven, all from different authors. She sprang up and hugged the books. "*Danki*, MJ. I left my books back home in Ohio."

"Come over any time and get more. Think of it as your own little library."

Lottie never felt lonely while reading and could relate to MJ. What a precious woman, someone who might become a kindred spirit friend.

~*~

Lizzie and Marge headed straight to the bargain bin in the craft section of Punxsy-Mart. Making a quilt for Ruth to comfort her in the days ahead not only would help Ruth, but them also, dealing with the loss of dear Claire. Lizzie shook her head. "The Amish don't talk about the death like the English," she confessed. "But Marge, I can talk to you."

Marge leaned towards Lizzie. "We're *BFF's* remember."

"*Jah*, best friends forever. Never had a sister and you're like one."

"I feel the same. So why don't the Amish talk about death?"

"*Ach*, we do, but we don't ask questions, at least out loud." Lizzie remembered Granny's warning about being too close to her English friend, but Marge was her kindred spirit friend, and they shared the same beliefs. "I don't question God exactly, since he's all powerful and can do what he wants, but sometimes, I just don't understand."

"Are we supposed to understand?" Marge asked, lifting a bolt of calico out of the bin and placing it on the nearby table.

"Well, I suppose not…"

"Our new pastor, Phil Darby, gave a sermon on trusting God. He said that if we understood all of God's ways, he'd be a small god, human sized, and we wouldn't want that."

Lizzie grabbed the plain black cloth and sat with Marge at the table. "Granny says that if we look real close at a quilt, we can't see the pattern and beauty. When we step back, we can. Some things we won't see clearly until we get to heaven."

Marge smoothed out the calico pieces. "Lizzie, are we talking about Claire dying or something else?"

Marge could see through her, obviously. "Same old thing. Not being pregnant and most likely not going to be."

"Same here. Joe wants a child, too, but after the miscarriage and my age, we're feeling pretty hopeless. But a lot of good came out of that miscarriage, in a way. I confessed for the first time about having an abortion as a teenager and found healing. But I still would like my own kid."

"Have you thought of adoption? Maybe one of the boys at Arbor Creek?"

Marge grabbed Lizzie's hand. "I just love Brian Adams. Was there ever such a sweet kid? And he's twelve, just like Anne-Girl."

Lizzie chuckled. "Do not tell anyone else that you're still looking for Anne of Green Gables."

"Why not? I already call him Brian-Boy but he has no clue why I do."

Lizzie started to shake, now laughing. "Marge, when Granny gets concerned about me having a BFF that's not Amish, I tell her you make me laugh."

Marge's brows furrowed. "Granny doesn't approve of me being a good friend?"

The hurt on Marge's face made Lizzie chide herself. *Measure your words Lizzie Weaver.* "It's not you, Marge. It's me. I'm changing and Granny's concerned."

"That I'll corrupt you?" Marge blurted.

"*Nee,* that I'm speaking my mind too much and getting too opinionated concerning homeschooling. She won't say it, but I know she thinks I'm going overboard wanting to home school Millie and Tillie come fall."

Marge looked sideways down at the floor. "Having a town half Amish and half English is a challenge. I have to admit, your dad pushes a lot of Amish ways on Joe and me, but we take orders from Phil Darby and I'm glad."

"Many of the English are trying to adopt Amish ways. We live a slower paced life and have more community." Lizzie felt so defensive all of a sudden, and this blurting out whatever's on her mind just had to stop. "I don't mean to fight."

"Fight? This isn't a fight. We're discussing something that's touchy. Nothing wrong with that…"

Lizzie met Marge's eyes and they both grinned.

"Still *BFF's*?" Lizzie asked.

"*Ach, vell,* I suppose," Marge said in a strong Pennsylvania Dutch accent.

"I'm glad. Now, back to what we were talking about, concerning God. You know about the attempted assault on me when I was engaged to Roman years ago."

"Thank God a hunter came by. Oh, Lizzie, the thought makes me shudder."

Lizzie stared at the black material. "Well, I had such a fear of God back then. I wish I could have talked to him as easily as I can now. I would have told Roman and he would have married me anyhow. I could have had *kinner*…"

"Well," Marge said, "Granny helped me see there's no use looking back. You turn into salt, like Lot's wife, not able to move forward. When I think that I aborted my little one, I hate myself, but then I think of a loving God who forgives and wants me to…I don't know, love myself in a good way. I have scars though."

"Me, too. Do they ever go away?" Lizzie asked.

Marge put a finger to her cheek. "I don't know. Jesus had scars on his hands and they helped Thomas believe. God can use scars."

Lizzie searched Marge's face. "Now that's profound…"

"That's Phil Darby's Wednesday night Bible study. He's awesome, Lizzie. A better preacher than Jerry, but do not ever tell a soul I said that. I love Jerry and Janice, but Phil's the best Bible teacher ever."

"Sounds like it. I never heard any teaching on past wounds and God leaving scars on purpose."

"Me neither! So, we goof up and get scars, or someone leaves us scarred, but Phil said we'd never be able to help hurting people if we weren't ever hurt ourselves."

Lizzie wanted to raise her hands and shout hallelujah, like the Baptist did. "Marge, maybe God brought us together because we're both wounded and can help Charles and Brian. Adopt them! What do you think?"

Marge pat her heart with her hand. "I do want to adopt my Brian-Boy."

Lizzie laughed. "And I want to adopt my Charles...Boy."

~*~

Phil peered around church, not knowing if he was boring this congregation, or if they were in deep thought. *Maybe on the verge of a deep sleep?*

"I'll close this thought. The cross of Christ isn't being preached in many churches. It's not a happy message. The cross calls us to die to our selfishness, greed, lust, and follow Christ, no matter the discomfort." He gulped, and then held his Bible in the air. "We need to live by this book, not just talk about it."

"Amen!" Joe yelled from the back. Brian, Greg and Charles, who were sandwiched in between Joe and Marge, all lowered their heads.

"Yes, preach it Darcy, I mean Darby," Marge said, nodding towards her husband.

Darcy? When would this mix-up end? Phil pondered, knowing he was beginning to blush. He never even thought of himself as handsome, someone out of a Jane Austen novel. *How ridiculous.* As he nodded his head, appreciative of Marge and Joe's encouragement, the back church door opened, a woman with red hair, head down, slowly slipped into the back pew. *Lottie?* He saw red hair peeping through her Amish bonnet, but why was she here, in English clothes. No, it couldn't be. But with her head down, how could he know?

Relieved that this Wednesday night Bible study was over, feeling rather worn out, he was glad to be refreshed by Ginny Rowland and her closing song, *The Old Rugged Cross*. As Ginny started to pluck at her guitar, he took a seat in the front row and followed the words to this classic hymn beamed up on the wall by an overhead projector.

On a hill far away stood an old rugged cross,
The emblem of suffering and shame;
And I love that old cross where the dearest and best
For a world of lost sinners was slain.
So I'll cherish the old rugged cross,
Till my trophies at last I lay down;
I will cling to the old rugged cross,
And exchange it some day for a crown.
Oh, that old rugged cross, so despised by the world,
Has a wondrous attraction for me;
For the dear Lamb of God left His glory above
To bear it to dark Calvary.

As Ginny continued to sing, Phil made his way to the back so he could shake hands with folks before they left. What criticism would he get tonight? Too much doom and gloom, most likely. He grabbed some fliers to hand out for the church picnic off the back table, but when he turned around, he was not prepared for who he saw. "Judith?" He almost choked on a throat lozenge he'd been sucking. "What? I mean, why are you here?" How could he have missed this red head, thinking it was Lottie? This was his ex-fiancé.

She took his hand. "I made a mistake. Can we talk?"

~*~

The next morning Granny paused to watch the sunrise out the window. The changing hues of pinks and magenta made her wonder about the colors heaven would have in store. Heaven, a place she'd thought she'd be nearing, until she talked to Angelina. The woman was as fit as a fiddle at eighty-one. Angelina wanted to teach her how to make Italian spaghetti sauce, and Granny felt special somehow. Did her girls feel this way about her?

That Angelina was going to mentor her in the art of Italian cooking made her feel young. *I feel like a kinner around Angelina, and I like it,* Granny thought. *Lord, bless this woman, and thank you for opening my eyes to something: Jeb makes me feel like an old woman!* His hovering and fussing about making pies for the boys over at Arbor Creek hit a nerve, and now she knew what it was. She was still a spring chicken in many ways, married to an old crow!

Lord, I love Jeb. Help him see he's not as old as the hills around us!

She heard feet shuffling and turned to see Jeb. "Morning, old man." She cupped her mouth. "I mean…young man."

Jeb moseyed over to the coffee pot on the woodstove and poured a mug full. "Something wrong Deborah?"

"*Nee,* nothing at all."

He eyed her before taking a seat at the head of the massively long oak table. "Smells *gut*. Berry pie for breakfast?"

She wagged a finger. "Oatmeal's for you. *Gut* to lower your cholesterol. Pies are for the boys at Arbor Creek."

"I'll have oatmeal with a side of pie, how's that?"

Granny opened her black cook stove. "Well, another few minutes and the pie will be done. Start on the oatmeal now."

"No eggs?"

"Need to lower your cholesterol."

"Deborah, ever since Claire was taken from us, you fear I'll keel over from a heart attack. I may die of hunger first."

"You're supposed to watch what you eat."

"Moderation in all things, Deborah Byler Weaver."

When he called her that, his dander was sky high. Well, she had to admit she did fear Jeb having such high cholesterol and it could shorten his life. "Alright, how about when we see the doc in town, he makes a diet for you."

"Diet?" He rubbed his thin middle. "I'm a rail."

"You know what I mean. A diet for your heart."

Jeb slowly closed his eyes, as if he could make her disappear. "Alright. Now, I'm starving. Can I have a *smidgen* of jam on my oatmeal?"

Granny nodded and scooped up piping hot oatmeal from the pan. "Blackberry jam or currant?"

"Blackberry. So, what plans do you have today?"

She placed his breakfast in front of him and went back to her stove to check on the pies. "Taking a walk."

"A what?"

"A walk. Over to Arbor Creek."

"It's a mile from here."

"Angelina walks to Ruth's and she's *old*."

At this, Jeb started to chuckle. "*Ach*, I see. Keeping up with the Italians, *jah*?

Granny couldn't help but laugh on Jeb's play on words. "*Jah*, I am. Should have walked over to see Nathan and Lavina when they lived there. Jeb, we're not as old as we think."

"Then stop calling me old man."

She grinned. "All right. Same for you. No more *old woman*."

~*~

Granny felt her knees would explode in pain as she hobbled up the steps of Arbor Creek. Denny ran out onto the porch and put an arm under hers, lending support. "*Danki*. I'm…tired."

"Why'd you walk? Is your horse sick or something?"

"*Nee*," Granny panted. "I, ah, decided to walk."

Denny cocked a brow. "To lug that big basket over here?"

She nodded, touched by this young man's concern. "*Jah*, I did. I'm not old, you know."

"You're not? Aren't you a grandma?"

"*Jah*, I am, but it doesn't mean I'm a…fossil."

Denny took the basket from her. "I didn't say fossil, just elderly in a good way."

"Elderly in a *gut* way? You mean respectful way? Being respectful to your elders?"

Denny nodded. "I never had any contact with my grandmas and wish I did. I think it's a good thing that the Amish have so many relatives. Becca said she has too many cousins to count."

Granny followed Denny into the kitchen, where he put the basket on the counter. "I'll tell Marge you brought these. Or, we could hog one up now and no one would know."

A smile slid across Granny's face. "You like my pies?"

"I could live off them. If I was deserted on an island and could take one thing, it would be enough pie to live forever."

Granny took a seat at the new table Marge raved about. *Retro 1950's style kitchen*, she's said. Well, Amish kitchens looked the same in the 1950's as they did now, so she supposed hers was retro, too. "With all the red in here, red cherries on the curtains, towels, red chairs and whatnot, I feel like I'm in a cherry pie."

Denny burst into laughter. "Marge has gone nuts on this kitchen. Joe said only the kitchen could look like this, not the rest of the house."

"Almost hurts the eyes, so bright"

"Marge sewed the curtains along with Lizzie. Came home last week from shopping with a ton of material."

Marge and Lizzie spend too much time together. "So, how did Lizzie sew? By hand?"

"No, on Marge's machine. You know, the electric one."

"What?"

"She comes over and sews with Marge. Isn't that alright?"

"*Jah*, I suppose," Granny mumbled.

"Want some lemonade? I made it myself."

Granny, trying to get over Lizzie's secretive ways, spending more time with an *Englisher* than any Amish friend, nodded. "I'd appreciate something sweet and cool to drink."

Denny took out a glass pitcher from the refrigerator that had a smiley face etched on it. "Marge flipped out over this Jell-O pitcher. Said it was like the one on TV years ago."

The Amish used plenty of Jell-O and she recognized the face. "Well, she's trying to make this a nice home for you boys, *jah*?"

Denny put two glasses on the table and sat across from Granny. "She's doing her best. But she has her favorites…"

A shadow skimmed over Denny's face. "Favorites?"

"Brian Adams. She L-O-V-E-S him. And Charles is Lizzie's favorite. I get under Joe's skin."

"How so?"

"I don't know. I heard him say it. He didn't know I was on the steps."

This blond haired, blue eyed boy yanked Granny's heart. "I think you're a fine young man."

"Really?"

"And Jonas feels the same way. He talks about you all the time."

"What's he say? I'm a bully?"

Granny searched Denny's mischievous eyes. "Is there truth in it?"

"Charlotte, I mean, Charles, gets on my nerves. He acts all...he sucks up to Jonas and Lizzie. Trying to get adopted."

"And you're jealous?"

"No. He's two-faced. What you see is what you get with me."

"I see," Granny said. "Are you too old to be adopted? Jealous that Brian and Charles are younger?"

Denny froze, his lemonade half-way to his mouth. "I don't know. They have it easier."

"How so?"

"Well, they got out of foster care younger. Charles never was in a home for misfits. I was in five. And yes, it makes me mad. I have no one. In two years, I'm out of here," he said, chin jutting out.

"I'm sorry, Denny. But if it's any consolation, you always have a home in Smicksburg."

"No I don't. When I turn eighteen, I have to leave. I'll have to go into the military."

"Military?" Granny croaked. "And kill people?"

"I don't have a choice. I get fed and paid and a chance of getting a college education."

Granny took a church bulletin that was on the table and fanned herself rapidly. "Do you want to go to college?"

"Not really, but I have to make money."

Granny thought back to how wretched Anne Shirley felt in Anne of Green Gables. Marilla and Mathew were up in years and took her in. She wasn't old and neither was Jeb. Could they make a difference in this young man's life? She reached across the table and took his large hand. "Ever think of being a farmer? Or someone who works with wood, like my son, Roman?"

"I used to make fun of Smicksburg, thinking it was boring. But now I feel, I don't know, like I like nature. Maybe major in nature studies at college."

"Why not be a farmer...or carpenter? We apprentice our youth. They learn better one on one."

"I'd love that. Especially the carpenter part. Ya, I think I'd like to work construction or be able to make furniture like Roman."

"Well, I'll ask Roman and others if you can be apprenticed.

To Granny shock, Denny grabbed her, clinging tight. "Thank you."

~*~

Nestled in her knitting circle, Granny felt her chest expand in pride. Her circle wanted to make a quilt for Ruth and Lizzie and Marge were initiating it. The aroma of berry cobbler that Granny placed on the new picnic table Roman made her, wafted across the circle, begging her to get up and cut a piece. But her legs were jelly, having walked too much.

She listens to Lizzie explain about the black material, representing those valleys in life, the shadow of death experiences.

"Granny taught me they were needed in life to make a beautiful picture. Up close, you can't see the design, but as we step back over time, we can see the beauty." Lizzie glanced at Granny, admiration filling her chestnut brown eyes.

Lizzie really did take to heart everything Granny said. *Why do you fret so much Deborah Weaver?* she admonished.

"Are we still making the quilts for the *bopplis?*" Lottie wanted to know. "I think everyone has their squares done, *jah?* We need to finish one thing before hopping over to another."

"Lottie," Marge said evenly. "Ruth just lost her mother. I think it's only right we get this done pronto."

Lottie face flushed and she remained seated as Lizzie and Marge continued to run the circle. *Was Lottie hurt? She was the expert quilter, not Lizzie and Marge,* Granny wondered. "Lottie, I think you'd be the best help in teaching us how to make this quilt for Ruth. Marge, do you know how to quilt?"

"You just follow the pattern, right?" Marge asked, looking bewildered.

"There's much more to it," Granny informed. "And we'll be hand-stitching it, not using an electric sewing machine..."

Marge pursed her lips, cheeks bulging.

Lizzie nudged Marge. "You knew we'd be quilting Amish style, right?"

Marge glanced over at Suzy. "Outnumbered again..."

Suzy groaned. "Marge, this is a rare skill to learn; quilting from expert Amish quilters."

"We can use a trestle sewing machine," Maryann said. "Some of us can sew, some embroider, some stitch appliqué..."

"You're right, Maryann," Granny said. "We all have our own talents. I love to embroider and am better at it than appliqué."

"I love the feel of the batting," Becca said.

"And I love having a teenager here," Suzy quipped. "Having the young and old in one circle. How cozy."

Old? Granny knew that was referring to her. How she wanted to boast about not only walking over to Arbor Creek, but also walking back, Denny at her side.

"Speaking of young," Lizzie teased. "I saw Gilbert the other day. He's not young anymore, but a man. Appears to be working mighty hard on that land he's inheriting. Will we have a wedding come fall?"

Granny gawked at her daughter-in-law. "Lizzie. It's a secret."

"What's a secret?" Maryann asked. "Surely if my daughter is making wedding plans, I'd know, right?"

Becca leaned her head on her *mamm's* shoulders. "Don't worry. Lizzie's teasing. I'm not marrying Gilbert in November."

Maryann patted her *dochder's* head. "*Danki*, Becca. You know how your *daed* and I feel."

"I'm sorry," Lizzie said. "I was teasing. You've been seen with Gilbert on Sunday night buggy rides."

Marge sighed. "That's like something out of an Amish romance novel…"

At this Lottie burst into laughter. "Some of those Amish novels are *furhoodled*. You'd think we lived a utopian lifestyle."

"What's that?" Marge asked.

"An ideal perfect world. And we can't have it because we don't have perfect people. Some of those novels make the Amish so perfect, or so evil. The bishop's always mean and rules with an iron rod."

"How terrible," Granny said. "Jeb's not like that at all."

Suzy spoke up. "I have to admit, I love Amish fiction. It's innocent compared to other books, making it all the more romantic. Speaking of, did you hear about Mr. Darcy's girlfriend showing up at church last night?"

"Is that his name for real?" Maryann asked.

"No, we tease him and call him Mr. Darcy," Marge said, giggling. "I think it's getting old. He just wants to be called Phil. Anyhow, he was engaged to Judith. I met her. Wow, what a nice couple they'd make."

Lottie shot up. "Can we start quilting? Split up into groups? Who's going to cut and do piecework? And who wants to embroider?" She fidgeted with the ends of her untied *kapp* strings. "I'll help cut while you all decide. Can I have the pattern? She asked Lizzie.

Lizzie appeared too stunned to move, but she did, handing the pattern over.

"Lottie, what's wrong?" Suzy asked.

Lottie's blue eyes brimmed to near spillover. "Nothing. Nothing at all."

Granny had heard rumors through the Amish grapevine that Lottie had been spending time with Phil. Did she care for him? Is that why she was mum whenever she invited a young fellow from church over for dinner, making a foursome? Jeb called it matchmaking, but she called it helping the young ones see what they can't see. *What's gut for them.*

Granny felt sorry for Lottie somehow, her standing there, a statue, ready to cry. "How about you help me get more lemonade out here on the porch?"

"We have enough," Marge said.

Granny stared hard at Marge. "We'll get some ice then. Hot out here." She grabbed Lottie's hand and yanked her towards the door to the kitchen like a ragdoll. Once inside, she pointed to the bench. "Lottie, sit down."

"What's wrong, Granny?"

"It's obvious the Amish grapevine is right. You're seeing Phil Darcy and care for him."

"Phil Darby's his name." She slowly shook her head as if trying to dislodge something.

"Tell me," Granny commanded, softening her tone.

"I like Phil. He's a great man. Knows his Bible through and through and is teaching me a lot."

"And?"

"Well, he's helping me forget something horrible."

Granny cupped her cheeks. "You mean counseling you? Are you hiding something like Lizzie went through? Did someone try to hurt you?" Granny rushed to Lottie's side and sat next to her. "It's best to tell someone."

Lottie's eyes narrowed. "I don't know what you're talking about. Was Lizzie in counseling?"

"*Jah*, out in Lancaster. You didn't know?"

"*Nee*, I did not."

"If you need counseling, we can arrange it, but women should counsel women, you know that."

Lottie tapped her foot rapidly. "Phil is kind and loving. Love heals wounds, *jah*?"

"Love? *Ach, nee*. Not you and Phil."

"He's helping me is all. Granny, remember when I told you I was engaged and my old fiancé is living with another woman?"

"*Jah*, go on."

"I still love him. I don't think the pain in my heart will ever go away, neither will I ever be able to love someone else."

Granny embraced Lottie. "I understand more than you think. Jeb wasn't my first love. Mine left for the world, too." She pulled Lottie back and smirked. "All over a clothes dryer."

Lottie didn't speak, only looked eager to be advised.

"I was engaged to a man who left the Amish in 1963 and became Mennonite. I was so sick of hanging clothes on a clothesline and wanted to leave, thinking the Amish were backwards. When that machine came out and was affordable, it was like the forbidden fruit and I wanted to bite it."

"But you didn't…"

"Well, thanks to my parents, I didn't. They sent me here from Ohio and I met Jeb." She touched Lottie's pretty cheek. "You're so young. Let me help you find a *gut* Amish man. You can't continue letting Phil help you."

"Why not? It's like our own Bible study…"

"The Bible has a way of making us talk about our deepest thoughts. Intimate hidden thoughts. We bond over our minds and then our bodies." She wagged a finger.

"Granny!" Lottie gasped. "I'm pure. A virgin."

"I supposed you were, but the best of us can be tempted to do things and emotional attachment can lead to, well, love and marriage. *You* are Amish. You *need* an Amish man.

"I still love Peter…"

"Well, when I met Jeb, I was still in love with my old fiancé. Maybe God put us together so I can help you." Granny thought of all the single men in the *Gmay* and ran through them like a Rolodex. *Ezekiel. Of course!*

~*~

After her knitting girls filed out one by one, heading out to their buggies or cars, Granny felt fatigued. So many emotions running through her, she knew a casting off prayer time was in order. She went to the rocker in her bedroom, finding solitude, Jeb being outside hoeing their vegetable garden. She closed her eyes to pray, but her mind raced to Jeb's concerns over Angelina tending to Ruth's *kinner. He took out his anger on weeds, pounding the life out of them.* It went against the grain of Amish culture to depend on *Englishers* for help; the Amish gained an opportunity to bond closer as a community, not unravel at such times. Suddenly, Lottie telling her about Phil Darby flashed before her. She tone of voice about this *Englisher* was tender, loving. No, this was not being knit together in the right way, this kind of bonding needed to loosen. And Lizzie's outspoken behavior, it was not Amish...

Unable to calm her mind, she reached for her Bible on the nightstand and flipped it open to Psalm 23, reading it three times to soak it in. The first verse seemed to leap off the page into her heart:

"The LORD is my shepherd; I shall not want."

Not want? For anything? She knew Jeb had other translations of the Bible tucked away in his little bookshelf on his side of the bed. Granny was curious to see what this verse said in modern language, the "goodness" and "mercy" parts. Granny slipped over to Jeb's bookcase and noticed a book with a new bright yellow spine. *The Amplified Bible.* She opened the new book, and as usual, sniffed the interior. *Ach, nothing like the smell of a new book. So inviting.* She riffled through the book until she was back in her rocker, reading Psalm 23 again. The first verse read:

The Lord is my Shepherd [to feed, guide, and shield me], I shall not lack.

Shield! She wanted to raise her hand in praise, but the walk to and from Arbor Creek kept it down; mighty fatigued she was.

God would shield Lottie from an English love. He would shield their *Gmay* from interference, but maybe for a time, let a lonely Italian woman in, blessing Angelina as she freely gave support to Ruth. God would shield Lizzie from English influences, but allow her to glean many lessons from Marge. *Gut* lessons, to be sure.

Feeling calm now, she closed her eyes to pray:

Lord,

Here I am again, your ever fretting child. Danki for your Word which calms my soul. When anxiety overwhelms me, your Word is a comfort. I want to thank you for how you knit all your children together in love. You're the master designer, and even though I wish You'd unravel some relationships I see being spun, I trust you. I can trust you like my sheep do me. I am their shepherd and you are mine, only You have infinite love and patience

I cast off Ruth, Angelina, Lottie and Lizzie on you. You care about them and see their hearts. Fix what needs fixing and keep together what you're pleased with. Help me to take the plank out of my own eye before I try to take one out of another. This takes humility, Lord, so help me.

I also lift up Denny. Ach, Lord, he breaks my heart. I read about elderly people adopting. It's a foolish notion, to be sure, at our ages, but I am your servant. If you want us to take in Denny on a permanent basis, and the laws of the land to permit it, we're willing. If not, help Denny accept our love. Help him soak in Jeb's mentoring down by the fishing hole. I believe you have a special place for fisherman, many of your disciples always wanting to be near the water, waiting for a bite. You said you'd make them "fishers of men." Help Jeb catch Denny in those teachable, tender moments, and help Denny realize he has a Heavenly Father who loves him.

I ask this all in Jesus name,

Amen

Dear readers, I hope you're enjoying Granny's fourth circle. As it is July in this episode, berries are ripe for picking in Western Pennsylvania, but, maybe not where you live. Here's a more flexible basic fruit cobbler recipe. "We'll meet again in a few weeks when *Amish Knit & Stitch, Episode 3 ~ Against the Grain* is released. Blessings to you! And if you have any comments or prayer requests, send me a message by filling the contact info at www.karenannavogel.com *Danki!*

Fruit Cobbler

½ c. butter
¾ c. sugar
2 c. flour
2 tsp. baking powder
2 tsp. baking soda
½ tsp. salt
1 c. milk
1 quart drained berries, any variety
½ c. sugar
2 c. fruit juice

Cream butter and ¾ c. sugar until fluffy. Sift next four dry ingredients and slowly mix into butter mixture, alternately with milk. Pour into greased 9 inch x 13 inch pan. Spoon drained berries over the top. Sprinkle with ½ c. sugar (or less if too sweet). Pour 2 c. fruit juice over the top. Bake at 400 degrees for 45 minutes. Serve warm.

EPISODE 3:

Against the Grain

Granny knocked her mug of morning coffee up against Jeb's. "*Salute.*"

"What?"

"*Salute.* It's like saying best wishes or whatnot. Angelina clicks my water glass every time we have iced tea." The scent of roses, now clinging onto the trellis around her porch, lifted Granny's spirits. "*Ach*, Jeb, how I love July."

Jeb rubbed his eyes. "*Jah*, I suppose so."

"You suppose so?" She leaned back into the cedar glider they shared. "What's wrong, old man?"

"Tired, is all."

"*Nee*, something's got you flustered. What is it?"

After taking a long swig of coffee, he said, "Angelina's overbearing. Telling Ruth this and that, how she lost a sister in Italy and how staying busy will make her better."

"That's true. Don't you agree?" Jeb started to tap his foot and the ruby throated hummingbird Granny was admiring darted out of the porch. "You don't like Angelina or her advice?"

"Truth be told," Jeb confided, "she irritates me to no end. There, I said it. I need to ask the *gut* Lord for more grace. She's so…"

Granny nudged Jeb, trying to get him to brighten up. "*English?* And we Amish help each other in a crisis."

"She's not English, she's Italian." His voice possessed a lilt, happy with his play on words.

Granny fought a smile. "Old man, you know my meaning. She's not *Amish.*"

"*Jah*, and we survive as a People by teaching our *kinner* our ways. We carry each others burdens within the *Gmay*. It's a lesson that needs to be lived out. What is Angelina's interference teaching my whole flock?"

Granny sipped her coffee. "But we let the local fire department and ambulances help in our time of need. What's the difference? I think what folks will see is that we're letting an elderly woman be a part of something. A *lonely* woman, at that."

"She's probably lonely because you can't get a word in edgewise." Jeb shook his head and then took a bite of his pastry. "Bet she can't bake like you."

"That's called fried dough. Angelina made it," Granny quipped. "She gave me the recipe. It's from the Old Country."

"Old Country?"

"*Ach*, she calls Italy the Old Country." Granny shifted. "Jeb, she's *gut* for Ruth right now. It's a link to Claire. Angelina's telling Ruth all kinds of stories, ones she needs to hear. How much Claire cared about Luke. Loved him like a son."

"Claire said that?"

"*Jah*. He made her bluebird boxes and did all kinds of handiwork around the house. Angelina said Ruth was headstrong to raise, and had her faults, too. She's helping Ruth see this so she's not so hard on Luke."

Jeb held his coffee mug up, frozen in mid-air. "Really?"

"*Jah*. So don't be judging Angelina."

"I don't judge her," Jeb defended himself. "I just don't find her as sweet as you to be around." He nudged her playfully. "Let's get this day off to a better start. How about a silent prayer?"

Granny scooted closer to Jeb and leaned her head on his shoulder. "I'd like that."

They both bowed their heads and Granny slowly said the Lord's Prayer and then Psalm 23, the Bible portion she'd been mulling over for the past month:

The LORD is my shepherd; I shall not want.

He maketh me to lie down in green pastures: he leadeth me beside the still waters.

He restoreth my soul...

The trickle of rain water being collected in a barrel off the side of the porch always calmed Granny's soul to a sacred hush. Still waters...*water*, something needed for life was what her Lord gave her daily. Her daily bread...a *wunderbar* husband that she loved, despite his headstrong ways. He clashed with Angelina because they were alike. *Lord, help Jeb deal with Angelina, my new Italian friend who makes me feel like a kinner.*

The rumbling of buggy wheels was heard in the distance and Jack darted off the porch, his deep woof menacing, although he was gentler than their little Pomeranian, Bea. When Jack met the buggy his tail wagged and barking ceased. A friend had arrived.

~*~

Maryann wrung her hands. "Becca's never kept things a secret."

"Well, she's *gut* at math and is helping Denny, to be

sure," Granny said. "And is company for him. He's a lonely boy."

"A lonely *man*, I'd say," Maryann grumbled. "A man who could steal Becca's heart with those big blue eyes."

"I agree," Jeb said. "They take walks in our woods. Not afraid of Old Bull."

"*I'm* not afraid of Old Bull," Maryann blurted. "He's as old as the hills and can barely walk."

Jeb winked. "We thought the boys would stay off our land if they knew we had a bull. I think they feed him."

"So Becca and Denny don't stay at Arbor Creek but take walks?" Maryann asked evenly, one hand over her heart.

Granny rose and got her pinking sheers, cutting off some roses from her trellis and handed them to Maryann. "Here, the scent will calm you down." She took her seat next to Jeb on the glider and watched as Maryann put the flowers up to her nose. "Denny's a *gut* boy and the woods are a *gut* place for boys to be." She gazed up at Jeb. "I told Denny and the boys, now that we know them better, to feel free to walk the path to our place. Summer will fly away like geese before we know it."

"So you think I need to trust Becca more?" Maryann's brown eyes yearned for understanding.

Jeb scratched the back of his neck. "Keep the communication free between *yinz*. We found that helpful in raising our boys. Ask Becca why all the secrets and tell her it hurts your feelings."

"But she's sixteen and in her running around years."

"That's why I'm in agreement with New Order Amish."

"What?" Granny and Maryann crowed in unison.

"No *rumspringa* in the New Order. I never did believe there was an age that you didn't need the safety net of the

Gmay. Makes no sense."

Granny sighed and then pat Jeb's cheek. "I was thinking New Order as in electricity or something. Best keep to ice boxes and live off the grid."

"New Order seem more lenient with electricity for businesses. And they fly in planes."

"What?" Granny asked in disbelief.

"They've changed a few things," Jeb continued, and one is no *rumspringa*...and bed courtship."

"*Ach*, Jeb, no one does that bed courtship anymore, lying on a bed while talking."

"*Jah*, they do, but most Amish have done away bundling, and some are rethinking *rumspringa*. Times are changing. *English* teens are more rebellious and downright violent today, and to let some of our lambs associate with them can be dangerous." He hit his knee. "I don't know what it is today, but I'm being a stick in the mud. Lots of *gut* in the world, and we need to think on that. As far as Becca's concerned, just have a motherly talk with her. Becca's one of those teens with her head and heart in the right place."

"*Gut* morning," Lizzie yelled from her house. "Jeb, we're going over to Ruth's soon, jah?"

Jeb nodded. "Jah, soon."

"What's going on?" Granny asked.

"Lizzie wants to help with Ruth's *kinner*. Feels like I do about Angelina. The Amish take care of their own.

Granny slowly closed her eyes. *Stick in the mud for sure and certain.* Jeb's upbringing was still at his core at times. The Schwarzentuber Amish and their odd rules and extreme isolation, not even allowed to marry someone Old Oder that wasn't Schwarzentruber. And no planting of flowers because it showed pride. How *furhoodled!* But Jeb's steadfast ways had won her heart, and kept her on the straight and narrow. She had been a lukewarm Christian when she met Jeb, but that all changed, thanks to her dear husband. *Lord, help Jeb to be wise as a serpent but gentle as a dove*

~*~

Suzy knit one, purled one, making a seed pattern on the prayer shawl for an ailing church member. Lord, help Rita overcome this horrible cancer. Help her through the brutal chemo treatments. Thank you, Lord, Maryann is cancer free.

A ding of the little gold bell made Suzy look up at the front door. "Morning, Lottie."

"*Gut* morning, I suppose." Lottie's tone was flat and her shoulders slouched.

"And what does that mean?" Suzy remembered having Jane Austen teas in the back room with Colleen, talking over her problems. "Want some tea?"

"Had three cups of coffee to wake up. Don't need anymore caffeine."

Such hollow, unsettled, deep blue eyes, Suzy thought. "Oh, no. Has Hezekiah had a setback? Were you up helping him?"

Lottie hooked her cape on the antique coat rack and shook her head. "Hezekiah's almost back to normal. Colleen hovers over him, tending to his needs." She stiffened. "Such a happy couple…"

Suzy wanted Lottie to spill the beans, but knew she wasn't as free with her emotions like other Amish friends. No, you had to pry open oyster-like Lottie. "Is everything okay? Need to talk?"

"*Nee*, I can't."

Getting out the mental pliers, Suzy tried a different angle. "Have you heard from back home in Ohio? Are they having a heat wave there, too?"

"Only a letter from my *mamm*. Nothing new."

"Have you been up late quilting? You have such dark circles under your eyes."

Lottie walked past Suzy as if she was invisible and entered the back room. Suzy followed. "Lottie, something's obviously wrong."

Lottie read the clipboard, her finger sliding down her list of jobs to get done in three short hours. "I best get busy." Her face scrunched in pain and she grabbed her middle.

"What on earth?"

"My nerves." She plunked down in a chair around Suzy's tea table. "I wish Granny would stop all this matchmaking. I'm having a noon meal with her, and Ezekiel Coblenz is invited."

Suzy took the pitcher full of iced tea from the counter and poured Lottie a glass. "Guess a Jane Austen tea can vary. Colleen used to tell me all her woes about Hezekiah here, over hot tea. We'll have cold."

"Her woes? What woes?"

"The girl had plenty of hardship in her life," Suzy said. "An abusive home, being a homeless single mother, cutting herself because she didn't know how to cry. She needs to write a memoir about overcoming life's obstacles."

Lottie stared at the glass of iced tea Suzy set before her. "Colleen never told me any of that. I knew she had a child out of wedlock and all, but repented and is now Amish."

"Well, she's not one for self-pity and her past is best kept right there. Hezekiah brought such healing to her heart."

"So Amish and *English* marriages can work, right?"

Suzy *knew* exactly where Lottie's mind was now. *On Phil Darby, aka, Mr. Darcy, the perfect man.* "Lottie, are you seeing Phil? Is that what this is all about?"

Lottie tied her loose prayer *kapp* ribbons. "We talk…"

"And?"

"Well, his ex-fiancé, Judith, wants a second chance. And for some odd reason, I want to strangle her."

Suzy cocked her head back like a chicken. "Amish are pacifists."

Lottie smirked. "It was a figure of speech. I wouldn't hurt Judith, but I'm afraid she'll break Phil's heart again. I told him to be careful."

Suzy poured herself a glass of tea and sat across from Lottie. "Did he ask your opinion?"

"*Jah*, he did. And I told him anyone can act a part, but watch how they react."

"Granny taught you that, right?" Suzy asked.

"*Jah*, she did. So Phil needs to put himself in a situation where he gets a reaction from her."

Suzy reached across the little table and squeezed Lottie's hand. "You care for Phil. Is that what this is about?"

Lottie avoided eye contact and let nervous laughter spill out. "We're friends. Of course I care about him."

Suzy gripped her hand tighter. "You love him."

"I, ah, admire him. I like him a lot."

Suzy's mind went to *Sense and Sensibility.* Didn't Eleanor say something similar about Mr. Ferris? And she was in love? Such insipid, safe words. "Spill the beans, Lottie. You're in love with Phil Darby, or think you are, right?"

"I can't. He's not Amish, but likes our ways," she exclaimed.

"*And…*" Suzy pried harder.

"He brings out the best in me. Maybe he'll turn Amish.

Suzy bit her lower lip and counted to ten mentally to calm down. She'd seen Amish families torn apart by an Outsider coming in and sweeping an Amish woman off her feet with the promise of converting to her faith. But, usually the woman left the Amish after "falling in love." Suzy shook her head. *Wait a minute. Phil is level-headed and would never lead a woman on.* "Does Phil have any romantic feelings for you?"

Lottie withdrew her hand and took gulps of iced tea. Her face became flushed and she fanned herself with a stiff hand. "I think he does. He's really nice."

He's nice to everyone, Suzy wanted to say. She'd have words with Phil, making him realize his good looks were charming many a single woman in town. Although Phil would laugh it off, really believing he wasn't anything to look at; he was a very attractive young man.

The front door bell jangled and soon a "yoo-hoo" from Marge was heard. "Anyone run this joint?"

Suzy had to stifle a laugh. Marge was a hoot. "Come on back, Marge," Suzy yelled.

Marge was soon leaning over the Dutch door. "Came to buy some yarn. Making my Brian-Boy a sweater."

"*Your* Brian-Boy? And a sweater? It's morning and already eighty degrees," Suzy said.

Marge patted her heart swiftly. "It's for Christmas. Found a manly man sweater I can crochet. He'll love it."

"Are you making one for the other two boys?" Lottie asked. "Phil wouldn't want you to show partiality."

Marge arched her neck cat-like, trying to appear bigger, ready for a challenge. "I work with Phil daily. Of course he knows."

Lottie straightened. "So he'd want you to make something for the other boys…"

"And what makes you an authority on Phil's thoughts?" Marge barked, and then covered her mouth. "Sorry, Lottie. But you're catching me off guard. You're acting like you have the corner on Phil. Why?

Suzy sighed. "Something to do a casting off prayer about...."

Marge's eyes pounced on Lottie. "Let me guess. You have a crush on Phil like half the single women in town. Well, I'm getting to know Judith, his ex-fiancé, and she's a woman who made a mistake. She bought all kinds of stuff for the boys, since she's a well-paid doctor. Judith works cuckoo hours, so she let Phil go, afraid of being a bad wife." Marge shifted. "She's learning balance, moderation in all things."

Silence. Suzy glanced over at Lottie, who had pain etched into her eyes. *Lord, help Lottie.*

Marge continued after taking a few breaths. "Judith is willing to be a rural doctor, all for Phil. She's even going to talk to Dr. Pal today, since he's only here on Wednesdays."

"But," Suzy blurted, "Phil's an interim pastor. Jerry and Janice will be back come fall. Why would Judith want to get a job here?"

A shadow formed across Marge's face. "I'm only relaying what I know. As far as Jerry and Janice, they're giving Phil more responsibilities."

"Oh," Suzy groaned, having to take a chair. "They're not coming back?"

"You get emails all the time. Don't you know?" Marge asked.

"Know what?" Suzy asked, panicking.

Marge held both hands up as if being arrested. "I don't know anything except that Phil's making more plans and they extend...into the fall."

"Janice emails me almost every day. Jerry does like it down there, for sure, but she's homesick for Smicksburg." Suzy took a deep, cleansing breath. "If they don't come back…" She wanted to measure her words. She and Ginny Rowland next door nearly ran the church now, and Phil was a wonderful teacher, but Janice was like a sister. How could she go to the Smicksburg Baptist Church if they didn't return? *Lord, why do things always have to change?*

~*~

A few hours later, Lottie closed her eyes as a slight breeze swept up from the pond. Having a picnic outside in the shade of a willow was refreshing, but this Ezekiel that Granny invited had the personality of a tree branch. Could he even speak? She looked across the picnic table at Granny and Jeb. *Lord, I want a marriage like there's.*

Jeb's eyes met hers. "Awfully quiet today, Lottie. Tired from working in the yarn shop?"

Wiping her brow with a napkin, she sighed. "It's the heat. Almost ninety."

"It's over ninety," Ezekiel said. "Was ninety-five when I left home. Sun's more powerful now."

"We need more iced tea," Granny quipped. "I'll go inside to make a new batch while *yinz* take a walk in the woods. It's much cooler there."

"*Jah*, let's take a walk," Jeb agreed.

Granny tugged Jeb by the elbow. "Need your help inside, old man."

"But I want to show them where I found some arrow heads."

Granny's brow furrowed. "Jebediah, I can't do all the work in this heat." She nudged him with her hip and then grinned. "Just tell Ezekiel and Lottie where the arrows are."

Jeb told Ezekiel which path to turn on to, while Lottie eyed Granny. *She'd arranged for them to be alone.* Lottie wanted to stomp a foot and cry. *What a horrible day.* She got a letter from Millersburg that Peter was seen in town with another woman, not the one he was living with. Was he a complete womanizer? And then Marge saying Phil was giving Judith a second chance made Lottie realize that yes, indeed, she was falling for Phil Darby. How couldn't she? He was so attentive to everything she said, accepted her, respected her...and she thought he felt something for her. Was he a womanizer, too? Could any man be trusted?

Granny and Jeb headed towards their little white clapboard *dawdyhaus* and Ezekiel drew closer. "What do you think?"

"About what?"

"What Jeb just said." Ezekiel took off his straw hat, revealing matted raven black hair, cut in the traditional bowl cut, and fanned himself. His bangs lifted and Lottie noticed a scar that extended above his left eye to his hairline, forming an indentation of a few inches long. *What was it? A bruise? Did he get hurt?*

"Lottie, quit staring," he said, sheepishly.

Sad for being insensitive, she averted her attention. "Didn't mean to be rude."

"Farm accident." His chest expanded, as if needing air and headed towards the path that led into the woods.

Lottie chided herself for making him feel so uneasy. "I'm sorry, Ezekiel. I thought it was a bruise."

He picked up his pace, making it hard for Lottie to keep up, so she ran. "I said I'm sorry."

He spun around, digging his heels in the path. "I know Granny's trying to set us up, but the whole town knows about you chasing an *Englisher*."

Lottie's heart jumped into her throat. "Who said such a thing?"

"Country gossip...the Amish and *English*. Twice as fast and juicy." He shook his head. "You were seen with him in his car."

"We visit a shut-in and I'm helping Arbor Creek with their garden. I have a green thumb, you know."

Ezekiel stepped towards her. "Lottie, be careful. He's not Amish. You're baptized, *jah*?"

"*Jah*, I am. But Phil's helping me...trust...people."

Ezekiel went over to a nearby fallen tree and took a seat. "Don't you trust Granny and Jeb?" Patting the area next to him, he encouraged Lottie to take a seat.

Was he making advances? "I'll stand, *danki*."

He spun his hat on a finger to a regular rhythm. "I'm sorry I was short with you. I feel deformed when people stare."

Deformed. Lottie felt deformed in her soul, which was probably worse. She was painfully shy.

"Do you forgive me?" Ezekiel asked.

Lottie shifted and then went and sat next to Ezekiel. "It's rude to stare. I'm sorry. But everyone has things they wish could change and can't, don't you think?"

He raked his fingers through his hair, dividing it where the scar lay, revealing the extent of the damage. "I have no one to relate to," he mumbled.

Lottie was taken aback that the scar ran up near the crown of his head. But then again, it was only seen when his hair was parted and his thick hair grew in over much of the injury. As his face contorted as if in pain, she reached for his hand. "My face turns red. I'm shy. So, I have a scar, too."

He gave a forced smile. "You don't have to be shy..."

"How do you know?"

"Because I overcame it. It's fear of people. There's a sting in it, like the Good Book says. I only blush now when someone new sees my scar, but then I reckon if someone thinks less of me because I have a five inch mark on my head and face, they're the one with a mark on their soul."

Lottie felt like she was talking to Jeb. Somehow Ezekiel was wise for his twenty-five years. Had adversity made him mature faster? Had trials made him appear to have a depth of character that surprised her?

~*~

Becca twisted stems of chicory into a wreath and plopped it on Denny's head. "I crown thee with the title of most improved math student in a month." She giggled, and Denny threw off the crown and said he needed to thank his teacher with a big hug and kiss. Becca dashed to a nearby tree and, being the tomboy she was, climbed it nimbly. "You stay away you bad boy," she teased.

Denny crossed his arms. "I can climb a tree, Becca. How does that saying go? About two people up in a tree, K-I-S-S-I-N-G? First comes love, then comes marriage and then comes –"

"Denny! Stop it." She'd heard this rhyme before and it wasn't funny, even in jest.

Denny got down on one knee. "Marry me, fair lady."

Becca climbed higher in the tree, but when Jonas shouted for her to get down, she was relieved that someone else was out in the back yard at Arbor Creek. Denny always had a way of leading her into secluded areas, 'where he could concentrate,' but she knew he was developing a crush on her. Becca had made it clear she was courting her Gilbert and would marry him in a few years, when she was ready to settle down, after a bit of traveling and learning herbal medicine from Reed Byler.

She descended the maple, but near the bottom she lost her footing and Denny broke her fall. In his arms, the scent of his peppermint breath so near, something stirred deep within. *Was she attracted to Denny in a wrong way?* Their eyes locked, and somehow Becca wanted to linger, being nestled in his arms.

"*Danki* for helping Becca, Denny, but you can release her now," Jonas snapped. "You're not getting much math learning out here, are you?"

"Yes, Sir," Denny said sarcastically. "Becca said I'll be up to par when school starts."

"Up to par for what grade?" Jonas asked.

"Ninth," he murmured. "Should be in tenth, but with the moving and all..."

"Well, ninth grade's higher than we go," Jonas encouraged, "and you won't be moving again."

Denny cocked his head forward in disbelief. "Someone wants to adopt me?"

"*Nee*, but you can stay until you graduate, if you want. Up to twenty-one years old. You know that," Jonas said.

Becca eyed Denny. Was he milking her sympathy? *On his own at eighteen with no one?* He told Granny this and had her in tears. "Denny, why'd you go on about having to leave in two years?"

"Because I do...have to."

"*Nee*, you don't," Jonas said, ambling closer, wobbly leaning on his arm braces. "You just want to. Is that it? Don't think you have the smarts to graduate from high school?"

"I'm an idiot! We all know it. Some kids my age are in eleventh grade. It's embarrassing."

"You're smart, Dennis Boles," Becca said. "And between me, Granny, and some of the other knitting circle women, we'll *make* you finish school."

Jonas chuckled. "You don't want to mess with that there group. They work as one mighty force."

"We're united," Becca declared. "We get things done."

Denny shuffled his feet and plunged his hands into his jean pockets. "Why do you care, Becca? It's not like we're kin or anything."

Becca clasped her sweaty palms. "I like a challenge, Dennis."

"Dennis the Menace," Jonas teased. "That's in the funny papers."

At that, Denny glared at Jonas and darted away, out to the path that led to Granny's.

Jonas shrugged. "Must be awful sensitive about being called that."

Becca shook her head. *Why did she care?* But the next second, she found herself running after him...*caring*.

~*~

"I'm glad we got to talk," Lottie said to Ezekiel. "And I do understand. Being shy is being scarred in the heart, but everyone thinks you can make it go away. Just pick yourself up by the britches."

"You wear dresses, *jah*? Not britches with suspenders."

Lottie laughed. "You know my meaning. "

Ezekiel pulled a small New Testament from his pocket. "I carry this with me all the time. It makes me see what's real. Things that are true about me."

Lottie asked if they could meander over to the creek and get cooled off. When they trudged the path a short distance, they both took off their shoes and sat along the creek bank, soaking their feet in the brisk water. "That'll cool me right nice."

"*Jah*," Ezekiel agreed. "Now, I want to show something from this here Bible." He riffled through the pages and looked at her pensively. "Am I being too preachy?"

"*Nee*, not at all. I love learning new things."

He gawked. "Me too. I lost count on how many books I own. *Daed* wishes I had the passion for woodworking like I do books. So, I buy books on building things to appease him."

Lottie somehow felt at home with this man she'd misjudged. A personality of a twig? *Nee!* Ezekiel seemed to be so genuine. "Go on and read what you'd like from the Bible."

He cleared his throat. "There is no fear in love; but perfect love casts out fear, because fear involves torment."

His eyes shone as he stared at the pages that appeared to be highlighted with different colors. He flipped back to another section and read, "For you did not receive the spirit of bondage again to fear, but you received the Spirit of adoption by whom we cry out, 'Abba, Father'." He slowly closed the little book and held it to his chin. "Lottie, the love of God's a powerful thing and it can heal any type of scar." He tapped the book. "You need to read this and let it soak in."

"I, ah, do," Lottie said, feeling defensive all of a sudden. "I read three chapters a day and get through it in a year."

"But, do you meditate on just one or two verses, slowly, letting the meaning sink down into your heart to change you?" He chuckled. "I have a fascination with words and it's hard not to break open the Greek Lexicon to find word derivatives, but what I'm really doing is running from the simple truths in the Bible. They're hard to believe. God loves me and so I don't fear. Perfect love casts out fear, like I just read."

"And it works, just like that?" Lottie was thirsty to know.

"Well, not overnight but in time, you'll see a change." He pointed to the massive oaks in the woods. "These guys didn't grow overnight, and neither do we."

Somehow this struck a chord with Lottie. The truth in the Bible, she'd been told. That it would set her free. Was she thinking truthful thoughts about herself, or hearing the voices of kids teasing her on the playground still? Lottie knew the answer. She'd been wounded quite young, and Peter rescued her. Was that why she was so attached to him? Lottie looked over at Ezekiel. "So, how long did it take you to feel comfortable being yourself? To be an oak?"

Ezekiel leaned back against a tree, cushioning his head with his hands. "I'm still a work in progress. It's only when I meet new people and they stare that I have a problem. Folks say they don't notice the scar anymore."

Lottie decided Ezekiel's face was one of the most handsome she'd seen, he could have a flaw and he'd still be good looking. His large, light blue eyes were now mellow as he gazed at her. Why hadn't she seen this when first meeting him? Then she thought of his hat. He'd buried his face behind his hat and it appeared he was aloof.

"Gotcha!"

Lottie jumped at the sound of a man's voice, followed by a girl's giggle. Across the creek she soon saw Denny and Becca. *She was in his arms?*

"I said let go, Dennis Boles," Becca shouted.

"Let her go!" Ezekiel yelled over.

Denny spun around, lost his balance and slid on a muddy slope. "Okay. Chill out. We were playing tag."

Becca covered her cheeks with her hands as she ran back down the path towards Arbor Creek, and Denny followed, asking her to wait up.

Puzzled, Lottie looked over at Ezekiel. "Should we tell Phil Darby?"

Ezekiel's eyes darkened and appeared sunken in. "Why Phil?"

"He runs Arbor Creek. Well, Marge and Joe do, but Phil's Denny's pastor."

"Tell Marge. You're too friendly with Phil for my liking."

For his liking? Lottie didn't know if she was appalled or liked his protective, strict Amish ways.

"Are you going to the Singing this Sunday over at Miller's Pond?"

Lottie had heard this before, a hint that he wanted to take her home. Could she open her heart up to this man? Men were as changeable as the zigzagged creek in front of her. Her *mamm* had always said life was full of changes, the seasons being our examples. She closed her eyes and shot a prayer up for peace and then stared into the rippling water. If God created this world full of change, she needed to dive in, not have her nose in a book, something she could control, not finishing it if it had no happy ending.

"Lottie, it's not a trick question." Ezekiel's tender voice broke into her mind. "Are you going to Miller's Pond on Sunday night?"

Chin up, she said, "*Jah.* I am."

A grin broke over Ezekiel's face. "*Gut.*"

~*~

Granny quickly hid the binoculars when Lottie and Ezekiel came into view. She was following the red-tailed hawk, not them, and seeing the majestic bird dip towards the woods, she wondered if it was nesting there. With her wrap around porch, she could do her birding hobby from so many angles, yet have a knitting project on a chair nearby.

She waved at them as the approached. "Have a nice walk? See much wildlife? See Old Bull?"

Lottie laughed. "*Nee*, but if I did, I'd pet him and he'd most likely purr like a kitten."

"Who's Old Bull?" Ezekiel asked.

"His name says it all. He's an ancient bull that's now only a pet," Granny said with a grin. "I have a weakness for animals of all sizes. Birds, dogs, cats, pigs…bulls. I remember when he was young and I feared him, but now he's like a lamb." Granny realized both Lottie and Ezekiel had a skip in their step. When they came on the porch, the radiance in Lottie's face was undeniable. They took seats in the Amish rockers across from her and it appeared they wanted to talk. "Did being out in the woods cool *yinz* down?"

"*Jah*," Lottie said. "Where's Jeb?"

Granny scratched her chin. "He's taking a short cat nap. Was out last night late, ministering to one of the flock."

Lottie peered over at Ezekiel and then fixed her eyes on Granny. "We saw Becca in the woods with Denny. Thought Jeb would want to know."

Granny picked up her knitting. *Why was everyone afraid that Denny was a hooligan?* "He's a lonely boy and they're like brother and sister. He's not a hooligan."

The screen door opened and Jeb, hair all disheveled, plopped a straw hat on his head, smashing it down into place. "Deborah, who you talking about?"

Knitting a bit quicker, she said, "Denny. He's a *gut* boy. Man, actually."

"*Jah*, he is," Jeb said. "Has grown on us. You two don't like the boy?"

Again, Lottie seemed to need Ezekiel's support as she looked over at him, as if a secret signal to something. Granny knew married couples had this covert language. *Seems like they picked it up right fast.*

"Well," Ezekiel started, "we saw Denny embracing Becca in the woods. We spoke up and Denny got defensive, saying they were playing tag."

Granny reached over and took Jeb's hand as he sat next to her. "He's never had a real family before, so he's finding his footing."

"But little stitches make a quilt," Lottie said contemplatively.

"What's that mean?" Jeb asked.

Lottie's face grew crimson. "My attempt at a parable of sorts? You know, one sin leads to more, until you're living in full sin. I see sin that way, one leads to another until you have a…large quilt-full…and it's time consuming taking that quilt apart, stitch by stitch."

Granny wanted to ask Lottie if she stopped making stitches, closer ties to Phil Darby that needed cut, but didn't dare say anything in front of Ezekiel. "We'll talk to Denny. *Danki* for telling us."

Jeb shot up and started to pace. "Deborah, did you hear this right? They were embracing." He pulled off his hat and fanned himself. "I don't want to rule with an iron fist, but there are boundaries." He eyed Lottie. "Did Becca back away or hug him back?"

"*Nee*, she said to let her go."

Granny inwardly rolled her eyes. Of course she did. It's Becca, a girl who's Amish to her core.

Jeb plunked down onto the glider next to Granny. "Maryann has her suspicions. Maybe she senses something's not right. I've never seen her so on edge."

"It's her first *kinner* to enter *rumspringa*," Granny said evenly, her breathing matching her knitting pace. She needed to calm herself. Roman had agreed to let Denny come over and watch rocker-making, the old-fashioned Amish way, and also woodworking of all sorts. *Lord, help Denny walk the fine line between living among the Amish and English*. She noticed Jeb leaned back, meaning he was calming down.

Jack darted off the porch, kicking up stones and dirt as he raced down the driveway. Soon Granny saw the Baptist Church van. The image of Janice driving that van down her driveway made her heart ache. Was the country gossip true? Jerry and Janice may be moving? At times like this, she envied Suzy's ability to communicate with Janice on the internet.

Jeb slumped. "It's *that* Phil Darby."

"*That* Phil Darby? What's wrong with him?" Granny asked, feeling her nerves unravel. "He's picking me up to go visit MJ. I'm teaching her how to bake, remember?"

Phil came to a slow stop, seeming to be afraid of hitting Jack. He nearly ran up the porch steps, but when he saw Lottie with Ezekiel, his countenance fell. "Hello. Am I interrupting an important meeting?"

"*Nee*," Granny said.

"Well, being in the ministry, I know problems don't happen as scheduled." He glanced over at Lottie. "Are you alright?"

Did Phil care for Lottie? Granny wondered. She'd find out.

~*~

Granny asked Phil to turn off the air conditioning, as she felt a headache come on. She rolled down her window and took in the scents of a sweet July afternoon. The air was dry, not so humid, and so it seemed crisp. Rows of corn always took her back to her childhood, living in Ohio farm country. "Knee high by the Fourth of July," she said.

"What?" Phil slowed the car as she talked.

"The corn. It's knee high by the Fourth of July, but it's the third week in July, and its shot up to head high, wouldn't you say?"

"Depends on how tall you are," Phil grinned. "For you, yes, the corn is up to your head. For me, it's chin high."

Granny playfully slapped Phil's arm. "I like you. Easy to talk to."

"Well, I'm glad. People need to be able to talk to a pastor. Some call it the gift of compassion."

Granny pondered his words. *Jah,* some people were more giving. Was this a gift? *Did she have it?*

"But," Phil continued, "as with any strength, there's a down-side."

Granny leaned her head back on the comfy seat. "What do you mean?"

"Well, some people with the gift of compassion can find themselves overlooking sin too much, or getting attached to people a little too much. Sometimes when I counsel someone, I want to do all the work for them, but they'd never learn to walk through their valleys on their own."

Granny's neck turned like an owl. "Really? You can care too much?"

"Yes, I believe so. Jesus was the greatest teacher and counselor, but he still had his disciples go out to learn on their own."

Granny now knew why young women's hearts fluttered around Phil Darby. He was a *gut* listener, sincere Christian, and wise. How did he learn so much in his thirty years? "I suppose you've had some valleys to go through to be so wise?"

Phil grimaced. "Yes. I'm going through one now, actually."

Granny hugged her middle. "Can I help?"

"Well, I don't know if anyone can help."

"Give me a try," Granny implored.

He looked in the side mirror and adjusted it. "So many deer out here, you need to keep your eyes on the roads."

Granny supposed Phil didn't want to talk about his valley.

"My mom has cancer. *Fourth stage.* Judith came here, to help me get through it. I...don't think I need her help, though."

Granny gasped. "*Ach*, I'm so sorry. Is it terminal?"

"Yes. She's in a hospice center in Cleveland."

Granny leaned towards him, wanting to take away his pain. "Is your church helping you?"

"My church back home, yes, but not the people at Smicksburg Baptist."

"But," Granny ventured to say, "how can you get through something without...community?"

Phil pursed his lips as if he bit into a lemon. "I'm used to it."

"You shouldn't be. It's not what the Bible teaches, and you know it."

"I know it," Phil said, "but I'm the pastor."

Granny's eyes misted. "I know many in your church. You should tell them you need help. Tell them to pray for your *mamm*."

Phil quickly glanced at her. "Pastors are supposed to be strong."

"Even Jesus asked for prayer in the Garden of Gethsemane. He was let down, his disciples all falling asleep, but nonetheless, he did ask for prayer."

Phil's face became a stone. "I don't know if I can. I hardly know these people."

"Well I do. Take my word for it, you'll get so many casseroles you'll gain ten pounds. But it's hard to admit you need help. It goes against our grain, if you know my meaning. Do you know I started my knitting circles because I needed help? Reaching out to those girls sure went against my grain."

His face softened. "Really?"

"*Jah.* Getting old, turning seventy, made me feel...not needed. Everyone needs to be needed." She thought back to when she wrote each girl a letter on her rose embossed stationary. She feared no one would come, that they'd think she was a pathetic old woman begging for a visit. How her life changed by knowing and helping her girls. How much her 'Little Women' helped her! "Phil, please let others help carry your burdens...."

Phil took her hand and squeezed it. With misty eyes, he said, "Thank you. I'll think about it."

~*~

Jeb winced when he thought of Denny flirting with Becca. He was as protective of that girl as if she was one of his own *grandkinner.* Knowing Denny walked over an hour ago and was at Roman's Rocker Shop learning a new skill, bending hickory wood, he felt he needed to have words.

As he moseyed over to the shop on the other side of Roman's large farmhouse, memories of he and Deborah building the place, raising their boys, flooded his soul and filled it with joy. *Jah*, the right helpmate can make a man's life a joy. He thanked God for Deborah, who seemed to understand Lottie so well, getting her fixed up with Ezekiel, a man who was as straight as an arrow in his Amish ways. *Was Lottie winking at worldly ways? At Phil Darby?* More memories of Deborah almost leaving the Amish and how she despised his strict ways when they first met passed through Jeb's mind. *Lord, help Lottie not to be as hard on Ezekiel as Deborah was on me.* A chuckled welled up from within him. How spirited Deborah was when they met at the new Smicksburg settlement. And how they helped scrape off each others rough edges. Deborah was indeed a helpmate of the *gut* kind. *Bless my wife today and help her not be too attached and compassionate to Denny. The boy needs to know some boundaries in life.*

He knocked on Roman's rocker shop door, and then shook his head. *Why am I knocking? Is this heat melting my brain?* He stepped inside to see Roman and Denny hovering over a piece of dark walnut wood. "Not making rockers today?"

Roman wiped his brow with his handkerchief. "Too hot to be around boiling water to bend the wood. I'm teaching Denny how to carve. Starting him on a rose." He leaned a plaque up to show Jeb.

"Looks *gut*. Making a present?" Jeb asked, eying Denny.

"No. Just learning."

"On a *gut* piece of walnut?" Jeb probed.

Roman leaned on the table. "*Daed*, it's a scrap piece. What are you getting at?"

Jeb crossed his arms and huffed. "Denny, word has it you were cuddling with Becca in my woods."

"We were playing tag and I caught her."

Jeb bit his lower lip, pausing to find the right words. "Do you like Becca?"

Denny peered over at Roman as if asking for help, but Roman had plunged his hands into his pockets, eyes ablaze. "Sure I like Becca. She's a friend and I don't make them easily."

"What about the other boys over at Arbor Creek?" Roman asked.

Denny rolled his eyes. "They're all suck-ups. Pansy-boy suck-ups."

Jeb leaned forward. "Care to translate that?"

"They're all goody-two-shoes' around Marge and Joe, but cuss and even hide cigarettes in their rooms. But they'll get adopted because they're sly."

"Charles smokes a pipe?" Roman pulled at his chestnut beard. "We Amish smoke pipes. Is that what you're saying?"

"No, real cigarettes."

Jeb cringed. "And no one smells it?"

"They smoke outside. I think Phil Darby's onto something, though. Cool guy. Can't fool him."

Jeb didn't smoke pipes like many Amish, Deborah warning him about the dangers. "Besides the smoking, do you think Charles and Brian are sincere in wanting to change?"

Denny looked down. "I suppose so. And they're younger and people can change them more than me."

Roman stepped forward and clamped a hand on Denny's shoulder. "The Lord can change a man at any age. He's still changing me. I was as stubborn as a mule." He smirked and looked over at Jeb. "Still am, I suppose."

Denny's shoulders seemed to relax. "All this talk about God is creepy." He put both hands up. "I think Jesus was a good guy from the movies I've seen. He was pretty cool, really."

"From the movies you've seen?" Jeb sighed "You can't learn about him there."

Roman cleared his throat. "*Daed*, the Baptist Church took a bus load to see a movie in Punxsy. They've been putting up posters about that movie, *Son of God*, all over town. Seems like it was a *gut* thing." He turned to Denny. "Did you like it?"

Denny nodded. "It's hard, you know. All I've known is a dad who was abusive. In the movie Jesus got hurt by people, too. I mean, they killed him and he forgave them." Sincerity was etched into his eyes as he met Jeb's gaze. "Is that what Christian men are like? Not some sappy wimps?"

Jeb's eyes clouded. Denny's acute understanding of Jesus, the God man who had feeling just like any human, must have been a powerful revelation. Jeb hadn't seen a movie his whole life but these Baptists had a way of expanding his imagination. "Denny, *nee*, Jesus wasn't a sissy, if that's what you mean. It takes a real man to forgive."

Denny shook his head rapidly. "I want to forgive my folks and foster parents. When they spit on Jesus he didn't retaliate, but I socked the guy."

Roman gasped. "What?"

"One of the foster parents spit in my face, so I hit him."

Roman looked over at Jeb, eyes wide. "I'd be tempted to do the same. Weren't there any *gut* foster homes for you?"

Denny's face softened. "Nora. She was old, in her fifties, and lost her husband. Nora was the best."

"Why couldn't you stay?" Jeb asked, his heart sick over what Denny was revealing.

"She took in a few kids and we put her in the hospital. Had to take care of herself, being old and all."

"Do you remember where she lived?" Roman asked. "Would you like to visit her?"

Denny shrugged his shoulders. "I don't know if she'd want to see me. Almost burnt her house down playing with matches."

Jeb groaned. Most likely Denny was his own worst enemy. If he listened to rules, he'd maybe be adopted by now. Denny *was headstrong*, Jeb pondered....*just like Roman.* Is this why Roman had a liking towards Denny more than Charles?

~*~

Suzy sat in the front pew, as usual, helping change the plastic sheets on the overhead projector. She flipped through the file of music to retrieve the lyrics to the last song, when Phil asked for everyone to please give him their full attention.

He tapped his Smart Phone and then looked hesitantly out at the packed-out congregation. "I got an email from Jerry that he wants me to read to you all, so here it is.

"Dear Church Family,

"Janice and I are having a grand time down here in the South. I've enjoyed every aspect of teaching classes at the Bible College, and I'm considering an offer they've made for me to be a permanent teacher. Of course, Janice and I won't do anything unless it's bathed in prayer. We mean dunked in prayer. Like the scripture says in Proverbs 16:25, "There is a way that seems right to a man, but in the end it leads to death." So, there's a way that seems right in our own eyes, but it doesn't mean it's right. It may end up destroying us somehow. Now I don't think God will strike me dead, but it's just not the very best path to take."

Phil scrolled down on his phone and continued.

Actually, Janice and I love yinz all so much. Yep, I haven't forgotten my Pittsburghese. I use yinz down here and people think I'm from a different country. When I say, "Let's get this classroom redd up, they stare. I mean they S-T-A-R-E.

Okay, I'm off on bunny trails as usual. Be nice to Phil Darby. I'm hearing good reports. Pray for us to make the right decision. We send our love to you all and don't think for one minute we love the folks down here better then...yinz. Yes, there's more people of color, like us, but we've become color blind over the years, not even noticing. And we have the kind folks of Smicksburg to give thanks for that.

Oh, I almost forgot. Continue your outreach to the least of these, the widows and orphans. I encourage you all to get involved with little acts of kindness that mean so much to the single moms and their kids over at Forget-Me-Not Manor and the new boys home, Arbor Creek. I hear from some of you that the knitting circle reading Anne of Green Gables is making some of you want to adopt. I endured last winter Janice talking about classic literature until I came to my senses and learned a thing or two. Remember, Arbor Creek got its name from Pilgrim's Progress, when Pilgrim found an arbor to rest under on his weary journey. And there's a creek out back.

Off on bunny trails again. I'll get to the point. Let's all pray for each other that we make the right decisions. Big decisions like moving away from our beloved quaint town or adopting. I depend on this scripture for guidance. Proverbs 16:3 "Commit your works unto the LORD, and your thoughts shall be established."

So, let's commit all we do to God and when the dust settles, what do our thoughts say? God puts his plan into our hearts and thoughts, is what I'm thinking.

I send you one of my bear hugs with this email.

Jerry

As sad as Suzy felt, her heart sank for Phil. He just stood there, his head hung as if in silent prayer...*or was it rejection?* The mumbling in the church, the gasping that accompanied every hint that Jerry may not come back must have hurt Phil's feelings. Suzy boldly got up and met Phil at the altar. "We have Phil here, the best Bible teacher around. Let's pray for Jerry and Janice and be thankful we have such a fine young man to fill in. Permanently, if need be."

Phil gave Suzy a side hug. "I want what's best for this church. I know you're all attached to Jerry and Janice."

"We appreciate you, too, Phil," Joe bellowed from the back. "Doing a mighty fine job over at Arbor Creek."

"Amen," Marge added.

Phil pat Suzy's shoulder, telling her to take her seat as he had another announcement to make. Suzy, ill at ease, wondered if she'd done the right thing in going up to the platform. Was she babying Phil?

Phil's chest expanded and he let out a cleansing breath. "I have an announcement. No, a prayer request. Being around the Amish, I see they have community not only at their barn raisings and quilting bees, but on a heart level. They carry each others burdens by being transparent. I'm not saying this church doesn't, but I haven't. I'd like to ask prayer for my mom. She has cancer and is in a hospice facility."

He gripped the wooden podium, leaning on it for support. "I'd like prayer. I've come across as happy-go-lucky, hiding my pain, because I thought a pastor wasn't supposed to share his sorrow. That I'd appear weak. A dear Amish woman told me even Jesus asked for prayer, and I'm no better." A sob escaped Phil, and with trembling words he asked, "Can I have a week off to visit my mom? She may only have a few weeks left." He shook his head, willing the tears to stop falling, but they didn't.

Judith ran down the aisle and up to Phil. She slid her arm through his and then turned to the congregation. "I've known Phil's mom for ages. She asked me to come here and see how I could help Phil. Mrs. Darby is the sweetest woman and I don't understand why her life is being cut short, but it is. Please pray for her."

Phil put his arm around Judith. "Thank you," he said, leaning his head against hers.

Suzy felt a pit in her stomach. How she hated cancer. It took her mom. When would there be a cure? She grabbed her green leather journal and put Phil on her prayer list. She wrote next to it, *Judith*. It was apparent she still loved Phil. Who would win this fine man's heart?

~*~

Granny held her morning coffee up to Fannie's. "*Salute.*"

"Sa...what?" Fannie asked, green eyes seeming like emerald gems this summer morning.

"It's Italian. Sorry, I say it all the time now. Get's Jeb's dander up. It means cheers, or good wishes...lots of meaning for one little word."

"*Ach*, Granny," Fannie quipped. "I've missed you more than I should have. I don't see how Ella can live so far away from Smicksburg." She shifted to lean closer to Granny as they share her cedar glider. "Is that *furhoodled* of me? I'm such a *boppli.*"

Granny pat Fannie's cheek. "You're my girl."

"Woman. One of your 'Little Women', *jah*?"

Warm glee filled Granny's heart. How this girl had grown from an immature twenty year old to a *mamm* and wife in two short years. Growing up too fast, for Granny's taste. "*Jah*, my little women will all be here at the circle. I sure do wish Ella was here, though. She and

Ruth are two peas in a pod, and Luke needs his brother's help."

"I hear Ruth's being…ruthless. I'm not making a joke, but seriously, badgering him about his past, all confessed and forgiven, making him feel responsible for her *mamm's* death. I never thought she could be so mean."

Granny put a finger up, meaning Fannie needed to hold her tongue. "Grief is a strange thing. We strike out at those closest to us."

"But Luke's been such an angel. I hear he's turned the cheek every time Ruth lashes out."

"Who said that?"

"My husband. Luke told Melvin he's held his tongue…so far. I think he's fed up. And I don't think that Italian woman is helping, being over there all the time."

"Angelina's her name," Granny informed. She just loved the elderly woman, challenging her to try new recipes, walk more, and what love she had for poor deceased Claire. Was she trying to fill Claire's shoes, being a *mamm* and *oma* to Ruth's family? "You say Luke's like a gum band, ready to break?"

"*Jah*, just like a gum band. We need Ella and Zach to move back home. Ella has such a calming effect on everyone. Zach, too." She took a sip of coffee. "How can we get her to move back?"

Just when Fannie seemed like she'd matured into a grown woman, she was saying something *furhoodled*. "Make them move back? *Nee*, we're not God. It's His job to pave the way home for them if He sees fit. Trust me, Fannie, I've wasted years trying to 'help' God and it's futile. Just yesterday, I feel I may have wasted time."

"How?" Fannie implored.

"Had one of my special meals. Really a meal to get Lottie and Ezekiel together."

"And you don't think it worked?"

"Well, I thought I saw a spark, but I think I have an imagination that just flaps like the clothes on the line. I see images of Lottie married to Ezekiel, and then in horror see her trot off with an *Englisher.*"

"Phil Darby?" Fannie sighed.

"*Jah.* He's a *wunderbar* man. I can see why the girls like him so, but Lottie's baptized, and I believe Amish in her core." Granny admired the ruby throated hummingbird that darted in and out of her porch, sipping nectar from her many feeders. The glider started to rumble and she glanced at Fannie. She was giggling so hard, she had to set her coffee on the little cedar table. "What's so funny?"

"Mr. Darcy comes to Smicksburg. It's so odd that the ideal man after our circle reading *Pride and Prejudice.*" She hooted so loud, Jack started to howl. "I hear people call him Mr. D-D-Darcy, *jah?*"

Granny's brow rose nigh high her hairline, deepening her wrinkles. She didn't see the humor in it at all. *Nee,* she was concerned for Lottie.

~*~

"Whoa now," Jeb advised. "Luke, calm down."

Luke plunged a stone into the creek near their house. "I can't take one more visit. Ruth's worse than ever and Angelina keeps bringing things up that aren't her business."

"Like what?" Jeb asked, taking a seat on a log.

"She's telling Ruth things best left unsaid. Like marital problems her parents had, of all things."

Jeb plopped a pebble in the creek. "Is Angelina saying private-like things about Claire and Jacob?"

"*Jah*, she is. And it's making Ruth cry. Then she goes and asks her *daed* and he denies it. We do *not* need this now."

"What's she saying? I am the bishop and know a thing or two."

Luke squatted down and started to poke the ground with a stick. "That Jacob had a problem with alcohol."

Jeb moaned. "It was a long time ago. Maybe Jacob's forgotten his wild days…"

"When he was in *rumspringa?*"

"*Nee,* when Ruth was a *kinner.* I've never said a thing, but maybe this is for the *gut.* I think Claire was the best support Ruth could have, knowing that God gives beauty for ashes. She was happily married later on in life, but not when she was young. The alcoholic rages Jacob flew into were pitiful. And he left scars…"

Luke's pensive blue eyes seemed to soften. "Scars? What do you mean?"

"He got violent. I was his friend and intervened quite a bit. Ever notice Claire never came to knitting circle?"

Luke pulled at his short blonde beard. "She never did. Ruth asked her but she wasn't interested."

"*Shame.* She knew Fannie was invited and thought Mona would be there. Now that woman's a metamorphosis if I ever did see one, a worm into a butterfly, but back then, Mona was mean as spit. And Claire thought she might blab something out."

Luke cracked his knuckles and stared hard at the ground. "How come no one ever told me this? When I was feeling like pond scum for the way I treated Ruth. It would've been nice to know Ruth's *daed* was a jerk like me."

Jeb wagged a long finger. "He confessed to the entire *Gmay.* Gave up the bottle and repented. And we never bring things up again, *jah?*"

Shame swept over Luke's countenance. He sighed and threw a stick in the water. "You're a *gut* man, Jeb. Never to say anything about the past. You never bring up mine, neither."

"If God can throw our sins as far as East is from West and remembers them no more, why should I?"

"That's an awesome thought," Luke said.

"It's in the Bible. Don't know where, but it is. Now, back to Angelina, I'll talk to her. I believe the woman has *gut* intentions, but is a little too outspoken. And she's lonely, too, so she needs someone to talk to."

"Maybe I should suggest she come over...every other day?"

Jeb chuckled. "*Gut* place to start."

~*~

Granny dragged her tired bones out on the porch where the knitting circle was meeting. Why she had a hankering to visit Denny and take him a pie before circle bewildered her, but she followed her heart and did it. Everyone seemed so leery of the poor boy who was alone in the world. Her dear daughter-in-law, Lizzie, had noticed her hunched shoulders and offered to make the treat for circle. *Bless her, Lord.* As she entered the circle, she forced a smile to all her 'Little Women'.

Fannie ran up to her and held her by the elbow. "Need help?"

Granny cringed. Did she look that bad? "Fannie, I'm fine. Legs are a little achy."

Lizzie took a tray of sliced lemon sponge pie around the circle and mentioned that iced tea was on the little cedar table by the glider.

"*Gut* to have Fannie and Mona back with us," Granny said. "Lottie, have you ever met Mona?"

Lottie tilted her head, looking confused. "*Jah,* of course. At *Gmay.*"

"You're tired," Mona said. "Running around, or should I say walking all over kingdom come. What's gotten into you?"

Granny sat up poker straight. "Angelina, my new friend. She walks a lot. Two miles to your house, right Ruth?"

"*Jah*," Ruth said, head down, not making eye contact with anyone.

"And," Granny continued. "She's teaching me how to crochet doilies." She picked up her knitting that had stayed on her glider all day. "So glad we're just knitting today. It's such a solace."

"We're so sorry about your *mamm*," Maryann said to Ruth. "It's a wonder that you were preparing me to face death two winters ago and perhaps the Lord was preparing your heart…"

Ruth glared at Maryann. "What?"

"You know. Remember when you came and sat with me before my breast cancer surgery? We talked about how life was never to be taken for granted, that life was fragile."

"*Jah*," Ruth snapped. "And you told me reading the Bible with Luke would make a permanent bond. Well, it's breaking."

Granny grimaced. Maybe it was too soon for her to come to knitting circle. Her grief was so raw and she didn't make for *gut* company. Granny looked down at her wooden knitting needles that rubbed against each other. This is what the girls did. They stuck close together and together God was making a masterpiece. "Ruth, we're all missing Claire. And what Maryann said is true. I'm thinking that the stages of grief are wearing hard on you."

Ruth shrugged her shoulders. "I don't know. I've bottled up a lot. Angelina's told me some things, some past hurts my *mamm* endured and grief keeps piling on."

"Your *mamm* wasn't happy?" Fannie asked. "Sure seemed like a peaceful, calm woman to me."

"My *daed* had his secrets…"

Fannie gasped. "What?"

Mona shot up to get a glass of iced tea. "Jacob's a *gut* man. Everyone has their struggles." She poured two tumblers full and handed one to Ruth. "I've been hard to live with, and Fannie's forgiven me."

Ruth's mouth gaped open and she searched Fannie. "So you had a 'healing time' up there in New York?"

"*Jah*, for sure we did," Fannie beamed. "We all make mistakes. I'm making mistakes with Anna and *Mamm's* helping me. But I don't know if Jacob has any big faults."

Mona cleared her throat loudly. "It's all in the past and so long ago, I can barely remember what it was."

Granny's heart did a flip. Was this the same Mona who last year would have tar and feathered Jacob publically all over again? *Lord, be praised.*

"I suppose my *daed* did have a problem with alcohol but Jeb and others gathered around him and helped. Just like they did for Luke a while back."

"And Luke's such a fine man," Marge quipped. "He helped Joe believe there was a God, do you know that, Ruth?"

She shook her head, looking impatient.

"Well, he told Joe how God turned his stony heart into a soft one of clay. Joe didn't think anything could change him, but look at him now," she laughed. "He's like putty dough, but in a good way."

Ruth's shoulders shook and soon tears were falling on her knitting. "I can't help but think the stress Luke put on my *mamm* two years ago was too much for her. People have heart attacks because of stress."

Maryann hugged Ruth and rocked her like a *mamm*. "God's ways are a mystery. He must have wanted your *mamm* with him."

"Yes," Suzy said. "Phil gave an excellent sermon on Enoch. The man was so close with God, he was raptured out of here. Phil said Enoch couldn't be any closer to God unless he went to heaven."

"That sermon blew my socks off. Seriously, Phil is the best Bible teacher ever," Marge declared.

Suzy looked across the circle at Ruth. "When my *mamm* passed from cancer, it took a while. The stages of grief are real. Anger, crying, denying it happened, and some days accepting it. Then it can start all over again, any one of those emotions hitting like waves at the least expected time. I had to run out of the store crying..."

"Really?" Ruth asked. "I've been so angry. First at Luke, now at my *daed*. Today, my words to Luke were harsh and Micah heard." She sniffled and closed her eyes. "He left."

"He what?" Granny asked in disbelief.

"Luke left. Said he'd come on home when he knew he could control himself."

"Was he mean to you?" Maryann asked.

Tears spilled down Ruth's cheeks. "*Nee*. He was calm, but said he feared his patience was wearing thin."

Granny snapped her fingers. "I want you to get counsel from MJ and Andy."

"*Englishers?*" Maryann asked, aghast.

"*Wunderbar gut Enlishers* that have daily trials due to MJ's health. I've never seen a marriage so strong under such circumstances."

"But the Amish should be helping," Maryann persisted.

"I want to meet them," Ruth said boldly. "If heart disease is hereditary, like Doc Pal said, I need to learn how to manage stress better for Micah and Little Debbie's sake, so I'm not taken young."

"And Luke's sake, too," Lizzie added. "He loves you more than you realize. And he's hurting, too."

Ruth groaned. "Not like me…"

"He lost both his parents long ago," Granny gently said. "If anyone can relate, it's Luke."

Ruth knit frantically. "Like I said, I'll talk to your *English* friends…. alone. Seems to be my fate in life, to be alone."

The women looked at each other, the situation so fragile, no one wanted to break the silence. Nesting sparrows swooped down into Granny's porch rafters. The baby birds had their beaks wide open, all vying for the food their *mamm* so freely gave. "I think we need to keep an open heart to God. All of us. When trials come, He shows us the path to take, *jah*? Remember *Pilgrim's Progress* and how dangerous it was to get off on the wrong path? *Ach*, lions can eat you."

"I know that feeling," Mona said. "That evil foreboding feeling or whatnot, it made me so fearful a lion may as well have been standing in the road. I was so afraid of driving a buggy and getting close to others." She smiled at Granny. "So glad you all welcomed me into this circle with all my prickles."

Granny's eyes felt moist. "You're not prickly any more."

Mona pointed toward the heavens. "The *gut* Lord made me and my Freeman once again a happy couple." She grinned. "I think I was driving him crazy."

"*Jah*, you were, *Mamm*," Fannie said.

"Fannie," Suzy gasped. "I can't believe you said that."

Mona put an arm around Fannie's shoulder. "We're learning the balance between speaking up and when to keep our mouths shut."

All eyes were glued to Mona and Granny knew they were shocked. Mona had changed from a person everyone avoided to an encourager, one who people were flocking to like geese to the North in summer. Granny glanced over at Lottie. "You're awfully quiet today. Hot or tired…or both?"

Lottie looked at Granny, eyes hollow. "I talked to Peter today."

"You what?" Granny felt her heart flutter and she started to breathe evenly to calm herself. "He's a shunned man, *jah*?"

"Well, my *mamm* gave him Suzy's phone number and he called this morning. Suzy told me and I called back. I figured if *mamm* wanted me to talk to him, he must have repented."

"And did he?" Granny asked, her throat tight, believing Ezekiel was the one for Lottie.

"Well, not really. He wasn't living with a woman in sin, though. She looks young but is old enough to be his *mamm*. She took him to some Mennonite church services. He's been involved in her church. He's been fellowshipping with lots of Mennonites. Word had it he was seeing another girl, but it was in a group outing with his church."

"If you read the Bible that's all that matters," Marge pronounced. "Lottie, maybe you should be Mennonite."

Lottie's eyes became two large lollipops. "*Ach, nee.* I made a vow to God and the People to be Amish. I take my vow seriously as if it were a marriage vow. I told Peter to never speak to me until he repents and returns to the Amish."

Granny didn't realize she wasn't breathing until she gasped for air. "*Ach*, Lottie. That's so *gut* to hear." She clasped her cheeks. "You're so much like Ella and the *gut* Lord will reward you."

"Who's Ella?"

"Who we were visiting in New York," Fannie quipped. "She's very Amish."

Lottie's brow furrowed. "What does 'really Amish' mean?"

Granny spoke up. "She's a gentle soul. Loves the Lord with her whole heart and it comes out in all she does. She lives out the Beatitudes us Amish hold so dear. Forgiving, turning the cheek…"

"*Hello*," Marge blurted. "We Baptist believe the same thing."

"But," Suzy interjected, "the Amish take their vows more seriously than we do. No divorce, no breaking a vow of any kind."

Marge slouched. "We believe all the Bible says. Amish ways can be too strict."

Granny set down her knitting and scanned the circle. "We agree to disagree, remember."

Marge looked over at Lizzie. "All the time. My BFF's Amish, remember?"

Bff's. Best friends forever. Granny had heard Marge and Lizzie say it many times. It was baffling to Granny, but she knew the Lord spun together every member of her knitting circle as He saw fit.

Lizzie motioned for Marge to follow her and they made their way into Granny's house. How odd, Granny thought. Was Lizzie correcting Marge's blunt behavior? Were they drifting? Was it not possible to be a best friend with an *Englisher*? She heard the screen door slam and turned to see Marge and Lizzie holding up the quilt the circle had made for Ruth.

"Ruth," Lizzie's soft voice said. "We all made this for you. I picked out the black, since I was pondering the dark moments in my life." Lizzie's chin quivered. "We have dark valleys but someday we'll see a beautiful design God's making." Lizzie glanced down at Granny. "Or something like that."

"*Jah,*" Granny said. "We have those black valleys. I had one I could scarcely crawl out of when my girl died."

Marge and Lizzie folded the queen size quilt up and placed it in Ruth's lap. Ruth mechanically slid her hand across a black patch. "*Danki.*" Although a complete statue, her chin quivered and then followed her body as tears spilled onto the quilt.

Many of the circle members got up and embraced Ruth, but Granny's legs didn't co-operate, feeling numb. But she rejoiced that Ruth was taking a step forward in allowing the knitting circle help carry her burden.

~*~

When the rambling of buggy wheel and rubber tires ceased and only the distant sounds of her granddaughters laughing as they played in their tree house, did Granny realize just how tired she was. She leaned her head back on the glider and closed her eyes. She just could not keep walking over to Arbor Creek. Was she jealous of Angelina's fitness? Granny did feel better after a brisk walk, but maybe she needed to walk shorter distances. Being Amish, she was always on her feet, but not walking long distances without a break. She'd have to pace herself better.

Her mind flew to Ruth. How close she was with her *mamm*, now deceased, and her sorrow was so deep, as was her anger. Was Ruth still in shock? Then she thought of all Phil Darby told her about his *mamm* being in hospice. *Danki, Lord, that you've given me these seventy-one years to be here for my kinner. I shouldn't complain about my age. Every year's a gift.*

A buzzing sound startled her. *Bees?* She opened her eyes to see the hummingbirds and relaxed. The image of Lottie and Ezekiel sitting across from her yesterday entered her mind. *Lord, they are perfect for each other. Ach, please, help them see this. And bless Lottie for keeping her vow to the Amish faith and People, telling Peter to stay away. Flee from evil, Your Good Book says. I'm not saying Peter's evil, but breaking a vow is.*

She closed her eyes again to take a nap, but, as usual, all the buzz at the knitting circle swirled around her. Mona had changed as if she was born all over again. Mona was not a concern at circle now, but Marge was. Her cheery English friend seemed too outspoken and contrary, or was she afraid she'd rub off on Lizzie since they were *wunderbar* friends? *Lord, I give Marge to you. Lizzie, too. You create friendships and put us together to glean from each other. Help me with my fear of Lizzie being too independent minded and outspoken. Help Marge to be her gut natured self. I miss that in her. Give her grace to work with the boys at Arbor Creek.*

She soon thought of Jerry and Janice, who started the mission to foster boys. Arbor Creek was turning the town on its head, but it was a *gut* thing, Granny thought. Shake people out of complacency and see there's hurting people in the world. Hurting teens like Denny. But as much as she liked Phil, she yearned to have a heart-to-heart with Janice. *Lord, bring Jerry and Janice back to us, if it be Your will. I miss them so much. And help Denny find a home. You brought him here for a reason. Roman being so keen on the boy isn't by happenstance. You're at work, giving Denny a place to call home. Praise be.*

Feeling fatigue wash over her, she started to mull over Psalm 23 again, and soon drifted off to sleep.

~*~

Dear Readers,

Thank you for reading this episode of Amish Knit & Stitch Circle. Look for the next episode 4 next month. I leave you, as always, with the recipe for the dessert the women enjoyed at the circle. Most likely Lizzie made her pie in the cool of the night, since there's a heat wave going through Smicksburg and the Amish don't have air conditioning. Enjoy!

Lemon Sponge Pie

Grated rind and juice of one lemon
1 c. sugar
3 Tbsp. flour
1 ½   Tbsp. butter
2 egg yolks
1 c. milk
2 egg whites, beaten stiff

Mix together lemon rind and juice, along with sugar, flour, butter and egg yolks. Add milk and continue to mix. Fold in stiffened egg whites. Pour into an unbaked pie crust. Bake at 325 for 45 minutes.

EPISODE 4

Mending Days

*G*ranny positioned a white prayer *kapp* on her damp gray hair and hoped this would keep the August heat wave at bay for part of the day. This was the only month she fought discontentment; the *English* had air conditioners and she did not. As she looked into the little mirror on her bedroom wall, she grinned at herself. *Deborah Weaver, you almost lost Jeb over your hankering for a clothes dryer in 1963,* she mused as she viewed at her reflection. *Ach, you almost left the Amish, wanting to turn Mennonite. Now, you will go through August with gratitude that you are Amish and know all the tricks to keep cool.* She was appreciative for a porch shaded by rose trellises, and mature maples that surrounded the house. Granny gave thanks for a *gut* husband who was just now closing the windows that let in the cool night air, holding it captive. He'd keep the windows open on the shady side only, hang a wet cloth to serve as a "swamp cooler" free of charge.

And they'd set up a little table downstairs as the Amish knew to build basements into a bank. With the earth cooling it, and the cement floor felt *wunderbar* on bare feet. And to think that she and Jeb would be making ice cream tonight. Granny pat her heart. *Ach,* it was romantic making ice cream at night.

But as her heart fluttered a tad, she winced. The report Jeb got from Doctor Pal, wanting him to go on high blood pressure medicine, was not a welcome thought. Jeb had only been on cholesterol pills years ago and he hated being dependent on pills more than his craving for salty snacks, pretzels in particular.

Jeb leaned on the door frame. "No cooking today, for sure and certain. Cold cuts are made for days like this."

"And ice cream, *jah?*"

"*Jah.* Tonight." Jeb winked. "And I don't want you walking over to Arbor Creek or any such nonsense, love."

"You'll be downstairs over at Roman's working, *jah?* He's not going to be using the diesel today in the woodshop?"

"*Nee.* We'll whittle some toys for kids to sell in the shop."

Granny smiled. "If you go out, keep the buggy sides down to keep cool. And use the fan Suzy gave you."

Jeb swatted at the air. "Battery operated fans. Don't need one."

"*Jah,* you do." Granny tied the loose strings of her *kapp* under her chin. "I'll do my mending down here but then I will be out with some *English* friends. Phil's taking me over to MJ's for a baking lesson, but I think he needs to talk."

"I thought you weren't cooking today."

"I'm not. I'm baking in an *Englishers* house that has air conditioning." Her heart plummeted into discontent, so she forced a smile. "Phil even has air conditioning in his car…"

Jeb pursed his lips and then began to chuckle. He drew near her and scooped her into his arms. "You know

Deborah Weaver, I'm sure glad air conditioning didn't come out the same time the clothes dryer did. It would have been too much for you."

Laughter erupted from deep within Granny. "*Jah*, you may be right." She put a hand up to his handsome face. "Jeb, I've had a weakness for modern conveniences, but some are necessary."

He studied her face as his brow knit together.

"Blood pressure medicine," Granny prompted.

Jeb slowly closed his eyes as if trying to block what she'd just said. "I know. I'll do it for you."

"*Danki*, Jeb." She kissed his cheek. "And let me take care of the burdens you carry. The womenfolk problems."

He gulped hard. "You mean Ruth?"

"*Jah*, Ruth and Lottie, too. Women that come here for advice, you take the backseat and rest and let me do the advising. You care too much and it's affecting your health."

Jeb's body tensed as if he were turning to stone. "I can't help it. I'm their shepherd."

"The Lord is their shepherd, *jah*?"

Jeb frowned. "We're his hands and feet though."

Granny patted his face. "Okay, then let me be the hands and feet to the womenfolk. Okey dokey?"

Jeb wearily kissed her cheek. "*Danki*. They sure do have more problems," he said with another wink and Granny playfully slapped his arm before he enveloped her in a long embrace.

~*~

Lottie rubbed her hands and jumped on her toes. "Suzy, do you think we could turn down the air conditioner?"

Suzy turned from the large pots that held boiling dye water. "I'm dying yarn and can't take the heat."

Lottie wanted to say it felt like December in the little store, but just turned back to stocking shelves with the new yarn shipment. Maybe the freezing conditions would give her a cold and she could tell Peter not to meet her today. Her stomach tightened just at the thought of her old beau being in Punxsy, having hired a driver in Ohio just to see her. His letters were begging her to reconsider the Old Order Amish ways. More progressive Amish lived in Punxsutawney, Peter discovered through the Amish grapevine. They used cell phones, and natural gas for most kitchen appliances. Peter thought it would be a stepping stone if they lived in Punxsy after they had wed to ease their way into a more lenient Old Order Amish lifestyle. He was willing to meet her halfway, not turn Mennonite, just an Order not so strict. But someone had to draw a line in the sand and say enough was enough. Living off the grid was essential to Amish living; no debt to the world. And with debt came a form of dependence and then what could happen was their culture would dissolve into the fast modern lifestyle. Lottie shuddered and pulled her shawl around her tighter.

Suzy, face wet from perspiration, turned to her. "Lottie, if you're too cold, go ahead and turn the air down." She wiped her stained hands on her apron. "And hot tea will warm you up, too." She tilted her head. "Something's wrong again. Think you'll ever adjust to Smicksburg if you have to share it with Phil Darby?"

Lottie sighed, her voice coming out a miserable monotone. "Peter's taking me out to lunch today."

Suzy hit her head. "Duh. I forgot. It's today?"

A purple mark now lived on Suzy's forehead and Lottie ran to the sink, getting a wet cloth to blot it off before the stain took. "You look like you have a port wine stain. Stand still." Suzy obeyed as Lottie rubbed at the mark. "Well, now its violet, but you can hardly notice it."

Suzy chuckled. "People stop asking anymore. I had some black dots on the side of my face and a customer said I had the best beauty marks. I thanked her."

Lottie's mind went to her first visit with Ezekiel. His scar took her back at first but the purplish mark seemed invisible to her now. Actually, he was in her thoughts lately more than anyone knew. But then, so was Phil Darby ever since she found out about his *mamm's* illness. But when she tried to comfort Phil, he seemed distant. Was this part of grief that the knitting circle talked about? Anger, denial, crying, acting numb. Or was this the reaction Granny had talked about, that the true nature of a man comes in not how he acts, but reacts. She swallowed hard. How could she go from wanting to marry Peter last winter, to being attracted to an *Englisher* and Ezekiel by summer? Was she that shallow and fickle?

"So," Suzy said. "Need a back-up? I could be at the Sampler, next table over…"

Lottie gripped Suzy's hand. "Could you?"

"I was kidding, Lottie. Aw, my poor girl. And I thought after Colleen left me to get married I wouldn't have a girl who needed me."

Lottie smiled shyly and then stared at the floor. "Do you think Granny needs to eat out at the Sampler? Mighty hot with no air conditioning and all. Maybe I could invite her?"

Suzy took Lottie's slouching shoulders and pulled them back. "Chin up. You are stronger than you think. And you know what you need to say, right?"

7. "*Jah*, I do. But Peter has a way with words…"

"A smooth talker?" Suzy asked.

"What's that?" Lottie wondered.

"Someone who will promise you the moon but not deliver." Suzy took a seat at her little tea table. "You know, guys that wear you down with flattery and persuasion?" She reached over to her little display of Jane Austen books she often read snippets of from time to time. "Ever read *Persuasion*?"

Lottie had read *Pride and Prejudice* after all the jokes about Mr. Darcy being Phil Darby. Then she went on to *Sense and Sensibility* but she never heard of *Persuasion*. "I haven't read it but I know you want me to learn how not to be…persuaded?"

Suzy grinned. "Yes, exactly. So, don't let Peter do it to you. You're so Old Order Amish, you hesitated when I asked you to make coffee in my electric coffee pot, remember?"

Lottie nodded. "But the percolated kind tastes better and you do have the burners going when you dye yarn."

Suzy laughed. "Ach, vell, it does, jah?"

When Suzy started to imitate "Amish talk" as she called it, Lottie knew she had to change to subject or Suzy would go on. "Read me something from *Persuasion*."

~*~

Lizzie took a wet tea-towel out of her gas powered refrigerator, thankful that Roman agreed to go "liberal" and not use an icebox like his parents. She draped the towel around her neck and let it do its job: cool her down. No baking, Roman had said, so she was preparing sandwiches and would open jars of pickled eggs and chow chow for sides.

"Guess what?"

Lizzie jumped and spilled some red pickle juice on her counter. She spun around to see Marge, jumping on her toes and clapping her hands. "Sorry, Lizzie, but I'm so excited I could bust."

Lizzie gasped. "*I* almost busted a canning jar." Trying to collect herself, Lizzie trembled as she reached in the refrigerator again for the pitcher that held her iced meadow tea. "Sit down and have a glass of tea."

Marge scrunched up her face. "That stuff taste like grass."

Lizzie shrugged her shoulders. "It's all I have and there's honey in it and peppermint, too. Try it."

After Lizzie poured a glass full, Marge took a sip. "Hmm. Tastes better. Not so herbally."

Lizzie noticed Marge's bouncing knees and smile that split open her face. "So, what's your news?"

"We did it!" Marge blurted.

Taking a glass of tea and sitting at the kitchen table, Lizzie wiped her face with the tea towel. "Did what?"

"You know. Joe and I had a decision to make about Brian-Boy and we made it. Remember I told you Joe needed some coaxing? Well, Phil Darby got a message from a couple in Cleveland who wanted a Brian-Boy, too. Bet they read *Anne of Green Gables*. Well, when Phil told us, we nearly keeled over with panic. Joe said to Phil, give us twenty-four hours to make a firm decision, and we did, this morning. Can you believe it?"

Lizzie couldn't believe Marge could say all she did without coming up for air. "So, you and Joe have no doubts?"

"Not a one. Brian is sweetness itself and I imagine if, you know, had the child I, you know...aborted...well...he would have looked and behaved like Brian."

Lizzie reached for Marge's hand, lending support. "You don't have to keep bringing up the abortion you had so long ago. I can see it casts a shadow over a happy occasion."

Marge squeezed her hand back. "I know. Joe wanted me to make sure I wasn't paying penance by adopting, gaining forgiveness from God for what I did. I still struggle at times, but when the dust settles in my head, I know I'm forgiven. Scarred, but forgiven. And I can help others who are scarred, like we talked about."

The tranquil glow on Marge's face was like that of an expectant *mamm*. What some *Englishers* called "The Pregnancy Glow." "I'm happy for you, Marge."

Marge held the iced glass up to her face to cool down. "I'm sure Roman will come around, Lizzie. I know you want Charles and I can see why. He's a buttercup."

Lizzie almost spit her meadow tea out as she laughed. "Buttercup? He's a boy…a man soon."

"Oh, I have pet names for everyone."

"You call him Buttercup to his face?"

"When Joe's not around. I pinch his cheek and ask how my Buttercup is. I do need to stop it though. That Dennis Boles calls Charles 'Charlotte' as if he's a girl or something."

"That's nasty," Lizzie croaked. "We Amish have nicknames like Corner Joe who lives on the corner, but not ones that embarrass someone. Roman's taken a real liking to Denny. Sees him more than his own girls at times." Lizzie shot up to resume making lunch, wanting to change the subject. "Are we going to make another quilt anytime soon?"

Marge slouched in her chair. "Lizzie, don't change the subject. We're *BFF's* remember? I can tell you're upset."

Was she upset? Nee, the heat was getting to her. "I'm just hot is all."

"Hot towards Roman? Mad at him because Joe's more flexible?"

Was Roman as stubborn as some teased, Lizzie wondered. *Like he admitted at times?* "Well, Roman moves slowly but surely. When he gets his mind on something, he follows through."

Marge groaned. "If he gets moving. How many times have you asked him about adopting Charles?"

"Marge," Lizzie said evenly, trying to calm herself and not overreact to Roman shelving the idea of adoption. "We're Amish. It's a different life-style, hard to live, as you know."

"I know. But Joe at least tried one of my whims and took the plunge. We did live off the grid for a while. And you know Charles doesn't have to be an Amish convert to adopt. He doesn't have to be baptized. He needs love, Lizzie, and he gets it here. Jonas is like a grandfather to him."

"*Jah*," Lizzie blurted, surprising herself that such emotion erupted in her. "I love Charles, too. He thinks of me as a *mamm*. But it seems like Roman's head is turned by Denny." She plopped a spoonful of chow chow on a plate so hard she almost cracked the edge of the plate. "*Ach*, Marge, I say white and Roman says black. I say up, he says down. He is a stubborn man! I do want to have Charles live with us, but all Roman talks about is Denny. And he doesn't pay attention to Charles anymore." She stomped a foot. "He's as stubborn as a mule sometimes."

Marge clapped. "Get it out, Lizzie. You pent up your emotions too much."

"I do. I like a peaceful home, but lately I have nothing but anxiety swirling in me. I want to just pop!"

"Tell Roman this. Tell him you want to adopt Charles, have him stop spending every waking hour with Denny, and give him a clear picture of what's going on. Sometimes you just have to spell things out to men. Don't take for granted they understand. Just say, '*Roman, I want Charles and not Denny, plain and simple.*'"

Lizzie gulped, her spurt of strength faltering. "I will," she decided, "even if I have to wave one of those orange flags the men use when fixing the roads."

"Penn Dot workers?" Marge asked. "Yes. With all their florescent gear, you can't miss them. You do that, Lizzie. Wave a flag to let Roman know you're not to be run over."

~*~

When Lottie saw Peter come into the Sampler, she was thankful for the air conditioning because she knew she was blushing profusely and perspiration was lathering her. She had pictured him in *Englisher* clothes, but here he was, dressed Amish. Had his trip to Punxsy make him believe in Old Order ways again?

When he came near her table, Lottie gripped her water glass. *Lord, help me. Help me see clearly.* Before he sat across from her, the image of Phil Darby and then Ezekiel Coblenz shot in rapid succession. Was she so nervous she couldn't even keep her thoughts in order? Or was it that she knew both men were praying for her for boldness to say what needed said? *Good-bye.*

"How are you Lottie?" Peter asked,. "You look great. I always liked mint green on you."

Lottie didn't remember that and certainly didn't wear this dress to impress him. It was made of a lighter, cooler material. "*Danki.* Mighty hot out there."

"*Jah,* it is."

Lottie realized she should have picked a bigger table. This tiny one in the corner was too intimate. Peter seemed so near. Too near. "I've made a new life here in Smicksburg, Peter. And I don't plan to return to Ohio."

He reached for her hand but she put both around her glass. "I like it here, too. Nice place to settle. Land's cheap with so many Amish moving to New York from these parts."

Lottie tried not to gape. "Settle here? So, you want to be Old Order Amish and settle here?"

"*Jah.* They said they're Old Order up in Punxsy, but more open-minded. But they still hold to the old ways." Peter scratched his clean-shaven cheek. "Lottie, I know you see things black and white with no gray, but there are gray areas in the Amish. You can be Old Order and still have a cell phone."

Lottie felt her head spin. "Peter, I'm confused. You go to a Mennonite Church in Ohio but will be Old Order for me. Is that what you're saying?" She straightened. "And when I say Old Order, I mean... like it's always been. Can you imagine a cell phone interrupting dinner?"

"You can turn them off. Can even keep it in your workshop, so what's the difference if it's a phone shanty or cell phone?"

Lottie felt her face screw up. "I don't even like phone shanties. When I read books written ages ago, I thought the Amish would always live like before the Industrial Revolution."

Peter's brow's shot up. "Well, you're the reader, not me."

"You don't know what the Industrial Revolution has done to our way of life?"

He leaned on one elbow. "*Jah*, I do. We made the split with the Mennonites, rejecting cars, electricity, phones... everything. And with the 'tech boom' as the *English* call it, we're at another crossroads, and there's division." Peter cupped his hands on hers as she clung to the glass. "We can find a common ground. That's what my Mennonite friends told me. We can find things in common and overlook the rest. Its things in our hearts that matter most. Lottie, I know I hurt you. I didn't have a clue about what the Bible said, and when I saw you read it, I got mad."

Lottie felt her resolve dissolving. *Lord, give me strength.* "So my bookish ways didn't bother you like you said?"

"*Nee,* not at all. I was convicted by your bookish ways, to read the Bible, but you know my folks and their *no reading the Bible unless Daed reads it out loud* rule. I'm a grown man and it was insulting. The Mennonites have helped me tons. I've learned a lot."

Lottie leaned forward. "I think that's *wunderbar.* So you understand about how to talk straight to Jesus?"

Peter put an index finger up. "Don't tell anyone." He chuckled. "I'm a silent seeker among the Amish. See, that's changing, too."

"What is?" she asked.

"Talking openly about faith and studying the Bible. You know our parents were forbidden, saying only silent prayers and hiding a Bible. It's changing, so why not change with having cell phones? It's just a phone, Lottie."

She wanted to believe him, but his capricious behavior not long ago, when he broke things off, still stung. "So you're saying you've always loved me, but how could you break our engagement and live with a woman —"

"We weren't living together like you think."

"*Jah,* I know that now, but the community, our *Gmay,* didn't know that. You made no effort to explain, to keep unity with the people, and it hurt so many..."

Peter licked his lips and his gaze darted over to the waitress. "Is she ever going to wait on us?"

"I told her we just wanted water. Too hot to eat."

"Well, I'm hungry now. Arguing with you always wore me out."

Lottie clucked her tongue. "How can you say that?"

"*Ach*, I didn't mean it. I'm nervous."

"Peter, I have to confess, I have a wall up to guard my heart and it must be exhausting to have to try to tear it down, but I erected it because of you."

His eyes begged for understanding. "I'll keep trying…"

Lottie knew a seed planted didn't struggle to grow if tended to. Love should naturally grow, but slow and steadily. She thought of a book she was reading and decided right then what she'd do.

~*~

Granny sprinkled white flour on the dough before applying her rolling pin to it. "Too sticky, so you need to dry the dough out a bit. Now test your pastry dough, MJ."

Phil wondered when he'd get a chance to talk about his dilemma with baking classes going on. He glanced up at MJ's apple clock on the wall. One-thirty. Andy should be back anytime now, but he had to get Granny home by two. He cleared his throat. "Can I get some advice?" he asked sheepishly.

MJ and Granny dusted the flour off their aprons and took a seat at the table across from him.

"I was wondering when you'd let us know what's bothering you," Granny said.

"Yes, Phil," MJ added, "you look a bit harrowed."

Harrowed beyond belief. "Well, you both have been praying for me and Judith. But there's something that came up. A red flag, I think."

"Watch for those red flags," MJ said with a wag of a finger.

That's what his mom said. How he'd miss her.... "My mom surprised us all, still being... with us, and I'm glad. Hospice and medical treatments have been steep and she had to sign the house over and most of her savings for her care." He cracked his knuckles out of nervous habit. "When Judith found out about it, her reaction was... odd."

"Odd?" Granny asked. "I don't follow."

"My mom was wealthy and I was to inherit everything. Now I only have debts. When Judith found out, she freaked out."

"Oh," MJ blurted. "I'm sorry. That's sad. Andy and I sure do know how medical bills can add up. Andy sold his coin collection he started when he was a little boy to pay off one bill."

Granny shook her head. "Such a shame," she said, patting MJ's hand. "Phil, you don't believe Judith was marrying you to gain wealth, do you?"

"She has lots of student loans," he said, "but she was never concerned since 'we'd have enough'. I should have seen it sooner."

"But didn't she break off your engagement?" MJ asked. "That doesn't add up."

Phil felt heat rise to his face. "Judith had befriended another man and was confused."

"Was this other man wealthy?" MJ pried.

Blinking rapidly, Phil sighed. "Yes. A surgeon she worked with that was twenty years older. And well-established in his practice."

MJ pounded the table, startling Granny. "You're too good for her, Phil. Look at all the girls vying for your attention here in Smicksburg. Maybe God sent you here for a reason. Forget Judith and move on."

"*Jah*, to a nice *English* woman," Granny was quick to add. "And you'll be here longer than you thought, right? Until at least Christmas?"

"Yes, until the end of this year." Phil shifted, finding it hard to digest what these two good women felt so vehemently about Judith. "I find it hard to think Judith could be so… calculating and greedy."

"Love of money is the root of all evil," Granny said, "and it makes people do despicable things. We Amish have rules on how much income you can make because it's so wicked."

"Well it's nice to have," Phil quipped. "Look at all the good money can do."

Granny swooshed her hand. "I mean the *love* of money, not money itself.'

Phil found it hard to swallow that Judith could be so conniving. They shared so many happy moments of the past several years. As his parents aged, they relinquished more of their wealth, which he'd shared it with Judith, but when his mom became so ill, Phil used any experimental medicine, no matter the cost. Many times Judith protested but he'd forged ahead, trying to cure his beloved mom, and now he was in debt. Big debt. Granny's gentle voice broke Phil's train of thought.

"You look years older, Phil. How can we help you?"

He shrugged. "Make enough pies to sell and pay off my mom's medical bills," he said with a forced laugh.

Granny's eyes were dancing. "That's a *wunderbar gut* idea, although pies don't bring in much money. But quilts do."

Phil studied Granny's face. *She must be joking.*

~*~

Ruth tasted salty sweat and put a handkerchief to her mouth. "*Ach*, we need air conditioning like the *English*."

Luke pulled into MJ and Andy's driveway. "Quit talking like a teenager, Ruthy."

Ruthy? He hadn't called her that since she was fifteen. Was he saying she was acting immature? Ruth bristled. Everything Luke did grated on her nerves. "Well, *Lukey*, looks like MJ and Andy have company. Best not go in."

He ambled out of the buggy and tied the horse to the white picket fence. "We promised Granny and Jeb."

"*Nee, you* promised."

"You promised, too. Now, we only have an hour since Becca needs to get back home quickly. Can't babysit all day."

Ruth found it so strange that Becca was over at her house so often. Jeb said it would be *gut* for her since she was spending too much time with the *English*. Ruth clenched her fists. Her cousin was a fancy *Englisher* in Ohio and with one call, she could have a driver take her there in no time.

Granny came out of the house to greet them. "You're doing the right thing in coming. You'll see."

"I hope so," Luke stated flatly.

Granny pet the chestnut brown mare's mane. "I'll give her a drink while *yinz* go inside and enjoy the air conditioning."

Nausea washing over her, Ruth clung to the picket fence. "It is hot."

Rushing to her side, Luke put an arm around her. "You're so pale. Are you alright?"

"I don't know. So weak." Guilt pinged Ruth's conscience. She'd felt every sign of pregnancy imaginable, but said nothing, willing it all to go away. How could she be pregnant again with Little Debbie only six months old? Ruth shivered. She'd performed her marital duty on her good days, when she and Luke had devotions and she'd

150

pour her heart out. When there seemed to be a bond, only to be broken by bitter words. She recoiled from his touch. "I'm fine. I don't need help," she snapped.

Granny spun around, hand on her hips. "Kind words, Ruth. They go far."

At Granny's advice, Ruth found herself running over to the woman who was like a *mamm* and nearly collapsing into her arms, sobbing.

~*~

MJ and Andy said their good-byes to Phil and Granny and then set themselves across the living room from Ruth and Luke. MJ met Ruth's hollow eyes. "You're sure you're okay?"

"The heat. I felt faint."

"You almost fainted," Luke corrected. "You're outside too much."

"I visit my *mamm's* grave in the woods," Ruth said evenly.

Andy hit his knee and ran out of the room, but could be heard from the kitchen, the house being tiny. "I bet you want a Popsicle, Ruth. How about it? Luke, do you want one?"

"Good idea, honey," MJ cheered. "I'll take grape."

"I knew that," Andy laughed. "But guess what? Out of a box of sixty popsicles, no grape left. I wonder who ate them all."

Chuckling, MJ confessed, "I had a craving for them all month."

Cravings? Ruth slowly closed her eyes. She craved pickles mixed with vanilla iced cream for a week. She shook her head rapidly. "*Ach, ich bin so ein idiot. Ich bin so ein idiot.*"

Luke slid closer to her on the loveseat. "What makes you say that?"

Ruth was visibly shaking now. MJ called for Andy to bring the popsicles quickly, saying that she knew all the signs of low blood sugar.

"She's upset," Luke said.

MJ put a hand up in protest. "I have lots of sick friends. Has she ever had her sugar tested?"

"I'm an idiot," Ruth said again, now in *English* for MJ and Andy to understand. "And it's not the heat."

Andy handed her a cherry popsicle with a napkin. "What is it then, doll face?"

Ruth accepted the cool treat and sucked it, trying to drain any sweetness which was in complete contrast to what she was about to say. "I think I'm pregnant," she said, trying to sound calm, but couldn't.

"Pregnant?" A smile slipped across Luke's face. "Well, we're blessed, *jah*? And it explains why you've been edgy."

"I don't want…" Ruth needed to measure her words. She didn't want anything else tying her down to Luke and Amish life. Thoughts of taking the *kinner* and leaving for Ohio were too often in her mind of late.

Andy slouched in his seat. "Children are a blessing, Ruth. Many can't have them." He took MJ's hand, squeezing it.

"Looks like you'll need more glue to build a happy home," MJ quipped.

Ruth remembered what MJ had said when she'd met her last week for a female talk. Christ was the glue that held a marriage together. She'd shared her health issues and Andy taking on the hands and feet of Christ as he cared for her.

The sound of a car engine emerged and soon after the back door flew open. Phil Darby ran in the room, panting. "I took Granny home, but had to come back. Ruth, are you alright?"

Ruth darted her eyes away from Phil. He was stunningly handsome and guilt always accompanied her when she saw him. "I'm fine."

Phil bit his lower lip. "Ruth, you're grieving pretty hard. I can tell."

"How?" she asked.

MJ pulled at Phil to sit down, and he obeyed. "She's pregnant," MJ exclaimed.

Ruth covered her cheeks. "We Amish don't announce things like that." Shame filled her as quickly as guilt. Was she going crazy? It wasn't a sin to look at a good looking man and it wasn't shameful to be pregnant, but the Amish didn't talk about it so freely.

"I'm sorry," MJ said sincerely. "I didn't know."

Phil hunched over, studying Ruth. "You know I'm grieving my mom's death, right?"

"*Ach.* We didn't know," Luke said. "We're sorry for your loss."

Phil's face contorted in pain. "She's not gone yet. But she will be. She's too tired to talk much and I'm grieving the loss of our talks. Ruth, do you understand?"

"*Nee,*" was all she could muster.

"I met you before you lost your mom. You were a happy, content woman. I think you're not only suffering from grief, but shock. My mom's death won't take me by surprise, but your mom's death did, so your grief is more... complicated."

Luke leaned forward. "How so?"

"It's like someone shocks your senses and they stay... raw. You're ability to cope is greatly hindered. Extreme mood swings, feeling helpless, anxious, depressed, and self-reproach are common."

When he said self-reproach, Phil seemed to be able to see into her soul. "What do I do?" Ruth found herself asking, Phil being so easy to trust.

"Be good to yourself. Don't rush a recovery, but if you start to think erratic thoughts, tell your doctor. You may need some medicine or supplements to cope."

Hand up to her throat, Ruth gasped. "I have been thinking... awful things."

"Suicidal thoughts?" MJ asked.

"*Nee*, but wanting to run away." Ruth somehow felt a lift in her soul just by this knowledge. Had sudden grief made her unstable? She turned to Luke and his blue eyes were filled with compassion and love. How could she think of leaving him? She felt as guilty as if she had left. He took her hand and kissed it. "When my parents died, it was sudden. I understand, Ruth."

"What?"

"Anxiety. Rage. Obsessive thoughts." Luke pulled her to himself and cupped her head to his shoulder. "We'll get through this together."

A sob escaped and then another as Ruth poured out on Luke tears of deep sorrow.

~*~

Granny tapped the gray-painted wooden porch to make the swing keep its pace. Jeb offering to clean off the dishes and whatnot was a blessing, as she was wrung out, a day full of emotion and heat waves. Ruth's health, emotional and physical, caused Granny to do many a casting off prayer all afternoon. Phil Darby's sad news of his *mamm's* condition and Judith's horrid behavior sunk her heart, but she had a plan. A plan she hoped the knitting circle would approve of.

A red sports car whizzed down her long driveway, but Jack was too hot to chase after it. *Marge, when would she ever slow down?* In lickety split time, Marge had entered her home and was jabbering to Jeb. She hadn't seen Granny as the swing was tucked away on the far side of the wraparound porch. *Danki, Lord. I need solitude.*

But Marge's tone was frantic and it moved Granny off her swing out of concern. As she moseyed into the house, Marge was waving a paper above her head like flapping towels on the clothesline. "What's wrong?"

Marge turned to face Granny, tears on her cheeks. "Denny. He ran away and it's my fault."

Ran away? Her Denny? Granny searched Jeb's face for answers, but he was hunched over the table, head hung.

"Marge, what makes you say it was your fault?" Granny wanted to know.

"He overheard Lizzie and me talking this morning. He was downstairs in the basement, due to the heat and all, and Lizzie and I were right above them and he must have heard. Oh, I have such a big mouth!"

Granny led Marge to the table, motioning for her to sit down. "What did you say?"

"How Joe and I decided to put in adoption papers for Brian-Boy and Lizzie said she wanted to adopt Charles, but Roman was too attached to Denny and Lizzie said she didn't want to adopt Denny."

Granny let the words sift until they made some meaning. "*Ach*, Denny feels unwanted? Unloved?"

Marge slid the letter across the table. "He left this letter addressed to Roman. I couldn't help but read it since it was on his dresser without an envelope."

Granny noticed that the letter wasn't scribbled but painstakingly nice handwriting was displayed. *He'd given this lots of thought.* Granny read aloud:

Dear Roman,

Thanks for teaching me how to carve. Never thought I could do anything so hard. Wish I could do all the things you do like pound a nail straight through a board with two hits. And you know how to fix anything. Thanks for teaching me some plumbing stuff. You're a patient teacher. Never had one before, and I'll miss you.

I know your wife wants to adopt Charles and all. Hope it works out. He's not as weird as I made him out to be. Only smoked a cigarette once. I brought out all his faults so you'd think I was better and adopt me, but I understand. I'm too old. Marge wants Brian and your wife wants Charles. So does Jonas, I think. But that's OK. I'm used to being on my own. Just wanted to say thanks. Oh, and tell Jeb thanks, too. He's as nice as you. Oh, and tell Granny I'll taste her pies until the day I drop dead. Oh, and tell her she's as sweet as Nora.

Thanks

Denny,

P.S. Tell Becca thanks too. She's good in math.

Granny swiped a tear and closed her eyes. She needed to keep her tears at bay because she needed to think. Think of where Denny may have gone. But her mind kept going back to the letter. "Jeb, who's Nora?"

"The only foster *mamm* who showed him real love."

She didn't even try to stop the tears when hearing this. How could a boy at sixteen never know the love of family? "I want to adopt him," she hollered between sniffs. "We need to find him."

The screen door slammed and Lizzie walked in. "*Ach, Mamm*, you're crying. What happened?" She ran around the oak table and scooted on the bench near Granny.

"Denny's run away," Jeb said evenly. "Seems like you and Marge need to mind your tongues."

"What?" Lizzie gasped.

"The boy heard you say you don't want him. He ran off," Jeb said with a firm jaw and then darted up, shook his head and grabbed his straw hat off the hook near the door. "We need to go look for him."

Granny gripped Lizzie's hand. "He didn't mean to say that. He's upset. Loves that boy." She handed Lizzie the letter and told her it wasn't her fault.

Lizzie sighed in parts, gasped in others, but was pale when done. "It is my fault. I did say all that."

"Oh, Lizzie," Marge sniveled. "I was egging you on to stand up to Roman more. You do love Charles and I wanted us to adopt at the *same* time." She clasped her heart. "Roman's not as stubborn as I thought, being so kind and gentle to Denny. I'm sorry."

Granny swallowed the lump in her throat. "We need to look for Denny, not waste time regretting words."

Lizzie rubbed Granny's back. "*Danki, Mamm.* You're too kind." She shifted. "Charles hitch-hiked here. Do you think Denny's doing the same? And if so, where would he go?"

Marge sprung up. "I need to go to the church. Phil will be there getting ready for Bible Study. We can have the church drive around and look. You Amish can... take your buggies down all the dirt roads. Sound like a plan?"

Granny wearily nodded. "*Jah.*"

~*~

Suzy followed Phil as he paced back and forth between picnic tables in the outside recreation area. "It's not your fault," she said.

Phil stopped, making Suzy almost run into him. "I know that. Just thinking."

"We'll find Denny. The church is out looking and the Amish are on back roads. He couldn't have gone far."

Crossing his arms, Phil leaned on a table. "I've seen how much this church cares about my mom. Every card she received lifted her spirits. I just wish I could get through to Denny what just got through to me."

Suzy leaned on a table opposite him. "Which is?"

"It's not a weakness to reach out to strangers. You might just find help."

Suzy didn't want to bring up dirty church laundry, but felt it was time. "Do you know why Joe sleeps in Arbor Creek at night?"

"To watch the boys."

"Well, out of necessity. We had a great guy here named Clark. He was in love with Colleen, and probably still is, since we haven't heard a peep from him since her wedding. He was to live at Arbor Creek and watch the boys."

Phil clutched his chin. "Hmm. So, what are you saying?"

"Well, Joe wanted to wait until Jerry got back to bring up such an issue: hired help. We can't afford anyone else on church pay." A slight breeze swept through and Suzy breathed in the musky sent of the woods not far off. "But ever since Denny left, my mental wheels got turning. Why don't you move in with the boys?"

"What? I'm watching Jerry and Janice's place."

"They're generous. They said 'house sit' in exchange for free rent. Understand?"

Phil's face softened. "Wow. That was nice. No wonder everyone misses such fine people." He crossed his arms and resumed pacing, head down, looking like a robin finding a worm. "I could move into Arbor Creek and maybe mentor Denny. Give him the attention he needs."

A car pulled into the church parking lot. It was Marge. She screeched her car to a halt and ran out towards them.

"Did you find Denny?" Phil asked.

"No," she said, looking deflated. "I was hoping someone had." She stomped a foot. "When will I ever gain control over my tongue?"

"You're being too hard on yourself, Marge," Phil said. "We all make mistakes."

Marge planted her clenched fists on her hips. "Thanks, but I did some confessing about my mouth and know I need to get a muzzle."

Suzy scrunched her lips to one side, forbidding herself to laugh. Marge was serious. "Well, fears of yesterday and fears of tomorrow are twin thieves, robbing us of the present."

Phil and Marge stared at her, bewildered.

"An Amish proverb. Think I got it right, but seriously, there's lots of truth in it. And I think regrets over yesterday can rob us, too."

Marge bit a lower lip. "I think that's how that saying goes. It's about regrets."

"Well, at any rate, they rob us of today and today we need to find Denny and make a plan so this doesn't happen again." Suzy looked over at Phil, her eyes still wondering. "So, Phil, you'll move into Arbor Creek and watch the boys?"

"Yes, if need be. I can come to the church to study and whatnot."

Marge danced on her toes. "Thanks so much, Phil. I miss sharing a bed with my honey."

Suzy grinned at them both. "Phil, since when do you say 'whatnot'?"

He laughed. "Since I moved to Smicksburg."

~*~

Granny unthinkingly put in an extra tablespoon of vanilla into her forty year old hand cranked ice cream maker. "*Ach*, Jeb, this won't be gut."

"Why?"

"I'm so absentminded, I don't even know what I put in here."

Jeb sat in the swing next to her and tapped her shoulder. "We need these times of rest, love. Can't let the stress of life ruin our ice cream making." He nudged her. "We've done this for ages."

Granny knew traditions pulled families tight. The girls would be over and crank the iced cream and intermittently catch fireflies to fill their mason jars, creating lanterns. And Jonas needed to feel more a part of the family unit, looking lonely at times. But Lizzie and Roman were still out looking for Denny.

"Jeb, why do the *English* treat their teens like *bopplis*? Denny's sixteen. Can't he leave Arbor Creek?"

Jeb closed the wooden ice cream maker and began to crank the handle. "I don't know. I think *Englisher* kids are babied too much. Our fourteen year olds are apprenticing for a trade."

Granny stared at a single rose. "Jeb, why can't Denny live here?"

"Suppose he could. We've had many live with us for a while."

"I'd like to adopt him," Granny prodded.

Jeb's turquoise eyes shadowed. "Me too. But we're in our seventies. Too old, love. Need to face facts. But Denny can stay here for a while if the Baptist let him."

"*Danki*, Jeb," Granny said with a shaky voice. "I know I can care too much, like Phil says, but if I don't follow my heart, I don't feel right in my... conscience."

"*Ach*, you're right. And Denny needs a home. Our Lord said when we do it to the least of these, we do it unto Him."

Granny's heart warmed. She was married to the best man on God's green earth. A man who saw hurts and wanted to mend, like a shepherd. "Jeb, God will reward you someday."

"Taking in Denny isn't such a big deal."

"I don't mean that. You are vexed at times, being a shepherd to the flock. And I may add to the burden by having so many *English* friends, but still you never chide me."

The crank finally stopped and Jeb took her hand. "It's what I love about you, love. You know how shy I am deep down and you reach out. We balance each other out."

Granny leaned into him. "Jeb, you're not shy anymore. Not like you used to be. And not a stick in the mud, like I tease."

"*Jah*, at times I am. Maybe not shy, but reserved, and not a stick in the mud, but set in my ways."

"Amish ways, and you keep me in line," Granny said softly. "When I hanker for an air conditioner, I know how to quiet my soul. You taught me that. Be content with what I have…"

Jeb took her chin and kissed her. "I love you, Deborah."

"And I love you, Jebediah Weaver."

Giggles were soon heard and Millie made her presence known. "*Ew.*"

"Ew, what?" Jeb asked.

"I've never seen you kiss… on the lips."

Jeb winked. "Kissing never wears out, no matter how old you are."

Jenny came around the corner, face red. "I'm never kissing a boy."

Granny and Jeb were silent and then howled, laughing. Jeb put his arm around Granny. "*Jah*, you will."

Horse hoofs stomping on gravel were heard and the girls started to shout. "Denny! It's Denny and he's riding a buggy!"

Granny sprang off the swing and ran, she could not contain herself. This boy had gripped her heart, there was no denying it. And to her shock, Jeb followed. As Denny jumped out of the buggy, they were nimbly there to greet him, embracing him, kissing his cheeks.

But Denny was stone stiff. "I'm sorry for leaving. I'm an idiot."

Granny took him by the shoulders, having to get up on her toes, and looked him square in the eye. "Now stop that. You are not an idiot. You are Denny, a boy we love... like our own *kinner*."

He remained emotionless.

Jeb clamped a hand on his shoulder. "What's wrong, Son?"

Denny fumbled for words, but got out, "I don't know how to... act. Take in what you're saying."

"A wall's falling down," Jeb explained softly. "A wall you built up around you from years of hurt. When the wall comes down, it may hurt a tad, too."

"I can't trust anyone..."

Granny looped her arm through Denny's and led him to the porch. "Let's talk over homemade iced cream." The sun cast an orange and magenta glow across their little farm and Granny thanked the Good Lord for Denny's return. She shooed the girls home, as they clamored around Denny, needing some one on one talk with the wayward teen. Granny wondered who's buggy Denny was using and he said Ezekiel Coblenz's.

Pondering this, Granny led him to the ice cream maker and sat next to him on the swing, Jeb pulling up a chair.

"Ezekiel Coblenz found me near his place. We swapped," Denny said.

"Swapped what?" Jeb leaned forward in wonder.

"Secrets. He told me some of his and I told him some of mine. I learned tons."

"Like what?" Granny asked pensively, knowing Ezekiel's fine character was forged by fiery trials.

"Well, it's sort of a secret, but you can see Ezekiel's scar, so I guess it's not a secret. He had problems like me. He told me to never run from my problems. It's a long story, but he made me go back to Arbor Creek for now."

"For now? You're not staying?" Jeb asked.

"Well, I'm sixteen. I went on the internet and learned I could be in the ILP. I just need a home. "

Jeb took of his straw hat and twirled it on his fingers. "What's an... IUP?"

"ILP," Denny corrected. "Independent Living Program. I have to live with a family but I can be on my own in a way, considered an adult, but still get money from the government."

"*Ach*, you don't need money from the government," Jeb said, "not when you have family and friends."

Denny slouched back into the swing. "Well, it comes in handy if you don't have either."

Granny took his hand. "You look into that program and come live with us."

"What? You're so..." His eyes were twice the normal size. "Do you qualify?"

"Qualify for what? Being your family?" Jeb asked, bewildered.

Denny's head swung from Granny to Jeb, back and forth like a pendulum clock. "You'd be my family?"

"*Jah*," Granny said, putting a hand to his cheek. "God's carved a special place in our hearts for you."

Denny's face was somber as he stared aimlessly, and Granny knew that a wall was coming down and it was painful, like Jeb had cautioned. Letting in love was a new thing for Denny, and he appeared to be in shock.

"I don't feel... adequate. That's the word Ezekiel said. He didn't feel adequate because of his scar, but said it was a good thing."

"Really?" Jeb asked. "How so?"

"He said people can talk to him about their problems better. His face shows he has a problem right off the bat. He has a scar that people can see, so they tell him all sorts of things and he's a real good listener."

"That's why he's the one for Lottie," Granny blurted, and then covered her mouth.

Denny laughed as Jeb rolled his eyes. "*Yinz* don't seem...old. Maybe you're not too old to be my family."

Jeb chuckled. "So, that's what's on your mind."

"Well, yes," Denny acknowledged.

Granny and Jeb chuckled and Denny's face lifted into a smile.

~*~

Lottie breathed in the musty summer dew that would soon evaporate as the morning broke over the world. Red-winged black birds sang from the woods their simple two-note melody. The rhythm of the horse feet clopping along Granny's long driveway calmed her. Simplicity was all around her, but not inside. Nature had a rhythm, a sync that was natural, but she had not stayed in step with the Almighty's tempo.

When she saw Granny out in her kitchen garden on the side of her little house, Lottie sighed. *I want a home like*

Granny's, a marriage like Granny's. Maybe she could give guidance that would lead to both.

As she approached, Granny waved and soon Jack's tail was flapping to greet a visitor. Jeb appeared to be busy fishing and since this was going to be a 'woman talk', Lottie was relieved. Jeb was a wise and kind bishop, but only women understood… romance in a woman's heart. The ache and joy.

Bringing her horse to the hitching post, Lottie swiftly got out and tied him, patting his black mane. "*Gut* boy. Maybe Granny has a carrot for you." As the sun poured onto her face, she raised a hand to shield her eyes as she made her way over to Granny. "*Guten murning*, Granny."

"That it is, Lottie. Hope the heat stays under one-hundred, though. Mighty hot already."

"Well, you're working." Lottie tilted her head to one side, wringing her hands. "Have time to talk?"

"*Jah*, sure. Always." Granny pulled off her garden gloves and threw them in the basket at her feet that carried her gardening tools. "Want some iced tea?"

"Do you have coffee? I haven't had my morning cup yet."

Puzzled, Granny looked up at the sun. "What time is it?"

"Only seven."

"Seems like noon. Jeb and I get up early on hot days, get all the work done and then rest. This heat isn't too *gut* on *old* people, *jah*?"

Her emphasis on old was odd for Granny. "You? Old?"

"Well, *jah*, according to Denny," she chuckled. "But it's all in how you look at it. My Italian friend, Angelina, thinks I'm young, so I agree with her."

When Granny's eyes twinkled, Lottie always thought there was a *kinner* trapped in her body. "You're young at heart and that's what matters, don't you think? Some people my age act old."

"*Jah*, they do." Granny wagged a finger. "Folks who see the bad in life. Don't you be like that."

"Am I?" Lottie asked.

Granny pat her back as they made their way into her kitchen. "It can happen to anyone. I was just saying something my *mamm* said."

"So, you have a choice on how you see things?" Lottie asked.

Granny touched the side of her speckleware coffee pot. "Want cold coffee? Angelina drinks hers cold sometimes. Must be an Italian thing."

"*Jah*, that's fine. Don't heat the house up."

After Granny poured a cup, she put it before Lottie with a sugar bowl and milk. "Now, I believe you've come for advice. And, *jah*, you have a choice on how you see things. God gave you free will."

Lottie fixed her coffee and took a sip. "How about feelings? How come I don't have a choice on them?"

Granny folded her hands on the table. "Feelings can be fickle, for sure and certain. When it comes to so-called romance, they're downright untamable at times. Is that what you're having trouble with?"

Could Granny read her so easily? Was she a complete open book for the world to read? Lottie wondered. "My mind goes from Peter and then to Phil and back to…" *Nee*, she would not reveal she was thinking of three men, Ezekiel being the third. "How do I know which man is right for me?"

"Well," Granny said carefully, "Phil's not Amish."

"But he could be. He loves Amish ways. Look at Colleen. It took her more than a few months in Smicksburg to make the jump but —"

"Did you hear about Phil's troubles?"

"That's what's so baffling, He used to talk to me a lot and when I tried to comfort him, he was distant, acting like I was a pest, a fly that couldn't be swat."

Granny's face scrunched up. "When Phil talked to you before, what did you talk about?"

"Well, little things. Nothing in particular, but he sure did teach me a lot. He's a great listener."

Granny reached for Lottie's hand and she took it. "Phil gave *gut* advice like Jeb?"

"*Jah*, like Jeb. I could talk to him like Jeb. And I want a man like Jeb, someone solid in their beliefs and… consistent."

Granny squeezed her hand. "Jeb's a bishop. Phil's a pastor, understand?"

"Understand what?"

"Phil was helping you like a *gut* pastor. You've told me how he made you feel more confident and all. You accept yourself more, *jah*?"

These words stung Lottie. Was she just one of Phil's flock? Memories dashed through her mind and in almost all, Phil was giving advice… helping her. "*Ach*, I feel like such a fool."

"Well, it was foolish to fall for an *Englisher*," Granny said softly, "but like I told you, I did, too."

Somehow the revelation that Phil was playing the part as pastor didn't sting her, only shame her. She'd been flirting with forbidden fruit, like Eve in the garden. "It needs to stop."

"*Jah*, your attraction to Phil needs to die on the vine; don't feed it."

"*Nee*, I will not." Lottie sipped more cold coffee. "And then there's Peter. He confuses me to no end. He's Mennonite in Ohio and then comes here saying he'll be Old Order like the Amish in Punxsy for me. Just for me..."

"A double-minded man is unstable, Lottie. You know that. He's two people, really. That's why I think Ezekiel would be *gut* for you."

Lottie lifted her hands to hide her cheeks as they grew warm. She did like Ezekiel, but how could any woman like three men at once? Granny would think her daft. "I hardly know Ezekiel."

"I thought you were courting, secret-like."

"He takes me home from Singings, but I feel guilty when I think of Phil and then Peter."

Granny grinned. "When I met Jeb, my mind was on two others. Maybe three. Marriage is the biggest decision in a person's life so you have your mind on it a lot at your age."

Three men? Granny? "How did you know Jeb was the right man for you?"

With misty eyes, Granny's eyes twinkled again. "I let the dust settle and my heart needed some mending time. It was wounded, so it needed some healing. It was a trial, but when I came through, it was easy to see who the right man was for me. As clear as day." Granny got up and replenished Lottie's coffee mug. "Letting the dust settle takes time."

"But my *mamm* thinks I'll be an old *maidel*."

"*Ach*, I didn't say it would take years, just some time." Granny sighed. "That Ezekiel is a *wunderbar gut* man, not that I'm trying to sway you. He not only found Denny, but talked to him for a long while. I think Denny learned more from Ezekiel in one night than all his years in counseling."

"Really?" Lottie asked, despite the fact that she was wary of Granny always bringing up Ezekiel. Not trying to sway her? *Jah, she was.* "What did Denny learn?"

"Well, not to run from problems, for one. And who better to teach him that than a man who can't, since Ezekiel wears his on his face? Ezekiel's glad for that scar, according to Denny. It's built compassion in him, making him able to understand those who hurt." Granny gripped the little black Bible that was on her table. "Ponder this scripture out of Ecclesiastes. *'For everything there is a season'.*" She slid her finger down and continued. "*'A time to tear and a time to mend. A time to be quiet and a time to speak.'*"

Lottie's mind rolled around this familiar scripture. But she never thought she'd be applying it to Peter…. She needed to make a clean tear from him. Their relationship was beyond mending.

~*~

Granny entered Suzy's yarn shop at eleven. The knitting circle's time had been changed along with the location. Suzy had air conditioning and Granny let it cool her smoldering body. When Suzy appeared behind her Dutch doors that led to her back room, Granny sighed. "*Danki,* Suzy. I just can't move in this heat."

Suzy winked. "You didn't walk over here did you?"

Jokes around town that Granny and Angelina were out walking together, making for an odd couple, were getting old, but she smiled at Suzy, her dear friend. "*Nee.* Not today."

"Do all the girls know they need to be here early?"

"*Jah,* I believe so. If someone shows up at my place, Jeb will direct them here." Granny breathed deeply, but it must have been her imagination because she smelled flowers. "Smells like... honeysuckle in here."

"I have a candle burning to freshen up the place." Suzy opened the bottom of her Dutch door. "Can I take your basket, Red Riding Hood?"

Granny frowned as she peered at her shoulder. "I'm wearing burgundy, not red."

Suzy sniggered. "*Ach, vell,* we *English* have saying you Amish don't understand, *jah?*"

Granny didn't know what on earth had overcome her friend. Couldn't be the heat. "Suzy, are you alright?"

"Couldn't be better," she chimed, taking her basket. "Yum. These look good."

"Couldn't fire up the oven so No Bake Cookies will have to do."

"I love chocolate," Suzy said. "And did you hear the health benefits of dark chocolate?"

"Jah. Read about it in Family Life Magazine."

"Yoo-hoo," Marge nearly sang as she entered the shop. When she met Granny's gaze, she pressed her hand on her heart. "Denny told me about what you want to do. Are you serious?"

"Jeb and I wouldn't have said it if we didn't mean it," Granny said, confusion obvious in her voice. "It's a big commitment."

"I've raised five boys. I know," Granny said as she took a seat at Suzy's little tea table.

"Anyone want to inform me about what you're talking about?" Suzy asked.

"They want to raise Denny," Marge informed, one eyebrow raised.

"He's already a grown-up," Granny said evenly. "You English treat men like *boppli* sometimes."

Suzy gawked. "Denny's only sixteen. A minor. And you and Jeb are…"

"Our bodies are wearing out, but we're young inside. Anyhow, Roman and Lizzie will be next door. Roman's excited."

Marge planted her hands on her hips. "Is Lizzie?"

Granny hadn't seen Lizzie's reaction last night, it being dark out on the porch. "Lizzie didn't say she wasn't happy. She was awful tired, coming in late, out trying to find Denny."

Marge's face seemed to expand and then slowly grew red. Her mouth was a thin line, and Granny thought she'd pop. "Marge, anything wrong?"

"Nope," she said through tight lips, and then spun around and left the room for the yarn shop.

Suzy's eyes were two large marbles. "I seem to be missing things today. Best not to interfere."

"Suzy," Marge called from the store. "Any yarn on clearance?"

"Yes, it's on the basket by my desk."

"I need help," Marge demanded.

Suzy shrugged. "I think she wants to talk."

"I'm sure she does," Granny said slowly, pondering Marge's behavior. Obviously she and Jeb were insensitive to Lizzie. And Lizzie said she wasn't feeling well enough to come to circle. Was she upset about Charles again? Well, Charles was only fourteen and Denny was a man. Maybe in a few years Charles could live with Jonas, the two being like peas in a pod.

Soon Lottie's voice could be heard and Granny hoped their early morning talk had helped the poor girl whose heart was easily swayed by romance. "Hi again, Granny," she said as she took a seat at the table near her.

Leaning closer, Lottie whispered, "You helped me see

something."

Granny grinned. "What's that?"

"Well, I'm reading a book about dating Jesus, and that's what I'm going to do."

Granny's heart turned over. "What's that supposed to mean? Sounds sacrilegious"

"*Ach,* what I mean is not 'date' Jesus, but… court him. And what I mean by that is I'm putting Him first, like a beau, and try to find friendship and contentment in Him alone."

"So you'll never marry?" Granny crowed.

Lottie laughed. "Of course I will. But I'm focusing on the scripture, 'Delight yourself in the Lord and He'll give you the desire of your heart.' It's my desire to marry, so I'm just going to delight in God and let the dust settle, like you said."

Granny felt dizzy in her mind, sorting through what Lottie said. Dating Jesus had taken her aback, but she was slowly deciphering what Lottie truly meant. "Sounds *gut.* Spend time with the Lord and His Word and He'll lead you. But it's obvious to me who's *gut* for you."

Lottie picked up an embroidery hoop and started to stitch. "*Jah,* Granny. I know. But we'll just be patient and see."

Marge and Suzy entered the little room and Marge appeared to have calmed down. Suzy tapped her wristwatch. "Where is everyone?"

Granny's mouth went dry. "*Ach.* Jeb can't tell the girls to come over here now. They'll go to my house at one o'clock. How could Jeb and I be so daft?"

"It's the heat," Suzy said softly. "You and Jeb are sharper than most people my age."

Lottie nodded in agreement, but Marge settled in at the table and was staring at her embroidery hoop.

Suzy picked up Granny's basket from off the counter. "Well, we have Granny's goodies for our Jane Austen tea, so let's begin."

"Too hot for tea," Granny said. "Unless it's iced."

"This air conditioning makes me cold enough. I want hot tea," Suzy said. "Anyone else?"

"I'll take hot," Marge said.

"*Jah*, me too," Lottie said.

Granny thought is so odd to drink hot tea when it was nigh one-hundred degrees outside. But she did wish she had her shawl, feeling a tad chilled. "Okay. I'll take hot, too, if you're making a pot-full." Granny took her embroidery hoop out of her tote and started to stitch. "I like to see lots of satin stitch on a quilt. I'm thinking we can sell it for a *gut* price."

All eyes landed on her, but only Marge spoke up. "Sell it? Not donate it to the homeless shelter?"

Granny resumed stitching. "Amish quilts fetch a high price, and I was thinking it could help Phil Darby."

Suzy slowly sat at the table. "Phil Darby? He needs more money than he earns?"

"I'd like to have a benefit auction to raise money for Phil's debt."

"His debt?" Marge exclaimed. "You can't raise money to pay off someone's debt. A benefit is for charity, right?"

Granny lowered her hoop and eyed Marge. Why was her dear *English* friend so confrontational all the time? "Phil's *mamm* is dying. We can make money for her treatments."

"But she's in hospice and that's covered by insurance, right?" Marge's matter-of-fact tone broached no argument.

"Well," Granny continued, "Phil told MJ and me something in confidence. Let's just say he's a hurting man who loves his *mamm* and miscalculated his finance's due to compassion. His love for his *mamm* made him try things insurance didn't pay for. And, we can help pay for it in *community*."

Marge groaned. "We took up a love offering for him at our church, which has plenty of community."

"It's not enough or Phil wouldn't be in debt, *jah*?" Granny said, her voice shaky.

"I agree with Granny," Lottie interjected. "Phil's been helping *English* and Amish alike and has never been paid. I say we help him." Lottie eyes misted. "I confess to having a crush of sorts on him, but I'm over it."

Marge scoffed. "You mentioned him yesterday all dreamy eyed."

Granny lowered her hoop. "Marge, what has gotten into you? All you want to do is quarrel."

Marge met her gaze evenly, like a dog being challenged. "I say what I mean. And I'm not apologizing for it."

Suzy gasped. "Marge, what's wrong?"

"Lizzie is… upset. She cried on my shoulder like a child. She blamed herself for Denny disappearing because he overheard her saying she wanted to adopt Charles. And Jeb yelled at her for speaking her mind when she was in her own kitchen?"

Marge poked at her embroidery too hard and the hoop slipped and fell to the floor. Granny was quick to retrieve it and her hand landed on Marge's. "You're right, Marge. We blamed Lizzie and you, and I'm asking for forgiveness. We spoke out of fear. Afraid we'd never see Denny again and it hurt Lizzie. When I get home, I'll apologize."

Marge stared at Granny. "Really?"

"Of course. And I'll find out if she's upset about Charles, too. She was mighty quiet last night."

Marge lunged at Granny and embraced her. "Oh, Granny, thank you. And I'm so sorry I've been a pain."

Granny hugged her back, glad to see the old happy-go-lucky Marge again.

Suzy clapped her hands. "It's about time," she giggled. "Marge, welcome back to planet Earth."

Marge laughed. "The stress over at Arbor Creek has gotten to me, I suppose, but Phil's moving in. Sure do miss Clark, but he's so hooked on Colleen still, I suppose."

Lottie frowned. "What? She's married."

"Well, he loved Colleen and put up a front that he was happy for her at the wedding and all, but then up and left town. Always was a wanderer, though. But anyhow, Jerry and Janice's house will be vacant, so we'll need to keep an eye on it."

Suzy moved gingerly to make tea. "I got an email from Janice, asking if I could find someone to give a new coat of paint to her house to spruce it up….in cream."

"And?" Marge probed. "Not everyone likes colors as much as you, Suzy."

Suzy had sorrow splashed across her face. "When people sell their homes, they always paint in neutral tones. Do you think… they're going to sell their house and stay…" Tears glistened in Suzy's eyes. "If they do… I'll… I won't be able to bear it."

Granny got up and slipped her arm through Suzy's. "We bear one another's burdens. We'll be here to help you as your wounds mend. And they will… mend."

~*~

Granny was relieved that no one strolled down her long driveway at one. The Amish stayed out of the heat, and so she wasn't too surprised that they'd be skipping knitting circle today. The little circle of friends that met over at Suzy's was beneficial. They would sell the quilt for Phil and make other items to sell for a benefit. The whole town owed Phil love and support.

Granny hadn't gone over to talk to Lizzie yet, and would ask for forgiveness after gaining strength from the Almighty. She bowed her head and prayed:

Lord God in Heaven,

I do thank you for Marge. She sees things I don't, like the need to be more sensitive to Lizzie. I love Lizzie and it pains me that she carries the heavy burden of being barren. Give me strength to help her. Help me see needs at home first; things that need mending.

And Lord, help Lottie see she needs Ezekiel. They are salt and pepper. During this time when Lottie dedicated herself to you, open her eyes to… Ezekiel, if it be Your will. Danki that she told Peter to go home and not write. Peter's on the fence, waffling about his baptismal vows, and keep him far from our Lottie.

And Lord, help MJ during her pain. Her little needlepoint pins she makes for others are charming. And her painting little knick knacks and whatnot just shows your love to others in deep ways. She doesn't wallow in self-pity but takes action against it by giving to others. How much I've learned from her. Bless her.

In Jesus name,

Amen.

Dear Readers,

Thank you for reading *Amish Knit & Stitch, Episode 4 ~ Mending Days*. When the girls meet for their knitting circle again, it will be the end of August and a drought has swept across Smicksburg, making the fields dangerously dry. What do the Amish do during a drought? Find out in Episode 5.

As usual, I leave you with a recipe served at the knitting circle. Enjoy!

Amish No Bake Cookies

1 ¾ c. sugar

3 Tsp cocoa

1/4 c. butter

1/2 c. milk

Mix and Boil 1 Minute. Remove and add:

1 c. nuts optional

3 Cups Rolled Oats

1/2 Cup Peanut Butter

1 Teaspoon Vanilla

Drop teaspoon full on wax paper. Cool and serve.

EPISODE 5

Steam Allowance

$\mathcal{D}$edicated to stabbing victims of the Franklin Regional High School on September 4th, 2014. As my Alma Mater, this hit close to home. Praise God no one was fatally wounded. But emotional and physical scars remain. Please continue to pray for S. W. Pennsylvania, as such violence is not common. Thank you.

~*~

Granny gingerly climbed the cellar steps, eager to see the sunrise.

Jeb, close behind her, grabbed her ankle playfully. "Always had nice ankles."

At the top of the steps she spun around. "Old man. I'm seventy-one and have cankles."

"What?"

"My calves have slid down over my ankles, hiding them." She wagged a finger. "Flattery is deceitful. What do you want?"

He cocked his head back, eyes wide. "Nothing. Peace and quiet. A nice cup of coffee with my wife."

Trying to hide a smile, Granny made her way to the blue speckleware coffee pot that lived on the stove, even in summer. "Sure glad it cooled down a tad by the rain last night."

"*Jah*. Thankful for the rain, but it didn't soak clear through to the undergrowth. Roots are still drying up." Jeb opened a kitchen window. "But, it's cooler for sure and certain. Only about seventy out."

Granny poured two mugs of coffee and motioned for Jeb to follow her out onto the porch. Once settled in their glider and sipping the java, she sighed. "It's for moments like this that I live for."

He nudged her. "Now who's using flattery?"

"Old man," she said, "I was talking about the sunrise and the magic of morning."

"Magic?" he blanched.

"Can't describe it any other way. Seems impossible that every day the earth circles around the sun. We sit in this here glider and never get tired of the colors that spread across the sky."

Jeb chuckled. "I know what you mean. I like how morning smells. Fresh and clean."

"Every day is fresh with no mistakes in it. Anne of Green Gables said that. *Ach*, Jeb, what if we hadn't read so many classics last winter? Our imagination wouldn't have grown."

Jeb groaned. "*Jah*, and with *English* friends over here all the time, they want me to imagine a movie picture. I tell them it's forbidden to the Amish, but they keep on describing it anyhow."

The ruby throated humming bird that nurtured herself on the many roses soon could be made out as dawn lifted the darkness. Before long a rooster crowed, and Granny tapped her toes together as she reveled in this blessed morning. "The *English* miss out so much by having television and whatnot. But, they're our neighbors and I do love them so. And Phil needs us more than ever."

"His *mamm* passed?"

"*Jah*. He came back to Smicksburg last night and he'll be here for the noon meal, along with MJ and Andy, if MJ is up to it. She wants to see my stove."

Jeb slouched. "Wanted a peaceful day with only you here."

She scooted closer to him. "We'll have the rest of the day. It's only for an hour or so. Any meeting for you today bishop?"

"*Nee*, and I was hoping we could have a picnic…"

"We can have it tonight. How about a bonfire, just you and me?"

Jeb took her hand. "*Nee*. Like I said, the undergrowth is straw dry and a fire could catch." He put an arm around her. "But I know you love roasted marshmallows, so I'll dowse the ground around the fire pit and we'll have a small fire."

"*Danki*, love." Resting her head on his shoulder Granny was filled with joyful contentment. All the years of marriage hadn't been bliss, but they'd learned to iron out their differences. "Sure do hope Ruth and Luke can find love again."

"Find love? *Nee*, we work at it. I can say that Luke's awful committed, but Ruth writing to her cousin out in Ohio has my nerves frazzled. I told her to be cautious."

"They bonded again at the funeral, Jeb. Ruth needs family ties more now than ever."

"But," Jeb continued evenly, "the woman left the Amish for the fancy *English* world and Ruth almost went to live with her when things got sour with Luke."

Granny cringed. She'd forgotten this and wished Jeb's words hadn't stirred up worry in her, ruining this glorious morning. She closed her eyes and let a portion of Psalm

46 roll around in her mind.

Goa is our refuge and strength,
A very present help in trouble.
Therefore we will not fear,
Even though the earth be removed,
And though the mountains be carried into the midst of the sea;
Though its waters roar ana be troubled,
Though the mountains shake with its swelling.

After saying it slowly a few times, her mind wandered to the newspaper clipping she'd read. "Seems like the world's getting mighty violent. If it's not guns, it's knives."

Jeb pat her knee. "The knife slayings in China or here in America?"

"Both. When we were young, who ever heard of such things?"

Jeb shifted. "The KKK tried to hang Carl from a tree. Remember?"

Granny nodded. But it was an unusual thing to be hiding someone who was going to Martin Luther King rallies. "The KKK is over, Jeb. Things are more peaceful."

He shook his head. "If that were only true. *Nee*, there's still KKK's and there will be hatred in this world until..." he pointed to the sky, "the Prince of Peace comes."

Granny stared in wonder at the radiant sky. Shades of pink, magenta, hues of oranges and purples swirled together. "*Ach*, Jeb, what colors. Most unusual."

"Lack of rain."

"But it rained last night."

"Just a sprinkle, love. *Nee*, we'll be out watering the kitchen garden today. You'll see."

Maryann poured rainwater over her lengthy dark brown hair. *Makes it so soft*, Michael will say. As the water drops hit the stone path that led to her kitchen garden, she breathed in heavy air that hung from the rainfall, and gave thanks. *Danki, Lord, that I didn't lose my hair during radiation therapy as I feared.*

As the morning sun cast shadows across the path, a darker one caught Maryann's attention, along with Becca's whimper. Maryann let her hair fall over her, making little rivulets fall down her dress and faced her daughter. "What's wrong?"

Becca stood there helpless with eyes like a little girl begging for comfort. But she said nothing.

Taking her hand, Maryann forced out the words she dreaded. "Did someone die? Did you get news of...?"

Trembling, Becca shook her head. "*Nee, Mamm,*" she blurted. "No one's died."

"Is anyone hurt?"

Suddenly sobbing uncontrollably, Becca pointed to herself. "Gilbert. He broke up."

Trying to decipher her daughter's faltering words and outburst so uncharacteristic of her oldest daughter, Maryann stared. "Gilbert called off your courtship?"

"*Jah. Mamm.* He thinks I love Denny."

Maryann knew many went to Granny and Jeb with emergencies and marveled at their composure. Right now, words failed her and anger arose. Gilbert? The eighteen year old that wanted to marry Becca only a few months back was calling things off? Because of Denny? "That's absurd, Becca. Why would he do that? I mean, why would he think you cared for Denny?"

Becca only cried harder and doubled over as if in pain. Maryann ran to embrace her dear daughter and sat her down in the grass. "I'm sorry. I said the wrong thing."

"*Nee, Mamm.* Gilbert's so selfish. I just didn't see it."

"Tell me."

"He kept asking for a wedding in the fall. I said I wanted to wait a few years. When I brought up herbal medicine and wanting to travel first, he accused me of loving Denny."

Wanting to hide her shock, Maryann purposefully didn't let her eyes grow round. "Did you explain why you're so fascinated with herbal medicine? How it helped my cancer?"

"Did I have to? I mean, he knew what happened. I helped with the cleanses and he watched me make them."

"*Jah*, he was here quit a bit but it's almost two years ago. Does he remember?"

"He doesn't want a wife that's educated is what." Becca clenched her fists and pounded her thighs. "I told him he wants a barefoot and pregnant wife."

"A what?" Maryann gasped, looking over at her bare feet. "Like me?"

Becca offered a forced smile. "It's a saying I picked up off the *English*. It means the only thing a man wants in a wife is a cook, cleaner and *boppli* maker." She ground her teeth and growled. "That's not me. I want to learn all there is to know about so many things, not only herbal medicine. I want to be a master quilter like Lottie. Maybe have women over to knit the yarn I spin and sell in my own shop."

This disclosure made Maryann's heart warm. "So, you want to be like Granny. I planted that seed quite young in you."

"What?" Becca asked, brows furrowed.

"I wanted many kinner but I saw in you a keen mind. Not that I don't have one, mind you, but who was it that begged to learn how to knit and went to circle before me?"

Becca's face softened. "I did."

"And who dropped you off at Granny's quilt shop to be her helper when only ten?"

"*Daed* did. *Ach, Mamm*, did you see it then? That I was like Granny and not you?"

Maryann laughed. "Would that be a bad thing? Me wanting a dozen kinner or more?"

"*Danki* Lord you didn't," Becca quipped. "I've changed enough diapers." She cupped her mouth, eyes showing shock. "*Mamm*, you wanted more kinner?"

Maryann tapped Becca's nose playfully. "And I might just have them. I'm in my forties, but if the *Gut* Lord blesses me with another *boppli*, it'd be a joyful day." She took Becca's hand. "But not all women are like me. If God made you more like Granny… *praise be.*"

Becca squeezed her *mamm's* hand. "*Mamm*, when we read all those books during the winter, I think you're like Mrs. March in *Little Women*. I may be more like Jo, being a book worm and keeping a journal and all, but everyone at circle wanted to be like Mrs. March, a godly *mamm*." She swiped a falling tear. "I hope to be like you in many ways, especially being happily married like you and *Daed*." She paused, her face clouding again. "But… what if I never find a man like Gilbert? Am I being foolish?"

Maryann shook her head. "You can't change Gilbert. Never marry a man thinking you'll change him. You'll only bicker."

Becca tilted her head, eyes wide. "*Mamm*, did you court someone before Daed and break up?"

Maryann nodded. "He made me feel not *gut* enough, always trying to change me, and it hurt. After a while, I told him he couldn't take me home from a Singing…"

"Was it hard? Did you cry like a *boppli* like me?"

"*Jah*, I did. And I felt so hopeless. I tried to please my beau and it wasn't *gut* enough. So who would want me?

Or so I thought, until I went to a Singing a month later and met your *daed*."

Becca sighed. "Did you know he was the one for you that night?"

Maryann smirked. "*Nee*, I'd had a guard around my heart. It took lots of patience on your *daed's* part to... love me to wholeness? *Jah*, I believe that's what happened so subtle-like. After a few months of talking, I looked at my Michael and felt... at home. Fearless. Perfect love cast out fear."

Becca clenched her hands to herself. "I want a man like *Daed*. A marriage like yours."

Maryann's heart lifted like a bird takes flight. "It's worth waiting for. But always remember, love is patient. Be patient and wait for a man who complements all your talents."

Becca lunged towards her, hugging her neck. "*Danki, Mamm.*"

Maryann held her daughter, reveling in the moment. Something she was sure to record in her journal tonight.

~*~

Lottie draped pink, mint, and purple summer scarves over antique hangers and mused about the teenage customers that came in for "bling bling" yesterday. They thought the Amish looked hot wearing three-quarter length sleeves in August, yet they wore scarves.

"When you're done, Lottie, take a break," Suzy said, ambling in from the back of the shop. "The air is on high but it's still too hot to dye yarn today."

"The rain helped a little, I think," Lottie said.

"Precious little. Only a sprinkling." She stopped in mid-stride. "I should water my garden before noon." She spun around and headed to the back room again to gather her gardening supplies.

The door bell jangled and Lottie froze. *Ezekiel? What's he doing here?* Not even a Sunday courting day. And a yarn shop? His mellow, deep blue eyes held no apology for entering a woman's shop alone, not accompanied by a woman. "Ezekiel," she blurted. "Do you knit?"

He cocked his head and then a smile split his face. "*Nee.* Never learned." After scratching the back of his neck and staring at her, eyes unflinching, he crossed the room to be near her. "Actually, my *mamm's* a knitter and I thought I'd buy her some yarn."

"Is it her birthday?"

"*Nee.* No special occasion, just was driving by and… thought of my *mamm.*" Ezekiel winked. "Wanted to say hi, too."

"Suzy's in the back."

He took her hand. "I mean you. You've been dodging me like a skunk. Am I repugnant?"

Lottie wanted to throw her arms around him and declare the opposite. He was growing on her and in her thoughts often. After hearing all he did to help Denny, her heart was putty. He could ask for her hand today and she'd say yes, but she was putting God first and not courting anyone until things became clear. "I only broke up with Peter three weeks ago. It was hard."

"But you were broken up when you came here last May. What a fool Peter is."

"A fool?"

"*Jah.* To let you go."

"I broke it off with him, remember?"

Ezekiel fumbled for words but let out, "*Jah*, I also remember first seeing you at Hezekiah and Colleen's wedding." He took her hand and led her through the store out to the front porch. "Look at my new buggy. Nice, isn't it?"

Lottie's heart leapt. Men tried to impress girls with their courting buggies and this one beat any one she'd seen. Glossy black to match a strapping black stallion. The reins and brindle were black, hardly visible. She couldn't help but run down the steps to the horse. "He's magnificent. Perfect."

Ezekiel put a hand up. "It's not a present, ya know."

She laughed as she ran her fingers down the horse's lengthy mane. She knew it wasn't a present, but she got his message very clearly. He wanted to court.

Ezekiel took the horse by the bit, revealing a scar on the left side. "We have something in common," he quipped. "Got him cheaper."

Lottie examined the wound on the horse's face. "How did this happen?"

"Farm accident. That's why I bonded with him at the auction in Dayton."

"You went to Ohio to get this horse?"

"*Nee*, Lottie, just four miles up the road in Dayton, Pennsylvania." He put a hand under her elbow as if lending support. "You okay?"

She was and she wasn't. Lottie realized at that moment that she did care for Ezekiel more than a little. If Phil Darby walked by she wouldn't even care, her eyes would be on this black-haired, dark blue-eyed man who was more masculine and he… cherished her. Treated her as something worth winning, a treasure. It was the first time she'd felt this way.

Ezekiel gripped her around her waist. "You need sugar or something. You're swaying a bit."

"What? *Nee*, I'm fine. Just thinking." His arm around her waist made Lottie want to lean up and kiss him, but she pulled away. "Maybe I'm too hot out here," she said, sprinting back up the store steps and into the store. *Lord, help me. I can't break my fast from courting. I'm putting You first for a while.*

Ezekiel soon appeared in the doorway, hands in his pockets, eyes downcast. "Your body language says it all, Lottie. No need to make excuses." He pushed his straw hat forward, making his scar disappear.

Lottie's eyes misted. "*Ach, nee.* That's not what I mean at all. I just broke up with Peter."

"An excuse. I met you in May at your cousin's wedding. I overheard Granny say she'd get you married off this summer."

"What? You heard that?"

"*Jah.* I've had my eye on you and maybe Granny saw that." He cleared his throat. "I'll take some black yarn. *Mamm's* making socks." He turned from her and examined the shelves of yarn.

Lottie clenched her sweaty palms. "Ezekiel, I'm not courting anyone for a while. No one. Understand?"

"*Ach*, Lottie, quit insulting me. I'm not daft."

His hurt was evident, yet his voice held no sarcasm or blame. It was almost playful. Is this how he dealt with rejection? But she wasn't rejecting him.

~*~

MJ knew it was God's grace that she had a few good days in a row. Wanting to see Granny's Amish kitchen was on her bucket list, so she accepted her invitation with glee. But before entering the little house, she paused to take in the shades of red roses that clung to the trellis all along the wrap around porch. "Andy, can you believe this?"

"Never seen so many roses. Jeb and Granny must have green thumbs."

"I'd love to have a rose garden, Andy." MJ produced a fake pout. "You said you'd do anything for me."

Laughing, Andy drew her near. "Anything in my power. I hear roses are hard to grow."

MJ leaned into Andy. "I love you. You're a keeper."

He stroked her hair. "You're happy to be out?"

"Sure am. Isolation can be torture, as you know."

"But you found how to battle it making all your crafts and sending them to friends on Facebook. And I'm your ever-faithful mailman." He chuckled. "Sometimes I feel like Santa Claus."

MJ sighed. "I don't miss getting out until I'm... out. Visiting friends is so rare and we've lost a few." She straightened. "But gained other ones. True friends, not fair weather ones."

Jeb opened the side door. "Deborah and I were in the basement cooling off. Didn't hear you knock."

"We didn't," Andy said. "We were admiring your roses."

Granny popped out on the porch and took MJ's hand. "So glad you could come."

MJ's face lifted into a smile. "It's a real treat. Can't wait to see your home."

Granny swatted at the air. "It's pretty barren. Mostly functional stuff. Hope you're not disappointed." Slipping her arm through MJ's, she led her into the dawdyhaus.

Off to the left was a living room with many benches and rockers with a bentwood table in the center. Off to the right was a massive kitchen as big as the living room, a long wooden table with benches taking up much of the space. MJ noticed there were no pictures on the walls but plenty of windows that had white curtains pulled to one side. A large doily with violets on it was the table centerpiece. MJ crossed the kitchen to get a better look at the black stove. "Do you use wood for baking?"

"*Jah.* Don't need much wood to keep it warm." Granny

informed. "Today it's too hot to fire up."

"*Jah*," Jeb said. "The rain last night didn't do much to stop this heat wave."

MJ couldn't stop admiring the black stove. "Do you polish it to keep it so black?"

"*Jah*, I do," Granny said. "It can fade over time to gray, and we blacken it up." She pointed toward the other stove near it. "That one's for heating purposes only. But she's a black beauty isn't she?"

Jeb moaned. "Deborah, don't tell people you named your new stove Black Beauty."

"Why not? It's a beautiful stove."

MJ's brows shot up. "I love that book. And I name things after books, too. I call my hospital bed Sleeping Beauty's Chambers."

"Is Sleeping Beauty a book?" Granny asked, eyes wide.

Shock ran through MJ. Granny had never heard of Sleeping Beauty? "Yes, it's a fairytale for children but I have the movie. Just love it. Happily ever after ending."

Jeb cautiously said, "We Amish don't read fairytales."

Andy was quick to put a hand up. "My mother always said, 'To each their own.'"

Jeb started to talk but Granny hushed him. "Should we eat dinner up here or down in the basement? MJ, can you take this heat?"

MJ wanted to admire this little house as long as possible. "Can we eat at your big table? I want to soak in this charming house all I can."

"Can I come in?" Phil asked through the screen door.

Granny ran to welcome Phil. "You never have to knock. Just come on in. Glad you could come."

Phil greeted Jeb and Andy but his eyes landed on MJ. "You're out of your house. Good for you."

"Having some good days. New meds."

"Well, maybe this will cure you," Jeb said. "We always have hope, right?"

MJ knew there was no cure for her illness. Having only one inch of her small intestine had altered her way of living permanently, but some medicines made life more bearable. Hopeless days filled with despair crept through her mind and she realized how much hope she did have. "Yes, Jeb, we have hope."

Granny asked everyone to have a seat at her long oak table and she and Jeb loaded it with cold ham, homemade bread, pickled green beans and little canning jars.

"What's in the jars?" MJ asked. "They're so cute."

"Chutney to put on your ham. Getting so many apples off our trees, I make apple chutney with raisins the most. Taste like pie filling and delicious smeared on ham."

"And you made this bread?" Phil asked, almost in reverential awe.

"I bake enough bread for a week," Granny said, eyes twinkling. "My *mamm* said I caught on to bread making faster than anyone she knew. I love making it."

Phil cut a slice and held it to his nose. "Smells delicious." He cut slices for everyone and then slowly began spreading the chutney on his own. "My mom liked to make bread, too…" he said quietly.

Granny gripped Phil's hand. "We're so sorry for your loss, Phil. But I have something for you."

"If it's a pie, I refuse. I'm putting on the pounds."

Granny slipped away to the living room and ran back in with an envelope. "This is from the knitting circle." She shoved it at him. "Open it up. I can't wait to see your face."

Phil appeared caught off guard and just stared at her for a few seconds. "Of course. I'll open it now."

Granny sat close to him on the bench, her face like a

child on Christmas morning. When Phil pulled out a check, his chin started to quiver. "I can't take this."

"*Jah*, you can," Jeb said. "It's a gift."

"It's too large. How can anyone afford this amount?"

Granny clapped her hands. "We sold quilts we've been working on. Suzy sold them on the internet. We had bids from England. Can you believe it?"

"Wait," Phil said forcefully. "I really can't take this money. Like I said, it's too much."

"Too much?" Jeb asked. "Let the giver decide that. Now, you put that there money towards the debt you have. Mighty *gut* of you to pay for herbal medicine and whatnot to save your *mamm*."

Phil looked numb, not able to speak. After a few moments he mumbled, "Thank you."

MJ remembered how surprised she had been when the people who showed the most love and support in her time of need weren't the people she expected. They were people filled with compassion who were like angels, visiting so much it was baffling. Her close friend surprised her, too, not coming around as much. "Phil, people surprise us. When I got sick, it seemed like everything shifted. You lost your mom and maybe God is allowing Granny and me to be like moms to you? Not that we could ever replace her, but I do care for you like a son somehow."

"Me, too," Granny said, "and I already have five boys. But only one lives around here."

Phil's eyes were glassy with tears. "God puts people together as He sees fit. And if he can do this small miracle here, then maybe I'll let you in on my secret."

"What secret?" Andy asked. "You look impish. Hope it's nothing needing confessing."

"No, not at all. If you're going to be like parents, then

pray I find the right girl. Now that I lost my mom, I'm lonelier than ever. And Judith's deceit made me a little cautious about women."

Granny pat his hand. "How can we pray?"

Phil took a bite of his sandwich and chewed slowly as Granny's eyes begged for information.

"I signed up for online dating."

"What's that? How can you sign up for dating?" Jeb asked, looking baffled.

"Well, you fill out a questionnaire about yourself and I put in what I'm looking for in a woman. Got some responses, one in particular. She lives in Pittsburgh and always dreamed of being a pastor's wife."

"What if she's…not attractive?" Jeb asked, scratching his head. "I've seen some ugly women in my day."

MJ burst into laughter. "Oh, Jeb, you're a funny man. He can see what she looks like on the internet, I'm sure."

"Not yet," Phil said. "I want a woman who will love me for what's in here." He thumped his chest with his hand. "I want a soul mate like you all have."

"But what if she loves you and you meet her and she's five-hundred pounds?" Jeb shook his head and furrowed his brows. "I don't understand the *English*. Why not ask the *Gut* Lord to put the right girl in your path, like he did for me? And I could see Deborah was someone I was attracted to right off the bat."

Granny grinned. "*Danki*, Jeb. I loved your turquoise eyes when I first met you."

Phil oddly burst into laughter. "I'm not marrying her. And if we email and we click, we'll exchange pictures. Lots of people meet online now."

Jeb groaned. "I'm glad I'm one foot out of this earth. It's gone crazy."

"Well, it's changing more than people can absorb. I

think that's the fascination with the Amish, and I have to say, living here, it works. Slows me down a bit and I'm reflecting more on what matters. Which reminds me, I have a book to drop off over at Jonas' place."

"What is it?" Jeb asked.

"Charles Spurgeon's *David's Treasury*. Three books on just the Psalms."

"*Ach*, the knitting circle is reading psalms and seeing how they apply to life. We share throughout the week when we see each other and they're so helpful."

"Well, it's a three book set with over five-thousand pages," Phil said, "so I think Spurgeon felt the same."

"Who's Spurgeon?" Granny asked. "Sounds familiar."

"I read his books. He was a Baptist pastor in the 1800's in England. You had to get to his church early just to get a seat."

"That's you, Phil," MJ said fondly. "You're the next Charles Spurgeon."

Phil started to cough uncontrollably. Jeb ran to pat his back but soon Phil could breathe again. "Me? Charles Spurgeon? I almost choked it's so funny."

"Well, you're our Charles Spurgeon, coming over to visit, teaching the Bible to the little group we formed."

Phil smiled. "You've given me confidence, and I'm thankful. Encouragement gives me… courage to preach." His eyes scanned every face and then he said, "Thank you."

~*~

Lizzie gasped. "Angelina, let me drive you home in my buggy."

Ruth pat Angelina's shoulder. "It's useless. She insists on walking."

"It's a *gut* for the health, no?" Angelina said in broken English, her accent thicker than jam.

"*Jah*, it is," Lizzie agreed, "but the heat."

"It no hot. I be fine. *Buena serra.*"

Lizzie assumed it meant good bye in Italian, so she said the same in reply. As the little Italian woman nimbly strode across the yard, Lizzie shook her head. "Makes me feel lazy. Angelina can run circles around me."

"Me, too," Ruth said, "but I know why now."

Taking their places at the two Amish rockers in the living room, the *kinner* asleep upstairs for their nap, Lizzie studied Ruth's expressions. They wavered from smiling to frowning to looking numb. "Ruth, what do you know now?"

Ruth shook her head. "What?"

"You just said you know now about what?"

Ruth's brows furrowed. "What were we talking about?"

Rummaging though mail on a nearby table, Lizzie held up what looked to be junk mail. "Do you need this?"

"*Nee.*"

"Use it for a fan then. You're overheated."

Ruth started to fan herself then sighed. "I know why I'm so hot, too."

"Why?" Lizzie asked.

"I'm pregnant. Doc Pal confirmed it. Can you believe it?"

The frown that made Ruth's face fall made anger rise in Lizzie. Here she was, a woman desperately wanting to have a *boppli* and Ruth acted like it was bad news. Fatigue washed over her and she grabbed a random flier from the mail pile and fanned herself, too. "How do you feel about having another *kinner*?" Lizzie forced her tone to be even.

Ruth shrugged. "Fickle. Up and down about it. Debbie's only six months and here I am, pregnant again."

Such piercing words to Lizzie's heart she could hardly breathe. *Lord, help me. I'm so jealous.* Fumbling for words, she was able to ask say, "You're a *gut mamm* and young."

"Young? I'm twenty-eight."

"Younger than me," Lizzie blurted. "I'm in my mid-thirties and my child bearing years are over."

"*Ach*, Lizzie, many women have *kinner* in their thirties."

Lizzie rubbed the back of her stiffening neck. "I've been married for fifteen months now. No pregnancy. I'm too old or I'm barren."

Ruth leaned back in the rocker. "What does Roman say?"

Not understanding her question, she just shrugged. What could Roman say except yes to adopting Charles, like she wanted?

Slowly rocking, Ruth said, "You have a *gut* husband. Not all of us are so blessed."

The stillness in the room accentuated Lizzie's pounding heart. She'd been so angry with Roman lately, him never wanting to discuss adoption, saying his girls were enough. And he believed she was being impatient. "Roman's a *gut* man but doesn't understand my pain."

"Really?" Ruth asked in disbelief. "That's how I feel about Luke right now. He doesn't know my pain at all."

Memories of Lizzie's own *mamm* who passed when she was so young flashed before her. She had long brown hair with almond shaped eyes that always made Lizzie feel like she was a rare rose. "I understand, Ruth. I lost my *mamm*, you know. It'll take time."

"But you have a *gut daed*."

Somehow Lizzie felt weighed down, spiraling into negative thoughts. Ruth was depressed and was pressing others down in the process. Could she not say one kind word about Luke or her *daed*? "Ruth, people are human. We make mistakes. We both still have *gut daeds*."

Ruth closed her eyes as if to block Lizzie's words. "I

forgive my *daed*, but in my heart I hold a grudge."

Lizzie's heart was pricked. This is how she felt towards Roman for weeks. The peaceful home they'd enjoyed was crumbling due to the rain cloud that never let up. Her infertility. How did Ella ever bear it?

The sound of the screen door slamming was Maryann and she soon made her presence known. "*Ach*, Lizzie, so *gut* to see you here. Helping Ruth, too?"

"*Jah.* I am."

"I can only visit when Becca's home and the little ones are down for their naps." Maryann held up two plastic grocery bags. "I brought over some ice cream. Michael and I made it last night on the porch. It's chocolate, which they say makes you happy. Well, dark chocolate's *gut* for you, so I indulge."

"*Danki*," Ruth said. "Want me to serve it up?"

"Do you want some right now? Didn't you have your noon meal?"

"I'm starving. Pregnant again."

Maryann nearly dropped her bags, then arched up on her tip toes. "*Ach*, so happy for you! A *boppli* will make the bond with you and Luke stronger"

"Really?" Ruth asked. "Won't another *kinner* be more of a strain?"

"Not at all," Maryann chimed. "Children are a blessing from the Lord. Having eight, Michael and I are more bonded than ever." She ran to put the ice cream in her freezer in the kitchen and yelled so they could hear, "I see Luke got you a propane powered fridge. That was thoughtful."

Ruth smiled at Lizzie. "I nagged Luke to no end, so he gave in."

"I heard that," Maryann said evenly as she crossed the room and took a seat on a bench. "Ruth, you helped me get through my cancer and I'm going to help you get through this depression you're experiencing. Now, have you praised Luke for anything today?"

"Praise him?" Lizzie said wryly. "We're supposed to praise our husbands?" As soon as she said this she knew it sounded just like something Marge would say in jest.

Maryann wagged a finger. "Lizzie, you know what the Bible says about the tongue. We can bring life or death into a relationship with a small member. I've told Ruth to make it a point to say something kind to Luke once a day, a word of gratitude or praise. Now bow down and praise him as God."

Lizzie felt heat rise into her cheeks and knew she was blushing. "I'm sorry. That's what I thought you meant at first, but now I see what you mean."

Maryann nodded and eyed Ruth. "This little family can be turned around just by saying kind words to each other."

Lizzie wanted to run. Was she as hard on Roman as Ruth was on her husband? She'd had a happy home with Roman's girls by so willing being the girls' *mamm*. Why was she so filled with jealousy and rage when she saw a pregnant woman? *Lord, let the words of my mouth and the meditations of my heart be acceptable to you,* she prayed. *Give me strength to carry the hard burden of being infertile....*

~*~

Becca rolled her eyes and repeated the answer to Denny's math problem. "To find the volume of an irregular prism is base times height. That's what *b h* stands for. You're supposed to know that b and h are multiplied."

Denny slammed his geometry book shut. "Okay, Bec, what's up? Tired of helping me?"

"You might not even stay in school," she murmured.

Taking a sip of her iced tea, she stared at the cheerful cherry curtains that adored the kitchen at Arbor Creek. If only her heart could be merry.

"What is it?" Denny asked, cupping his hand over hers.

Becca tried to hide any emotion today while tutoring, but obviously anger made an appearance and Denny knew pain. He recognized it in others. "Nothing." She put both hands on her glass and held her glass to her lips, avoiding Denny's touch.

"Bec, tell me. I've never seen you so hurt."

"Me? I'm fine. It's the heat. Really. I have a lot on my mind."

"Such as?"

"Well, in a few weeks it'll be harvest time."

"And?"

Becca wanted to scream that harvest time was filled with working not only on canning and putting up the harvest, a joyful event, but preparing for weddings. And this year, she didn't want to attend any.

"Bec, what's wrong with harvest time? Too much work?"

She shrugged her shoulders. "*Jah*, I suppose. Don't want the summer to end."

Denny slouched in his chair. "Me neither. I have a decision to make about school. I still want to drop out, take the GED when I'm ready and keep working at woodworking. You'll laugh, but all this geometry is clicking because Roman uses it all the time in the shop."

"Really? I thought he used patterns handed down. You know, Amish rockers have been around for centuries."

Denny leaned forward, eyes bright. "We carve wood. I know Amish don't make people with faces, but Roman has me carving nativity sets for Christmas. And I make little toys for the girls."

Becca noticed Denny's blue eyes twinkled just now. "You like kids?"

"Never really thought about it, but they're fun. Maybe someday I'll have a kid of my own. Have a real family."

Becca's eyes stung. Gilbert wanted a bakers dozen of *kinner*, but now there would be none, at least with her. She bit her lower lip as a tear slid down her cheek.

"Becca, you're crying. Did I upset you?"

"*Nee.*"

Denny narrowed his gaze and then crossed his arms. "Did that Gilbert guy hurt you?"

Fighting tears, Becca nodded.

Denny shot up and pounded a fist into his palm. "I'll hurt him. What did he do? Hurt you?"

Shocked, Becca couldn't help but stare at Denny. He was bouncing around the kitchen, swinging his fists. "What are you doing?"

"Hey, I'm good at boxing. One strike and he's out of here."

Denny cared about her like a big brother, she thought. Never having a big brother, this new feeling of being defended made her want to embrace him. "Denny, you can't hit Gilbert. Amish are pacifists."

Denny cocked his head. "I'm not Amish.. Tell me, what did this guy do? "

"*Ach,*" Becca said. "He broke things off between us."

Denny slid into a chair near her. "If I was Amish, I'd never let you go. Gilbert's an idiot."

Becca hid a shy smile. "Who said I'd court you if you were Amish?"

Denny reached for her hand again. "Becca, if I was, would it make a difference to you?"

Becca shook her head. "Denny, what are you saying?"

He pulled her out of her chair and led her out the

kitchen door. "Let's take a walk. I can talk better in the woods."

She halted. "Denny. People talk. Us being alone and all. It's one of the reason's Gilbert called off our courtship."

He continued to lead her, not looking back. "He doesn't trust you is what. Never liked the pansy boy."

The bizarreness of Denny's words made laughter erupt out of Becca's heart. "*Ach*, Denny you say the oddest things." Hand in hand, they nearly ran to the edge of the woods and entered the path to Granny and Jeb's. "I'm out of breath for Pete's sake."

Slowing down, Denny plopped down on a huge rock, taking a seat. "Becca, I can't hide it anymore. I care about you."

Becca leaned against a large maple pretending she didn't understand his meaning. "We're like brother and sister, *jah*?"

Denny chose a rock to chug into the woods. "Not like that. You know what I mean. When I think of having a family, I imagine you as my…wife."

Was Gilbert right? Was it obvious she was attracted to this *Englisher*? She'd fallen into a predictable relationship with Gilbert, but Denny's heart was an open book. One she felt more compelled to read. When Denny got up and cupped her cheeks in his hands, planting a kiss on her lips, she didn't resist, but leaned in to kiss him back.

Denny whispered in her ear. "I knew you cared."

"I do, Denny. But this can't be."

He kissed her on the cheek. "Why not?"

"You're not Amish," was all she was able to get out, leaning her head on his chest.

"I could be. Maybe that's why the Lord put Granny and Jeb in my life."

Becca pulled away enough to stare in disbelief. "You

just talked about the Lord. I've never heard you say anything about God before."

Denny pulled at her loose prayer *kapp* strings, tying them in a bow. "Phil and I stay up late talking. Never heard such things. Can't stop reading the Bible. It makes me feel...whole."

Becca gave a knowing look. "It's spiritual food. We need it like regular food."

Denny tapped her nose. "Jesus said he was the Bread of Life. He's filling me."

Longing for another kiss, which startled Becca to no end, she laced her fingers around his neck. "Would you be Amish?"

"Would you marry me?"

Becca looked down. "Denny, life isn't a joke you know."

"I wasn't joking."

His body stiffened and Becca realized he was serious. "Denny, I'm sorry. It's just that in the Amish culture, only a baptized member can propose to an Amish girl."

He took her hand and squeezed them tight. "Pretend I am Amish. Would you say yes?"

The love that poured out of this man amazed Becca. She gasped for air, not realizing she was breathing shallowly. *Yes*, she wanted to shout. How she'd struggled ever since she met Denny to keep her emotions at bay, spending all the more time with Gilbert to convince herself she loved him. She'd said in three years, but with Denny, if he learned a trade and was baptized, she'd wed him in the fall if they were allowed.

"What are you thinking?"

"You need to keep your apprenticeship with Roman and learn to be a master carpenter."

His eyes widened. "Why?"

"Because in two years, you'll make a *gut* living."

Denny kissed her cheek. "And why would you care about that?"

She giggled. "Well, Roman has a nice big house and I want one, too."

He swung her around and then held her tight. "I love you, Becca."

She pressed her hands on his chest. "Me, too. But you have to be Amish. Understand?"

He beamed. "I'll have an Amish family with Granny and Jeb, so I best be talking to Jeb about baptismal classes."

Becca knew Denny never said anything unless he meant it. She started to laugh and cry at the same time. The Lord had said He'd turn her mourning into dancing, but she never knew if could happen in one day.

Denny sniffed. "I smell smoke. Do you?"

Becca looked past Denny into the woods and yelled, "Fire!"

~*~

Granny gripped her middle as Jeb and Roman raced towards the smoke billowing from their woods. *Lord, send rain right quick to help put this fire out,* was all Granny was able to pray. As she stood on her porch, she became aware of the red-tailed hawk she'd been watching. It darted near its nest and then back out, making a dreadful cry. Were her babies in the nest and she couldn't get them? *Ach, Lord, help the critters out there that call our woods home.*

She scanned the area. "Old Bull. Where are you?" Granny yelled.

Lizzie ran up on the porch and joined her. "Are you alright?"

"*Jah.* Where's Old Bull?"

Lizzie ran off around the wrap around porch and was out of sight before Granny could speak further. Running after her, she yelled, "Lizzie, stay here. You can't go near the woods."

"The fire's way off. I need to get Bull."

Granny was struck dumb. Didn't Lizzie know how dry the ground was? The undergrowth could catch fire quicker than she could run. "Stop, Lizzie!" But Lizzie only ran into the woods, calling back for her to keep an eye on the girls.

"Lord have mercy," Granny whispered. Lizzie's heart towards animals touched her. Realizing that Lizzie wouldn't pay heed to her words, Granny ran over to Roman's, and chimed the old dinner bell that she used to ring when all five boys were living at home. She pulled on the rope, making the clanging bell scream out in warning, but it was drowned out by the sirens from the fire trucks over at Arbor Creek.

But soon the girls sprang off the porch and ran towards the woods. "Get back here," she yelled, but then gasped. There was Lizzie leading Old Bull out of the woods into safety. The girls met her, hugging her until Lizzie almost toppled over. *Lord, help Lizzie see that she's needed. She's ever bit a* mamm *to those girls as Abigail was. Open her eyes, Lord.*

~*~

As the fire trucks left the scene, Jeb and Roman stared in disbelief at the woods. "That fire ate up half the woods in no time," Roman said.

Jeb put an arm around Roman's shoulder. "Those berries will all come in stronger, *jah*? A *gut* fire is needed to take out the weeds."

"*Jah*, you're right," Roman said, a forced lilt in his voice.

Marge pulled into the driveway, screeching her tires

along the gravel, kicking up stones. "I got here as quick as I could. How'd this happen?"

Jeb rubbed the back of his neck, feeling soar from pulling the hose that nearly knocked him over when the water spouted out. "Brush fire. Land is dry."

"Is anyone hurt?"

"Well, some are being taken to the hospital for smoke inhalation, just as a precaution. Some minor burns."

Patting her heart, Marge blurted, "Was Joe one of them?"

"He drove," Roman said. "Can't remember who all went."

"Any of the boys?" Marge spit out.

"Boys are all here. Fire Chief is asking questions out back."

"About what?"

"Cigarettes were found. The boys were smoking in the woods and it could've caused the fire."

Marge groaned. "Dennis the Menace to be sure."

"*Nee*," Roman said sternly. "He was with Becca. Charles and Brian were the ones smoking."

"My Brian-Boy? I don't believe it. Denny was sure to be the instigator."

Jeb noticed his son's face contort and put a hand on his shoulder again. "Easy now."

"*Nee, Daed.* Marge, what do you have against Denny? He's the nicest kid that lives at this joint. If you treat kids like they're bad, they'll be bad." He shook his head. "Denny's a *gut* man. Like a son to me, so leave him be."

Marge glared at Roman. "Mark my words. Denny is behind all this." She spun around and marched toward the back of the house.

When Becca and Denny came around the other side, Jeb was relieved Denny had escaped the wrath of Marge.

When he saw that they were holding hands, he clung to Roman for support. *What on earth?*

Roman ran to Denny. "You alright? You're face is black with soot."

"Need help walking?" Jeb murmured.

Denny straightened. "I'm fine. Becca's shook up."

"About the fire?" Jeb probed.

"Gilbert was here helping and was mean," Becca said. "But I don't care."

"Aren't you two courting?" Jeb asked.

"Not anymore. It's a long story," was all that Becca offered.

Denny's eyes were dancing with glee and Jeb saw Becca's were doing the same. It was the look Deborah gave him when they knew they were the ones for each other. "Becca, you have something you want to tell me? I'm your bishop, *jah?*"

Denny raised a hand. "I do. Can I live with you for sure?"

Jeb nodded. "Offer still stands. We can be a family."

"Then, I figure I, ah, need to be Amish," Denny struggled to get out.

Roman stared hard. "We've all talked about that. We'd all be family but you don't need to be Amish."

"But I want to be Amish."

Jeb sat down on the spot, feeling water soak into his trousers. "Come again?"

Roman sat next to his *daed.* "He wants to be Amish, *Daed.* I say praise be."

Jeb studied Becca's face and again she was beaming...confidently. "Well, being Amish takes time, ya know. Years. Won't be baptized until you're old enough."

"How old is that?"

"I got baptized when fifteen," Becca chimed in. "So,

Denny, you're old enough. We'll both be seventeen in February, *jah*? Funny how we share the same birthday."

Jeb gulped and his mouth went drier than sand. He'd agreed to Becca being baptized at the young age of fifteen. Her *mamm* was battling cancer and Becca articulated so well how the brevity of life stunned her. She wanted her *mamm* to witness such a special occasion if Maryann's cancer took her young.

Jeb studied Denny's face. For some time now, he imagined him as an Amish man. The way he took to their ways was unusual. But be baptized? "Son," he said to Denny as he got up. "We need to have a talk."

~*~

Granny felt the life drain out of her as she took in the scent of her partial burnt woods. She leaned her head on Jeb, needing support. "*Ach*, the berries we had in those woods."

Jeb laced his fingers through hers. "That fire was kept a bay by lack of wind and this little community coming together, Amish and *English* alike."

Granny looked up, observing Jeb's face. "So you see we need each other, jah?"

"Jah, for fires and such, but rubbing shoulders too close can be trouble."

"Trouble? Jeb, what's on your mind?"

"Denny. He wants to become Amish."

Granny was too bone tired to have her normal animated reaction. "Praise be," she said.

Jeb clucked his tongue. "I talked to Denny for a short time. I see right through it all."

"Through what?"

"He cares for Becca and wants to be Amish for her."

Shock deemed Granny speechless. She closed her eyes and prayed for grace. God's lifting that helped through confusing times. Becca was like a *grandkinner* and as Amish as they came. "Becca's courting Gilbert, *jah*?"

"He broke it off. Doesn't like how cozy Becca is with Denny and her wanting to postpone marriage to study herbs and travel."

"Travel? What?"

"*Jah*, she wants to go to Pinecraft, Florida for a spell before she gets married. Why that notion's in her head I have no idea."

Granny sighed. "Suzy went down there two years back and maybe she told Becca about all the Amish and Mennonites there."

Jeb straightened and fiddled with his straw hat. "I think Becca cares for Denny. She's the one encouraging him to be baptized. Only a baptized Amish man can propose."

Granny pondered this thought. She did love Denny and how he took to Amish ways like fish to water. Time spent with Roman had given him confidence. "I think it's his natural bend. He loves the Amish lifestyle and the People. He wouldn't be attracted to Becca if he didn't, don't you think?"

Jeb pulled at his beard, brows knit together. "Never thought of it that way. Maybe he sees the goodness in Becca and that's what he's thirsting after." He put his arm around his wife. "You see things I can't see, like the goodness in the *English*."

"You care for Denny as much as I do."

"*Jah*, as long as he stays away from my flock. I need to be a gentler leader. I yelled at Denny."

Granny started to grind her molars. "You what?"

"Yelled at him. Told him to stay away from Becca, but he didn't reply back in anger but…understanding. He said he knew he needed to respect Amish ways and earn the right to be Amish. He's serious and I thought it was only to snatch a nice Amish girl. Feel kind of badly."

Granny knew Denny was verbally abused and would naturally strike back in anger. "I'm proud of our boy for not doing what's natural."

"Which is?"

"Well, he's admitted to retaliating in the past, but he turned the other cheek…when you struck it."

Jeb blew out a sigh that scared a hummingbird from its feeder on the porch. "I need prayer, like I said. I'm afraid Denny cares for Becca and I need to protect her. On the other hand, I can't keep a sincere man from joining the People."

Granny pat his back. "Sorry, old man. I'm tired. You know best. God gave you this flock and the wisdom on how to lead. You're as tired as I am, this fire's frizzled my nerves."

Lizzie came around the corner of the wraparound porch, lifting up a long tray. "I made dinner for all of us."

Soon the three girls were seen, following Lizzie like a mother duck. Tillie smiled as she climbed on Jeb's lap. "*Opa*, I'm glad you're okay."

"*Jah*, *Opa*, you were brave to get so near the fire," Millie quipped as she cozied up next to Granny on the porch swing.

Jenny tapped a foot. "*Opa*, can Amish girls be firefighters?"

Lizzie chuckled. "I told you *nee*. Your dress might catch fire and men are stronger than women."

"I'm as strong as Charles, though," Jenny protested.

"And how do you know that?" Granny asked.

"I beat him in arm wrestling."

Jeb let out a hoot. "He let you win. Nice boy."

Roman came around the corner and forced a smile. "Glad the fire didn't reach here."

"*Jah*, for sure and certain," Jeb said.

Granny asked Millie to help her up and started to lead the women to her kitchen where she'd open some chow chow and pickled eggs to add to Lizzie's dinner. But she soon spied Suzy's car coming down her driveway. She turned to Lizzie. "Hope nothing's wrong. I know some men were taken to the hospital for smoke inhalation, but nothing serious, I think."

Lizzie shrugged her shoulder, eyes wide. Suzy sped up to the porch steps and jumped out of the car in no time. "What a pickle," she blurted.

Granny ran down the porch steps to meet her frazzled friend. "What is it?"

"Well, I'm taking Ruth to see Luke in the hospital. Lottie's coming along."

"I'm sure they're fine," Lizzie said. "Roman was out there with them and it's nothing serious."

"Well, it is. The Fire Chief found the cause of the fire and it was kids smoking in your woods. Charles and Brian admitted to it. Now Marge is in an uproar wondering if she knows the boy she's trying to adopt at all. Her Brian-Boy, as she calls him. And I know how fond you all are of Charles, especially you, Lizzie. Your dad, too."

"Did Denny put them up to it?" Lizzie asked in a rushed, accusing tone.

"No, he was with Becca being tutored. Phil Darby grilled all the boys and it was Charles and Brian."

Granny put up a hand. "I say the boys didn't know how dry the ground was and it's all over and done with. We all make mistakes."

Suzy's eyes softened. "That's so kind of you, Granny. It's your woods they burnt down."

"I know," Granny said, "but it'll grow back."

Suzy embraced Granny. "Thank you. So you'll still bring pies over to Arbor Creek and visit the boys? They do love talking to you."

Granny was surprised that Suzy didn't know her better by now. "Of course I will. Like I said, we all make mistakes."

After another quick embrace, Granny made her way back to the picnic table near the willow tree and was shocked to overhear Roman's tone as he chided Lizzie for running towards the fire to save Old Bull. "Roman, she saved Old Bull."

Roman's face drained of color as he faced his *mamm*. "I know. But...what if Lizzie got hurt?"

Granny noticed tears forming in Lizzie's eyes. Was she hurt or touched by Roman's concern? Taking her hand Granny said, "Lizzie, what Roman's trying to say is he needs you. He's speaking out of fear."

Lizzie stiffened, her cheeks turned crimson red, and she eyed Roman with an icy glare and then ran towards her house.

Granny shook her head. "Roman, you yelled at her and she saved Old Bull. What's really wrong?"

Roman raked his fingers through his chestnut colored hair. "We're not in agreement about Charles. And now that he almost burned the woods down, I don't want to hear anything about adoption."

She took his hand. "Roman, I didn't raise you to judge others. What's wrong? Tell me the truth? Maybe I can help."

Roman's jaw jutted out. "I don't know her anymore. She's too *English*..."

"Go on..."

"She can't have *kinner*."

"And?"

"She's hard to live with it at times."

Granny pat his hand. "She's grieving, don't you know? When you lost Abigail, you were hard to live with, moody and whatnot."

Roman's eyes registered a glimpse of understanding and compassion. "I remember. You and *Daed* got me through." He put an arm around his *mamm*. "But Lizzie hasn't lost anyone. I don't follow."

"Roman, all her hopes for having *kinner* are dying. Understand? She's losing hope and as the Good Book says, *hope deferred makes the heart sick.*"

Roman stared hard at the ground, as if it was too much to absorb. "So you're saying I should adopt Charles to give her hope."

"*Nee.* Not at all," Granny said. "But she needs something. I don't know what, but she's sinking into hopelessness. Pray and love her. She'll open up like a flower.

Roman squeezed his *mamm*. "I will. And I know I don't say it enough, but I'm glad I have a *mamm* like you. One who cares." He kissed her on the cheek and then put an arm around her.

Granny felt a little slice of heaven slip into her heart.

~*~

The smell of antiseptics always made Lottie feel light-headed. As she walked down the hospital hall, visiting members of the Baptist Church with Suzy while Ruth spent much needed time with her husband was out of her comfort zone. But she wanted to get away from Colleen and Hezekiah's love nest. Her cousin was recovering and soon she wouldn't be needed. Her reason to stay in Smicksburg was becoming blurry, and she felt like a third wheel around the happy newlyweds.

"What's on your mind?" Suzy asked her.

"Nothing. I don't do well in hospitals."

Suzy stopped mid-stride and turned to face her. "We're friends. Is it seeing Phil Darby here that's got you so unnerved?"

"*Nee.* He's a friend, nothing more."

"Then what is it?" Suzy gently prodded.

Lottie tucked a few stray strands of strawberry blonde hair into her prayer *kapp*. "Dating Jesus is hard around Colleen and Hezekiah. I might not ever have what they have."

Suzy hooked her thumbs through her blue jean belt loops. "Remember our talk about marriage. It's forever, for good and bad. Putting God first and seeking His guidance will lead you to the right spouse eventually. Ever take a morning walk?"

"Plenty," Lottie said, confused by the odd question.

"It's dusk and you can't see too well. But as the morning comes, you can, right?"

"*Jah.*"

"That's how knowing God's will is for your life. Wait for high noon."

Lottie knew she had to wait on God, but what if it was for fifty years and she lived her life alone? She closed her eyes and prayed, "Lord help me."

Suzy took her hand. "I have Bible proof on this. Dave and I live our lives by it." She grabbed Lottie's hand and led her to the nearby guest room. Taking her phone out of her purse she tapped and slid her fingers and then said, "Here it is. Listen to this:

Open up before GOD, keep nothing back;
he'll do whatever needs to be done:
He'll validate your life in the clear light of day
and stamp you with approval at high noon.

"That's Psalm 37: 5-6 in The Message Bible."

Lottie asked to look at her phone and read it again. *Open up before God.* Did that means fears of being an old maid? *He'll do whatever needs to be done.* Did this mean her waiting and "dating Jesus" wasn't a foolish notion? The more she leaned on Christ, he'd work things out without her efforts? *He'll validate your life…stamp your with approval at high noon.* She supposed it meant he'd give her a life full of purpose and meaning.

Something solidified in Lottie's heart while pondering this verse, or meditating on it slowly as Granny was teaching her. And it was in Psalms, something the knitting circle was focusing on all summer. She gave a quick nod and smiled. "*Danki*, Suzy. I feel like I'm on the right path."

"*Vell, dat* is *gut*," Suzy said in a strong Pennsylvania Dutch accent which always made Lottie laugh. "Come on. We have patients to visit."

~*~

Ruth waited in a chair next to Luke's bed. Oxygen tubes were under his nose. Smoke inhalation was the only reason he was here in the hospital and he'd be home tomorrow, but she needed to say what was on her heart. Like Granny said, how a person reacts is the truth, not how they act. Hearing that Luke was in the fiercest part of the fire made her imagine a life without him and it was empty and grim. She loved this man and had taken her grief over losing her *mamm* out on him. Could he ever forgive her? Could their marriage mend?

"Ruth?" Luke said, head turned to her.

"*Ach*, Luke, did I wake you up?"

"*Jah*, but it's nice to wake up to your pretty face." He winked.

Feeling tense, she gulped and pain shot through her throat. "You were brave."

"I didn't want the fire to get to the girl's tree house."

Ruth frowned in confusion. "Their tree house is near the main farmhouse."

"They have two. Joe built them another one in the woods. I helped."

He's such a gut man, Ruth thought. *He was never disappointed when Little Debbie was diagnosed with Down Syndrome.* "That was nice of you to do."

"Joe doesn't know how to build like the Amish and I'm teaching him. It was nothing."

A sob escaped Ruth and she reached for Luke's hand. "You're a *gut* man, Luke. I'm sorry I took my anger over losing *mamm* out on you."

He squeezed her hand. "Hush now. You were shocked by a sudden death, which is harder to bear, just like Phil told us."

Tears ran down Ruth's cheeks. "I'm ashamed that I brought up your past. Now here I am on a prescription for anxiety to 'take the edge off,' as Dr. Pal put it. He was right about the brain only being able to take so much stress."

Luke pushed the button to make the hospital bed rise and leaned over, lips puckered. Ruth leaned in to give him a kiss he wouldn't soon forget. "I love you," they said in unison and then both laughed.

"So you forgive me?" Ruth had to ask for reassurance. She'd treated this man with so much contempt, he'd slept over at Joe and Marge's a few nights to escape her wrath, so it must have been unbearable.

"Ruthy, I love you. I see only the best, *jah*?"

"But you left for a few days."

"I spent time in solitude and prayer. Asking God for strength to help you. Wisdom to know when to talk and when to shut up. Understand?"

"So you weren't mad?"

"Well, *jah*, but not at you. Angry at God but I wrestled with it all and I'm fine. It's a mystery why your *mamm* was taken so young."

Ruth's jaw dropped. "Mad a God? Really?"

"*Jah*. The Baptists talk like that. They say God sees your heart, so why not admit what's on it. So I told God I was mighty mad that you were in such emotional pain and you lost your best friend. Our *kinner* lost an *oma*. I lost someone who was like a real *mamm*. *Jah*, I was furious."

Ruth pondered his words and had to admit this was the constant underground current raging in her. She was mad at God. "Luke, I'm mad at God, too, but isn't that a sin? We're not to question His ways."

"I think it's being honest. If one of our *kinner* is angry with us, I'd want to know. When they're older, entering *rumspringa*, I want them to feel free to talk openly, like I did with your *mamm*. And how I can talk to your *daed*."

Ruth moaned. "I've been so cruel to him when he needed me most."

"I think he understands, but an apology would go a long way. You did bring up his past to others."

"I'm so *furhoodled* at times."

"We've all got feet of clay, *jah*? We're all messed up in the head at times." He leaned over again for a kiss and Ruth was eager to give it.

~*~

Lottie entered a hospital room to see a Baptist Church member, but gasped when she saw a man with half of his face bandaged and a scar like Ezekiel's on the exposed side. When his crystal blue eyes met hers, her heart flipped. "Ezekiel?"

"Lottie. *Gut* of you to come," he said as he gripped the white sheets, pain apparent in his voice.

"I, ah, well…" Lottie could only stutter. She didn't even know he was hurt.

Suzy intervened. "I brought Ruth to see Luke and we're visiting men hurt in that horrible fire."

"But Ezekiel," Lottie blurted, "no one else has bandages…"

"Some do," Suzy said. "Don't you remember Harvey? On his arm?"

Lottie kept staring into Ezekiel's eyes. He was in pain. Was it emotional as well as physical? His face was scarred on the left side now. Or maybe not? How she wanted to hold this man and let him know how she felt. As if Suzy could read her mind, she closed the dividing curtain and said she wanted to talk privately to the roommate.

"Ezekiel, how did this happen?"

A shadow cast across his face. "I tripped and fell. The fire was close."

"Does it hurt?"

"*Jah*, it's painful. Third degree burns."

"Will it leave… a scar?"

Ezekiel's chest rose and fell. "It depends on how it heals. Glad my hands are alright. Need them for work."

Lottie gingerly took the seat next to his bedside. Ezekiel was the most confident, real man she knew. He'd helped her realize that inner beauty is what's important, making her less self-conscience about her looks. Some said she was beautiful, but she didn't see it at all.

"Can I get you anything?"

He held up the nurse call apparatus. "I just push a button and the nurse comes."

"How about I read to you? I don't know how much you can read and with one eye bandaged –"

"Stop, Lottie," he said in an even tone. "You made it clear this morning you didn't care for me like I care for you. I think it's best we not see each other."

"Not see each other? Ezekiel, *nee*, that would be horrible."

His eyes softened. "Forgive me. I don't want to be mean-spirited, but I can't be around you is what I'm trying to say. I care about you."

"I care about you," Lottie admitted.

"But you won't go in my courting buggy. You made that real clear."

Lottie bowed her head, asking God for strength and words to say. Silence filled the room but peace permeated for some odd reason. She slowly looked up at him. "Ezekiel, you're a carpenter and deal with lots of dust, *jah?*"

"*Jah.*"

"My life has lots of dust in it and it needs to settle so I can see things clearly. I do care for you, but I tend to be impulsive. I want you to promise me something."

His eyes were moist. "What?"

"That you'll not think I'm rejecting you. I care about you but am afraid of making a commitment to anyone. Peter hurt me badly and I can't trust any man right now."

Ezekiel reached for her hand. "I understand."

"You do?"

"*Jah.* It's like when I got bit by a stray dog when I was a kid, I was afraid of big dogs for a while." He smiled despite the pain it clearly caused. "So you care for me."

"*Jah,*" Lottie said tenderly.

"But not enough to court?"

She'd made a vow to God to not court until she was sure it was the right man for her. But looking at Ezekiel today, she felt at home. She imagined a family with this man. "I'm afraid."

"Me, too."

"Can we take it slow, like court to build a friendship? Granny says friendship is a good foundation."

"A foundation to what?" Ezekiel teased.

Lottie felt her cheeks burn but she didn't care. "It starts with an *M*," she giggled.

Ezekiel's face lit up. "Sounds *gut*. And I just thought of something."

"What?"

"I love playing hangman. Can we play?"

Lottie's heart enlarged with joy. "*Jah*. Let me find some paper."

~*~

Granny took a sip of morning coffee and then leaned her head on the glider back. "I smell burnt cherry wood."

"I smell apple. Best kind for smoking ham, but thank the *Gut* Lord no one was hurt."

"*Jah*, and it could have spread to this house." Granny shivered at the thought. One spark could light a whole forest on fire. "From a smoldering cigarette. Makes me think of the tongue and how the Bible says one unkind word can do the damage of a forest fire." She snuggled up closer to Jeb. "I hope Roman apologized to Lizzie like he promised."

Jeb took a swig of coffee and groaned. "Heard them having a pretty loud discussion on the porch last night. Can't help but hear."

Granny knew Roman had a soft heart but hard head. "He's against adopting Charles and I see his point.

Lizzie's pushing the matter in a frantic way and I wonder what's behind her behavior."

"Behind her behavior? That's why I need your help with women in the *Gmay*. Men just come out and say what they're thinking, but with women, you need to pry things out."

Granny humphed and scooted away. "I'm a woman...old man."

"*Jah*, but with age comes wisdom." He poked her playfully with an elbow.

"Women have more emotions than men, I'm thinking. It's why I have my knitting circle, it helps women open up. Women open up when ready, like flowers."

"*Jah*, they do. Men can speak too frankly. Maybe that's why marriage is such a *wunderbar* thing, we compliment each other."

Granny nestled back up with Jeb. "So, what are you doing today? It's still mighty hot."

"Work in Roman's basement. Denny's coming over and we'll give him a taste of what it's like to be Amish." Jeb chuckled and then sighed. "He has no idea what it's really like."

"What are you up to, old man? We all know there's the beautiful and the not so beautiful part of being Amish, like when the outhouse needs cleaned and whatnot."

Jeb's body shook with laughter and he placed his coffee on a nearby table to spare any spillage. "Did Roman tell you?"

"About what?"

"The outhouse cleaning we're having Denny do."

Granny scrunched her lips to one side to stifle a smile. "Be fair to him is all I'm asking. Don't drive him away." As the day lit up, the sun bursting over the horizon,

Granny saw the little hummingbird that seemed to live on their porch. "I wonder where her nest is?"

"He's a male. More colorful."

"*Ach, jah.* The female can be camouflaged better by blending in. I wonder where *his* nest is?"

Jeb's brows furrowed. "Mighty hard to find a hummingbird nest. They're so tiny."

"Jeb, pray that Lottie finds a place to nest. She has a strong desire to raise a family and I fear I'm failing."

"You? Failing? How?"

"Maybe I need to have another dinner with Lottie and Ezekiel, but she's determined not to court anyone, putting the Lord first."

"Well, that's wise."

"But I haven't told her that the Coblenz clan is moving to New York and Ezekiel may be leaving."

Jeb retrieved his coffee and took another swig. "They can always write. Many have found spouses by letter writing."

"I wonder if Phil's finding a bride on the internet. No different than we Amish writing letters, only faster. *Much faster.*"

Jeb pat her knee. "Now, Deborah, I know Suzy gets letters on the internet daily from Janice but you have to wait a whole week or more."

"I'm not envious, just miss Jerry and Janice. The Baptist Church members need them. If they stay down South, I'd be sad."

He put an arm around her. "I think you have more *English* friends that any Amish woman I know, but it's not just to get a ride somewhere, you really love them."

"'Course I do. Marge has toned down some and I'm glad to see it. There is a line not to cross."

"Like any relationship," Jeb said, tapping his forehead. "I'm sweating already. Going to get a Popsicle."

"Before breakfast?"

"Well, doing farm chores since four this morning has given me a sweet tooth."

"Jeb, your excuses to eating Popsicles could fill a newspaper."

Jeb slowly got up and held out a hand for her to join him. "How about I make breakfast this morning. You're tired from all the stress of yesterday."

Granny knew the fire had shaken her up and she was slow moving this morning. Stress made a body tired. She looked up into Jeb's turquoise eyes and playfully said, "I'll act like a man and be frank. *Jah*, make breakfast. I want pancakes, eggs, bacon and cinnamon rolls."

Jeb pulled her up into a sweet embrace. "Do I bark out orders like that?"

"*Nee*, old man. You meow them."

He leaned down and tenderly kissed her lips. "You know I appreciate all you do...at your age."

Granny whacked his arm and laughed. "You're two years older...old man."

~*~

I love air conditioning, Granny thought as she walked into Suzy's yarn shop. She was running late, since she dropped off pies at Forget-Me-Not Manor that she'd baked last night, her nerves still raw from the fire. Baking soothed a soul, along with the aromas exuded: elderberries, blackberries and cherries. With leftover berries, Granny made a fruit pizza that she thought the girls would enjoy. Entering the back room, her eyes shone as each girl was present, even Mona who was usually busy watching her granddaughter. Fannie quickly got up to unfold another chair that she plopped herself in, giving Granny a comfy padded chair.

"*Danki*, Fannie," she said fondly to the girl who was like her own.

Fannie took the dessert from her and kissed her on the cheek. "I need to come by and visit more. I miss you."

Granny thought back to what Roman said, that he was glad to have a caring *mamm*, and Granny's heart again expanded as she had real *kinner* and ones that were *kinner* by love. *Hearts knit together in love,* she thought.

After a round of greetings to all the girls, Lottie passed out quilting squares in muted shades of floral prints. "We have a surprise for you, Granny. A quilt will be made and all profit will go into replanting your forest."

Granny forced a smile. Didn't the girls know that a forest fire would clean the woods of weeds, a pruning of sorts? Like being in a fiery trial and coming out more refined?

"It's for blueberry bushes," Lizzie informed.

"And white raspberries," Suzy quipped. "They're rare but I found some online."

"Elderberry bushes, too," Marge said, cheeks propped up by a smile.

Fannie clapped her hands uncontrollably. "And a grape arbor. A long one that you can walk through."

Granny gasped as tears moistened her eyes. "*Ach*, it's not necessary."

Mona frowned. "Do you already have all these plants?"

"*Nee*," Granny said, "but it's too much."

"Too much for you and Jeb to keep up?" Mona continued to probe.

Granny put her head down, trying to hide the tears welling up. "It's… expensive."

Ruth came around the table that the women enveloped and hugged Granny from the back. "You deserve this gift, *jah*? You help us and it's our way of saying *danki*."

Granny's chin quivered and then she let the tears flow. The stress of the fire, staying up late to bake, and then receiving this gift was too emotional.

"Granny, don't cry," Fannie said. "Remember how hard it was for me to receive a compliment?"

Granny nodded, but didn't look up.

"Just receive our love," Fannie continued. "None of us would be where we are today if it wasn't for you."

"*Jah*," Lottie agreed as she passed out embroidery thread and needles. "If I ever get married, you'll be one of my attendants because with you're help, I'll get a man."

Granny started to laugh and cry at the same time. The women roared at Lottie's remark, knowing that it was only single women who were attendants and being chosen was a great honor.

"How's your love life, Lottie?" Marge asked. "Any word from Peter?"

Lottie's face drained to white. "*Nee.* I broke it off for sure and certain."

"But I thought he was going to be Old Order Amish for you," Marge said.

Lottie's eyes met Granny's and there was a twinkle in them. *Was she seeing Ezekiel? Ach, Lord, I pray so.*

"I'm putting God first and waiting for the sun to shine," Lottie said, smiling at Suzy.

"What's the sun got to do with this?" Mona asked, mouth puckered.

Suzy spoke up. "She's waiting for God to illuminate her mind as to what His will is."

"*Jah*," Lottie said. "I'm waiting on God for an answer to the biggest decision I'll make: who I marry." She shifted, obviously uncomfortable. "Remember allow room on your squares for a five-eight inch steam allowance."

Marge roared. "*Steam* allowance? Letting off *steam*, are we?"

"After that fire, I think we all need to let off some steam," Suzy said. "And knitting is good...to let off steam. Good for the nerves."

Lottie laughed. "I get tongue tied."

"We all do," Ruth admitted, squeezing Granny from behind again and went back to her seat. "I picked a *wunderbar* man."

"Really?" Marge asked, and then quickly covered her mouth. "I didn't mean for it to come out like that. I just know you shared about your problems with Luke with your mom dying and all and –"

"It's over. When I heard Luke was sent to the hospital, it made me think about a life without him, and it was grim. I've been so angry with God for taking *mamm* and took it all out on Luke."

"Angry with God?" Mona asked. "We're not to do that, are we?"

Granny put a hand up. "He knows our hearts. And he's did say 'come let us reason together.' Sometimes I'm mad when I reason with God." Granny remembered when she prayed for God to knock sense into Luke like being hit by a two-by-four piece of lumber. "I pray real honest-like. If I don't understand, I ask lots of questions."

The room fell silent and Granny looked around at the women stitching the squares. Did she say something wrong? Didn't everyone talk to the *Gut* Lord like this? She looked at the square before her. Lottie had ironed a picture of kittens playing with yarn and in cross-stitch it read *West Virginia*. "Are we making a State Quilt? They're huge."

"*Jah*, but they sell well."

"Lottie's quite the business woman," Suzy said. "Yarn sales have gone up lately."

"In this heat?" Lizzie asked.

Suzy's eyes bulged and her lips pursed as she gave Lottie a knowing look. "Well, she attracts male customers buying yarn for their moms."

Lottie clapped her cheeks in shock. "Suzy, that's not true."

Suzy laughed. "Oh, yes it is. How about yesterday morning. A customer bought loads of black yarn for his mom."

"Who?" Fannie asked. "Noah Miller?"

"Harvey Miller?" Mona asked.

"Moses Miller?" Lizzie asked.

"So many Millers in this town it's baffling," Marge blurted, and laughter echoed off the walls.

"Not a Miller," Suzy said.

Lottie stiffened and Granny knew this sensitive girl needed rescued. "Lottie has that rare beauty of strawberry hair and blue eyes, but it's her inner beauty that really makes her special. Don't you all agree?"

"I do," Fannie said. "*Ach*, how I hated my round face until I reconditioned my mind. Now, it's silly even to think that I was so obsessed with my weight, it's vain."

"*Jah*," Lizzie added. "When we look to the outside appearance too much, we do become vain."

"Vanity, pride, conceit," Granny said, "no one wants to label it as harmful thinking. Fannie, remember how depressed you were when you thought too much about yourself?"

"*Jah*, I sure do."

Marge shifted as if uncomfortable. "I like jewelry, gold in particular. And I wear make-up or I'd scare people on the streets," she chuckled. "Do the Amish think this is vain, proud, and conceited?"

"Well, the Amish don't wear jewelry as one of our rules," Lizzie said, "but I think it all comes down to the heart. I mean, we Amish can be vain and conceited without jewelry."

"Bingo," Suzy said, arms thrown up. "And that's why we all get along, Amish and *English* here in this circle. We're knit together in the heart."

"Aw, that was so sweet," Ruth said.

A sweet aroma seemed to fill the room. It was peace, unity, and love. And Granny was once again thankful for this circle of friends.

~*~

Granny saw that her outside thermometer read ninety degree, so she'd go downstairs to cool off. Grabbing the thin yarn and crochet hook, she decided to practice making a doily, something Angelina, her elderly friend was teacher her. She laughed. I have an elderly friend. But Angelina had wisdom beyond hers, making her feel young and eager to learn. That Angelina hung meat to dry into all sorts of **prosciutto**, salami and sausage amazed Granny. Angelina also gave her cheese that was aged two years, making it turn from mozzarella into something more like Swiss.

As she ambled down the steps, she put little wooden chair by the exposed side of the house which had window. She pondered the thought of "steam allowance". Although a slip of Lottie's tongue, it was something she'd believed in for many years. Pouring the heart out to God, letting steam out, was praying honest-like. She remembered Phil asking for prayer concerning getting an online wife. The fire saddened her as well, no one knowing all the trees she and Jeb watched mature over the past forty years. Nothing ever stayed the same. She bowed her head and prayed:

Lord,

I thank you that some day we'll have a place where there will be no change. When you come back and re-create this world, the New Jerusalem, as the Bible says, where the lion will lay down with the lamb, is mighty appealing. I thank you I have this blessed hope.

Hope, Lord, is what Lizzie needs. Her eyes are hollow and I know it's not fatigue or this heat. Give her hope and purpose. We all need this. Give Roman the words to say and pour love into his heart for his wife. Make their marriage strong.

And, Lord, I'm sad about the fire. Well, actually I'm fighting anger. How could Charles and Brian be so careless? Leaving smoldering cigarettes, not thinking a spark could set a forest ablaze. I'll miss my massive cherry trees...

Lord, I lift up Phil to you. He's needing a wife. It's not gut for man to be alone, like your Word says. Bring the right girl into his life. Lead him and bless him.

I pray this all in Jesus name,

Amen

Dear readers,

Do you think that letting off steam in prayer is sinful? Maybe this episode will help you see that God sees your heart anyhow, so confess your anger to him so he can help lead you to still waters. There's nothing like a still, quiet heart, but we're challenged daily to cast our cares, our honest emotions on God. I personally was outraged at the Franklin Regional school stabbings and I wrestled for a week. It wasn't until I talked to my friend, Kathy, who's also an alumni, that I felt better. A weight was lifted as we together shared our fears, hurt, and thankful hearts that no one was killed. We do need each other.

I hear from readers that knitting circles are starting, women being inspired by this series. I have to say that just makes my day to hear these things. Drop me a line if you're starting a knitting, crocheting, scrapbook club etc. being inspired by Granny Weaver. You can leave a message at www.karenannavogel.com Danki.

Fruit Pizza

½ c. butter
½ c brown sugar
1 egg
1 ½ c. flour
1 tsp. baking powder
1 tsp. salt
8 oz. cream cheese
1/3 c. powdered sugar
Cool Whip
Fruit for toppings

Cream the butter, brown sugar and egg. Add flour, baking powder and salt to form "pizza crust." Roll out into a circle and bake at 350 degrees until golden brown. Mix powdered sugar and Cool Whip. When the crust is cooled, spread on the pizza. Top with any fruit you like. Enjoy.

EPISODE 6

Patchwork

*G*ranny nestled Bea, her little black Pomeranian, closer. Early mornings in September had a nip to them, but the chill didn't keep her inside for a second cup of coffee. The changing of the leaves in all their glorious colors was unfolding before her eyes. Shades of orange, yellow and crimson dripped from the many trees across the field. Granny knew if she looked over towards the woods, it would only make her heart sink, as there were patches of black char marks. *I have a choice*, she thought. *I can pout over burnt woods and all in life that looks black, or I can rejoice over what I have, all things beautiful.* Before Jeb joined her on the porch, she thanked God for what she had:

Lord,

I have this here lovely spot in Smicksburg and I'm thankful for it. I rejoice over your creative power to take something burnt and give it new life. Lord willing, if I'm here, I'll see woods grow in much thicker than they were in ten years. The fire took out weeds and the decayed burnt wood has fed the earth, making it richer in nutrients. I can't see all you're doing, but I'm content in... knowing you. Jah, Lord, just being able to relish in a God who loves me is enough.

231

Granny heard the footsteps and opened her eyes, glad to spend this precious morning with Jeb. But Denny appeared before her, in Amish clothes and a straw hat. She gulped. Were they doing the right thing? Encouraging this man-child to be Amish? *"Guten marning,"* she said.

Denny leaned up against the porch rail. *"Jah,* it is."

Granny sighed. "Denny, you don't have to use an accent like us. Just talk like you're used to."

He grinned. "I like saying *'jah.' 'Nee,* too. Sounds cool."

Cool? Sounds cool? Did Denny see all the magazine articles about the Amish and think it would be 'cool' to be Amish? "Denny, God loves you even if you're not Amish, you know that, *jah?"*

"Jah," he said.

Granny's heart sank. "This is serious. If you get baptized next year and you leave the Amish, you'll be breaking a vow. God doesn't like that."

"But He forgives, right? I mean, he knows we have feet of clay."

Feet of clay. Something she and Jeb always said, meaning we can all fall into temptation and sin. No one was perfect, only the Rock, Jesus Christ. Granny bit her lower lip. "A vow is a promise you don't make until you're sure you can keep it. It's serious becoming Amish, just like taking a wedding vow. If we let people come in and go as they please, it would ruin our whole way of life."

Denny crossed his arms. "How? I can't do that much damage, I don't think."

"We live in community. We pay for each other's hospital bills, work together as one unit to get things done." She peered over to Roman's shop. "What if Roman sold rockers with only three legs?"

Denny twisted the toe of his black Amish shoe into the gray porch boards, looking down as if in thought. "Wouldn't rock too smooth."

"That's the way our community is and that's why joining the Amish is a solemn vow. We wouldn't live too smoothly if folks came in easy and left all the time."

"So you think I shouldn't be Amish?"

"Jeb believes he sees an Amish man in you. I won't be questioning his judgment. I just want you to know that you won't gain God's love and approval by being Amish. You know I have friends outside the Amish. God cares for them as much as us."

A smile broke across Denny's face. "I think I'm a born farmer. I never lived out in the country. I think I was Amish in a former life or something, or Amish."

Granny stroked Bea's thick black hair. "Former life? You don't believe in reincarnation do you?"

He laughed. "No. It's just a sayin.' Means that I have a farmer in me I never knew about."

"Well, there's lots of *Englishers* who are farmers, too."

Denny's eyes darkened. "Did I do something wrong? I fed all the chickens and sheep. Cleaned the manure out of the stalls…"

The look on Denny's face, fear combined with utter loss, gripped Granny so that she put Bea down and ran to embrace Denny. "*Nee.* You did it all *gut.*"

"But I'm imposing. You don't want me here?"

Granny cupped Denny's face in her hands. "We love having you here. Understand? You're doing a *gut* job farming and working with Roman. And if you want to be Amish, I'd say, 'Praise be.' But I want you to realize how serious becoming Amish really is."

His eyes misted. "So you *do* want me to be Amish."

Granny patted one cheek and then went to grab Bea again. "*Jah*, I like you, Denny Boles. And I'd be mighty happy to have you a part of the flock, but do it for yourself, not for Jeb and me. We're here for you whether you're Amish or not."

Denny was a statue for a few moments and then said, "You really mean that, don't you?"

"We didn't give you the two bedrooms upstairs for no reason. Just hope you don't bang you head too much off those walls. Mighty low."

Denny rubbed his head in mock pain. "I know. Why didn't you make the upstairs taller?"

"It's a *dawdyhaus*. The upstairs is like an attic, *jah*?" Granny snickered. "Maybe it'll keep you on your knees."

"It's the only way I can get to my dresser," he laughed.

Granny observed this fine man before her and the life she imagined him having... and peace flooded her. Maybe Jeb was right. *Denny's a born Amish-man.*

~*~

Lizzie huffed and then puffed. "That's not true."

Roman squared his shoulders and placed his clenched fists on his hips. "Is too. Now, I want Jenny to go to school tomorrow, *along with* Millie and Tillie. I'm the head of this house."

"And you have a hard head," Lizzie snapped. "I have all their school books ordered. And you agreed."

Roman collapsed into the chair at the head of their kitchen table. He swooshed his hand. "I gave in to homeschooling. You're becoming as bold as Marge."

"What?"

"I'm surprised you haven't asked for a red table and chairs and curtains with cherries."

Lizzie cringed. Roman thought she wanted to do everything Marge did? That she was overbearing? Didn't he realize her character was deeper, more solid than that? Yes, she had been tempted to add embroidery to the ends of her plain white curtains, but knew the *Ordnung* wanted them to have all things in common. But white flowers embroidered in a satin stitch would look so charming. "Roman, what you just said was insulting."

He ran his fingers through his thick chestnut hair. "You're always questioning me on major decisions. *That's* insulting."

Only the deafening honking of the geese outside as they made their trial runs, exercising their wings for the journey south, was heard. *Fly away*, Lizzie thought. She needed to get away. Her dear *daed* was now bogged down instructing Denny, something Roman decided. She planted her hands on her hips. "*Daed* mentioned he wanted to see the ocean. Watch the birds migrate. It would be *gut* for us to have a vacation."

"It's puttin' up time. Loads of canning to be done. And Jonas is teaching Denny."

Ready to pop, Lizzie took in a deep, cleansing breath. "*Daed* gave up Amish camp this summer for a reason. He's tired. And he hasn't seen the ocean in decades. The birds migrate in late September."

"*Jah*, I know. And it's harvest time. Lizzie, why say something so *furhoodled*?"

Roman had never called her *furhoodled* before and hurt threatened tears, but she gained composure. "I'm not mixed up. The birds do migrate early October, to be exact, and Jenny did the Audubon Bird Count, remember?" Lizzie shifted. "I want to take the girls to see bird banding."

Roman shook his head and blinked his eyes uncontrollably. "*Nee*. They'll be in school."

"But when the girls thought they'd be homeschooled, they saved money in their glass jars and we counted it out. And we found out from Fannie and Mona that train tickets are cheap. Very cheap."

Roman's face contorted. "I'm telling them they need to go to school."

Again they were drowned out by the geese and Lizzie was thankful. This conversation was painful, because this trip was also about getting away from Roman. Their bickering was causing her heart to become calloused and she needed a time of healing. Like Ruth, she too had learned that watching birds was *gut* for the nerves. It gave her a knowing that God would take care of her problems. He promised to care for sparrows, how much more for her?

Roman had his head resting on his clenched fists. "Lizzie, why do you always run away?"

"What?"

"You ran away to Lancaster last time we quarreled, but now we're married. We shouldn't be separated. We have to work out our problems."

His tone had softened and Lizzie was afraid her heart would, too. But she needed to stand her ground. "Take a log away from the fire and it'll go out." Putting a hand over her heart she said, "I need this fire to go out in me."

"Fire?"

She nodded. "I'm angry with you, Roman. You don't understand my pain. I can't have children."

"You're giving up too early. We've only be married for eighteen months or so."

She grimaced. "I'm too old, Roman. My childbearing years are over. I'm thirty-four now. And I just *know*."

Roman reached out a hand, but Lizzie didn't take it, only sat down at the table with him. "How do you know? Some women have *kinner* in their forties. "

"I just do. It's private."

"I'm your husband. How could it be private?"

Lizzie didn't dare tell Roman that Marge encouraged an exam by Doc Pal and he found scar tissue caused by endometriosis. Surgery could help but he said it was stage four; the scarring was intense and her ovaries were crusted over. She now knew why every month she experienced such pain. Not having a sister, she shared it with her adopted sister, Marge, who promised not to tell anyone. She was barren for sure and certain.

"Lizzie, answer me. Please. Don't shut me out again."

His reaction took Lizzie aback. He reacted with love and concern. How a man reacted was the real man, like Granny said. But he wanted a boy and she couldn't deliver such a gift and she felt utterly inadequate. "Roman, I need time alone."

"But if you take Jonas with you, you won't be alone."

She pondered this. *Nee*, she wouldn't be alone. "What I mean is, I need time away…"

"From me…"

She slid down the bench and took his hand. "Roman, we quarrel all the time now. It drains me."

He said nothing, only nodded as if in agreement. "You work too hard. We both do. You go on and take a vacation. I'll manage, but it can't be until early October after puttin' up time is done."

She wanted to run around Roman and hug him from behind, but she only nodded in agreement, adding a forced smile to show her appreciation.

"The girls will start school tomorrow. We can always pull them out if you're feeling the same once you're rested." He took her hand and ran a finger down a vein.

His eyes were her Roman's again, mellow puppy dog eyes that calmed her.

"Most likely the girls will want to be homeschooled." He grinned. "The new teacher is Sabrina Hostetler."

Lizzie froze. Sabrina didn't seem like the type to teach *kinner*. She was an old *maedel* for a reason; she was a crank.

Roman leaned over, pulling her closer and kissed her cheek. "Make you feel better?"

She could smell his peppermint breath and the desire to kiss him flooded her. He kissed her cheek and she turned and gave him a kiss from her heart. "Roman, I do love you. Don't ever doubt that."

He puckered his lips and kissed her hand. "I need more convincing."

She slapped him playfully. "I have things to get done."

Roman reached for her, cupped her cheeks and kissed her with fire. "I love you, too. And that burden you're carrying, is mine, too." He kissed her cheek. "When you're ready, you tell me. Understand?"

So he could see through her as Lizzie suspected. She leaned in for a kiss that lingered. "I will."

~*~

Lottie placed the new autumn colored yarn out on the display table. How different autumns were in Smicksburg. The rolling hills made for interesting scenery, but it wasn't Millersburg. Feeling like a third wheel over at her cousin's house only made her think of home more. Her dear cousin, Hezekiah, was back to normal, only a stutter from time to time, and she was so thankful. Colleen had forced him to exercise, use his mind in cross-word puzzles and played endless chess matches. And he beat her last night.

Lord, I want a marriage like my cousin, she prayed.

No one knew she and Ezekiel were talking quite a bit, and today she'd see him in Colleen's "Secret Garden." In the woods with plenty of privacy, she wondered why Ezekiel asked to see it. Did he want to be alone outside of a Singing? That was unusual, but he said there was something he wanted to show her... alone.

She gulped. Maybe he was leaving for Marathon, New York, with the other Coblenz clan. New York was farther from Millersburg than Smicksburg, much farther: seven hours in a car. Was this homesickness from God? Did he not want her to court Ezekiel as a friend? She'd promised to put God first and not get serious with anyone, but over the past weeks, helping him at his home, doing little chores, as his eye was still bandaged over, she couldn't help the affection she felt toward him.

Maybe God put Colleen and Hezekiah's marriage into her life for an example. Love bears all things, and the more you give, the more love grows. She saw this in her cousin's marriage. Lottie helped Ezekiel while his scar healed and they had grown only closer.

The gold bell on the screen door jangled and Marge appeared, cheeks red. "Lottie, a word?"

Lottie knew Marge lacked subtlety, but she would not step out on the porch, where Marge pointed, needing Suzy's support.

Suzy crossed the room and stood by Lottie. "Marge? Come in here, for Pete's sake. You're in a huff and I don't want bickering on my front porch."

Marge's eyes became too large for her face. "It's private. Well, sort of. Well, Suzy, maybe you need to hear this, too."

"What?" Lottie asked. She looked at Marge's bag with a SuzyB Knit logo on it. "Aren't you happy with a purchase?"

"Everything Suzy makes is fine."

Suzy put a hand up. "Marge, come to the back room. If customers come in here, it won't make for a pleasant shopping experience." She opened the Dutch door that led to the area where she dyed and spun yarn, along with having Jane Austen teas. "Want some tea?"

Marge marched back to the back room and Suzy motioned for Lottie to follow. Lottie felt heartburn coming on and a slight headache. *Why was Marge so upset? She was usually such a cheerful woman.*

Suzy put on the tea kettle and Lottie took a seat at the small round table, decked with a new tablecloth. "Like this material, Suzy," Lottie said.

"It's antique roses. I love that Shabby Chic look." She opened a cabinet and held up two pot holders. "Making these and then placemats. Lottie, all those sewing pointers really got me going. I'm hooked on sewing now."

Marge cleared her throat loudly. "Can we talk?" Without waiting for a reply, she glared at Lottie. "I saw you jogging in Old Smicksburg Park with Phil Darby. Don't deny it."

Lottie shot up. "I do deny it."

Suzy paled. "Was she jogging in an Amish dress?"

Marge fumbled for words, but then spit out, "No. She was dressed like an *Englisher*."

Lottie stomped a foot. "I've never worn pants in my life."

Marge looked through Lottie. "I'm not the only one who saw you."

"What? That's impossible. I haven't even been to the park in a month. It's our putting up season, you know. And I've been helping... a friend."

Marge's chest rose and fell. "Can you account for your whereabouts yesterday at dusk?"

"Marge," Suzy said evenly. "If it was dusk, maybe you didn't see things very well. Maybe it wasn't even Phil."

"Oh," Marge protested. "It was. He came into Arbor Creek with the same outfit. Alone. I wonder why..."

"There's other girls who have strawberry blonde hair," Suzy continued to defend.

"Down to her waist like the Amish? I don't think so."

Lottie felt rage simmer deep within. Did she want to live in this gossipy little town? She was reading the *Anne of Green Gables* series again and Anne's desire to break free from a small town resonated in her. Millersburg was bigger with more a variety of Amish. Maybe she did want to go home. Lottie wiped her sweaty palms on her black apron. "Marge, you're acting like Rachael Lynde."

"Who?" Marge barked.

"The town gossip in *Anne of Green Gables*," Lottie yelled, feeling brave like Anne.

Marge narrowed her gaze. "Well, Rachel was right about one thing. Girls with red hair have tempers. *Carrots!*"

"Stop this," Suzy gasped. She looked at Marge and then Lottie. "This is a little bizarre a conversation. First of all," she said, turning to Marge, "I am a red-head." She tossed her shoulder-length hair. "Lottie, I've never heard you yell so loudly."

"She provoked me," Lottie said, hurt that Suzy couldn't see this. She was Amish, but even Amish people got angry when interrogated for no reason. She didn't look at

Suzy because she feared she'd cry, but left the table and entered the store again to cool down.

Suzy followed her and took her hands. "Lottie, I wasn't scolding, only… in shock at this whole thing. You say you weren't with Phil and I believe you." Suzy pulled her back to the tea table. "I have some nice tea and some shortbread cookies. We're friends and will talk this out." She wagged a finger at Marge. "You need to apologize. Lottie doesn't lie."

Marge guffawed. "I saw her with Phil."

"You think you saw her but it was someone else," Suzy corrected in even tones.

"Then who is it? Lottie's twin?"

"That's not our business," Suzy said. "Maybe it's another redhead. Was it Judith? She has red hair. Maybe they patched things up."

Marge shook her head. "She had long hair. Really long. It was in a massive braid that reached her butt. Only Amish have hair like that.…"

"Some Mennonites don't cut their hair," Lottie said timidly. "Some do live around here."

"But they wear dresses, too, right?" Marge said, confusion etched on her face.

"Not all. Some where blue jeans," Lottie said, not able to understand why girls would dress in such a fashion, just like men.

Marge's eyes slowly met Lottie's and begged for forgiveness. "I'm sorry. Maybe he's seeing a Mennonite?"

Suzy banged a tea cup down in front of Marge. "Oh, I almost broke it." She groaned. "Marge, this was all so uncalled for. What's wrong with you?"

Marge stared into the tea cup that Suzy was filling with black tea. "Denny. The Amish. Sorry, Lottie, I mean the Amish in general. We Baptists didn't build Arbor Creek as a stepping stone to be Amish, but to further the boys' education and go on to college. I think Denny living with Granny and Jeb and dropping out of school is pathetic. And the Amish are encouraging it."

Lottie watched the black liquid trickle into her cup. "*Danki*, Suzy. Marge, Denny's studying for his high school diploma. Granny said he's real smart."

"The GED?" Marge gasped.

"Yes, the GED," Suzy informed. "I think if a kid is smart enough to pass it, he should be able to go right on to college. Homeschoolers do it."

Marge methodically put a spoonful of sugar into her tea and stirred it. "But Denny won't be going to college if he turns Amish."

"Roman's going to apprentice him to be a carpenter," Lottie said. "Jeb said he has a God-given talent with his hands. What's wrong with that?"

"Yeah," Suzy said. "Can't go to college to be a carpenter, right?"

Marge gulped her tea. "He could go to trade school or be an architect is what. Make blueprints and learn to follow them."

Lottie slowly closed her eyes as if she'd wished to block what Marge just said. "The Amish know how to make blueprints and follow them. Men working construction jobs know how to do the electrical and plumbing, too. We're not living in the Dark Ages."

Silence. Lottie looked down at her folded hands, glad that she could speak the truth in real love. She wasn't upset, but simply needed to inform Marge of all her misconceptions about the Amish.

"Really?" Marge asked. "I thought they only made barns and their own houses without electricity. But he won't get a college degree…"

Suzy sipped her tea. "Getting a college degree doesn't guarantee a job these days. We're in the Great Recession, remember, and it's the blue collar workers that have the jobs."

Lottie knew the Amish had blue collar jobs most of the time and they were hired for their craftsmanship. "Can I get back to work now?"

Marge looked at Lottie sheepishly. "If you find your look-alike, will you let me know?"

Lottie smirked. "If you see a gray-haired gossip like Rachael Lynde, I'll let you know."

Marge ran her fingers through her hair. "I just dyed my hair brown last week. Is some gray showing?

~*~

The trail to Colleen's secret garden was littered with yellow oak leaves, and Lottie's heart once again went back to Millersburg. Her *daed* had hung a tire swing on an old oak in their front yard and childhood memories flooded her heart. She was five and her cousin pushed the swing a little too hard and she started to cry, fear gripping her. Then the sound of her *daed's* voice from the porch saying, "You're fine, honey," soothed her. She could trust her *daed's* judgment, but why did she white knuckle life, not trusting God? Having a high-strung nature, she needed a steady, calm man. Ezekiel took life in stride and wasn't plagued by the anxiety she'd battled. Suzy told her she'd calmed down, not being a nervous chatterbox and wondered why. Lottie hadn't told her too much about Ezekiel, but he was the reason. She didn't have to shout for love and attention from this man.

A twig cracking startled Lottie and she jumped. Movement in a nearby bush and then a black bear, growing taller as it stood on its hind legs growled. Lottie cupped her mouth as if to hold in a scream. *Lord, help me to not run. Never run from a bear,* her *daed* had warned. Feeling faint, she forced herself to stand, eyes wide in fright. *What if I'm standing in the middle of this bear and her cubs?* Not daring to turn around, she saw her life fly before her and her funeral. She'd die before she'd get married. The children she longed for would never be born. Afterwards, at the dinner, the People would say, "Lottie, the old *maedel,* died. How tragic."

The bear only stared at her, so she looked down. Show submission, not aggression. But she did feel aggression. If this bear ruined her chances of getting married, she'd want to give it a good smack with a tree limb.

A thump and crash to her right, and the bear dove off to the left, running like a scared little bird. Lottie gasped in relief and then saw Ezekiel farther down the path. She did what came natural, not feeling very composed, and ran to him and threw herself into a protective embrace. "Did you see that bear?"

"*Jah.* Threw a rock to startle it. Are you okay?"

Releasing her grip on him, she stepped back. "*Jah. Danki.* You saved me from getting eaten alive."

He chuckled. "Black bears don't eat people, they're afraid of them."

"Really?"

Ezekiel repositioned the gauze that was still wrapped around part of this face. "Well, maybe that there bear was mean and I did save your life," he said wryly and then winked.

Lottie grinned. "Okay, you saved my life. How does it feel?"

He took her hand and stared at it. "*Gut.* A man is to protect his wife…"

Wife? Was he proposing? Lottie felt that old pressure on her face and knew she was blushing profusely.

He took her hand as they walked to the Secret Garden only fifty paces away. "I have some news," he said as he sat on a log and pulled her down beside him. "I can take this bandage off. Doc said it's healed up as much as possible."

"Why are you wearing the bandage then?" she asked.

"I wanted you to be the first to see the scar. My other scar." He stared at her intensely, and then unwrapped the gauze and slid off the bandage. "What do you think?"

Lottie stared into his eyes. Why so severe? The scar was on his cheek and side of his eye, making it a little discolored and wrinkly, but she still found him to be the most handsome of men. She liked *him*, not his looks anyhow.

He turned away. "You're not saying anything, so I understand."

"Understand what?"

"You can't stand to look at me."

"What? Ezekiel, not at all. Your scar isn't so bad at all."

His head spun around in disbelief. "Really? I think it's pretty ugly."

Lottie couldn't help but touch his face. "You're still so handsome. Honestly, the scar isn't that noticeable."

A smile slid across his face and his blue eyes twinkled. "Lottie, be my wife."

She wanted to say yes. Plant a kiss on his lips and scream "*Jah*, I'd be happy to be Mrs. Coblenz," but she couldn't say anything, too shocked to speak.

He gripped her shoulders. "We'd have a big farm with lots of cows."

"But you and your *bruder* are carpenters."

"*Jah*, because we can't get land, but there's plenty in New York. My *bruder*, Joshua, bought five hundred acres! Can you believe it? And he wants all the *bruder* to move up. We'd all have one-hundred acres each." He pulled her to himself. "Please say you'll be my wife."

New York? It was so far from Millersburg. So far from Smicksburg. A pit landed in her stomach. Yes, she wanted to marry Ezekiel, but did she love him enough to make such a sacrifice? She'd barely see her loved ones. "I, ah, I…"

"You think about it." He kissed her cheek. "God will lead you to me if you're the one."

This lack of pressure made her want to say yes all the more, not feeling trapped. "*Danki*, Ezekiel, I will be seeking the Lord. You know that's been my focus these past months and you've been so patient, courting without a good night kiss."

His face went limp. "Dating as friends has tried my patience, but you're worth it. I know lots of dust has to settle in that heart of yours."

He was so near she felt his breath and the desire to kiss him overwhelmed her. She turned her head and backed away. Kissing made her lack judgment with Peter. *Nee*, she wasn't going to kiss another man until their marriage night.

~*~

Phil nodded as he met two of MJ and Andy's friends who would form this little house church. *Where two or three are gathered in My name, there am I in the midst of them*, Phil thought. The Baptist Church board had hired an architect to draw-up ideas of an expansion due to numbers increasing. Many patted him on the back, saying it was due to his great preaching, but he knew better. Jerry Jackson had laid plenty of seeds around Smicksburg and now he was seeing the harvest.

In MJ's tiny home, however, he felt an intensity to preach to this small group more than a larger one. Was

God calling him to be a church planter in an area that didn't have a church? Maybe a different country? *Your will be done, Lord*, he thought, and shuffled through his Bible to get to his notes.

"I think we need to start with prayer requests so we know if anyone is hurting here," MJ said. "Sherry, are you all right?"

Sherry lowered her head, long auburn hair cascading. "I broke up with Jack. He's a jerk."

Andy guffawed. "Amen to that. You deserve better."

MJ, who was sharing the loveseat with Andy, nudged him until he let out a wail. "Hey, I'm only saying the truth." He looked across the room at Sherry. "Honey, you're a doll and young with your whole life in front of you. You're like a daughter, really, and I want to see you with someone like…" He slowly looked at Phil, and then MJ nudged him again and he huffed. "Sherry, the right guy will come along."

"I'm thirty-two," she sighed. "Getting a doctorate wasn't worth all this. I don't even like being a physical therapist." She groaned. "And my childbearing years are over."

"What?" Uncle Charley, an elderly neighbor to MJ, asked. Fiddling with his cane, he snickered. "You must think I'm a fossil."

"No, not at all," Sherry reassured. "My biological clock is ticking. I've always wanted six kids like my sister, and she started her family when twenty-one. Met Mr. Right in high school and has a lovely home. I was the brains in the family and Mom said a woman is more secure with a college degree."

"Well," MJ said, "many want to go to college and can't. And your mom's right in a way. A good education is never a waste. No one can ever take it away from you."

Phil had gotten his Masters of Divinity and wondered why at times. "I think I understand. I'm still paying off school debt when what I do could have been done with a three year Bible school degree. Education was encouraged by my father and I didn't want to disappoint."

"Yes, that's it," Sherry said. "Since my sister's real artsy, painting and playing the piano, Mom said that she had the right brain and I had the left, 'Good for doctors and lawyers.'"

"But," Phil continued, "God trusted our parents to lead. And if we're to honor them by listening to their advice, I find it's God's way of speaking to us."

"Sounds like a Psalm 131 message to me," Andy quipped.

"What's that?" Sherry asked.

"It's my and MJ's secret code. We have days when things don't make sense, and we read the Psalm." He reached over to the book shelf near him and grabbed a book. "The Message Bible says it best." He opened the wear worn Bible and read:

GOD, I'm not trying to rule the roost,
I don't want to be king of the mountain.
I haven't meddled where I have no business
or fantasized grandiose plans.
I've kept my feet on the ground,
I've cultivated a quiet heart.
Like a baby content in its mother's arms,
my soul is a baby content.

Andy's countenance changed to complete calm. "Ah, just reading this makes my blood pressure drop. God's in control and all we have to do is rest like a baby in His arms."

Sherry's eyes misted. "Like a baby." She looked up, keeping tears at bay. "When I hold my little niece, she is content." A grin broke across her face. "Maybe I'm called to be an aunt and not a mom."

"Amen," Uncle Charley said. "Never had my own but my name says it all. I've been Uncle Charley to kin, neighbors, kids in church, kids at the YMCA where I taught swimming back in the day." He scratched his short gray beard. "I think I'm an uncle to over a hundred kids at least. My quiver is full," he chuckled.

Phil admired Uncle Charley already. He was an optimist. Surely he'd wanted children of his own, but instead he shifted his attention to being an uncle. *Lord, help Sherry see this. Her perspective needs a shift.*

"What about you, Phil," MJ asked. "How are you doing? Can we pray for you and the grief you're going through?" She looked at Sherry and then Uncle Charley. "Phil lost his mother to cancer not long ago."

"Oh, I'm so sorry," Sherry said.

"That's a real shame," Uncle Charley added.

Phil's mouth grew dry and his chest tightened as usual when speaking about his dear mom. "It's still hard. Yes, pray for me."

"It will take time, Phil," Sherry said. "A broken heart is harder to get over than a broken bone."

"See," Andy said, "you're talking like a physical therapist. You like your job."

She grinned. "Yes, I do. I'm just emotionally whipped. Breaking things off with a man you thought was marriage material was tough."

MJ tilted her head as if confused. "How long did you two date?"

"Four months," Sherry informed.

"Four months?" Uncle Charley near barked. "You can't even train a good hunting dog in four months. That's not long enough to make a life-long commitment."

Sherry shrugged. "He had a good job and said he was ready to settle down."

"But he's arrogant," Andy groaned. "I don't care if he's a medical doctor or not, there's no excuse for bad manners. Coming into my house and telling me this and that, what needs to be done. I felt like screaming, 'Hello, I have a job and a wife who's ill.' He didn't seem to have the sense God gave geese."

Sherry burst out laughing. "You're right. He's all left brained and analytical, seeing faults and not having the social skills to know when to be quiet."

Uncle Charley laughed and he swiped his pencil across his notepad. "Well, I'm taking out your prayer request. You're over that guy but just need to move on." He turned to Phil. "I hear you've been seeing an Amish woman. Is that a fact?"

Phil knew Uncle Charley was up in age but didn't think anything was mentally wrong. "Me? No."

"That's not what I heard. Don't you know the whole town knows?"

Phil noticed MJ and Andy had their heads down, not able to face him. "I'm not seeing an Amish woman."

Andy cleared his throat. "You were seen walking through Smicksburg Park with Lottie. Will she be leaving the Amish then?"

Phil's brows knit together. *Lottie? Walking with Lottie in the park?* "She helps with the community garden at the church, but I don't think we went to the park."

"Oh, you did," Uncle Charley said. "I met the girl. The wife dragged me into the yarn shop to pick out what color I wanted for a winter scarf. She's a sweet girl and seems like your type."

Lottie was a sweet girl, Phil had to admit. And he did find her attractive, but he wasn't courting her. Then it all rushed in on him. *April.* "That wasn't Lottie, but a girl I met online. She has reddish hair. And long." Feeling stunned that the whole town would think he was seeing an Amish woman, he felt annoyed. Small towns were charming but could be suffocating.

Andy and MJ let out a sigh of relief in unison.

"I'm so relieved," MJ said. "I've seen Amish leave for an Outsider and it ruins whole families."

"Shunned, some are," Uncle Charley informed. "A kid lived with me after his shunning. Family treated him like he didn't exist. Don't agree with that."

Phil wanted to expound on all that he learned from Granny and Jeb about community and how their survival depended on taking serious vows, but he was still perturbed that this town was maybe a little too small for him. As he looked down at his notes for Bible study, he shot up a prayer. *Lord, put me where you want me. Either here in this gossipy little town or a huge city like New York. I'm yours.*

~*~

Jeb was cut to the heart as Denny finished telling his stories of life in the foster care system. Denny had acted out in rebellion as a cry for help. A cry for love and family. But here he was, at sixteen, saying he'd found what he was looking for. Could Jeb deny this young man baptism into the Amish faith? A vow's as serious as a wedding vow? "Son, what do think of how we live?"

"Like I said, it's cool driving a buggy," Denny said with enthusiasm.

Jeb crossed Roman's shop and took a seat on a new rocker. "I mean living with Deborah and me. No electricity. No cell phone."

"Never had anyone really to call on my phone. Mostly played games."

"And you say you don't mind the outhouse?"

"It's like the camping I never got to do as a kid."

Jeb leaned forward. "This is for life. Can you imagine having lots of *kinner*?"

"Kids? I guess so. Sure."

"No birth control allowed among the Amish. What if your wife gives you a dozen kids...or more? Would you be up to that?"

Denny's eyes rounded. "More than twelve?"

"*Jah*, you know Ida the female herbalist? She has thirteen. And many others do, too."

"I, ah, haven't met any. That's a lot of kids. Maryann has eight and that's a lot." Denny hooked his thumbs through his suspenders. "Never thought about that."

The pain in Denny's eyes made a lump form in Jeb's throat. "You said you wanted family. Having your own would be *gut, jah*?"

Denny plunged his hands into his pockets. "Are you trying to scare me? Is this part of one of your tests? I passed the cleaning the outhouse test, the shoveling manure test, cold shower test."

"*Ach*, son, Roman and I had some fun with you but we also wanted you to see how much work it is being Amish. At least we didn't make you shovel out the pig pen. Now that would've been cruel."

Denny peered out the shop window. "If I get twelve kids, does the whole community help in the expense?"

"Well, we help each other in lots of ways, but feeding your family and clothing and whatnot would be your responsibility. And no government handouts. No food stamps, welfare or cashing those new stimulus checks."

Denny groaned. "So no help from anyone, only family."

Jeb cracked a knuckle. "What do you mean?"

"Well, Michael and Maryann would be my in-laws so —"

"Hold on now. What does Becca have to do with this? You're not turning Amish for her, right?"

"No. I want this, but I do see us married. She has a big family and we'd help each other out, right?" Looking like a worn out scarecrow, he fell into a nearby chair. "Twelve kids? Are you kidding me?"

Jeb felt his face tighten. "I am serious. *Kinner* are a blessing from God and we take as many as we can get. Some women get pregnant in their fifties and we see it as a gift. A real gift."

"Fifty. That's just wrong. People that old do...you know."

Jeb let out an abrupt laugh. "*Jah.* We look at that as a gift, too, only in marriage."

Denny stared at Jeb unflinching. And then he covered his mouth in disgust.

"What's wrong with you?"

"You're in your seventies. And you still..."

"*Jah*, all parts functional."

Denny rolled is eyes and then slouched deep into the chair. "Wow." He shifted and rubbed his palms together. "Ah, maybe Phil's right. I need to slow down and take this one step at a time. Finish school and see where I'm at in two years."

Jeb hadn't seen Denny so mixed-up. He seemed to be Amish. Was Phil Darby discouraging him? Was he still talking him out of being Amish? All he'd said was twelve *kinner* and that they were gifts. As for how a woman got pregnant, surely Denny knew that, too. And it was a gift for sure and certain, only in marriage.

Jeb leaned his head on the back of his rocker. He'd be having a talk with Phil Darby.

"What do you think?" Denny asked abruptly.

"About *kinner*?"

"*Nee*, about me going back to Arbor Creek and taking this Amish thing slower."

Jeb's heart sank. He imagined this young man being a part of not only his life but Roman's. "Would you be going to high school then? Give up the apprenticeship?"

"Can't I still do the apprenticeship with Roman?"

Jeb moaned. "You wouldn't have time. It takes a while to learn a trade. *Nee*, you can't have one foot into the *English* world and one into the Amish. Now, you can live with Deborah and me and go to school and all. You know we're here for you. Understand?"

Denny chewed on his lower lip and seemed to fall into a trance-like state. After what seemed like an hour, he shook his head. "I need to think about all this. This test wasn't easy."

"Denny, you may not have twelve kids. Look at Roman. He's only got three girls."

"His first wife died."

Jeb scratched his head. "Look at Jonas, he's only got Lizzie."

"His wife died, too."

"Not giving birth. We use modern medicine so your wife will be safe. What's really wrong? You never had a family so you can't imagine being the head of one? Jeb wanted to know.

Denny jumped up and threw up both hands. "That's too many kids. I'm only sixteen and it's too weird to think about."

Jeb remembered how much fear he had about the future, but knew the trick to overcoming the enormity of the uncertain. "Son, God gives you grace when you need it."

"I need it now!" Denny nearly screamed.

"*Nee*, what I mean is that a lot of things I'm telling you won't happen for years. You do know a woman is pregnant for nine months, *jah*?"

Denny glared. "I'm not that stupid."

"I didn't say you were. You just seemed naïve about… well, women still having babies in their fifties… and whatnot. What I mean is that, well, look at me. I'm not a spring chicken and I know my time on earth is limited."

"Don't talk like that," Denny said in gripping fear.

"It's the truth. I won't be here forever. And when I think of passing on, I must admit, fear rises up in me. If Deborah would go before, more fear rises up because I wouldn't want to be here without her. But I don't worry about it because God will give me grace, or his strength to get through it when I need it, not a minute before. Understand?"

Denny crossed his arms. "Sort of."

Jeb thought back on his life when God's help, his supernatural enablement, had carried him through. "Well, I had a brother. He moved out West. I always was afraid of him dying and I'd have dreams about it and fear gripped me. Sometimes I'd cry just thinking about my brother not being around. When he did pass five years ago, God lifted me through it, just like a child being carried. I grieved, but deep down I had peace. It was supernatural. And then I realized that all the fretting about the future is futile and tiresome. There's no help from God until we need it. Maybe that's why the Bible cautions against worrying about tomorrow. We have enough on our plates every day."

Denny's shaggy blond bang hung half-way over his eyes, but Jeb saw a softening in them. "You understand, *jah*?"

He nodded. "You're saying God will help us, even if we have twelve kids."

Jeb smirked. "Or more… no birth control allowed."

Denny grinned. "And this grace will come in on time?"

"*Jah*. God's never failed me."

Denny got up and dusted off his Amish trousers. "All right. I see here on the farm a mother cat can have a litter of one or ten. No sense in fighting what's natural. I think that's why I like the Amish. They step in pace with nature."

Jeb laughed. "Roman taught you that, *jah*? But get it right. It's 'Adopt the pace of *nature*; her secret is patience.' Lots of truth in what Emerson said."

"Who's that?"

"Ralph Waldo Emerson was a writer in the 1800's. A good poet. We got that proverb from him."

"He was Amish?" Denny asked.

"*Nee*, not Amish. We take sayings if they're *gut* and teach them to our *kinner*. It helps form their character." Jeb snickered. "Think of how many of these proverbs you'll have to learn if you have a dozen *kinner*."

Denny laughed and then ran to Jeb, embracing him. "Thank you."

Jeb pat the boy's back. "For what?"

"Being patient with me."

Right there and then, Jeb felt like he'd just tasted a bit of heaven. He slapped Denny's back and pulled him away. "*Ach*, we best get on home. Deborah likes to watch the fireflies on the porch."

As they made their way out of the shop, Denny said with big brother love, "I'll help the girls make their canning jar lanterns."

"They'll like that," Jeb said, glad that night had covered the earth like a blanket. His tears he let drip down his cheeks, love for this boy overtaking him. He looked up at the crescent moon and thanked the Lord for his wife. If she hadn't reached out to start the knitting circle almost two years strong now, he wouldn't have changed. Changed into a man who saw the needs of those outside his small Amish community. *Jah*, Deborah, when he first met her, was a challenge to his thinking; his closed mind, stick-in-the-mud thinking. But over the years he'd softened, maybe a little too much. *I'd rather err on the side of mercy than judgment*, he remembered Deborah saying. It was a saying she'd picked up. Jeb's heart lifted. *Maybe it should be an Amish proverb.*

~*~

As the morning sun left streaks across Maryann's freshly mopped and waxed wooden kitchen floor, she strode over to the coffee pot to get her second cup. As footsteps descended her long stairway, four of her *kinner* of school age lined up to kiss her cheek and trot off for their first day of school. Being too young to help during harvest, they'd start earlier than her other sons in sixth and seventh grade.

Becca came into view, holding the hand of her toddler brother of three. "*Mamm*, before you know it, Sammy will be in that line out the door." Sammy ambled over to his Lincoln Logs to play, while Becca gave Maryann that look that said she needed to talk. "*Mamm*, are you busy?"

"Never too busy for you." Maryann shot up a prayer for strength. The knowledge that her daughter cared for an *Englsher*, Denny Boles, was a burden she and her dear husband talked about often.

Taking a mug of coffee, Becca pulled up a chair to sit by her *mamm*. "I heard you and *Daed* talking. We have thin walls."

Maryann stammered for words, but none came.

"I know *yinz* think Denny's not right for me, but Gilbert isn't the angel you imagine."

Maryann tried not to show shock. "What did he do?"

"Nothing bad, but he's a candle snuffer. Anytime I mentioned herbal medicine or traveling, he shut me down."

"He's controlling?"

"*Jah*," Becca groaned. "Denny's the complete opposite."

"The *English* need more control in what they can and can't do, that's why. He's *English*."

Becca sipped her coffee. "*Mamm*, can we have him over for dinner? You all could get to know him."

Maryann studied Becca's face. It lacked its usual brightness. "What's the rush?"

Fidgeting with her coffee mug hand, Becca said, "I'm more serious about Denny than I ever was with Gilbert."

Anger filled Maryann. "That's *furhoodled*, Becca. You've only known him for a few months."

"Three months and a week," Becca corrected. "But I can't stand to be away from him. I'd marry him today if I could."

A tightness went around Maryann's head, the sign of a stress headache coming on. "But you said you wanted to travel. Be an herbalist. I don't understand."

Becca reddened. "I love being with him everyday and don't want to be apart."

Maryann felt like she was sinking into the floor. "You see him everyday? How?"

Becca covered her mouth, knowing she was caught. The Amish only courted on Sundays. "I tutor him."

Maryann darted up. "You meet up on purpose and you two are kissing."

Becca's eyes widened. "What?"

Maryann felt dizzy and sat back down. "I thought I knew my eldest *dochder*, but I don't."

"*Mamm*, we do nothing wrong. He only kisses my cheek when we say good-bye."

"Kissing leads to other things. Kissing everyday is asking for real trouble," she growled. "You're lovesick which can make you half crazed out of your mind. That's not love."

Becca snarled. "You're not even listening. I'm not some immature thirteen year old girl. I know what love is."

Maryann was dazed. Becca had never taken such a tone with her. She sat staring, waiting for an apology, but Becca only jutted out her chin in defiance.

"I'll be talking to Jeb about this. You know our ways."

"Jeb knows. He sees us. He lives beside Jonas and when we take walks in the woods, there's open spots."

Jeb knows? If so, he needed to be approached by the elders. This was most definitely not their way of courting. Only on Sunday as passion and infatuation was tested, as was love. Love was patient to see each other, lust was not. Maryann had a sickening feeling that Becca needed church discipline if she didn't change her ways. What if Denny's desire to be Amish was only a cover? If they saw each other everyday for kissing, what else were they hiding?

"Becca, I don't want you seeing Denny until *Gmay* on Sunday, understand?"

"But he needs my help to pass the GED."

"And what's the hurry about that?"

Becca's cheeks reddened. "He wants to be done with school like me."

"And I ask again, what's the hurry? By getting this GED, can he get a job to start a family? With you?"

Becca turned her head, chin still protruding. "We keep those things secret, *jah*? It's our way."

Marriage? Maryann could take no more shock and simply burst into tears.

~*~

Jack ran out to the buggy nearly flying down her driveway. *What on earth? Is Marge driving a buggy?* But soon Maryann could be seen. Knitting circle wasn't for an hour. *An emergency. Lord have mercy.* Granny ran inside to get Jeb as he was surely most needed, but was blocked by the teenager living with them. "*Ach*, did I hurt you?"

He winced in pain. "Only my knee. You ran into me so hard," he said, and then burst into laughter. "How could someone as little as you hurt me? What's wrong?"

"An emergency. Maryann's come for Jeb, I'm sure. Where is he?"

"I don't know. Maybe his fishing hole."

"Go get him."

Denny pat her shoulder. "Don't panic. It'll be okay." He ran towards the front door and out onto the porch. Granny was quick on his heels and saw Maryann get out of her buggy. "What's wrong?"

Maryann glared at Denny and then Granny but said nothing.

"She's in shock," Denny said.

"*Jah*, I am Denny Boles, and I've come to talk."

Granny had never seen Maryann so lacking self-control and the fire in her eyes made her almost look like a different person. "Maryann, come on inside so we can talk."

She huffed. "I want to talk to my bishop. Make a complaint."

Her eyes never left Denny and Granny felt her dander go up. Denny was as fine a man as there was. She didn't realize until now, how she reacted, how much she cared for him as if he were her own son. "Maryann, self-control, *jah*? It's one of the fruits of the Spirit? Please come in and calm down."

"*Jah*, self-control needs to be preached more at our *Gmay*." She rigidly walked up the porch steps, head held high.

"I'll get Jeb," Denny said meekly, as if he'd done something wrong.

Granny knew Denny was used to being yelled at over nothing, and again a motherly love filled her heart. "Denny, did I tell you how much I appreciate you helping with the canning? You learn right quick." She turned towards Maryann. "We put up thirty quarts of pears this morning."

Maryann's glared was more ferociously, and she spun around and marched into the house.

"Denny," Granny said, "you did nothing wrong." She ran down to him and lowered her voice. "Change of life comes on quick like in some women."

Denny's eyes widened. "Hope it's not hereditary. Becca would never act like that."

Granny grinned. "Maryann's always been a bit more spirited. Becca's calmer like her *daed*. Most likely something awful has happened to upset her, but it's not your fault, understand?"

"What do you mean?"

"When someone yells at you, you cower. Just because someone's mad doesn't mean you're the one to blame."

He took a sigh of relief. "She sure was lookin' at me like she wanted me dead."

"Don't take it personally. Maryann's a bit uptight at times.

Denny squeezed her shoulder. "*Danki*."

She grinned. "I told you to stop that Amish talk. It's not necessary."

"*Jah*, it is *ven* I need to make you laugh, *jah*? *Ach*, you've been frowning."

Granny chuckled. "*Ach*, I didn't realize it. *Danki*."

Denny's face split into a smile and Granny made her way into the house to face Maryann. *Lord, give me words. Jeb wants me to help with the womenfolk.* She brushed flour off her black apron, smoothed it, and then opened the door. Maryann was huddled in a rocker, doubled over crying. "*Ach*, Maryann, what's wrong?"

Maryann continued to sob but when she was able to speak, she could only say, "I don't want to hate," over and over.

Granny rubbed her slumped shoulders. "Now, now. We'll talk this out. Jeb will be in here soon and we'll fix what's wrong."

Maryann's brown eyes glistened. "You'll send Denny back to Pittsburgh?"

Granny gawked, and then the defensive motherly love reared its head again. "*Nee*. He's one of us now."

"He's what? Amish?"

"*Nee*, not Amish, but a lost sheep Jeb and I took in. A lamb that was lost and found."

Maryann groaned. "A sheep in wolf's clothing."

Stiffening, Granny went over to fill up her tea kettle. There was nothing on God's green earth that calmed her more than the whistle of a tea kettle. As the water splattered onto the side of her kettle since she was now shaking, Jeb stepped in. *Danki, Lord.* "Jeb, Maryann wants to talk to *you*."

He lowered his gaze to the crying Maryann and then his eyes met Granny's. They said, "Please help me." As much as she wanted to be outside in her garden, another stress reliever, she knew Jeb needed her. She set the kettle on the stove and sat next to Jeb at her kitchen table. Jeb asked Maryann to sit across from them, which she slowly did. Maryann appeared to be like an old woman. Was she going through the change? In her forties?

"Now, what brings you here, Maryann?"

She didn't hesitate. "I want Denny to stay away from my Becca. She sees him everyday. And you know this. It needs to stop."

Jeb's gray brows furrowed. "Denny lives here. Jonas is teaching him along with Becca. Of course I know that."

Maryann pounded the table with a fist. "They're kissing!"

Granny looked up at Jeb, who had the same expression she wore. Shock. "We don't see them kissing," Granny informed.

Maryann's eyes darted wildly between Granny and Jeb. "You don't? Becca said you knew."

Jeb put up a hand. "Now calm down. Maybe she said we knew she came over here and saw Denny a lot. But those two have self-control."

"What?" Maryann nearly whimpered, eyes tearing up.

"*Jah*. They told us they knew what kissing led to. Denny has his regrets and Becca's a pure soul. Nothing to worry about on her account," Jeb said.

Granny noticed Maryann's eyes now held shame. "You thought Jeb and I wouldn't be keeping an eye on our...son?"

"Son? You're adopting him?"

Jeb's face brightened. "If we were a few decades younger, we would. He's like a son, though."

Granny went to her China closet to get her best tea cups. "Maryann, I'm a little defensive about Denny. He's a hurt lamb, like I said..."

"*Ach*, and I called him a wolf. I'm so embarrassed."

Jeb pulled at his beard. "You're a mother bear looking out for her cubs."

"I've been a bear for sure and certain. I mistook everything Becca was trying to say to me."

"It's prejudice," Jeb said. "You have a preconceived notion about Denny that isn't true. Don't pre-judge him. He's coming a long way and Becca has a lot to be thanked for."

Maryann cleared her throat. "I just wish Denny was normal looking. His *gut* looks can make a girl swoon."

"Swoon?" Granny asked. "Give Becca more credit than that. She's not a silly Bennett girl."

"A what?" Jeb and Maryann asked in unison.

"You know. The Bennet girls in *Pride and Prejudice*. The two young ones fainted over the handsome officers. *Nee*, Becca's like Elizabeth Bennet, the one with lots of sense."

"*Jah*," Jeb said. "I agree."

Granny ran around the table and hugged Jeb from behind. "You read it the whole way through?"

"Jah. Pride and Prejudice is a gut book."

The door opened and Denny walked in, trying not to be seen. "Denny," Granny said. "Maryann has something to say."

Maryann paled but said, "Would you like to come over to my house for…dessert some night?"

Granny winked at Denny. "She's making humble pie."

Maryann forced a smile and then sighed. "*Ach*, what a fool I've been."

Granny wanted to agree, but held her tongue.

~*~

Granny felt as aged as her Italian friend, Angelina, and wanted to stay in her kitchen and not step out onto her wraparound porch. She craved solitude. A *gut* book and another pot of hot tea, maybe snuggle under a light blanket now that September had relieved them of the heat and a nip was in the air. But she did what she knew to do; one foot in front of the other even when they needed put up.

Granny rubbed the kink in her neck, and upon hearing the screen door bang shut, she turned to see Lottie, eyes seeming wild. *Ach, Lord, I cannot take another woman throwing a fit today.*

"Granny, the circle's working on their squares and I told them you needed help in here."

"*Nee*, I don't. Just puttering around with canning this pear juice. Waiting to hear the ting of sealing jars."

"Is everything all right?"

"*Jah*. Just a little tired is all."

"Too tired to talk?"

Granny knew that one-on-one talks with her girls were sometimes needed, and today, she relished in less chatter. "*Jah*, I'd love to talk just to you."

"Just to me? Granny, are you upset with anyone in the circle?"

"*Jah*. Need to cool down."

"It's Marge and her...gossip, *jah*?"

Granny's eyes narrowed. "*Nee*. Marge isn't a gossip as far as I know."

Lottie plopped herself at Granny's table. "She flusters me to no end. Accused me of dating Phil Darby."

Granny took a seat across from Lottie. "I'm surprised that Marge can upset you. You've grown since I met you."

"Grown? How?"

"Well, you had that nervous non-stop chatter when I first met you, remember?"

Lottie's lips curled into a shy smile. "*Jah*. I was nervous. Meeting new people."

"Well," Granny continued, "I think you feel more at home in your own skin. You know that being a bookworm and wanting to stay home and quilt is all right."

"*Jah*, and it feels refreshing, really. It's exhausting trying to be someone else." Lottie shifted. "Marge isn't what I wanted to talk to you about. We patched things up."

"*Gut* to hear that. What's on your mind?"

Lottie looked at Granny, eyes starting to brim. "I'm homesick. And I don't want to move farther away than Smicksburg."

Granny folded her hands. *Lord, help Lottie open up to what's really wrong.* "Farther than Smicksburg?" she prodded.

Lottie's face drained of color. "Ezekiel has proposed marriage to me. And he wants to move to New York."

Granny's heart leapt for joy. She knew that Lottie was the one for Ezekiel just like she knew Roman and Lizzie needed each other. "*Ach*, Lottie, that's *wunderbar*."

"I didn't say yes."

Granny felt her heart plummet down into her toes. "What?"

"I didn't say *nee* either, just said I needed time to think on it. I don't know if I love him enough to live so far from Ohio and my friends here in Smicksbug. It was hard enough coming here..."

Granny took Lottie's hand and squeezed it. "I left my family for Jeb."

"But Millersburg isn't too far from here. Marathon is a seven hour car ride."

Granny sympathized with Lottie's parents. It near ripped her heart out when her sons moved to Ohio and

Montana. But they needed land and it wasn't because of some rift with the People. Then her mind went to Jeb. She'd move wherever he went, feeling at home with him. "Lottie, how do you feel around Ezekiel?"

She blushed, cheeks red. "What do you mean?"

"When I met Jeb, it felt like coming home. I can't say that happens to everyone, but it did for me. I would have moved to the North Pole if he was with me."

"I can't say that. I feel cherished by Ezekiel and I believe I care for him, love him. But I can't say I'd be willing to give up my roots for him."

Disappointment ripped through Granny. "Then you best be telling him your honest feelings. You can only be yourself. Some are more sentimental and prone to always want to live near their childhood home. Roman's like that."

"Turn down his proposal?" she gasped. "I don't want to."

"Well, you can't have it both ways. Unless he decides to give up New York for you. But his whole clan is moving up there, right?"

"*Jah*, they are. Have plans to split up land among family."

Granny remembered Fannie's trial and quickly got up. "I want you to talk to Fannie."

Lottie protested. "I don't want all of Smicksburg to know of this."

Granny twirled around. "We're spun together here, *jah*? We help each other?"

"*Jah*, but just Fannie."

Granny ambled out into the circle and pointed to Fannie. "Can we talk private-like?"

"Granny, aren't you joining us?" Maryann asked sheepishly.

"*Jah.* In a minute. Fannie? Can you come in?"

Guilt plastered itself across Fannie's face. "Am I in trouble?"

Granny laughed at this sweet girl. "Of course not. Just need your help."

She sighed with relief and followed Granny into the kitchen. Granny asked her to take a seat because Lottie needed advice. Fannie's shoulders straightened as if she was important. "How can I help?" she asked as she sat in Jeb's chair at the head of the table.

Lottie just stared at Fannie.

Fannie touched her shoulder. "What is it, Lottie?"

Lottie's eyes seemed to beg Granny for help.

"*Ach,* I'm sorry. You don't know. Fannie was engaged to Melvin and his family moved to New York. She had some decisions to make. She can help you decide."

"*Ach,*" Fannie quipped. "Has one of the Miller men proposed?"

"*Nee,* Ezekiel Coblenz," Lottie near whispered. "And his whole clan is moving to Marathon."

"That's where my in-laws are. It's pretty nice up there."

Granny spoke up. "Fannie, tell Lottie about how hard it was for you to think of moving from Smicksburg, but how you were willing."

Fannie scrunched up her face. "There's really nothing to tell. A man needs work to provide and a wife must follow." She tilted her head to one side as if going down memory lane. "I was upset at first. Talked to the bishop about my hard feeling towards Melvin's *daed* for wanting to sell the farm so quick-like, not giving Melvin much time to make plans. But it all worked out."

Lottie's eyes were wide. "So you had doubts about New York? Fears?"

"*Jah*, for sure and certain, but never about Melvin. I'd move anywhere for him to be happy. He didn't want to be a farmer, though, and boy am I glad. Milking cows twice a day is not for me." Fannie squeezed Lottie's hand. "Let it all simmer like a pot of tea. Give it time. You're probably in shock that Ezekiel proposed since you were giving up courting and all."

Lottie hung her head. "I broke that promise to God. When Ezekiel got hurt in the fire and I saw him, I knew I loved him. And we decided to court in secret."

Fannie snapped her fingers. "It's how you react that shows your real feelings." Her face shone as she lovingly gazed at Granny. "This *wunderbar* woman showed me that. *Ach*, Granny, where would I be without you?"

Tears threatened Granny, so she sprang up to put on her tea kettle. "I'd be a lonely old woman without my knitting circle."

"Well," Fannie continued, "Lottie, you just relax. God knows we're dumb sheep and leads us real clearly. Just relax. Let your mind relax. Our minds try too hard to figure everything out in a day. *Nee*, knit, quilt, read, and enjoy the things you like. Your heart will calm down and be able to speak."

Granny felt her chest expand. Turning form her stove, she beamed. "Fannie, that was *gut* advice. *Let the heart speak*. Where did you read that? Is it in the Bible?"

Fannie flustered. "I just thought it up." She grinned. "I think I have a wise teacher, *jah*? Being with you so much has rubbed off on me?"

Granny pursed her lips so not to smile and show pride.

"*Danki*, Fannie," Lottie said. "I try too hard to figure things out. I over-think it all. I'm going to read a good book tonight and embroider my Alaska square. We need to get this state quilt done if we're to sell it to replant Granny's forest."

Granny saw how much Fannie had helped and said, "Praise be." When she was gone, as we all pass on to glory, her "Little Women" would have each other to rely upon, no matter the distance that separated them.

A waft of air blew in and Granny saw a brown haired haggard Maryann amble in. "Do you want me to cut up your pear crumb pies?" She shifted. "Maybe I can do that without making a blunder."

Fannie near ran to Maryann. "Why so sad? You're going to cry. Or you've been crying." She glanced over at Granny. "Maybe I can help you. What's wrong?"

Tears rolled down Maryann's cheeks again. "I've been so horrible to Becca. I don't think she'll ever forgive me."

Fannie put an arm around her to sooth. "My *mamm* said things to me that were horrible, and look at us now. We still have our ups and downs, but we're on the up more than down."

Maryann humbly nodded. "You're right, Fannie. This was a Jonah Day, for sure and certain."

Lottie clapped her hands. "I know what that is. It's in Anne of Green Gables. It's one of those days when if anything can go wrong it will, *jah?*"

"*Jah,*" Maryann said with a forced smile, despite the tears. "Becca and I never quarrel, so it's shaken me to my core."

Lizzie opened the door and leaned in. "Are we having circle in here or out on the porch?"

Granny grinned. "I think we're being spun together in her right fine. Want to join us?"

"Well, I wanted a word with Granny but I can tell you all. *Daed* and I are going on a vacation to see the ocean."

Squeals echoed around the kitchen. Roman had told Granny but she embraced Lizzie as she came near her. If Lizzie knew how many times Roman came over to get "Woman Advice" it may hurt dear Lizzie. What Roman did tell her was a tad disturbing but she knew they'd work things out in time. *Time away.*

"What about homeschooling?" Lottie asked.

"The girls went to school today. Roman and I need to be in agreement on that and my trip away will help us both think clearer."

"Well," Maryann said, "I think the kids should be in school. Romans' right."

Granny leaned her head to the side until Maryann met her gaze. Granny shook her head slightly.

"*Ach,*" Maryann said, "I'm giving my opinion where it's not welcome, being a *neb nose.*"

"What's that?" Lottie asked, bewildered.

"A *neb nose* is slang in these parts for a person who gets their nose into other folks business." She turned to Maryann. "You've had one bad day and now forgive yourself. You're not a *neb nose*"

The door opened again and in came Marge and Suzy. Marge winked. "Having an Amish only party in here? We feel like *Outsiders.*" Her belly started to jiggle and then she leaned over, laughing at her own joke. "Get it? *Outsiders?* We were outside and you're in here? The Amish call us *Outsiders,*" she wailed.

Granny didn't get the play on words at first, but when she did, her heart smiled though she didn't get the humor. Her Amish and English knitting circle had its kinks, but they worked them out. When Marge calmed down, she said, "Let's all go out on the porch. We have a quilt to work on, *jah?*"

The women looped arms and Granny stayed at the rear, relishing the sight. *A three cord strand is not easily broken*, she pondered, and their cord had several strands. *Praise be.*

~*~

Bea repositioned herself on Granny lap and she awoke with a start. "What?"

Jeb, who was sitting at the kitchen table, reading *The Budget* said, "I didn't say anything."

Granny hugged Bea. "Sleep talking I suppose." When she realized she'd dozed off in her rocker, she sighed. "Jeb, why didn't you wake me up? I need to make dinner."

"*Nee*, you don't."

"*Jah*, I always cook."

Jeb smirked. "Maryann talked to me after circle. We're to be at her house at six for a wiener roast."

"Denny, too?"

"Denny, too," Jeb reassured.

"*Ahhh*," Granny near sung. "I do love a bonfire and hotdogs."

"Me, too."

Granny closed her eyes and recounted all that had transpired at circle. They'd worked in complete harmony on the state quilt and it would be finished by next week. She thought of each block and how different they all were. She really didn't think it would look so good but when they stitched the squares together, it looked right nice.

That's what her girls were, like patchwork squares. How they were all different, but when together, they were beautiful.

She thought Lottie looked more at ease as the circle continued out on the porch. Had someone said something that settled her mind? And Lizzie had a skip in her step. Was she that eager to get away from Roman. Knowing she had a God she could cast all her care on at any given moment, she bowed her head and prayed:

Lord,

I just feel deep down that Lottie and Ezekiel are meant to be together, but if I'm just an old neb nose, sticking my nose in where not needed, show me. I do love to see people happily married. It's been the joy of my life and I want the same for dear Lottie.

I want the same for Roman and Lizzie. The girls came home all down in the mouth today from school. Is Sabrina that awful a teacher? If so, Lord help soften her to be a teacher that loves kinner. I don't like seeing my little Tillie cry. Maybe Lizzie is to homeschool her, but more than anything, they need unity at the head, in Lizzie and Roman. They're both so different, but, like my Little Women, together they make a nice patchwork quilt. Lord, bind them together.

I ask all this in Jesus name,
Amen.

Dear Readers,

I hope you're enjoying this series as much as I am writing it. As usual, I leave you with the recipe for the dessert Granny served at her knitting circle. Enjoy!

Pear Crumb Pie

1 Lazy Wife Pie Crust (see recipe below)
2 ½ lb. ripe pears
1 Tbsp. lemon juice
2/3 c. sugar

1 tsp. cinnamon
1-2 Tbsp. flour
Topping
1 c. flour
½ c. brown sugar
½ c. melted butter

Place pears in pie crust. Sprinkle with lemon juice, sugar, cinnamon and flour and toss. Combine topping ingredients and mix until crumbly. Sprinkle on top of pie. Bake at 425 degrees for 15 minutes. Reduce heat to 350 degrees and bake for another 25 minutes.

Lazy Wife Pie Crust
1 cup flour
3 tablespoons powdered sugar
½ cup oleo (Crisco or margarine)

Mix ingredients to make crumbs. Press into pie pan

EPISODE 7

Stitched Up

*J*eb stretched his long arms over his head and then put one around Granny as they nestled on their glider. "Nothing better than harvest time. Seeing a reward for hard labor is mighty satisfying."

Granny was relieved that each year, when the hard work of putting up came around, Jeb seemed younger, not older and feeble as she feared. "You're mighty spry today."

"*Jah*, I am. Looking forward to the apple butter frolic."

"Why? It's the women who do it."

He nudged her and laughed. "And you use me for tasting it to see if it's just right." He pat his stomach. "Usually put on a few pounds."

Granny's heart calmed the more she had her second up of morning coffee with Jeb. And the air was crisp with the scent of apples and drying corn stalks, which also took her back to her childhood days, helping her *daed* load the apple carts. But then emptiness filled her when she thought of Lizzie's letter. How she missed her being next door. And Lizzie was running away from her problems again. Granny just knew it.

"Jeb, I want to share something with you. It's a letter we got in the mail yesterday from Lizzie."

He pulled at his long beard. "You know I've had Lizzie on my heart more than usual. I pray and cast her on God when it happens."

Granny sighed. "Saying a casting off prayer, like the circle calls them."

"*Jah.* Something's not right."

Granny took the letter from her apron pocket. "Well, you're right. Or at least I think so. I do hate to fret over something that's not worthy of…fretting."

"Nothing's worthy of fretting. It does no *gut.*"

"You're right, old man. Listen to this:

Dear Granny,

Daed and I had such a wonderful time at the beach. It was a much needed vacation. So much so that we're going to visit relatives in Lancaster for a while. Marge writes that everything is fine and how she's helping with the girls. What a good friend she is, making this trip possible.

You'll never believe who I saw the other day. Remember Amos, the man I courted? He came out to see Smicksburg and thought we were all too backwards? Well, he's doing fine along with his children. No wife yet, but he looked so happy when I saw him. He says hello.

Give the girls my love and with this letter I send my love. Oh, and give my love to Jeb, too.

Lizzie

P.S. Give my love to Charles and write to me this week about how he's doing.

She folded the letter and put it to her heart. "See what I mean?"

Jeb leaned back, mouth gaping. "*Nee*, I do not. There's nothing wrong in that letter."

Granny rolled her eyes. "Maybe you have to be a woman to see it. Do you see someone's name is missing altogether?"

Jeb's brow furrowed. "I don't know. She didn't ask about one of the knitting circle friends? Ruth's grief?"

Granny wanted to scream. "Roman. Not one word about her husband."

"*Ach*, Deborah, it's because she probably writes to him everyday."

Granny huffed. "I take Bea for a little walk to the mailbox daily, remember? I get the mail and there's been no letters marked for Roman."

Again, Jeb pulled at his beard. "Odd."

Granny took her coffee mug off the little side table and took a sip. "And she's talking about Amos. Remember him?"

"Who could forget? Had his nose up in the air over us cutting our own ice. Well, my *daed* did it and so did my *opa* and it's fun. *Gut* exercise in the dead of winter, too."

"Jeb, do you know that women who are not happy in their marriages live in the past, in their minds, daydreaming about former beaus?"

Jeb narrowed his gaze at her. "So you think her talking to Amos is wrong?"

"*Nee*, not at all, but notice how happy she says he is and makes light of his rude behavior while out here. And she added there was no wife yet."

Jeb leaned towards her. "Really? I didn't know that." He kissed her cheek. "Ever think of Samuel?"

Granny clucked her tongue. "Old man, we've been married so long, I can hardly remember his face. If I do, it's with a grateful heart that I didn't let him steer me away from the Amish." She leaned her head on his shoulder. "Lizzie's not happy with our son, I'm sure of it, and he needs to do something."

"*Jah*. Roman needs to stop being so stubborn, spending more time with Denny than we do, and he lives with us. Roman knows how much Lizzie loves Charles and wants to adopt."

"Well, there's something else in this letter, too. Ungratefulness. She credits Marge for making the trip possible? I see Roman working mighty hard out there in the fields and the shop to pay for her trip."

"*Jah*, that does bother me. Roman's looking haggard, I will say that."

"Denny's helping him, too. That's why he's with him so much, *jah*?"

Jeb sighed. "You're right." He pursed his lips. "Now that I think about it, that letter is disturbing. Best go show it to Roman.

"I will." Granny had something else that just kept hankering at her that she needed to discuss with her dear husband. "Jeb, do you think Jonas is unhappy here?"

He took a sip of coffee. "That's another one on my prayer list. We read together, lots of Spurgeon and Lucado, and books have a way of opening up a person. I think he needs a wife."

Granny hit Jeb's knee playfully. "We're turning into each other. I agree. Who can we match him up with?"

"No one. Let the *Gut* Lord do it."

Granny started to think of all the widows Jeb's age. "How about Serena Byler?"

"She's only in her thirties!" Jeb said in shock.

"Well, Jonas is young yet. Only in his fifties."

Jeb chuckled. "I think Serena has many options, such a pretty woman. She needs a young man."

"Ida Troyer?"

"Deborah, let the Lord do his work."

Right then and there, Granny prayed that Jonas would find a wife. She'd never tinkered with the notion of him marrying again, but maybe it was the loneliness she was seeing for the first time. Or maybe the Lord had simply put it on her heart to pray for him…and help.

~*~

Granny stepped into Roman's house, the girls all a giggle, and smiled as they kissed her on the cheek before marching off to school. Coffee wafted from the kitchen and so she made her way through the living area to the kitchen in the back. When she noticed Romans' downcast countenance and Marge's slumped shoulders, she wondered if they'd just quarreled. "Everything okay?"

Marge turned from the pile of breakfast dishes. "I'm fine. Think you all need to hook up a diesel engine to a dishwasher, but besides that I'm fine."

"Well, I appreciate your help in getting the girls ready in the morning. I know you have plenty of your own to do."

Roman grabbed the newspaper that was on the table and started to riffle through it.

"Son, wake up on the wrong side of the bed?" Granny nudged.

"*Nee.* Just being grumpy, I suppose."

Marge clapped her hands, soap suds flying, and burst into laughter. "Remember when Jenny met us? Was trying to find the seven dwarves? Roman, you are Grumpy."

He cocked his head back. "Now that didn't make any sense."

Marge wiped her hands on her red cherry apron. "Oh, I forgot. You don't know fairytales. Well, Grumpy's the name of one of the dwarves. They all have names that fit their personality like Sleepy, Dreamy, Dopey, and

Sneezy…" She laughed all the harder, now doubled over. "I'd say more than one of those names can apply to you, too."

Granny knew Roman didn't understand Marge's good-natured humor, so she spoke up. "Roman, Marge is just joking with you." She plopped herself in a chair. "Roman, I need to talk to you about something serious."

He folded the newspaper in half and set it down. "What's wrong, *Mamm*? Your voice is shaky."

Marge cleared her throat. "I'll finish these later. I'll leave you two to yourselves."

"*Nee*," Granny said. "You can hear. Lizzie mentions you in her letter."

"She loved the ocean. Did she write you about that?"

"*Jah*," Granny said, turning to Roman. "Did she tell you much about her trip?"

His brown puppy dog eyes sank. "She hasn't written."

"What?" Marge gasped. "She said you two left on good terms. You agreed to her going and all."

"*Jah*, we're *gut*. She's just busy and only writes to women, I suppose."

Granny waved the letter at Roman. "Read this. Women understand women and I say she's angry with you and not happy."

Roman slowly reached for the letter and read it silently. Marge turned and viewed him like a hawk on prey. The pendulum clock was all that was heard and its beat seemed louder to Granny than normal. Slower, too. Or was she nervous? Most likely she'd have to explain how to read in between the lines, like she did with Jeb.

Roman looked dazed when finished. "So? She's staying in Lancaster longer. She needs a break."

Granny bit her lower lip and darted a knowing look at Marge. Marge nodded. "Roman, can I read it? See what I make of it?"

"Sure. It really says nothing at all."

Marge took her red cheater glasses out of her apron pocket and balanced them on the end of her nose. After a few moments she moaned. Her lips moved but no sound came out, only another moan. Then a groan and then she covered her mouth as she gasped. Her eyes large as a full moon beamed on Roman. "You need to hire a driver or buy a train ticket and get yourself out to Lancaster, today!"

"Why?" Roman blanched. "I didn't do anything wrong."

"You're not doing things right! She mentions Amos in here, she doesn't mention you once. Hello, Roman, smell the coffee?"

He rolled his eyes. "*Jah*, I do." He put up his mug. "Can I have another cup?"

Marge growled. "It's a saying. It means to wake up! She's miserable."

"How do you get that from the letter?"

Marge froze like a mouse stunned by a cat. "Well, let's just say she tells me things in letters." Her voice softened. "Roman, Lizzie's struggling something awful. She feels like a failure."

Granny knew this, but knowing that Lizzie had divulged to Marge made her want to break down into tears. But she kept them at bay. "Infertility?" Granny guessed, her voice audibly trembling.

Marge clasped her hands nervously. "She wants to give Roman a son and believes she can't. She feels like she's a disappointment. I believe it's the reason why she wants to adopt Charles. It would fix the problem."

Roman darted up, his chair falling behind him. "She told you that?"

"Well, in confidence. Let's just say Lizzie needs to know from you that she's enough. That she's cherished."

"But," Roman protested, "I do that every day."

Marge sighed. "When a person is ill, you give more medicine at different doses, right? As a nurse, I'll answer the question. Yes. Lizzie has a wounded spirit. And she's angry at herself for not telling you about all her pain when you were engaged. She's mad at herself and ashamed around you."

Roman swiped the beads of perspiration off of his upper lip. "I was so stupid not to see the change in her. She was assaulted and I wasn't there for her." He leaned on the table for support. "I blame myself for that, you know."

Granny pat his arm. "*Nee*, don't. I'd say if you're both looking inward at your own faults, you'll never solve this problem. Learn to see each other clearly daily."

"How?" Roman asked, eyes filled with tears.

"Communicate. I agree with Marge. You go out and surprise Lizzie. Take her out to a nice restaurant and bring her home."

"Cut her vacation short?"

Marge went to Roman and took him by the shoulders, making him look at her. "She's only out there to run from her problem. *You*. Her problem is with you. Iron sharpens iron and you two need to cross blades. Cut off all the garbage in your marriage."

Roman's eyes narrowed. "I think I understand what you're saying. Cut the bad part of the apple out so it doesn't rot the whole thing."

"Bingo," Marge quipped, as she pat him on the shoulder.

When she turned to go back to the dishes, Roman said, "Marge, I'm glad Lizzie has a friend in you."

Marge took a tea towel, wiped her brow, and faked fainting into a chair. She closed her eyes for a minute and then opened one eye. "Roman, I thought I'd never hear those words."

Roman grinned. "And you're *gut* medicine for Lizzie, too. You make her laugh."

"Have you ever seen me impersonate Lucille Ball at the chocolate factory?"

Granny had no idea what Marge was talking about, and apparently Roman didn't either, since he was waiting for Marge to explain. But Marge only shrugged her shoulders and said Joe thought it was funny. Granny pondered the fact that the Amish and *English* didn't understand each other at times, and neither did men and women. She thanked the Lord Roman was bringing Lizzie home.

~*~

Lottie was relieved the Suzy's yarn shop was slow today and she was able to come home at ten. Now that Hezekiah had fully recovered from the coma that many feared had done permanent brain damage, she could ask for his advice. His dear wife, Colleen, had spent the entire summer helping him by using his five senses to awaken memory, and physical exercises, small walks around the house at first. Now long walks and calisthenics. Watching Colleen teach him to jump rope was a bit humorous, since she could do double skips, but Hezekiah soon was keeping up with his wife.

She'd also seen Hezekiah bond with Colleen's little girl, Aurora, a black-haired, spunky five year old. When it was safe, no fear of Hezekiah losing his balance, he took Aurora for piggy back rides to the apiary to see the hives and bees the Amish gave him to support himself if he didn't recover. As boxes of honey bear bottles came in, he gave Aurora the task of inspecting them for any "bad bears" as he called them, ones that were defective. Aurora had a daddy now and it showed in her smile that could brighten any gloomy day.

Aurora had lit up Lottie's visit here, until recently. There was something deep within that no amount of childhood laughter and play could chase away. She was homesick and was it God's way of saying she needed to go back to Millersburg, or was it just time for her to grow up? Lottie's heart was in two places, though. Ezekiel was up in New York looking at land with his brothers, and she felt an emptiness like no other she'd experienced. It was much worse than when she called off her engagement to Peter. No, this was a heart-sick kind of loneliness. Was God trying to make her realize she should accept his proposal and move to New York, much farther away from her home in Millersburg?

Hezekiah came into her bedroom, the place they'd agreed to have a heart-to-heart. His hair was much blonder due to the summer sun and his blue eyes twinkled as he looked at her. "Now, what's this all about, Lot?" He took a seat in a chair by her bed. "Are you cold? Need a fire already?"

"*Ach, nee*, why do you ask?"

"You're under your bed covers…"

Lottie smoothed the quilt. "*Mamm* made me this quilt. I feel closer to her when under it. And there is a nip in the air."

He leaned forward, eyes observant. "You're going back home, aren't you?"

Lottie slowly shook her head. "I don't know what to do. I need your advice, as a man."

He grinned. "So this is about Ezekiel?"

"*Jah.* I'm so confused. I mean, I love him, but I'm not sure I can move to New York."

He blew air upward, making his bangs flutter. "I remember when Colleen wasn't sure she could be Amish."

"Colleen had doubts?"

"Sure she did. Turning Amish is a big commitment. It took time. But I never met a girl I felt at home with, so I prayed a lot and waited."

"And you two are so happy," Lottie said. "But you were both living here. I'm homesick for Ohio so how can I move to New York?"

Hezekiah put up a hand as if to say 'slow down.' "Did he ask you to go there? Marry him?"

"*Jah.* Didn't I tell you?"

"*Nee,* you did not. That's something I wouldn't forget." His face split into a smile. "He's a *gut* man Lottie. The best they come."

"I know," she blurted, feeling exasperated. "But it doesn't make sense. I'm homesick for Ohio. Do you think God is turning my heart towards home and moving back?"

"What do you mean?"

She tapped her heart. "I've been crying at night lately, feeling homesick. Maybe God's showing me I need to turn down Ezekiel's proposal."

Hezekiah readjusted his straw hat. "You've been crying?"

"*Jah,* I have. Only at night, though."

"Lot, do you think God leads us by our emotions? They're not very reliable."

"Well, you seem steady enough," Lottie said, bringing her knees up and hugging them. "And Granny says to look at how you react to things. It's the real you."

After taking a deep sigh, Hezekiah took off his hat and started to fan himself. "Now that's tricky. I can see a reaction like a mean dog coming at you and you run. That's a reaction, *jah*?"

Lottie nodded.

Hezekiah stared hard out her bedroom window. "God gave us emotions for a reason, I'm just saying they shouldn't be the litmus test on major decisions."

"Litmus test?"

"A dirt test farmers use." He scrunched his lips to one side and then looked at her evenly. "You're not sure you love Ezekiel, is that it?"

She fumbled for words, but none came. Only a nod.

"Well, lots of folks are moving up to New York. Emma Miller did a ways back and I think she writes to Ezekiel."

"Who's she?"

"An old beau…"

Lottie gripped the quilt, eyes almost popping out of their sockets. "And you think he…cares for her still?"

Hezekiah shrugged. "He's a stable man and wouldn't propose to you if he did. But if you turn him down, she'd be ripe for the picking up there in New York. And she's a real beauty, I have to admit. Not as pretty as Colleen, but almost."

Lottie turned on her side and laid down, feeling ill. "I'm not feeling too *gut* all of a sudden."

"What's wrong?" Hezekiah prodded.

Tears formed in her eyes. "I could lose him. Just the thought of it makes me nauseated."

"*Ach*, you'll get over it. Lots of fish in the sea."

Lottie darted up and ogled at her cousin. "How can you say that? There is no man like Ezekiel. They're all fake, or mean, or stupid. He really loves me and I can't lose him. I can't!"

Hezekiah grinned. "I think Granny is right. A reaction tells all. You love the man."

Lottie narrowed her eyes, studying Hezekiah's face. "Did you make up that story about another woman?"

"*Nee*, I'd never do that. Emma moved there and has always liked Ezekiel. They're childhood friends and he thought it could turn into something else, but he told her it wouldn't."

"When was this?" Lottie asked, rubbing her sweaty palms on the quilt.

"Last May…when he met you at my wedding."

Memories of Ezekiel telling her about when he first saw her at the wedding flooded her soul. She felt her stomach flip. "I can't lose him," she gasped.

Hezekiah's eyes mellowed into pools of peace. "I'll miss you, Lot."

She cringed. "I love him but I can't move to New York!"

"What? Lottie, you need to grow up and stop acting like a little girl. Life is hard but rewarding."

"I'm homesick. I don't want to live in New York. I like the warmth of Ohio, not the tundra air of Upstate New York!"

He got up to leave. "Maybe you're not old enough to get married."

"I am, too. I'm –"

"Marriage is loving someone in a sacrificial way. You don't look out for yourself but your spouse. You just said the weather would keep you away from Ezekiel. That's not love. I'm sorry cousin, but sometimes the truth is painful."

Lottie huffed. *She was too immature for marriage? Nee*, she was not. She was confused. *Nee*, she was not confused. The thoughts of Ezekiel being with Emma made her physically ill. She needed to be with him. Suddenly an idea rushed in and she blurted it out. "Maybe we're supposed to get married but live here in Smicksburg."

Hezekiah groaned. "His whole family is moving up to New York. Do you think that's fair?"

Lottie had never been so angry with her cousin. "My whole family lives in Ohio. He can meet me halfway."

Hezekiah looked at her as if he pitied her. A knock on the door and Aurora's voice asking for her *daed* ended this miserable conversation and Lottie was relieved. *Men, what do they know about true love?*

~*~

Luke frowned. "Angelina's supposed to be here by now. Do you think she forgot?"

Ruth continued to roll pie dough. "*Nee*, she said she was coming at two. Can you take the buggy and check on her? She really has no one now that *Mamm's gone*."

Luke felt relief wash over him. Ruth had mentioned her *mamm* and her voice didn't shake. "Sure thing."

Ruth ran over to him with a smidgen of dough. "Taste this."

He let her pop the dough into his mouth, relishing their redeemed relationship. "Tasted different."

"It's rice flour. Do you like it?"

"Rice flour? Why not wheat?"

She leaned forward and kissed his cheek. "I'm trying a gluten free diet for Little Debbie. Some kids are misdiagnosed you know."

Luke kissed her and turned to go. Ruth somehow got into her head that a new diet could make Debbie's Down Syndrome better. Marge told her that Down Syndrome kids had a much higher chance of wheat intolerance. Well, he'd been eating wheat bread his whole life and hoped Ruth didn't expect them all to eat anything but. And Ruth was pregnant and craved pastries, so surely this food was only for Debbie. "I'll be right back with Angelina. I'm sure it's her age and she forgot."

He closed the door and waved to Micah who was on his tire swing. *How he's grown*, Luke thought. *Will be off of to school in a year. Hard to believe.*

He hopped into his open buggy to enjoy the fall leaves as he made the short trip to Angelina's. He could walk, like the little Italian woman, but what if something was wrong? What if he found her alongside the road, out of breath, not able to make the trek?

He inhaled the scent of apples and imagined Ruth making his favorite. Apple crisp. If he wasn't mistaken, he smelled apple pies in the oven. *Well, I hope they have real flour in them*, he mused.

He waved at his *English* neighbor and gawked at what appeared to be his new John Deere lawnmower. The women cut the grass in the Amish community and he always wondered why. Ruthy did sections at a time with her little motorless cutter. He'd talk to his father-in-law and ask why they didn't help. They were both there in the wood shop and could easily take the load off Ruth.

The grove of trees laden with shades of reds, yellows, and browns came into view, and Luke tried to take in the beauty while it lasted. If he had it his way, it would be autumn all year long.

A red flashing light caught his attention. Fire? He hastened his horse and soon he saw an ambulance entering Angelina's driveway. *Lord, have mercy. Ruth's gotten attached to Angelina. Lord, don't take her.*

He pulled over to the side of the road in front of her house and hitched his horse up to a nearby tree, and then ran into the house. Two paramedics giving commands in loud voices led him to the upstairs bedrooms. Angelina was sobbing as she watched the men do CPR on her husband.

Luke put an arm around her and to his shock, she clung to him, her strength crumbling. "It's my mistake," she said, sobbing.

Luke held her up and whispered, "What do you mean?"

"I leave him here and I downstairs. He say he sick and no feel the *gut* but I no pay attention."

Luke tried to understand her broken English, and he gathered enough to know that she blamed herself for not being upstairs. "Has he been sick very long?"

"Years. He no feel *gut* everyday."

Luke pulled her tight. "Then you'd never be downstairs cooking pasta for him then, *jah*?"

She looked up at him. "You right. He die of the hunger first."

Luke stifled a laugh, as Angelina had such quick wit, even under tragedy.

The medics started to yell at the victim and then checked his pulse. After a few moments and a few other vital signs taken, they asked to speak to Angelina in private.

"He like son. You can say it here."

The medic's face twisted but was able to say, "I'm sorry. We lost him."

Angelina screamed, her hands flung in the air. "We come to this country together. Together we come. I was a young girl." She clung to Luke, screaming and sobbing until the medics asked her to take something to calm down, which she rejected.

Luke held the little woman and prayed for God's comfort, the best medicine.

~*~

Phil flipped shut his cell phone and looked up into the blue sky with wispy clouds as he strode across the hospital parking lot. *Thank you, Lord. Maybe she's the one. Only two dates, but…*

Now, to the task at hand, he thought. He'd relished in hospital visits, compassion coming easy to him. He was in the zone while helping hurting people, but not seeing MJ suffer. Leading their little house church had made Andy and MJ like family, and as they treated him like a young kid, they took some of the sting out of losing his mom. Slight sting, as no woman he'd met was he able to call a confidante, even Judith. His mom he could spill the beans and she'd listened.

He looked up at the clouds again before entering the hospital. Lord, I need your help to get through this grief. And give me words for MJ.

He pulled at his all access clergy pass as he made his way to the elevator. In his peripheral vision, he saw black. Lots of black. He turned to see a group of Amish women and recognized one: Katie Byler, now Katie Hummel, since her husband converted to the Amish. Phil took a liking to her animated husband, Joseph, from day one, and respected his commitment not just to the Amish, but his story that led to his conversion. A homeless man reconnects with his sister, Ginny Rowland, their church worship leader, and finds a home among the Amish. Was Denny Boles' story going to have such a positive outcome? Then it dawned on Phil as he stepped inside the elevator with the five Amish women. "Katie, do you think Joseph could talk to someone wanting to convert to the Amish?"

Her large brown eyes danced. *"Jah.* Joseph loves to tell his story."

"Gut. I mean," Phil laughed. "Good. I'll stop by your place and set up a time."

Katie put a finger to her lips. "Hmm. It's apple picking season and we have an apple farm." She looked pensively at the floor. "How about the boys at Arbor Creek come over and help pick apples? I can pay them in apple pie and cider."

"Sounds great. I'll stop over your place in a day or two."

Katie said good-bye and the women exited the elevator. Jane reminds me of Katie. So lighthearted and natural looking… but she's Mennonite and we wouldn't be going on a second date, as much as I want to. He shook his head to dislodge the thought of her. No, he was Baptist from head to toe.

The elevator *dinged* and he knew he was at his destination. A pit lodged in his stomach, which took him by surprise. Memories of his mom in the hospital somehow made him lightheaded. *Lord, I need strength. It's like I'm reliving my mom's illness all over again.* Phil ran to a nearby chair in a visitor room and put his head between his knees. "Flashbacks," he growled.

"Are you all right?"

The room not lit, he jumped. When his eyes adjusted, he made out a man with a white collar. "I'm sorry. Is this the chapel?"

"No, just an empty room for an old priest to get his bearings."

Since the room had one window that ran the length of the room, he could see the view. "Nice day, huh?"

"Yes, I like to look up into the clouds when I pray. Do you need prayer?"

Phil nodded. "Lost my mom and usually don't have a hard time coming to hospitals until today."

The man nodded. "Grief. It comes when you least expect it. I'm sorry for your loss."

Phil sighed. "I'm here to help someone, but *I* need the help."

"Oh," the priest said, "that's why I'm in here, too. When you get to be seventy, you've lost more people and have more flashbacks."

Phil gawked. "You're seventy?"

"Yes. Have been a priest for thirty-three years. Got a late start, ignoring the call. But here I am and glad the Hound of Heaven tackled me."

Phil snapped his fingers. "C.S. Lewis, right?"

"Yes. I ran from God as much as him."

Phil stood up, knowing he still had to prepare for the Wednesday night Bible study at the church. "Nice meeting you. Best be going."

"Who are you visiting?"

"MJ Holzer. Dear woman."

"I'm her priest. I just saw her and the pain has gone down some," he said, shaking his head.

Phil crossed the room to shake his hand. "MJ's told me so much about you. Good job. She's so lonely."

"Yes," he said. "People volunteer for everything in church except hospital visitations. And MJ has been so hurt by this since she visited shut-ins when well, being a Eucharistic Minister."

"Someone who can give communion, right?"

"Yes. I fear she has emotional scars that run deeper than the scars in her body. Loneliness is cruel."

Phil thought perhaps this priest had a melancholy personality, being a bit too deep. "MJ has a small group of friends and a great husband."

"She lost many friends and it pains her," the priest corrected.

Phil nodded, wondering if MJ didn't tell her priest that they were having a non-denominational service at her house.

~*~

Phil leaned over MJ's bed, fear rising that she wasn't breathing. Her eyes popped open and he jumped back.

MJ chuckled. "Not dead yet."

Phil let out a long sigh. "Well, I'm glad." He took the seat next to her bed and once again admired this woman's ability to be so chipper under such dire circumstances. *Or was she hiding all her pain?* "I met your priest."

MJ raised the bed and repositioned herself. "He's a dear man, don't you think? I make him pins and bookmarks and he gives them as gifts to patients right here."

He wanted to take her hand, but IV's were attached. "MJ, he said you're lonely. That you carry a lot of hurt from people in your church."

MJ's eyes darkened. "And I thought I had pastoral confidentiality."

"Well, he slipped. But is it true?"

MJ nodded. "I tell Father Thomas things I can't tell Andy. Yes, I served so faithfully at my church and then when I needed help, friends seemed to fall off the planet."

Phil leaned forward. "Why not tell Andy? He's your husband."

"Andy? He has enough to concern himself with. Anyhow, what can he do? No, it would just add to his burden." She peered out the window. "Anyhow, Father Thomas doesn't know how much I gain from solitude."

"Why's that?"

"I only talk to him when I'm down in the mouth. You know, when I'm really going through a tough time." She smiled. "No, what I gain in my intimacy with Christ surpasses any hurt any human can throw at me."

"How?"

"Well, I have lots of time to read. I love the gospels and I see over and over that Christ was rejected and alone, yet He had the Comforter."

"The Holy Spirit," Phil quipped.

"Yes, and he fills all the cracks in my broken heart." She grinned. "Granny Weaver said that and I like it. We're all cracked up in one way or another and...scarred."

"Scarred?"

"Yes, all the ugliness in life that hurts us. God takes it and somehow and makes things better, but we still have battle wounds."

Phil gawked. "Thank you. I thought I knew what I was teaching on tonight, but there's several people who have cracks in their lives and I need to preach out of the book of James."

"On suffering?"

"Yes, and what we gain from it. Thanks, MJ. I always get so much from talking to you."

Her eyes moistened and a tear slid down her cheek.

"I'm sorry. Didn't I upset you?"

Her glossy eyes danced. "Tears of joy. It's nice to feel useful."

Phil carefully leaned over the IV tubes that hydrated his dear friend and kissed her on the cheek. He'd come to this hospital to give, not to get. But what he was getting from MJ, Andy, and many in the small town of Smicksburg was solidifying a call deep within, and he dared not ignore the still small voice of God, like MJ's priest. No, today he made his decision. He needed to call back Jerry Jackson, the pastor of the church he'd come to dearly love.

~*~

Maryann polished a plate so shiny she could see herself, and she didn't like the image. She was haggard. But a parent needed to set up firm boundaries, right? It just seemed she wounded Becca's spirit, accusing her of being immoral. And she was prejudiced against Denny, an outsider. No, she did not encourage this relationship and it was hard living under the same roof with a daughter that had turned from a warm summer breeze to ice.

"*Mamm*, can we talk?" Becca's flat toned voice came from behind her.

Maryann spun around. Did she want to talk or have a really loud discussion? Becca's eyes, though droopy, were tame, so she nodded her head. "*Jah*. Let's go outside." Maryann placed the plate in the cupboard and silently prayed that her relationship with Becca wouldn't crack because they'd become like delicate China, not sturdy stoneware. She followed Becca outside to the white porch swing that Michael attached to two trees. "*Daed* will have to move this swing into storage when the snow flies, but how I love autumn. Look at all these colors."

"*Mamm*," Becca blurted. "I don't want to move."

Maryann turned to Becca who just plopped down very close to her, and that bond they'd always shared seemed to reappear in no time. "Becca, you don't have to wed anytime soon," she dared to say.

"I think I made a mistake," she said, leaning her head on her *mamm's* shoulder. "Gilbert hurt me and I ran to Denny because he's so…"

Maryann held her tongue, but wanted to say 'Good looking' and an *Englisher* with no rules.

"Denny listens to me, takes my advice. I do care for him and all he's been through."

Maryann put her arm around Becca's shoulder. "You have a big heart, Becca. Do you think you feel sorry for Denny?"

"I don't know. Doesn't true love want to give all they have? I feel that way about Denny. I want to give him a family and be a wife to him…"

"Fix his problems?" Maryann asked. "Fill the void in his life?"

"*Jah*, I do. He deserves to be happy."

She squeezed her daughter's shoulder. "Let me ask you this. Do you feel anxious about Denny?"

"What do you mean?"

"Well, do you worry about him? Do you feel responsible for his happiness?"

"*Ach, Mamm*, I make him so happy. I care about him."

"Don't try to do God's job," Maryann said, relishing in their mother-daughter bond, feeling free to speak into Becca's life again. "Every person has problems and a void only God can fix."

Becca clenched her hands together and slouched. "I can't break things off with Denny. He may never be Amish. And down the road, if he's Amish, I can see us together, married with lots of *kinner*."

Maryann released Becca, leaning back and gazing up at the towering maple trees, decked in shades of scarlet. *God makes all things beautiful in His time.* She let this scripture roll around in her mind as she waited for words to say. Becca was a woman now and needed to figure some things out on her own or she'd never mature. "I think you need to talk to Denny about all this."

Becca turned, eyes wide "You're not going to tell me what to do?"

Maryann rubbed Becca's back briskly. "I have confidence in you. And you already know what to do, but just need to find the words…"

"Tell him I need time?"

"Do you?"

Becca nodded. "But he's been so verbally abused that he'll feel totally rejected."

"He's finding lots of healing over at Granny and Jeb's, *jah*? You may be surprised that he's not the same Denny that first came to Smicksburg."

Becca nestled back close to her *mamm*. "You really think so?"

"*Jah*," Maryann said, her heart full with motherly love. "I do."

~*~

Lizzie heard a familiar rapping on the door at her cousin's house in Lancaster. *How odd.* Hoping to let all the advice she'd received from the counselor sink in, having the house to herself, she sighed. Solitude was needed to digest all that she was learning, and now a visitor. Her cousin had many friends in the busy life of the Lancaster Amish and she missed the slow pace of her place in Smicksburg.

A familiar knock at the door.

Well, it's rude to ignore someone, Lizzie thought as she moseyed over to the door. *Lord, if it's chatter-box Ida, please give me strength!*

She turned the knob and peeked out the door. Roman! With a bouquet of purple wildflowers wrapped with purple ribbon. Lizzie felt her eyes get puffy as she bit back tears. "Roman," she nearly whispered.

His chin quivered. "Our secret, right? The purple ribbon?"

She flew at him and clung to his neck. "You love me."

He dropped the flowers and cupped her cheeks in his hands. "Lizzie, *jah*, I love you." He drew her lips to his and kissed her. "*Jah*, Lizzie, I've never loved anyone like I love you."

Astonishment dazed her. "Abigail gave you *kinner.*"

He let his forehead rest on hers. "Lizzie, I've had to come to terms that I half-heartedly loved my first wife. I still loved you but you shut me out and I'm so afraid you'll do it again."

She gripped him around the middle. "I came here to get fixed...again."

"What?"

"Remember when I came out here to see the counselor? I faced the assault and stopped blaming you for not seeing my pain?"

Roman's mellow eyes rested on her, patiently waiting for her to go on.

"Well, Roman, I'm barren. And I've felt like a failure as a wife. I've been depressed."

"But, Lizzie, look at Ella. She thought she was barren and she has a *boppli*..."

Lizzie's heart sank at the thought. "But I won't be." She took his hand and led him to the stuffed couch. "I had an exam and I can't have *kinner. Ach*, Roman, I feel like such a mess. I didn't have this condition when I was twenty-one when we were engaged. If I didn't hide the assault from you, we could have had *kinner.*"

Roman bit his lower lip and then kissed her cheek. "You really don't understand, do you?"

"What?" she asked, surprised by the gentle tone in his voice.

"I only need you. I've always only needed you."

She tried to hold his gaze but couldn't and looked away. "How could I be enough? Amish men want a boy."

He took her firmly by the shoulders. "Lizzie, listen to me. I'm not just an Amish man who wants a son. I'm Roman, the man who loved you as a teenager and didn't even think of *kinner*. We belong together, you and me. We're a family whether we have *kinner* or not."

This love from Roman was hard to contain. Was she really enough? The counselor had said she needed to accept love and quit blocking it. To stop trying to be in control but let life in all its beauty unfold naturally.

"Lizzie, do you understand that a love between a man and a woman is the most...awesome thing in the world?"

She smirked. "Awesome? You sound like Denny Boles."

He gripped her hands tightly. "You know my meaning, *jah*? You are my treasure." He reached down and fumbled in his pant pocket to retrieve a white box. "Open this."

She obeyed and saw a beautifully carved rose. "It's beautiful."

Roman took the rose out to reveal that it was really a trinket box. "We're going to start over again. I promise to write little notes in this box to remind you of what a treasure you are."

Lizzie remembered how Melvin had done this for Fannie and had half the men in Smicksburg do it for their wives. Melvin sold these boxes, but Roman had made this one especially for her. Fannie had healed from Melvin's words written in her trinket box. Could she heal from Roman's words?

"Do you like it?"

Lizzie leaned into him and clung tightly. "I'll never run away again. I need you."

He held her head to his chest. "Lizzie, I need...to feel needed by you. I want to protect you. It's my job."

302

So she had a protector in her best friend since a teen. They'd gone down wrong paths but ended up in the right spot. All this was too much to grasp, but in time, she knew she could contain it all if she kept an open heart.

He slipped her prayer *kapp* off and started to unpin her hair and she did what the counselor told her to do. Let life, her lovely life, unfold naturally in all it's beauty.

~*~

Denny jutted out his chin. He listened to Granny, Phil, and Jeb, agreeing to talk to this Joseph man turned Amish dude, but he wasn't going to budge. He was Amish, like Jeb said.

After a few knocks, a petite brown-eyed woman opened the door. So this was the Amish beauty that made Joseph turn Amish. This was like something off television because it was so predictable. This woman was drop-dead gorgeous. But so was Becca....

"Hello, Phil," she said. "And you must be Denny?"

Phil slapped Denny's back. "Yes. I know I just asked yesterday if he could talk to Joseph and I'm sorry for coming without any warning."

"Warning?" She laughed. "No need to make an appointment. Come in."

"*Ya*, gets as dull as tombs around here," a tall, lanky man with light brown hair and short beard said. He put an arm around Katie. "Just teasing."

Katie's face broke into a smile. "That's a line from *Little Women*. Better stay out of your sister's store."

"Why? *Persuasion* by Jane Austen got you...persuaded." Joseph laughed at his own joke and then squeezed Katie tight. "It's part of our story, but I'll spare you all the details."

Katie's cheeks grew crimson and she bumped him with her hip. "This is Denny. He wants to turn Amish and needs some advice." She motioned towards her kitchen table. "Would *yinz* like a cup of coffee?"

"I would," Phil said. "Thanks."

"I don't drink it, *danki*," Denny said.

Joseph sat at the head of the long oak table. "Making fun of the Amish lingo?" he asked Denny.

"*Nee*. I mean no. I just hear it all the time over at Granny's and picked it up." Denny noticed a smirk on Joseph's face. "You did it, too, huh?"

"*Jah, vell,* I made Katie *furhoodled* at times, mixing Pittsburghese and Dutch," he looked over at Katie and laughed. "*Aber sie mag meinen sag sinn fur humor.*"

"What?" Denny gasped.

"*Aber sie mag meinen sag sinn fur humor.*"

"You sin for humor?" Denny frowned. "That makes no sense."

"You my boy need to learn German, *jah?*"

Denny arched his back and yawned. "*Jah*, I suppose. But I've passed all the other tests. The outhouse and cold shower."

"Cold shower? Amish don't take cold showers." Joseph looked wryly over at Phil. "Did Jeb or Roman do that prank?"

"Prank?" Denny barked.

The room echoed in laughter and Denny soon joined them. "I got them back."

"How?" Joseph asked in anticipation.

"That's for me to know and them to find out...when they fall for it."

Katie served coffee and homemade donuts and took a seat. "So, Denny, what questions do you have for Joseph?"

"None, really. Pastor Phil's the one who...asked me to come over here."

"Well," Joseph said. "You said you've passed all those tests Jeb and Roman put you through, but have you done the Jeremiah 6:16 test?"

"It's painful and long," Katie added.

Denny's brows furrowed. "Jeb gave me lots of things to read and all, but I've never heard of that."

Joseph nimbly got up to retrieve his Bible near the woodstove. "Had to start a fire this morning. It'll be a cold winter." He riffled the pages of his Bible and then pointed to a passage. "Read the highlighted part," he said as he placed the book on the table in front of Denny.

Denny cleared his throat and read:

Stand at the crossroads and look;
ask for the ancient paths,
ask where the good way is, and walk in it,
and you will find rest for your souls.

"Ancient," Denny repeated. "The Amish do act ancient…"

Katie burst into laughter. "*Jah*, we do, but you're missing the point. You can't become Amish quickly. Joseph waited, 'stood at the crossroads,' and wouldn't become Amish until he knew the Lord led him. He didn't turn Amish for me."

"Why not?" Denny said abruptly. "Don't people convert for love?"

"I put God first, before Katie. If I did it the other way around, it would be idolatry."

Phil said an 'amen' but Denny thought what Joseph said was ridiculous. "You didn't bow down to her did you?"

Joseph took a swig of coffee and bit into a donut. "No, I only do that when I want homemade donuts." He blew Katie a kiss and she pursed her lips, hiding a smile. "Denny, my man, an idol is something or someone you put in front of God. When I met Katie, I was in love. I mean, I was a goner. But I didn't have peace after that."

"Why not? If you were in love, weren't you happy?"

"Well, Katie was Amish and I had no intention of converting. We called it our Dilemma but worked through it. Here's how it played out. God doesn't lead where he can't keep you. I needed to know deep down that God planned for me to be Amish because then I'd know he'd give me the strength to remain Amish. God doesn't lead us down the road to failure. So, I stood at the crossroads and waited, like the Bible says, and looked for God's way for my life. And it took time. Broke things off with Katie. It was tough."

Denny felt that all too familiar fear that kept crouching up lately. "I know what you mean. I don't know if I have what it takes to stay Amish."

Joseph's countenance grew grave. "You can do lots of damage to the woman you marry. If you leave after baptism, she'll shun you. You'll have to eat at a different table from her and your kids."

"What?"

"Yes, and you should be shunned. I finally believed that. You made a vow to God, your future wife and kids to raise them Amish. That's breaking a lot of vows and it's not right."

"*Jah*," Katie added. "You better be sure it's God wanting you to be Amish because it takes a lot of faith."

"Faith?"

"*Jah*, and patience only God can give. Living in a community is hard, very hard. We all live near each other for a reason. If we see someone straying or having some bad behavior, they have to answer to us. We keep each other on the straight and narrow."

"But at Jeb and Granny's, no ones always correcting someone."

"*Really?*" Phil asked. "I can tell you for a fact that they do have differences and work them out."

"It's behind closed doors, unless you outright sin and need to apologize to the whole *Gmay*," Joseph said. "But the people are forgiving."

"Oh," Denny could only offer.

Phil sipped his coffee. "I think Denny has some things to think about and I have an appointment in half an hour." He turned to Denny. "Was this helpful?"

"No," Denny blurted.

"What?" Phil asked, surprised.

"Now I'm more confused than ever."

"Oh," Joseph said. "That's a good thing. You've come to a crisis of belief and it leads you to your knees. Seek God. That's a good thing."

Phil extended a hand to Joseph as he got up. "Thanks. We should hang out sometime."

"Come help pick apples. I'm stuck here for the season."

Denny only heard Joseph say 'stuck' and it only made a pit lodge into his stomach.

~*~

Lizzie smirked. "Where you naughty when I was away? Why all this attention?"

Roman placed a tray full of pancakes with a tiny mason jar containing maple syrup on the bed beside her. He touched her face. "*Nee, Daed* and Denny didn't get me into many scrapes. Well, at least any you'd want to take a switch to my behind for."

Lizzie's heart smiled. "*Gut.*" She noticed the sunbeams dance on the wooden floor of her room, and knowing how to tell the time by the sun's position, she gasped.

"Roman, the girls need to get ready for school. It's eight o'clock. *Ach*, I slept in."

Roman placed the tray on her lap. "Eat up. You have a busy day ahead."

She blinked, wondering if she was in a dream. "*Nee*, I don't have more to do than any other day. Are you nudging me along to can more? I'm doing that with Granny today."

"After school's done. You're behind, you know."

The mirth in Roman's eyes enchanted her. He was like a little boy at times, eager to reveal a present or some blessed news. "Roman, what's going on?"

"Okay, girls, come in," he commanded, and soon Jenny, Millie and Tillie ran in, each taking a place on the bed.

"*Mamm, Daed's* letting us be homeschooled. Sabrina Hostetler's such a crank," Jenny exclaimed. "She hit Tillie's hand."

"With a ruler?" Lizzie felt anger rise as fast as a rabbit jumped into its hole when chased. "Tillie, are you all right?"

Tillie's tender eyes held shame. "I asked too many questions."

"But that's how you learn, *jah*?" Lizzie gripped the tray, losing her appetite. "I'll be having words with Sabrina Hostetler."

"I already did," Roman said, "and she can bark louder than Jack. Her face contorted like this." Roman scrunched up his face, making an exaggerated frown and turned up nose and the girls all giggled.

Lizzie took in the scene. These precious ones were in her keeping. She wasn't their biological *mamm*, but the bond between them was closer than many families. The stories Marge told her about new candidates for Arbor

Creek, an orphanage of sorts for unwanted *kinner* or ones at risk of being hurt by their own parents, made her rethink parenting and family. It seemed to her that a family was a real family when held together by love. This love for the girls and Roman came from above, she was certain. God must have planned this all out. She could focus on these dear girls who lost their *mamm* so young. Emotions overtook her and she reached out for the girls. "I love you all so much."

The girls would have piled on Lizzie if their *daed* hadn't made a protective barrier with his muscular arms. "Hold on now." He took the tray from Lizzie and then smirked. "Now you can all hug like girls."

Lizzie laughed, knowing Roman was annoyed at times that Marge always hugged her in greeting and Angelina, Granny's elderly friend, kissed both sides of her cheek and then hugged tight, the Italian way. Lizzie kissed each girl on the cheek. "You girls are my treasures, a gift from God." She eyed each one. "Want to go on a nature walk later today? We can collect and catalogue all the autumn leaves."

"Yay!" shouted Millie. "No more being cooped up in school! Everyday's an outside day."

"Hold on," Roman warned. "Today is an outside day for a wee bit, but you have lessons to learn. *Mamm* has the books and will need to make up for lost time and she also has knitting circle this afternoon."

A round of groans echoed off the white walls and Lizzie realized Roman was right. She best get up and plan lessons. She'd need to see what they'd learned over the past month. Joy enveloped her. To be with the girls, to nurture their minds, was so fulfilling to her. Reading *Anne of Green Gables*, she had to fight off envy as Anne got to be a school teacher in a one-room schoolhouse like their own. And then a thought overtook her. "Roman, I think Sabrina needs to be fired. You're on the school board."

"What? She just started."

"I know, but she'd never been fit for the job. People just pitied her loneliness, but it's of her own making. No one wants to get close to a prickly rose bush; she's a wild rose bush at that."

"What are you suggesting, Lizzie?" Roman asked evenly, arms now crossed.

"How about I become the teacher? I love *kinner* so much. Maybe it's why I wanted to adopt. Maybe being a teacher is my gift."

The girls all squealed with delight. "*Jah*," Jenny said. "That would be best. I'd miss my friends."

"You can see them after school," Roman said, "and you go to school to learn, *jah*?"

Lizzie saw stress marks on Roman's forehead and she chided herself for being so outspoken, getting the girls hopes up. "Your *daed* is right. You see your friends and we can learn outside as much as we want." She lifted the tray of untouched pancakes to Roman. "Lets all go down to the kitchen and eat together…*as a family*.

Roman pat her shoulder. "*Jah*, and that's what we are, for sure and certain. And I'll talk at the school board meeting next week. Other parents are complaining as well."

Lizzie wanted to pull Roman close but instead slipped out of bed and followed *her* family downstairs to eat. How her heart skipped with delight.

~*~

Granny bit her lower lip as she and Jeb pulled into Angelina's driveway. She leaned toward Jeb. "I don't know what to say."

"You? Deborah, you'll do just fine. Just being a friend is a big help."

"Jeb, this one is too close to my own…fear. My greatest fear: being in Angelina's shoes someday."

Jeb put an arm around her and kissed her head. "On the day I leave for glory, God will lift you up. And the same for me, if you go first. It's hard to fathom, but we'd survive somehow."

"I want us to go at the same time," Granny crowed. "It's possible, you know."

"Now, Deborah, settle yourself. Fears of tomorrow will rob us of this moment and we need to be strong for Angelina."

Granny shot up a prayer for strength as Jeb got out and tied the horse to a fencepost. She also knew gratitude chased fear and self-pity away so she started to list mentally all she was grateful for: a husband who was helping a woman-friend of hers who wasn't Amish, a husband who'd become flexible enough to accept all her *English* knitting friends, a husband who bought tickets to Montana to visit their *kinner* in a month. *Ach*, she was grateful for Jeb in so many ways and fear gripped her that she'd be a widow someday.

But what if she was? She'd have to start now doing unto others as she'd want done unto her, like the Good Book said. What could she do for Angelina though?

Jeb took her hand and half pulled her out of the buggy. "You're rigid as a stone. Love, don't be so nervous."

She inhaled the scent of dry cornstalks and damp earth. "Okay. I'll try."

Hand in hand they walked to Angelina's front door and knocked. It felt odd to use a front door and knock as the Amish walked in through backdoors. Loud talking startled Granny and she wondered who on earth was yelling at poor Angelina.

A middle-aged man with dark features opened the door and a broad smile broke open his face. "Welcome. You must be the Weavers."

"*Jah*," Jeb offered. "And you are?"

"I'm Angelina's son, Silvano. I hopped on a bus last night from Toronto to be with my mama."

"Real sorry for the loss of your *daed*," Jeb said.

Granny tried but failed to hold her tongue. "Why all the yelling?"

Silvano pat his chest. "Yelling? Who's yelling?"

"You were," Jeb accused.

Silvano's eyes darted from Granny to Jeb and then back to Granny, and then he chuckled. "Italians talk loud. At least we do. Mama and I are talking about funeral arrangements and the man at the funeral home is cheating Mama. My papa loved cherry wood, but there's a less expensive one that's just as good."

"Cherry wood's expensive for sure," Jeb said. "I work with wood and...my son and I could make you a right nice cherry coffin for next to nothing."

Silvano's eyes were round as a barrel. "Is it legal?"

Jeb took off his black wool hat and scratched his head. "We use them."

"Don't you have your own laws though?"

"Well, in some things, but we have to abide by the laws of the land. My son in Ohio makes caskets."

"Do they look like, well, a nice coffin though or just a pine box with nails showing?"

"We don't live in Colonial American times," Jeb said, annoyance clearly heard in his voice.

Silvano put up a hand. "I've never talked to an Amish person in my entire life. I didn't mean to offend, but I thought you really did live like long ago."

Jeb straightened. "Well, we do and it keeps things simple. But we're not against a nice looking piece of furniture or a nice polished casket, brass handles and all."

Angelina peeked out from around her son. "Deborah, so *gooda* to see my friend." She slapped Silvano. "Where be you manners? Ask them into *mia casa*."

Silvano put an arm around his mother. "I'm sorry. She's right. Come on in."

Angelina took Granny's hand and whisked her away swiftly into her kitchen, Angelina's haven. The smell of tomato sauce wafted through the air and Angelina ran to a pot on the stove. "I almost burn." Turning off the stove, she turned to Granny. "My son, he mean good, but he treat me like child." She poured a cup of coffee and motioned for Granny to take a seat at her little table. "Silvano say I need spend money on flowers. Fresh flowers and I say we have fall flowers out in the fields for free. The flower shop want hundred dollar or more for one bouquet. That's *isa* crazy."

"*Jah*, it is. When do you need flowers by? When's the funeral?"

"Never if Silvano and I stop this spending. I no rich lady."

Granny knew the talents her knitting friends possessed. They'd arranged quilt squares to balance color, why not flowers? "Angelina, you leave it up to me for the flowers. Jeb and Roman can make a casket in cherry wood in three days, I'm sure."

Angelina's eyes moistened and her gaze drifted upward. "He raise from the dead on day three." Her shoulders slouched and she waddled over to her stove again. "All my children, they come here and I need so much food."

"How many?" Granny asked.

Angelina tilted her head while raising up fingers. "Two hundred? I don't know these things. Everyone need the plane ticket and get time off their jobs."

Granny noticed the quiver in Angelina's voice. She was in deep mourning but not able to grieve like she should. Granny got up and embraced her Italian friend. "Tears can cleanse a body. I call them cleansing tears. Let me help you."

Angelina gripped Granny tight and let out a wail, sobbing and saying over and over, "I no see the signs. Heart attack, I just no see."

Granny held her close and asked the Lord of all comfort to be with her friend this very moment. Jeb was right. What Angelina needed was someone to just listen and be there. Someone who was strong so they could be leaned on and she was thankful that Jeb insisted she come, not letting fear rob her of reaching out to others who were now widows. Widow left such a bitter taste in her mouth while saying it, but not everything in life was sweet.

~*~

Suzy stuffed her *Denim Jean Blue* yarn into her tote as a reminder that she had to go straight from Granny's circle over to Elyse's house to give one-on-one advanced knitting classes. The woman had that same dreadful phobia of leaving her house as she suspected Mona still battled, the only difference was that Elyse was pleasant and Mona still...moaned.

Suzy sat behind her desk and stared at the walls full of yarn. Every nook and cranny was filled, displays in the middle of her little shop creating a circle for the many customers who came in to browse. *Her very tiny shop!* Although customers raved about it, she had a dream of expanding it triple the size, and raise her own alpaca and sheep so her yarn was fresh for the sheering.

Lord, here I am moaning again about the size of this shop. Nothing like pointing the finger and three are pointed back at you. I see moaning in Mona...

The little gold bell on the door jingled and in popped her best friend, Ginny Rowland, short brown wispy hair fluttering as she jumped up and down with a paper above her head. "Suzy, guess what!"

"You have a book order for a million bucks?"

Ginny animatedly lowered the paper and ran to Suzy's side. "What's the matter?"

"Nothing."

"Oh, I know you. Tell me. What's wrong?" She plopped into the chair for visitors near the desk. "*Joseph.* Did my brother make things worse with Denny?"

"What are you talking about?"

"Phil took Denny over to talk to Joseph about turning Amish. I think Phil wants to scare him back into Arbor Creek or at least slow down a bit."

"I didn't even know. Phil does what he thinks is best."

Ginny leaned an elbow on the desk to prop up her head. "Tell me what's wrong."

Slouching, Suzy twisted her mouth up, refusing to complain. "Just thinking."

"About what?"

Suzy counted to ten mentally and then sighed. "A sheep and alpaca farm with a huge shop."

Ginny's brows knit together. "I tell you all the time how people crave cozy, small places, like my store. It's not much bigger than this, and —"

"It's twice the size," Suzy corrected.

Ginny glanced around the room. "Maybe, but it's not one of the big brick and mortar stores. And the women come in here and –"

"Men come in too. There are men knitters and crocheters."

Ginny's eyes widened. "Okay, I see a man every once in a blue moon come in here, but remember, your knitting circles and lessons are on the porch, and I see women. Now, like I was saying, women need a haven. Someplace small where they can get to know the owner. There are some women out there who don't have a single bosom friend, can you believe it?"

Suzy knew this, but she still hankered for the store of her dreams.

"Just the other day," Ginny continued, "a woman came in and told me that she could forgive her husband for his 'transgressions' because of a book she read from my store, then broke into tears. I hugged the woman and prayed with her and we struck up a friendship. We're having coffee in Indiana next week to talk further. That, my friend, happened because my store helped people open up, just like a book." She scrunched her lips to one side. "That was corny, huh? Open up like a book in a bookstore."

Suzy couldn't help herself and burst into laughter. "Yes, that was corny, but thanks for trying to cheer me up. You really think women wouldn't come to a big yarn store?"

"I know it. I direct customers over to your place just to feel the ambiance. 'It's so lovely' is what they always tell me."

"I do hear that a lot…"

"And, Suzy, you know how crazy I am about visiting my relatives in Italy. Their stores are half this size. They make fun of Americans because everything has to be so big. They call a half cup of coffee Café Americana."

"A half cup of coffee?" Suzy wasn't sure if she heard this right.

"Yes, it's only four ounces, but it's huge to them. Hello, it's me, Ginny. The one who sold her big house to our church to live on top of my bookstore. Yes, smaller is much better."

Suzy's heart softened into a puddle and she reached for Ginny's hand. "Thanks. You always have a way of helping me see things from the sunny side of life. You're my Pollyanna."

Ginny grinned. "You know I see both sides of the coin: the good and bad but channel my energy into changing what I can. That Serenity Prayer really did me a world of good." She grabbed the paper and gasped. "I almost forgot to tell you. I had to run it off to show you. You'll never believe this."

"Slow down. Who's it from?"

"Janice. It's top secret church business, but you can know."

"Janice emails me everyday. I haven't' gone online yet. I'll check it later."

Ginny darted up. "I want to see your face. Here, read this."

Suzy took the offered white paper and read over the one liner. Her heart soared immediately and she ran around the desk and took Ginny's hands and they jumped up and down until Ginny knocked over a mannequin and they doubled over laughing.

"Do… not tell…a soul," Ginny said, in-between laughs.

"Cross my heart," Suzy said, and then raised her hands. "Hallelujah!"

Ginny grabbed her by the shoulders and looked severe. "Remember, top secret church news." But a smile soon slid across Ginny's face and she started to jump again. "Can you believe this?"

~*~

Granny motioned for Angelina to sit in her most comfortable rocker, one with cushy pads and armrests. "The girls will be here any minute."

"I should be at the home," Angelina said, looking trapped.

"Now, you need to rest. Jeb and Silvano are just out in the woodshop looking over designs for the coffin. If you want to leave, I'll just go back and get your son, *jah?*"

"I *capisco*," Angelina said. "Silvano, he good boy."

Lizzie skipped across the lawn, ran up the steps and kissed Granny on the cheek. "*Ach, Mamm,* I've had the best day."

"I'm sure the girls had a better day being out of Sabrina Hoffstettler's classroom. Something needs to be done and right quick."

"I know, but in the meantime, I'm homeschooling again. *Ach,* it's so fulfilling. The girls had a nature walk and I found some teachable moments along the way. Those special times when learning is caught, not taught, or something like that. Read it in a teacher's book."

"You make the good teacher," Angelina said.

Lizzie spun around. "*Ach,* Angelina, I didn't see you." She ran to take a chair next to her. "I'm so sorry for your loss."

Angelina put her head down and began to wrung her hands. "I so stupid I no see signs."

Granny crossed the porch to be near her dear friend. "Now, Angelina, stop being so hard on yourself. It was his time to go. We can't question God on that."

"Why not? I ask the question all day. Why no question?"

Granny scolded herself. Of course Angelina was in grief and her mind was swaying like dried cornstalks. "You're right. Being in a dark valley makes it hard to see, *jah*? We can't understand right now, but in time…"

"I lost my *mamm* when I was a teen," Lizzie offered. "Time does heal."

"I almost dead. I old woman. I go soon, too, and that be good."

Granny took Angelina's hand. "And until you go, you will be a grandma to many in California or Toronto. Have you decided where you want to go?"

Angelina's chin quivered and then looked forlornly at Granny. "I want to stay here."

Stay here? In my house? Granny found it hard to breathe and gasped for air.

"You want to stay in Smicksburg?" Lizzie asked. "You like it here?"

"Yes, I like the small town. My house for sale because my children think we, now me, too old to live on own. Now it just me and they right." She leaned over and wept and Lizzie hugged her from behind, lending comfort.

Granny, ashamed of herself for thinking Angelina meant to live at her house, collected herself and went into her kitchen, letting Lizzie comfort her Italian friend. She'd spent hours with Angelina, hardly understanding her broken English, and was mentally exhausted. She opened the icebox to retrieve the stack of cookies she'd made for circle, but when seeing an empty plate she clenched her hands into fists. *Denny Boles. You ate them all?* Wanting to go back to the woodshop to give Denny an earful but lacking energy, she moseyed out on the porch.

319

"Angelina, can I serve the bread tin full of Italian cookies you gave me to my circle friends?"

Angelina leaned forward, brows furrowed. "They're for eating. Why not?"

"All right then. Lizzie, can you get them out of her son's car? It's in a large tin that's too heavy for me to lift."

Lizzie obeyed and Granny was ever so thankful to have Lizzie next door. The girl she'd loved since birth had become nigh a stranger over the past few months, mood swings like flapping laundry, but the vacation had done her *gut* and she was her old self: sweet, kind and her ever-faithful daughter-in-law. *Danki, Lord, for Lizzie. Bless her.*

Jack sprang off the porch and barked the whole time he dashed down the driveway. Soon a line of buggies and cars were in a procession to her house. *And Lord, danki for my knitting friends.*

One by one the horses were hitched and cars came to a halt and women hugged each other and chattered. Granny made a fleeting look over at Angelina and wondered if she'd done the right thing. *Like one who takes away a garment in cold weather, And like vinegar on soda, Is one who sings songs to a heavy heart.* This scripture ran through Granny's mind and she knew the worst place for Angelina was to be among happy people. She'd just lost her husband. *Why was she being so furhoodled?* Granny ran over to Angelina. "Would you like for me to get your son?"

Angelina cocked her head back. "I just get here."

"Well, my girls can be...well...happy."

"I hope so," Angelina said with a glint in her eyes. "It no bother me. They young and no see too much sorrow yet."

Granny sighed in relief and sat next to her dear friend, the girls one by one coming over to give their condolences or meet her for the first time. Angelina seemed to be lifted by Granny's circle of friends and her heart swelled. *We do need each other*, she thought.

Lizzie yelled for Granny from the car. "I don't see a tin in here." She shifted then planted both hands on her hips. "The men took them."

"*Ach*, I cannot believe how much men can eat," Granny cried out.

"*Mamm*," Lizzie continued. "I have some apples rolls at my house. I'll get two and be right over.

Again Granny gave thanks for Lizzie. *What would our lives be like without her?*

Out of the corner of her eye Granny spotted a lone buggy coming down the driveway and Granny squinted to see who it was. *Colleen!* She'd come back to circle. After being cooped up all summer in her house, helping her new husband recover from a coma, she'd returned. Granny had always called Colleen "Honey Girl" since her dark amber hair and eyes were the color of honey, and she was sweetness itself. Colleen waved vigorously as her buggy neared and soon all the girls ran off the porch to embrace her. Her "Little Women" were so neatly spun together, Granny pondered.

~*~

Ruth sat near Angelina at Circle. "Luke will stop by and do any fixing up around your house."

Angelina nodded a thank you and continued to crochet a cream doily.

"Angelina, can I see what you're making?" Fannie asked. "I've never seen such delicate work."

Angelina held up the ten inch round doily. "It no hard."

"I wouldn't have the patience for that," Becca spouted. "It would take me a year to do that much."

Maryann leaned towards her daughter. "Becca, your *oma* made trim like that to edge pillowcases. They're in the attic. I'll have to get them out."

"You should enjoy using them," Mona said. "Such art wasn't meant to be hidden in an attic. Mice or moths could eat them up right quick."

Fannie peered across the circle at Granny, one eyebrow cocked. Granny knew what that meant. Her *mamm* was becoming irritable again. Well, seeds don't sprout up overnight, but need lots of watering and sunshine. "Mona, I like that color on you. It matches the crimson leaves."

Mona's stern face softened and colored like reddish leaves. "*Danki*, Granny. And you look *gut* in green, like the grass."

"How come Amish wear no *pasta* colors?" Angelina asked.

The circle stared at Angelina and then looked blankly at Granny to interpret. *Pasta?* Granny sifted *pasta* and *colors* swiftly through her mind and soon said, "*Pastel* colors. Angelina, some Amish do wear pastels, but our group wears darker colors."

"Lottie wears mint," Colleen said. "She looks so pretty in pastels. Granny, why can't we wear pastels?"

"Well, it's something we can bring up in April during the vote. When we can add or change the *Ordnung*."

Angelina placed her doily in her lap. "I wear black for a year to show grief."

"Really?" Lizzie asked. "Some Amish do that, but I never knew a...someone not Amish did it."

"In the Old Country, in Italy, we wear the black all year. We also hang the wreath on the door to show mourning. I no understand why American's put wreaths on doors when no one dead."

"It's for a decoration," Marge said. "I love hanging up my fall wreath. It has tiny pumpkins in it. So cute."

Granny knew Suzy decorated her whole porch and sidewalk for autumn and she thought it lovely. "Suzy, where do you store all those autumn decorations?"

Suzy looked up pensively from her embroidery. "You think my store's too small?"

"*Ach, nee,*" Granny said. "Why would you think that? You know I like small. Look at my house."

Suzy sighed. "I'm sorry. I just feel like I need to expand somehow."

"Never," Colleen said, hand on her heart. "I agree with Granny. Small places make us closer. You know, it forces us to interact. I don't like big stores anymore."

"You've been so cooped up all summer," Mona stated, "and you need to get out more. I did, going the whole way up to New York. Don't let fear make you a prisoner to your home."

Again, Fannie shot a look over to Granny, a cry for help. But Angelina intervened. "I have no fear of going out. I never have car in Old Country. We walk to the church and market. We stop and talk. I miss. Americans, they have no communism."

Communism? Granny shot this through her mind again and said, "Community. Communism is not so *gut, jah?*"

Angelina grinned. "I get the words mixed. No. No communism, community."

Suzy got up to take a slice of the apple roll that Lizzie had brought to circle. "So, what you're all saying is that you think tiny is good."

"Well," Maryann said, "I have eight *kinner* and it's not *gut* for me, but Michael and I will go into a small *dawdyhaus* like Granny's when the kids have all married and grown."

"What about big churches?" Suzy asked. "Do you think that's not good for community?"

Granny noticed a lilt in Suzy's voice and understood the meaning behind the words. "Your church has doubled since Phil Darby has come, *jah*? And it concerns you."

Suzy puffed her cheeks out and then exhaled. "I cannot tell anyone, and I'm ready to just explode. Granny, you see right through me."

"I do not. I don't understand why you're so excited."

Marge cocked her head back. "Suzy, I'm a church member. Is there something I should know?"

"I can't tell a soul."

Marge huffed. "Must be for the frozen chosen."

Lizzie gasped. "Marge, I can't believe you said that."

Granny nodded. "There's plenty Jeb and I know, him being bishop, that's confidential."

"I run Arbor Creek, though. If it concerns the boys, I should know," Marge defended.

Suzy rolled her eyes. "It doesn't concern Arbor Creek." She gave a fleeting look at her watch and sprang up. "I need to run over to Elyse's for a knitting class."

"So soon?" Granny asked. "I wanted to share something with you all."

Suzy put her bag of denim colored yarn on her lap. "I have a few minutes."

"Well, you all know that Jeb and I are going up to Montana in November."

"Now that will be one long train trip," Mona blurted.

"*Jah*," Granny agreed. "And we're staying for three weeks...or more."

Fannie cupped her mouth as tears sprang to her eyes. "You're moving, aren't you? You miss Nathan and

Lottie." Fannie ran across the circle and knelt down before Granny. "You can't. You're like a *mamm*."

"I didn't say I was moving."

Fannie leapt onto Granny, embracing her. "*Danki.*"

Angelina again set down her doily. "We all say the good-bye sometime…"

"*Jah*," Ruth said, putting an arm around this dear Italian widow.

Fannie straightened and went back to her chair. "I'm sorry. So emotional."

"That's all right," Granny said. "What I was getting at is that I want the circle to continue while I'm gone. If Jeb and I want to stay a month, we'd like to do that. I believe my 'Little Women' can make a plan for the winter circle."

A round of "*jahs*" and "yeses" ensued. Granny's heart was lifted.

"I can have it over at my place," Lizzie said. "Homeschooling doesn't take all day and the girls can join us."

Maryann gawked. "You took the girls out of school?"

"Roman did," Lizzie said, rather carefree. "It was his decision. Sabrina is not fit to be a teacher."

"She's just a hurting person," Maryann said. "She can't help it."

"Hurt people hurt people," Suzy said and she picked up her yarn tote. "I read that in a book and it's true. The girls are too young to let a hurt person…hurt them."

Lizzie got up and hugged Suzy. "*Danki.* I can't explain it. Roman's mighty upset. He's addressing the school board about her."

Suzy winked. "No problem." She turned to the group. "We can have winter circle at my store since you all think it's big enough. I do have my Jane Austen tea collection. Might buy some Regency tea cups."

"That would be so nice," Colleen said. "You started those Jane Austen teas to hear all my woes. What a mess I'd be if it weren't for you, Suzy. *Danki.*"

Suzy wagged a finger. "You turned Amish but you're still my girl. Say it right. *Thank you.*"

Colleen laughed. "*Thank you,* Suzy."

"Well, my house is big," Mona said. "I can have it at my place."

Silence. A starling crowed from the rows of dry cornstalks left in the fields for pig food in the winter.

"I say we all think about the commitment involved and talk about it another day," Lizzie said, turning the conversation.

"Yes," Marge agreed. "Let's hear all about your trip to Lancaster and the ocean."

Suzy said her good-byes and Lizzie sat back down in her seat. "I love birds more than ever." She turned to Ruth. "I see now why you watch them so much. I don't think I was ever calmer than sitting along the beach, watching eagles with my binoculars. And then Lancaster was splendid. My cousin took *Daed* and me to Lititz to get chocolate and pretzels. Can you imagine living there? A chocolate and pretzel factory in one town?"

"I'd balloon out," Marge quipped. "Can't move there."

"But I did miss Roman and the girls. Some distance made me see things more clearly."

"Like what?" Marge prodded. "Remember, we're BFFs and I haven't even heard about your trip yet."

"Roman came and got me." As she flushed, she fanned her face with her embroidery hoop. "I see now that I'm enough for him, barren and all."

"But you really don't know you're barren," Maryann corrected.

"*Jah*, I do. Dr. Pal ran tests and I am. It made me want to run away. I do that when I'm upset. Cobwebs were cleaned out of my mind though, out there by the ocean, which was *gut*, but when Roman hired a driver to come get me, well, some things are personal, but I just feel so loved."

"Has Roman changed his mind about adopting Charles, too?" Marge asked, eyebrows up, challenging.

"Charles has bonded with Phil Darby and wants to stay at Arbor Creek. Feels really at home there."

Marge gasped. "He does? Oh, I love that boy. So glad."

Lizzie sat back real comfortable-like in her chair and said, "Roman is a *wunderbar* husband. He's real sensitive to how I feel, and if Charles is supposed to be with us down the road, we're open to it. For now, I'm just basking in a *gut* marriage.

Angelina, although through glossed over eyes, smiled. "My husband, he was a good man. I was loved. I lucky. Some women, they be nags and the husband no love. I was loved."

Granny was afraid to move for it might break this beautiful scene before her. Angelina was thinking straight; she did not kill her beloved, and her grief, though fresh, would be healed because she had very little to feel guilty about. How they'd talked about her many adventures as a couple, coming from Italy and her being a seamstress and baker to make extra money during hard times. Angelina now had the balm of a clear conscience, not regrets over words hastily said that could tear down her spouse. And her Lizzie and Roman were like teenagers again, so in love. *Danki, Lord, for you keep us all stitched up.*

~*~

Granny nestled up next to Jeb on the glider after the girls left. "Old man, you know I love you, *jah*?"

He frowned. "Not when it's nigh suppertime and my stomach's growling and whatnot." He nudged her playfully. "*Jah*, I know you love me. Do you know I love you?"

"Every day. And I'm mighty thankful."

He kissed her cheek and rose. "I'm going to put feet to my words. I'm making supper."

"But you aren't a *gut* cook," Granny said.

"It's easy. Just get a jar from the pantry of your stew and heat it up."

Granny laughed. "Well, okay then. Can you make biscuits?

Jeb tapped his foot. "*Nee*, but you have bread. What's the difference?"

Granny chuckled. "Stew and bread is fine."

As Jeb left to "cook," Granny looked over at the big old farmhouse that Roman and Lizzie occupied. *Bless them, Lord. Bless my Lizzie. You give and take away, but bless Your name. Lizzie is barren, but she has three girls who love her as much as Abigail. I'll never understand why Lizzie is denied the joy of giving birth to her own kinner, but you fill in the holes in our lives somehow. Jenny, Millie, and Tillie fill Lizzie's holes so she doesn't know she has one.*

Lord, bless Angelina. Help her make the right choice, whether to move to California or Toronto. Help her during the funeral and danki that Lizzie and the girls are making wildflower arrangements, the yellow in golden rod and the hues of purple in chicory will look lovely.

Ach, Lord, I was so happy to see Colleen, my Honey Girl, I nearly jumped for joy. Bless her for her dedication to her husband, sacrificing her summer to help with his rehabilitation. That he's whole again is of your doing, but he needed the care of his wife. Bless Colleen, Lord.

Lord, I see Mona regressing into her pessimistic self. I see pain in Fannie. She was so tearful today. Hold her tight. Give Mona a thirst for your Holy Scriptures that clean us out, rooting out bad thinking. You give us good news in the Bible, not bad. And if Mona's going through some trial, help her to open up and get help. Help her to be humble enough to know she needs others.

I ask all this in Jesus name,

Amen

Dear Readers,

I also brought a characters from my first book, *Knit Together,* into this series (It is a small town; the they tend to bump into each other) *Knit Together: Amish Knitting Novel* tells the story of Joseph, a homeless man suffering from Post Traumatic Stress Disorder due to 9/11 and he reconnects with Ginny Rowland, his sister. This book tells the story of Ginny and husband James selling their house to the Baptist Church to create Forget-Me-Not Manor, a refuge for homeless moms. So much can be learned about the Amish faith and beliefs in this book, too, since Joseph converts to be Amish. Much research was put into this book and it would benefit you to read it to dig deeper.

As always, I leave you with the recipe of the dessert served at the circle:

Apple Roll

1/3 c. milk
½ tsp. salt
1 egg
2 c. flour
2 Tbsp. sugar
4 tsp. baking powder

3 Tbsp. melted cooled butter

Cinnamon

Brown sugar

4-6 apples diced and chopped

Mix milk, salt, egg, flour, sugar, baking soda and butter in a bowl to make dough. Roll out and spread with butter. Sprinkle with cinnamon, brown sugar. Place apples evenly on dough and make into a roll. Put in loaf pan. Puncture dough into "slices" and pour syrup over the top. Bake at 400 degrees for 45 minutes or until golden brown.

Syrup

1 Tbsp. flour

1 ½ c. sugar

½ tsp. salt

1 c. boiling water

1 Tbsp. butter

Mix all ingredients in sauce pan and bring to a boil.

EPISODE 8

Spinning Out

Granny tilted her morning coffee to her lips and she felt its warmth go down into her cold feet. "*Ach*, Jeb, nothing like coffee when there's a chill outside."

"*Jah*. We expect the seasons to change but get our fill of each here in Smicksburg, so they still come by surprise. Can't remember last fall, much, can you?"

"*Jah*, I can. You were brooding over me wanting to have a knitting and reading circle combined...reading classics."

Jeb chuckled. "And you started with *Pride and Prejudice*, your favorite."

Granny smiled. "I have many favorites now. MJ's library has all those Amish fiction books in it and I have to admit, some are *gut*. And Lottie has many books, too."

Jeb pat the gardening magazines on the table. "Well, I'll stick to 'true' books. So, we have a few hundred dollars to replant, *jah*?"

"*Jah*. The State Quilt fetched a *gut* price. The girls all said they wanted us to have a grape arbor and some fruit trees, so we'll need to wait until spring to plant. Best keep that money aside."

He put an arm around her. "Deborah, remember when I asked you to be my wife?"

"*Jah*, but what's that got to do with planting trees?"

"The smell of pines always takes me back…."

Granny nudged him gently. "Old man, as you age your long term memory improves. Everything takes you back."

"*Nee*," he protested. "When I smell pines, I feel young. Like I was in the one-room school house helping you decorate it real fancy-like."

"*Ach*, Jeb. It was a relief that you weren't the stick in the mud I assumed. You thought I was a liberal Amish woman for putting up red candles." Granny chuckled, thinking back to when Jeb came into where she was teaching, all shy and backwards, ruled by the strict *Swartzentruber* Amish, thinking even planting flowers was too fancy. "So, you want to buy pines to make you feel young?"

"Well, the wind whips down the hill and I thought a row could make a windbreak."

"But we always donate to Arbor Day and get some pines real cheap."

"Well, how about cedars?" He took her hand and kissed it. "Come on. Meet me halfway."

She looked up into his loving turquoise eyes. "Of course. If you need to feel younger." Granny winked.

She heard thunderous stomping descending down the steps and soon Denny was seen, not in Amish clothes. "Denny Boles. You have on blue jeans."

Sheepishly, Denny took a seat at the table across from Granny and Jeb. "It's my final decision and I have to stick by it."

Jeb nodded. "Not *gut* to be double-minded. But you're young and always can come back here, *jah*?"

Denny bit his lower lip. "I don't want to leave."

Granny held her hand over her heart. "Then don't. You can go to *English* school and live here. You're like our son, remember?"

Denny swiped at a runaway tear. "I think. I think that....I like Phil Darby and the other guys over at Arbor Creek. I like toilets that flush and driving cars and all."

Granny reached across the table and he took her hand. "Denny, that's not family."

Jeb placed his hand over theirs. "Deborah, like I said, he's young and can always come back here in a few years."

Granny gulped and bit back tears. "So, what grade will you be attending?"

"Twelfth. Can you believe it? I almost passed my GED and am only taking the classes I need to graduate. Nothing too complicated." He squeezed her hand. "So, maybe I'll be back here next year as a graduate and...be Amish or go on to college. It's in God's hands."

Jeb released their hands and flapped his arms in the air. "Hallelujah. You've given over the horse's reigns to the Lord."

Granny poked Jeb in the side. "Old man, you're acting like a Baptist."

Denny laughed despite his ever quivering chin and glum eyes. "I guess I finally did give God...the steering wheel of my car." He grinned. "No more buggies for a year, at least."

"Well," Granny said contemplatively, "you've made this summer real special for two old folks."

Denny stared, not flinching. "You really wanted me here? You weren't just saying it?"

"'Course not," Jeb said. "That would be a lie."

Denny folded his hands and then started to crack his knuckles. His Adam's apple jumped up and down and it appeared that choking back tears was painful. Granny stood and ran around the table and hugged him from behind. "We love you, Denny Boles. And don't you ever forget that. When you think everything you do is wrong, or you're not wanted or whatnot, you just know your Amish *mamm* and *daed* love you with all our hearts."

He took her hands and wept.

Jeb came around the table and planted a hand on Denny's back and prayed:

Lord God Almighty,

As our English son goes to school today, lead and guide him, and let him know You're his father who will always be there 'til the end. You're our Comforter, Counselor, Everlasting Father and Prince of Peace. We commit Denny to you and ask you to lead him over these next few years. If it be your will, back to us here in this home, but if not, we know you have a better plan.

Amen.

Denny turned and let Granny and Jeb fall into his arms. Granny never wanted to let this boy go again into the *English* world that had been so cruel, but she kept her mouth clamped shut, and simply said, "Amen."

Denny sniffled and then got up "I need to run out and catch the bus." He hugged Granny and then Jeb. Slapping his back, he made a joke through glossy eyes. "You pray better than the *English...Daed.*

Jeb pulled at his beard. "*Danki,* Son."

Granny tried to breathe evenly as Denny left and then buried her head in Jeb's chest. "Why couldn't we keep him here?"

"He's not ours, Love. He's not ours..."

~*~

Suzy bit a nail and then stomped a foot. "I just can't take the suspense."

Lottie placed the box she'd just received from the UPS man on the floor. "Will you leave your church if Janice isn't there, like you said before?"

Suzy sunk into her desk chair. "I don't think so. Phil's really done a great job. I like him. Great preacher and the church has doubled in size. I'll get all the details tonight. Jerry insisted driving straight to church, not giving Janice the opportunity to blab out the info beforehand." She wrung her hands. "I don't see Jerry being able to handle a church of three-hundred. He'll flip out and leave. I know it."

"So you'll split off into two church districts?"

Suzy frowned. "Why would we do that?" Then Suzy remembered how the Amish only had two-hundred or so people in a church and then broke off into two groups if it got any bigger. "No, we *English* like 'big', big churches included. But I don't. Those mega churches of thousands of people are not for me."

"Thousands? How can the bishop know the needs of a thousand?"

"Well, they have elders and small group meetings, but I'm small town, small church…small store, too, but I'm starting to just accept that. It's cozy in here, right?"

"*Jah,*" Lottie offered.

Suzy noticed Lottie looked pale. "Something wrong, Lottie? Have allergies?"

"*Nee,* why?"

"Well, lots of people have seasonal allergies…and they make you tired. You look tired."

Taking an x-acto knife, Lottie opened the box and started to unload the red yarn on a shelf. "It's Ezekiel. He's been avoiding me."

Suzy knew Lottie was hard to open up at times, like an oyster, but she was getting better. "He's only been home from New York for a week, right?"

"*Jah*, and he has only come by to talk to my cousin. They go off to the beehives and sit and talk, and he avoids me."

Suzy leaned an elbow on her desk. "Do you love him?"

Lottie threw a ball of yarn on the shelf. "*Jah*, I do."

"But not enough, is that it? Not enough to sacrifice?"

Lottie's big azure eyes misted. "*Jah*, I do. But he's ignoring me. I can't just go up and say I'll marry him when he might have...you know."

Suzy glowered "Ezekiel is feeling rejected. Go figure. 'The most incomprehensible thing in the world to a man is a woman who rejects his offer of marriage.'"

Lottie frowned. "What?"

"Oh, that's a Jane Austen quote. Men don't understand why women say no to a marriage proposal. They don't take into consideration that the girl's more attached to her family and doesn't want to move. Men just up and move." Suzy exhaled loudly. "Lottie, can you imagine your life without Ezekiel?"

"*Nee*, I cannot."

"Then tell him. You two together can work out where you live, but the core of your marriage is the two of you. Everything else will fall into place."

Lottie lowered her eyes. "He's been writing to a girl up there. My cousin told me. From what I gather, he's courting her..."

"I'll gather him and throw him in the laundry for a good scrubbing," Suzy snapped. "Are you serious?"

"I don't know," Lottie said almost in a whisper.

Suzy jumped up. "Where does he live? Exact address. I get all these Amish farms mixed up."

"I can't remember the road number. Why do you ask?"

Suzy grabbed a red knit scarf off a display nearby, pulled off the sales tag, and flung it around her neck. "It's nippy out," she reasoned. "And I can use this to strangle Ezekiel Coblenz."

"*Nee*, you can't go over to his place."

Suzy bolted across the room towards Lottie. "Oh, yes I can. You mean a great deal to me. You've become my Anne-Girl." Wrapping her arms around Lottie, she whispered in her ear. "You're like Colleen. Like a daughter."

Lottie hugged Suzy around the middle. "I love you like a *mamm* and I don't want to leave…you. Leave Smicksburg. Granny, Colleen, Ruth, the whole circle."

Suzy pulled her back and eyed her evenly. "I want you happy in the long run. Of course we all want you to be here with us, but imagine your life in twenty years. Granny will be ninety-two and…well, I'll be older."

"*Ach.* I never thought of Granny being so old."

"Or dead," Suzy said, a tinge of pain coloring into her voice. "It's inevitable. We all die sometime." She ran to the front door, flipped over the sign that now would read "Closed" and took Lottie by the hand. "Now, we're going to have words with that Ezekiel Coblenz, understand?"

"*Nee*, we are not. A girl does not pursue a man."

"A man who asks a girl for her hand in marriage waits patiently for an answer, not go off and date someone else. Grab your bonnet. We're going for a ride."

~*~

Granny grabbed Little Bea to avoid a mud puddle on her way back from the mailbox. "So muddy and you won't be messing up my floors," she said. Skimming through the mail, she mentally categorized it into junk mail, pen pals, and Roman's Rocker shop orders. But one marked for Jonas? Return address was Lancaster from a Sarah Peachy?

Granny gripped Bea tighter and nigh skipped to deliver the mail to Jonas. Was this an answer to her prayer? Jeb's, too. She mused. *Jeb is becoming a matchmaker. He wants to see folks happily married, knowing their settlement's well-being relies on strong families.* But thinking back to Jeb calling her "Emma" the matchmaker out of Jane Austen's book made Granny know she'd had a *gut* influence on her dear husband.

As the wind whipped, Granny saw Lizzie fighting to hang laundry as blankets whipped around her, wrapping her up. Putting Bea down, she said, "Lizzie, you look like a cocoon."

Lizzie clung to the line and stuck a clothespin into place. She turned to Granny. "Makes my arms sore. This wind's fighting with me something fierce today." She picked up the empty basket beside her. "Come on in for a second cup of coffee."

"I'd like that. Have some mail for *yinz.*"

"*Ach*, letters? I do love letters."

Granny handed a letter to Lizzie. "This is for your *daed.*"

Lizzie gawked and then held it to her bosom. "Praise be."

"*Gut* news?" Granny prodded. "A relative out in Lancaster?"

"*Nee*," Lizzie was quick to say. "We have no kin named Peachy." She flapped the letter with delight. "This is from *Daed's* friend."

"What?"

"We went to Lancaster after the beach. Well, let me back up. We went to the beach because *Daed* wanted to see it and then go visit Sarah in Lancaster."

"Really?" Granny could hardly believe this. "Is Sarah a sweetheart?"

Lizzie nodded. "I hope so. Well, I believe so. She's young. Only ten years older than me. Has a teenager at home still, but two are married. She's a widow and a real beauty. Her name suits her. Sarah in the Bible was a beauty in her old age and so is Sarah Peachy."

Granny linked arms with Lizzie as they ascended the steps into the house. "Now, Lizzie, being in her forties doesn't make her old."

"She's in her late forties, I believe. Took a real liking to *Daed*. They both read Spurgeon and C.S. Lewis. Both are deep into theology. You should hear Sarah talk. Could be a female preacher."

Granny took a seat at the table. "But we're not Mennonites, having female preachers, *jah*?"

"I did hear that some Mennonite women can be preachers up in Canada, but Sarah is Amish to her core. Lovely woman."

Granny gazed over at the door that led into Jonas' *dawdyhaus* connected to the main farmhouse. "Where is Jonas?"

"*Daed* has a cold. Still in bed."

Granny slouched, wanting to see Jonas's reaction to this letter, but then she scolded herself for being nebby. "Well, Jeb and I have noticed Jonas is lonely. We've been praying for a wife."

Lizzie froze, the speckleware coffeepot in mid-air over a mug. "*Daed*? Lonely?"

"*Jah*. You and Roman and the girls fill up his time, but he's so young. Needs to share the rest of his days with a *gut* wife."

Lizzie poured the coffee and set it on the table in front of Granny. "I don't want to see *Daed* hurt. Like I said, she's a beauty and many men come by to visit. She's the most eligible widow in Lancaster, my cousin said."

Granny tapped the letter Lizzie had placed on the table. "But she wrote to Jonas. And it's thick."

"Maybe she needs someone to talk to about the Bible…"

"Well, didn't Maryann tell Ruth to read the Bible with Luke? It's the glue that holds a marriage together and something that pulls our emotions out, helping us bond?"

A smirk slid across Lizzie's face. "You keep on praying, Granny. *Daed's* talking about a train trip at Christmas to see the lights in Lititz. The Moravian lights."

Granny wanted to clap, but restrained herself. "Lizzie, don't you see? Your *daed* is courting by letters. Visits are planned during the courtship."

With raised eyebrows, Lizzie asked, "Really? Are you sure? Not something you got out of a Jane Austen book? They do write a lot in those books."

"They courted much like we do and how the world has always done it."

Lizzie reached for Granny's hand. "I'd be so happy if *Daed* remarried. But where would we fit them?"

Granny hadn't thought that far. "Well, houses are for sale in Smicksburg, unless they settle out in Lancaster."

"What? I've never been away from *Daed* my whole life," Lizzie blurted, her face contorted. "I know all about his medicine, exercises, braces and whatnot. What does Sarah know about all this?"

Granny pat her hand. "Lizzie, Roman needs you, remember? And the girls, too? You have a family to care for." She hesitated, not sure to reveal what she thought, but then decided she best. "Lizzie, I think your *daed* lacks purpose. Maybe it's why he's so giving to Charles."

"But it's a *gut* thing to be like a *daed* to Charles, don't you think?" Lizzie asked.

"Of course I do. But Jonas may feel like he needs to move on, feeling like an imposition here."

"But the girls love him. He's not in our way, but adds to the family…"

Granny forced a smile. "Just look at us. Borrowing trouble when they may never marry."

"But it would be *wunderbar gut* if he did," Lizzie said slowly. "And the weather is milder in Lancaster. They have closed in buggies, too."

Granny saw the wheels turning in Lizzie's mind and knew how futile it was to try to figure everything out. "Now don't you think too hard on this, Lizzie. It saps you of strength. Things will happen naturally, in the *Gut* Lord's timing."

Lizzie pursed her lips. "The counselor said I need to let life unfold naturally. You're right. We'll just put this all in God's hands and pray for the best outcome."

Granny's heart widened with more love for Lizzie. "I'll miss you when I go up to Montana."

"I'll miss you…. You are coming back, *jah*? I know they'll try to convince you that Montana is better than Smicksburg."

Granny's eyes twinkled. "Better than Smicksburg? *Nee*, nothing's better than Smicksburg."

Lizzie slid the sugar bowl down to Granny. "Need sugar for that coffee? Haven't had a sip."

Granny offered a weak smile. "My mind's churning like butter."

"I saw Denny walking down the driveway with *English* clothes on."

"*Jah*," was all Granny could say.

Lizzie shook her head slowly. "Roman is so much like you. He's blaming himself about Denny, too."

"I don't blame myself," she said. "He's taking things slow and waiting for a year to see if he should turn Amish. He's doing Joseph Hummel's Jeremiah 6:16 test."

"*Jah*. I know. Stand at the crossroads and wait and you'll find peace, or something like that."

"The ancient paths," Granny added. "All these modern problems we have are because we don't stick to the old ways, when right was right and wrong was wrong. Well, the Amish still do."

"Well, I've learned a lot from our *English* friends, especially Marge. I think we can glean a lot from them."

Granny nodded. "*Jah*, we can. The right *English* friends." Granny sipped her coffee and then with cloudy eyes said, "Pray for my Denny. I do love him and there're lots of bad influences out there. My nerves are on edge something fierce."

Lizzie grinned. "Then let's do something fun to beat the stress. How about we ask Marge to drive us to Musser's Nursery?"

"Why?"

"Jeb was over talking to Roman about wanting pine trees. Isn't that odd? We have them all around us."

Granny felt her cheek heat up. *Blushing at seventy-one over a romantic memory over forty years ago.* "Jeb wants a wind break on the north side."

Lizzie sprang up and pulled a little yellow device from her kitchen cupboard. "I'll call Marge."

"A cell phone?"

"*Nee*, a walkie-talkie. Nothing in the *Ordnung* against them, *jah*?"

Ancient paths, Granny thought, need to be reinforced among the ones we least suspect of going too modern.

~*~

Lottie had never been more embarrassed in her whole life. Suzy dragging her around from The Country Junction, The Sampler, and now Jeb Weaver's to find Ezekiel? He wasn't home, as Suzy assumed, and was on a mission to give Ezekiel a piece of her mind.

"It's time for the noon meal," Lottie squealed as Suzy flew down Granny's driveway. "Suzy, slow down. I feel carsick."

"I'm only going twenty miles an hour," Suzy huffed. "You can talk to Granny while I tell Jeb Weaver the behavior of one of his flock."

As they pulled up to the little house, Jack soon greeted them with his huge wagging tail. *Dogs. Animals in general calm me down. Like the cats over at Colleen's.* After shakily getting out of the car while Suzy fiddled with the gear-shift, Lottie went up the steps, opened the door and hugged Jack around the neck. "Hi, boy."

Suzy sprang from the car and flew up the steps, but stopped short. "This is odd. No signs of life anywhere." She rapped on the door, but no answer came. "Lottie, go over to Lizzie's and see if they're over there."

"I'd just rather go back to the store, Suzy. This is embarrassing."

"Why do you keep saying that? Don't Amish women expect more from men? One month they propose, the next month give up. Love is not constant when alterations find," Suzy said as she made her way back to the car. "That's Shakespeare, I think. Anyhow, you need to tell Ezekiel that love isn't fickle. It's steadfast and patient. You didn't say no to his marriage proposal, did you?"

"*Nee*, I did not. But I hesitated and said I needed time. I miss Ohio."

A door squeaked over at Roman's and soon Jonas, with the aid of leg braces, came out onto the porch. "The Weavers went into town. Can I help *yinz*?"

Suzy marched over to Lizzie's and Lottie followed like a baby duckling. "We're looking for Ezekiel Coblenz. Well, I'm looking for him and want to report something to Jeb."

Jonas's merry eyes seemed to be laughing at Suzy's behavior. "Report him? What's his crime?"

Suzy huffed. "Do Amish men lead on women?"

"Come again? What do you mean, lead on?"

"You know, one minute make them think they love them, the next leave them dangling."

Jonas took a seat. "Well, some would, being human and all, but not Ezekiel. He's as steady as they come."

Suzy clenched her fists. "Well, his behavior has been odd, to say the least."

Jonas scratched his black beard. "Need to talk to him, you say?"

"*Jah*. I mean yes," Suzy blundered. "Yes. Where is he?"

"Well," Jonas said. "Lots of men are out in the woods, putting up tree stands and scanning their hunting site for signs of a buck."

"Where does he hunt?" Suzy asked.

"Ezekiel and his *bruder* have lots of land. Can't really say." His eyes twinkled all the more. "Seems like you'll have to be patient and wait. You *English* sure are in a hurry to fix things."

Suzy's brows shot up. "Fix things?"

"*Jah*. Ezekiel will come around when he's ready. Men pursue the womenfolk."

"That's what I said," Lottie said evenly. "Suzy, this is ridiculous. Let's go back to the yarn shop."

Suzy deflated as she slouched and hit her knee with her hand. "I'm sorry. Really. I care about these Amish girls who I mentor like they're my own flesh and blood." She turned to Lottie and took her hand. "Colleen was so hurt and I did fix her problems. Honey, I want to do the same for you, but it seems like Ezekiel just doesn't have my confidence. He doesn't have the character that your cousin Hezekiah has."

"Hold on now," Jonas spoke up, and got up again, leaning over the porch rail. "Now that boy I know. He's as trustworthy as Hezekiah."

"Really?" Suzy asked, meekness resonating in her voice. "I don't understand him then. He proposed marriage to Lottie and since he's gotten back from New York last week, has been ignoring her completely."

"Maybe he's afraid of getting hurt."

"What?" Lottie asked.

"Well, he's had a hard life, one filled with…hurt. His character was made solid in the fire of affliction."

Suzy's eyes rounded and she snapped her fingers. "So he's hiding, isn't he?"

"Why would he hide from me?" Lottie asked before Jonas could speak.

"Well," Jonas interjected, "we can get hurt the most by those we love."

Love for Ezekiel exploded in Lottie's heart. "Suzy, let's go find him."

"But you said this was all ridiculous. You were embarrassed."

Lottie darted to the car. "Never mind what I said. Let's get going."

~*~

Becca, having finished washing supper dishes, swished the soapy water in the basin and then popped a bubble. "*Mamm*, I'm bored."

"Bored? You?" Maryann covered a dish with aluminum foil and slid it into the icebox. "I've never heard you say you're bored before. Maybe you were getting too used to too much excitement being with Denny....and the *English*."

"What do you mean?" Becca challenged, not liking her *mamm's* tone when she mentioned Denny...who was *English*.

"Well, the *English*, not all, but some, are addicted to entertainment and pleasure. They run to the store just to get new outfits and movies. VDV's."

"DVD's, *Mamm*. They have lots over at Arbor Creek and some are *gut*."

Maryann shook her head. "I knew you were watching television over there. You got antsy."

Becca smashed her lips together, not wanting to discuss this any further. She didn't watch television shows with their immoral commercials, but only DVD's that Marge and Joe approved of, and she loved them.

Maryann took a seat at the table. "Becca, you're discontent, *jah*? And the Bible says be content with what you have so you don't covet anything."

Becca, knowing she was going to pop, slowly poured the water down the drain. *Slow down. Measure your words, like Granny said.* "I need to take a walk. Crisp air out there."

"I'll join you."

"*Ach, Mamm*, I need to have a quiet time. You know, walk and talk to God time."

Maryann clasped her hands in satisfaction. "You're turning into such a grown woman, Becca. I'll be thinking

346

about your discontentment. Sometimes we do need a change."

"Really?"

"*Jah.* Now, you go on and take that walk. But please stay out of the woods as hunters are out getting ready for deer season, shooting their guns and all. A bullet can ricochet."

"I know, *Mamm.*" Becca wanted to say she wasn't a child, but grabbed her black knit shawl and headed out the back door. "I'm too old to be here anymore, Lord. I feel like a bird in a cage." She rounded the house and headed towards the road. "Granny said to talk to you like a friend and be honest. Well, I am discontent and I'm not used to it. Maybe it's my age. Maybe it's the excitement over at Arbor Creek, and Denny…*Ach*, Lord, I miss him. We only kissed once on the lips, so I know I don't' miss that, although….although I found great pleasure in it. Kissing on the cheek is for a greeting, but for a mature…love?"

A pale blue car with rusty spots came slowly down the road and she soon made out the driver. She waved vigorously. "Denny!"

As the car slowed to a halt, he flashed a brilliant white smile like a kid in a candy shop. Rolling down the window, he said, "Becca. Hop in. It's my new car."

She ran toward him, laughing. "Doesn't look too new."

"I'll fix her. She's old but I got her cheap. Get in and we'll take a spin."

Should she get in? Kissing doesn't wear out, the Amish always said. What if they found themselves tempted again? "Let's walk in the corn maze. *Daed* made one for the *kinner.*"

He parked the car. "I've never been in one. Saw some signs along the road to an *English* one, but didn't know the Amish had them."

Becca put her hands on her hips and couldn't help but let the smile inside burst forth. "Denny Boles, we have more in common than you think."

He looked down and kicked a stone. "I know." He took her hand and kissed it. "I have to do this, Becca. You know that."

"Be *English*? *Jah*, I know. You're a fancy man."

He gripped her hand tight. "I'm doing a test. Talked to Joseph Hummel, the man who turned Amish. He said I needed to slow down and wait at the crossroads and pray. Not turn Amish for you."

Hand in hand they headed toward one of the openings to the corn maze. "I agree. Denny, I need time, too. You're so handsome and I need to know I'm not infatuated."

He stopped abruptly, yanking her back. "Me, handsome? Are you serious?"

"*Jah*, Denny. I want to love you for the inside, not just the outside."

"Really? I feel the same way. Becca, you could be on a magazine cover." He pulled her close and kissed her on the nose. "You have the cutest nose. And those big brown eyes…" He turned away and then took her hand again. "Joseph and Katie prayed for almost a year to test their love. And Joseph made me see how serious turning Amish is if I get married. You could shun me if I left."

"*Jah*. I could, but don't know if I would."

"What? What are you saying?"

"When I marry, I'll stick with my husband. My marriage vow is until death. I'd see signs of my husband

348

being unhappy, wanting to stray from the Amish and I'd help him stay on the straight and narrow."

"Oh. And you think you could handle a wayward, worldly man like me?"

She neared him and fidgeted with the buttons of his jean jacket. "I don't know, so that's why we'd need to wait and pray."

Denny cupped her cheeks and made her look at him. "Will you wait for me like Katie Byler did for Joseph?"

Becca met his desperate blue eyes. What fear of abandonment they held, and it yanked at her heart. "Denny, Katie almost accepted a marriage proposal from a man in New York after she met Joseph. She didn't think he'd turn Amish and she did care for the other man."

He blinked wildly. "You still care for that Gilbert dude?"

"*Nee.* I'm just saying I don't want to be tied into a secret courting relationship…an understanding between us. Let's just wait and pray and see where we are in a year."

Denny released her and plunged a hand into his jeans, pulling out a white paper. Unfolding it, he read:

"Stand at the crossroads and look;
ask for the ancient paths,
ask where the good way is, and walk in it,
and you will find rest for your souls.

His countenance fell. "Becca, it starts with stand. That means not moving, right? Don't leave me, Becca."

Becca didn't know what overcame her. Was it love or pity, but she blurted out. "I don't think I'm infatuated with you one bit, Denny Boles. I love you. The real love kind of love, so yes, I'll wait." She flew at him, clinging to his neck.

He embraced her and soon his body was shaking. He was crying. "*Danki.* I mean, thank...you. Becca....I know....I love you the right...way. In a year...I think I'll be Amish. But...what if I'm not?"

She put her hands to his cheeks and kissed his forehead. "We'll cross that road together."

He leaned forward to kiss her, eyes eager, but she turned her head. "No kissing for a year. No walks alone for a year. You finish high school."

"And what will you do?"

Becca fumbled. "I don't know. I do need something to keep my mind off of all this." Then an idea that had been mulling around in her mind came to the forefront. Yes, how perfect!

~*~

Suzy sat next to Janice during the Wednesday night church service. She grabbed her hand and observed the contrast in color: black and white. Was she forever seeing colors to dye her yarn? Her skin was more cream colored, really, and Janice was the color of milk chocolate. "I've missed you something fierce. This church isn't the same without you."

Janice's eyebrows arched. "Suzy, Jerry will announce the news as soon as this song's over. Now, we can't gab during worship."

Suzy agreed and looked up at the colorful screen. The words to the song had a swirly border around them and it looked like old parchment paper. *So much better than that old overhead projector,* she thought. *And to think the church teens set it all up.* She glanced over at Phil, who looked mighty grave. "It was nice having him here. So many changes for the better, more up to date everything. When they showed him their flannel graph board they used for Sunday school, he'd insisted on a new DVD player. And so many programs for the teens and small groups were available, why hadn't they done it sooner?

Ginny strummed her guitar's final cord and then looked over at Suzy pensively. *Ginny's as nervous as I am. Lord, help us bear any news. We're staying here. You planted us here in this church and we'll bloom where we're planted, like the kid's story goes.* Was that a flannel board story she'd taught? Well, it stuck.

"Welcome to our Wednesday night Bible Study. Good to be back," Jerry started. "And I see so many new faces. A bon-fire with yummy s'mores will be provided after the service to get acquainted." A smile slid across his face. "Yes, I need to get to know all the new folks at *my* church."

A gasp and then chattering spread across the church and then clapping. Lots of clapping and cheering. Suzy turned to hug Janice and then put two fingers in her mouth to blow out a loud whistle.

Jerry beamed. "Janice and I had a decision to make, but all that glitters isn't gold. Yes, we love the South and I could have popped buttons over the job offer the college gave me, but deep down, Janice and I were in turmoil. In a nutshell, we were homesick and missed Smicksburg. But was it because this little town is cozy and safe and familiar? Change is hard and in your fifties, getting old, it gets harder."

Janice squirmed and then shouted out, "Speak for yourself!"

Laughter erupted and Suzy glanced over at Ginny, but it was Phil who grabbed her attention. He wasn't laughing. *Lord, help Phil move on.*

"Okay, honey, I'm a few years older than you, so I'm the elderly one," Jerry chuckled. "But being homesick wasn't the clincher. It was the emails *yinz* sent. Some of you are going through trials and a shepherd doesn't desert his sheep in their time of need. I felt this very strongly. Then it deepened into something, well, deep. Deep as a rabbit hole...but I won't be hopping off on bunny trails as many of you know I have a tendency to do. No, Janice and I have a sense that there's great need in American cities, but also in rural places. The girls from Forget-Me-Not Manor wrote to Janice faithfully and told her about their friends. Single moms living in poverty. Then Janice went to Pittsburgh with some of the Amish and they saw children in line to the food bank. And this was in the suburbs, not downtown. I believe we have a real army here that can make more of a difference than ever."

Joe yelled from the back a hardy "Amen" and Marge echoed him.

"We have so much work to do, I need help. And we need to put something to the vote. Can we afford an assistant pastor? And can Phil Darby be that pastor?"

Suzy darted her gaze over to Phil, who looked pale. But when the congregation got to their feet and started to clap, tears welled up in his eyes.

"I don't even think we need to have a committee meeting, do we?" Jerry asked.

"No," the church all blurted in unison.

Jerry motioned for Phil to come up to the altar and he hesitated, but then Ginny ran to him and led him up. Phil, with dazed eyes, stood like a statue until Jerry nudged him, giving him the new church microphone.

Phil cleared his throat. "I don't know what to say."

Jerry slapped his back and Phil nearly lost his balance. "Go on. Just tell them you accept the position."

The teens who sat in the back started to clap and shout. Shy Brian Adams stood up and yelled, "Don't leave."

Phil bit his lower lip. "I want to thank you all for this summer. As you know, I lost my mom, and this church, along with some fine Amish people and a shut-in named MJ, helped me see I needed to be more transparent. I don't know who benefited most by being here, you or me."

Suzy clenched Janice's hand again and leaned towards her, whispering, "He's accepted the position, right?"

"Honey," Janice said lowly, "I hope so. I can't believe all these people are here. Three- hundred? Lord have mercy. "

Phil looked over the church. "So, I've grown spiritually and a calling deep down has formed in me. Jerry has included in my job title Youth Pastor, but I said I had to follow my heart, my calling."

A groan waved across the congregation, but Phil put a hand up. "Pastor Jerry agreed. We need a ministry to shut-ins who can't make it here. Small group Bible studies in homes and hospitals. So, I'd be happy to accept this job offer if I can take the teens on short term mission trips once a year, head up small groups, and the church start a decent mercy ministry to the sick and dying." A tear slid down his cheek and he swiped it. "My eyes have been opened to these needs I'd never experienced before. Of course, I'd also oversee Arbor Creek and Forget-Me-Not Manor."

The church erupted into applause and Phil couldn't hold back, but raised both hands in praise. Suzy did too and shouted out a hallelujah. Ginny pointed to the new sound booth and yelled out a song name, strummed her guitar and the whole church sand in unison a song of praise.

~*~

The full moon's glow helped Ezekiel make out his brother's face as they trudged through the woods, their dogs close on the scent of raccoons. "I know. I have to talk to Lottie soon, but the woods calm me."

Samuel slapped his back. "*Gut* excuse to hunt. Coon hides aren't fetching much in price, but still you insist on going."

"Well, it's a family tradition, *jah?*"

"*Jah*," Samuel said. "Too bad *Daed* can't stay up all night anymore." He looked up at the moon. "Must be two o'clock."

Ezekiel, legs sore from tramping through woods all day, plopped himself on a log. "*Bruder,* can we talk?"

Samuel unloaded his rifle and leaned against a tree. "*Jah.* Something's bothering you."

Ezekiel nodded. "It's about New York and Lottie. Do you think Emma's more suited to be my wife?"

"You asked two women to marry you?"

"*Nee,* but Emma's made it clear she's interested and she loves New York."

"And Lottie's still homesick for Ohio?"

"I don't know. I've been avoiding her since we got back."

Samuel gawked. "You fool. Why not talk to her?"

"Because she might say no to marriage and I've never loved anyone so much."

Taking a seat on a nearby log, Samuel sat and took out some chewing tobacco. "Want some?"

"*Nee.* Gave it up."

"How come?"

"Lottie doesn't like the habit. She said it's carcinogenic."

"What?"

"Causes cancer."

Samuel stuffed a wad of tobacco in his mouth and chewed. "*Opa* chewed and lived to be eighty." He shifted. "You say you love this girl?"

Ezekiel groaned. "And you think she's controlling me, *jah*? Making me give up tobacco."

"*Nee*," Samuel said. "Not at all. I can't believe you did it, but you steer your own ship. That's one thing about you I know stubborn mule." He chuckled and then started to twiddle his thumbs. "Do you think Lottie's controlling you?"

"I don't know. I need the advice of a married man. When do you give in on major decisions? Shouldn't the husband lead?"

"Well, Anna and I talk things through. I'm to love my wife like Christ loves the church, and so that's a lot. And I also know her heart, what will break it and all. I'd never want to do that, so I'm not one to rule with an iron fist."

Ezekiel leaned forward, eager to learn more from this brother of his. When he thought of marriage, he wanted one like Sam and Anna's. "Lottie's homesick for Ohio to the point where she may say no to marriage. She said she loves me, though, but love puts the other person first."

Samuel stared at the ground for a few moments. "If Lottie's so attached to Ohio, what's she still doing out here?"

"Well, she came to take care of her cousin, but now that he's fine, she wants to either stay in Smicksburg or move back home."

"Maybe she'd marry you and go to New York and be depressed. Would you want that?" Samuel asked.

"*Nee*, not at all. I want her happy." He groaned. "So, she's not the one for me, *jah*?"

"Well, she's put you in a pickle. If you marry her, you can't take her to New York, so you'd be missing our family. If you move to New York, you'd lose Lottie."

"But why can't she move to New York? Be a submissive wife?"

Samuel smirked. "Women can be submissive on the outside but fuming mad on the inside. You don't want to crush your wife's spirit. Lottie's real attached to her family, and being in New York could crush her. Best give her up."

"What? Just like that? It's not easy!" Ezekiel yelled, and a falcon flew out of a nearby tree. "I love that girl."

Samuel stared at Ezekiel and then his countenance fell. "I'll miss you, *bruder.*"

"What?"

"I've never seen you so adamant about any girl. Lottie's a dear girl with a tender heart. Maybe that's why it gets so attached to others: her family. But she's changed you by all that sweetness."

"How?"

"You accept yourself, scars and all. She's a balm for you, Ezekiel. Don't let her go and make her a nice home here in Smicksburg or Ohio."

Ezekiel and Samuel rushed towards each other and embraced.

~*~

Lottie clung to Granny as she greeted her at dawn. Was she intruding? A visit too early? But she needed to talk. Granny motioned for her to sit down at her table. "Want some pancakes with real maple syrup?"

Lottie rubbed her stomach. "Can't eat. Smells *gut* though."

"Well, try some, then. And tell me what's ailing you?"

"Do I look sick?"

Granny gave her a knowing look. "Heart-sick. And your eyes are red, so you've lost sleep and have been crying."

Lottie felt her lips tremble, and pressed them together, willing them to still. "Granny, I am tired and I've lost sleep. Suzy and I have been trying to find Ezekiel, but he's nowhere to be found. Jonas said he might be hunting. What if he's hurt?"

Granny poured coffee and sat it on the table alongside a plate heaped with pancakes. "He has kin and men hunt together usually. It's safer. Why does Suzy want him?"

"*Ach*, she wants to give him a piece of her mind. He proposed, you know, but since he came back from New York he's been avoiding me."

Granny couldn't hide a smile. "I knew you two were the right ones for each other."

"But Granny, he's avoiding me and I hear Emma Miller is after him and –"

"If he loves you, he'll come around. Lots going on in that head of his, moving to New York and all." Granny sat across from her. "I'll miss you so."

"I'm not moving up to the North Pole."

"What? Who said you were?" Granny asked, eyes wide.

"I call New York that. Marathon gets ninety-three inches of snow a year, Smicksburg only gets forty. It's cold enough here."

Granny shook her head. "Lottie, don't chatter about nonsense. Speak what's on your heart. Remember how we talked about nervous chatter?"

Lottie knew full well that when she first came to Smicksburg she was a nervous wreck and spoke non-stop, her nerves so on edge. "Wait. I just thought of something."

"What's that?" Granny asked.

"I moved here only knowing my cousin, but I made lots of new friends. I was nervous, but not now."

"Well, we're glad you came. But what does this have to do with Ezekiel or New York?" But soon Granny wagged her finger. "I see. You were nervous to come here and you're nervous to move to New York if you marry Ezekiel."

Lottie slowly nodded. "*Jah*. I don't like change or meeting new people, but I did it...for Hezekiah. I love my cousin, so I came here without giving it much thought."

Granny's eyes twinkled. "So you'll move to New York? Be Ezekiel's bride?"

Panic shot threw Lottie. "I had to give it too much thought, don't you think? How I react is the real me, right? I came here without any hesitations because I love my cousin and he needed me and because I hesitate with Ezekiel, I must not love him."

Granny planted both hands on the table as if Lottie's barrage of words would blow her over. "*Ach*, Lottie, your cousin was in an accident and you were moved by shock, not love. Now with Ezekiel, you're not in shock, but have had a long time to think about marriage."

"*Jah*," Lottie said sheepishly. "I'm overtired, I suppose. I can't think straight."

"*Nee*," Granny challenged. "I think what you just said makes a lot of sense. You made friends in a new place before and you can do it again. The weather has nothing to do with it. The real thing you're afraid of is change."

Lottie had to admit, Granny hit it right on the head of a nail. The foreboding dread that enveloped her when thinking of moving to New York was the same dread that accompanied any big change. Hiding in books and quilting was her refuge from an ever-changing world, but it was a lonely world.

She reached for Granny hands. "I'm so afraid."

"I know. I was, too, when Jeb asked me to marry. It's the biggest decision of your life."

"So how did you make up your mind?"

"Well," Granny continued, "I thought of a life without Jeb and that brought more gloom than anything."

"*Ach*, I can't lose Ezekiel. How *furhoodled* I've been. And so selfish. Maybe he doesn't even want to marry me anymore."

Granny patted her hands. "Hush, now. We all make mistakes. If he loves you, he'll overlook anything you said that was selfish. Love covers a multitude of sins."

Lottie winced. "You think it's a sin to be selfish?"

"*Ach*, my girl. We're all selfish in one way or another. We feel like we have to look out for our own interests, but the Lord does all that. We just need to trust him."

Lottie darted up. "I do trust him. And I love Ezekiel. And I will find him and get on my knees and beg forgiveness."

As Lottie withdrew her hands, Granny yanked her back into her seat. "Now, slow down. Don't be hasty. Adopt the pace of nature: patience. Now, you eat up some pancakes and then go home and get some sleep. You don't want Ezekiel seeing you in such a mess."

Lottie put a hand to her cheek. "Do I look that bad?"

Granny nodded. "You have such dark lines under your eyes, you look like a raccoon."

Lottie accepted the plate of pancakes and coffee Granny pushed towards her. Pancakes always had a calming effect, after all.

~*~

Phil crossed the hospital room to shake Andy's hand. MJ, though pale, oxygen tubes under her nose, gave a faint smile. "I'm so sorry you two are in here so much," Phil said, feeling his words were weightless. *How lame*, he thought. But what could he say to these fine friends who'd become like family in a short time?

Andy gripped his hand firmly. "Visitors always cheer MJ up. Helps the time pass."

Taking a chair on the other side of MJ's bed, Phil knew what he was going to say would be difficult. Sharing what was deep within was hard, especially if it didn't make sense. "I came by to let you both know how integral a part you've been in my life."

Andy gawked. "Why so formal? What's wrong?"

"Nothing," Phil blurted. "I have good news. I'm just a little, I don't know, emotional about it."

"Getting married?" MJ asked.

"No, not yet. But I, well, want to just tell you both thank you. I keep a journal. It helped me see God's trail in my life. When I was reading about coming to Smicksburg, my fears, inadequacy and all that, I found an entry that mentioned you two. How amazed I was at MJ's courage and how giving she was, making gifts for authors she appreciates." He got up and paced a bit, clasping both hands behind his back. "And then I saw it wasn't just MJ, but her best cheerleader, her husband."

"Hey, and I have great legs," Andy chirped, raising a pant leg.

Phil laughed. "And then I kept reading and saw how we all need those people who cheer us on, and you two were there encouraging me when I felt like I couldn't fill Jerry Jackson's shoes. Remember that?"

"Yes," MJ said. "You felt too young."

"Inexperienced," Andy said. "You were comparing yourself to Jerry. But I can see why you felt uneasy in Smicksburg at first. Half the women were chasing you down."

Phil felt heat rising from his neck. "They were not."

"Yes, they were," MJ said with a wink.

"Well, I didn't notice that, but I don't think I'd be hired as assistant pastor at the church and running Arbor Creek if it wasn't for you two. Our little home church, too. I've learned to be more open and…I can't describe it, like I said, but I know I'm different."

"Transparency," MJ said softly. "You've let people see the real you."

Phil snapped his fingers. "Yes. And I don't feel so alone anymore. Does that make sense?"

"Sure does," Andy said. "MJ's illness made our marriage stronger, more open. Something that could have ripped us apart drew us together because we were honest. We showed our real selves." He bent over and fidgeted with his hoodie strings. "I can tell her anything now and there's something comforting in that."

MJ nodded. "Unconditional love. It's a rare thing, almost divine."

Phil took his seat again. Divine. Yes it was. God placed people together because they needed each other. And when relationships got hard, God bound them together by love. "MJ, I think you're right. It's divine, something from above."

"It's called koinonia fellowship," Andy said.

"What that?" Phil asked.

Andy grinned. "You theology majors aren't the only ones who can dig into a concordance or study Greek and Hebrew. Koinonia fellowship is a deep communion with other believers. And communion, the word we use for taking the sacrament, its root is common. So we share things in common deep down inside, well, it's friendship the way God intended." He scrunched up his lips comically. "Too deep?"

Phil laughed at his play on words. "No, not too deep. Deep of the good kind." He raked his hands through his sandy blond hair. "And I hoped to have a deep marriage like you have. At least you've given me an example of what to hope for."

"Your parents weren't close?" MJ asked.

"They got along," Phil said, "but it wasn't a warm home. My mom and I were close, but Dad, well, he lived for golf and was rarely home. Died on the ninth hole. I think he was losing."

Andy's mouth gaped. "Are you serious?"

"Well, he did die on the ninth hole, yes, but I don't know about the losing part." Phil got up and kissed MJ on the cheek. "I'll see you two in a few days. Have to prepare for Sunday's sermon. I'm preaching."

"That's my boy," Andy said, reaching across the bed with an outreached hand.

MJ put her hand on Phil's as he clasped Andy's. A tear slid down her cheek. "You've become like a son. We love you so much."

Phil gulped the lump that suddenly formed in his throat and tried to speak, but nothing came out, only gratitude from his heart.

~*~

As she neared the two scruffy men walking along the side of the road at dawn, Lottie's throat tightened and she urged her horse to pick up the pace, passing them up. But then she turned and thought she saw Ezekiel's face, although smeared with mud. *What on earth?? Was he hurt?*

Turning the buggy to the side of the road, she couldn't help but stare. "Are you all right?"

Ezekiel darted back into the nearby woods, leaving the other man looking dumbfounded.

Lottie felt a sharp pain rip through her stomach. No, her heart. Ezekiel was avoiding her…

The other man ran up to her, panting. "I'm Ezekiel's *bruder*, Samuel" He took a hanky out of his pocket and wiped his face. "Camouflage. Did it work?"

"What?"

"The camouflage. Didn't recognize me, *jah*?"

Lottie felt her eyes sting and then cloud. "*Jah*, it worked."

Samuel looked over his shoulder. "I don't know what's gotten into my *bruder*. Wait here for a minute."

"He's avoiding me," Lottie said evenly, trying to appear calm. "I understand. Nee, I don't really understand how men can be so fickle, but I will move on."

"*Nee*, wait," Samuel blurted, running to take her horse by the bridle. "Don't move. Stay here."

Lottie pursed her lips and tried to breathe, but found it hard. "Samuel, I meant move on in life. Hope all you Coblenz's have a *gut* life up in New York."

Samuel groaned. "Can you just wait here for a minute? Please."

"Why?"

"It's a surprise. Please just wait."

Lottie didn't know how much longer she could keep her composure but simply nodded. Images of Ezekiel proposing at the Secret Garden after she ran to him, fearful of the bear, flashed though her mind. She loved him, but it was too late. And she couldn't blame Ezekiel if he didn't care anymore. First it was Phil Darby. Why had she acted so cozy towards Phil? *Such a silly schoolgirl crush!*

Lottie chided herself. And then Peter coming out and going out to lunch with him. *Ach, what a fool she was!* And then having the nerve to say she didn't want to move to New York. Lottie felt as limp as a wet noodle. "I've pushed him too far…"

"Lottie, can we talk?" Ezekiel asked, head down.

Stunned by his sudden appearance, she blurted *"Jah."* His mud smeared face was hard to read. Was he upset with her?

"I look like something out of a pig pen. Didn't want you seein' me like this." He fidgeted with his suspenders. "Samuel said I needed to face you in camo or not."

Lottie gripped the reins, ready to face his revelation. He no longer cared for her.

"Can we take a ride?"

"Jah," she croaked, mouth dry.

"I've been rude," he said as he hopped in the open buggy and took the reins from her.

Lottie tried to ignore the odd smell that exuded from Ezekiel. What was it? Packed with mud and stains on his blue trousers…and blood. "Ezekiel, you're bleeding?"

He cocked his head back. *"Nee.* I've been hunting all night."

She sighed. "I love deer. Poor creatures can't even feel safe at night."

Ezekiel turned onto a dirt road and slowed the horse to a walk. "We were hunting raccoons."

"To eat?" She pat her heart. "Some ways here in Smicksburg are so odd. Men in Millersburg don't –"

"Lottie, we don't eat them. We trap and sell animal furs." Ezekiel stared ahead, dazed. "This is embarrassing. Samuel insisted." He took her hand. "I've been hiding in the woods. It's my escape. And I have something to tell you."

She slowly closed her eyes, wanting to shut out information about Emma Miller. "Ezekiel, I've been a fool. I don't like change and am shy deep down."

"What?"

"I didn't want to move to New York, but I will now."

Even under the camouflage, she saw Ezekiel's eyes widen. "What?"

"Don't marry Emma Miller. Marry me," she exclaimed, and then cupped her mouth.

A bright white smile broke across Ezekiel's grimy face and he pulled her tight and kissed her cheek. "You'd make me a happy man. But I don't want you unhappy. I won't force you to move to New York if you'll be my wife."

Despite the fact that she now had mud on her cheek and his clothes reeked, she embraced him and her heart felt so open to loving this man, she barely knew what to say. He'd forgo New York for her? She looked into his crystal blue eyes and touched his cheek. "Wherever you go, I will follow."

He gripped her hand. "I don't want to be a tyrant husband."

"Your people will be my people." She kissed his hand. "It's out of the book of Ruth. Remember?"

"Ruth's promise to Naomi? Her mother-in-law."

"*Jah*. In her time of need. I'll do the same."

His eyes misted. "I don't want pity. I may have a scarred face, but I'm whole."

Lottie let out a laugh. "I know you're not in need like a poor old widow like Naomi." She shook her head. "It's all coming out wrong." She took out her handkerchief and wiped his face, and then tenderly kissed the new scar on his left cheek. "I love all of you, Ezekiel Coblenz, and I want to make you a happy man...in New York."

He cupped her pink cheeks in his hands and kissed her. "I love you so much. I thought you'd never say yes."

She wrapped her arms around him. "I love you. And we'll move to New York so you can be near your family. Like I said, your people shall be my people. Reading the Book of Ruth helped me see God provide. We follow God and he provides."

Ezekiel whispered in her ear. "And He's given me the woman I prayed to be my wife last May. And it all happened so quickly." He took her by the shoulders and looked at her evenly. "You're sure about New York?"

"*Jah*, I am."

"And you want to be a farmer's wife?"

She bit her lip. "I'd like to make quilts and sell them. Could a shop be built?"

"*Jah*, no problem. Anything else?"

She looked at him coyly. "No hunting raccoons all night."

He paled. "What?"

She let out a hearty laugh and put her nose up in the air. "No hunting raccoons unless you scrub down outside before entering my house. You stink." She kissed him and then pinched his cheek. "Understand?"

"*Jah*, I do. Like I said, Samuel made me do this. I wanted to meet you in the Secret Garden, not like this, having two day old clothes on. But the animals can smell soap and I blend into the musky smell of the woods more…"

Lottie tilted her head to one side. "We'll look back and laugh about this. But for now, let's get you home so you can get cleaned up. Then we can share our good news."

~*~

Fannie let Granny's arms embrace her, congratulating her on the good news. She was pregnant again.

366

"*Ach*, to think you and Ruth will be carrying *kinner* again, just like before," Granny exclaimed. Sitting back at the long oak table, Granny placed homemade donuts in front of Fannie. "Eating up."

Fannie's mouth started to water as she grabbed one of the sweets. "*Danki*, Granny." She took a nibble and then exhaled loudly. "I want to talk to you about something else."

Sitting across from her, Granny, with wide-eyes, leaned forward eagerly.

Fannie felt like a child around Granny. She felt nurtured. Why did she feel like her own *mamm* was a burden? Shame and guilt over images of her *mamm* dying had consumed her. "Granny, I am so wicked."

"What did you do?" Granny asked slowly.

"Nothing. I have these thoughts that are wicked. About someone dying. My *mamm*. And I'm relieved."

"*Ach*, Fannie, she's stressing you to the breaking point. I see that. What you're imagining is having the stress gone, not your *mamm*."

Tears welled up in Fannie's eye. "*Jah*, that's it. I'm anxious, I guess. But these thoughts make me feel guilty. I keep thinking of horrible images of her buggy getting hit or her having a heart attack like Claire. If I had thoughts like that about *Daed* or Eliza, I'd cry, but I feel relief about *Mamm* dying. That is wicked, right?"

Granny reached for her hands and Fannie grabbed them. "There is no condemnation to those who are in Christ Jesus. Romans 1:1. Write that down and put it in your scripture memory box."

"But I should be condemned to prison for some of my thoughts," Fannie huffed.

"*Nee*, only when you act on evil thoughts. Everyone is tempted by thinking something wicked. I'd say women have a harder time with it, especially if they're pregnant, hormones all jumbled up and tired."

Fannie still could not forgive herself. No normal person would think such things.

"Fill your mind with good thoughts," Granny suggested.

"I can't. I feel too guilty."

"And that's the danger of guilt and condemnation. It's like planting a flower in a toxin. It'll absorb all the poison. Now, you go out on a buggy ride and spend some time in silence. In solitude your mind can rest. You rest your feet when tired, *jah*?"

"*Jah.*"

"Why not your mind?"

"Because your mind is always working?"

"Not a fretful mind. Let yours settle and be still and know God is God, in control. Control over our emotions as well. And be kind to yourself. If I told you I had thoughts like yours, what would you say?"

"*Ach*, Granny, you wouldn't have such thoughts."

"*Jah*, I do. Any idea can drift into my mind. Sometimes I know it's because I'm tired, other times I know it's the enemy of my soul planting thoughts to plague me. He tempted Jesus to jump off a cliff, remember?"

"*Nee*. What are you talking about?"

"When Jesus was tempted for forty days and nights in the wilderness, Satan came to him when he was hungry and tired. He comes in when we're feeling weak. Then the devil puts in thoughts like, 'bow down and worship me,' 'change a stone into bread,' and 'jump off this cliff and let the angels catch you.' Show the world how powerful you are. And it says that Jesus was sorely tempted. His mind had a battle in it."

"A battle? In Jesus' mind? Sounds too...."

"Human?" Granny asked. "Well he was tempted in every way a person could be so he could sympathize with us. I take comfort in that. I do get some wicked thoughts, but I rest and put my mind in some fertile thoughts. I give thanks." Granny grabbed the black Bible that was the centerpiece of her table and riffled though some pages. "I love this verse: Philippians 4:6-7

"Don't worry about anything; instead, pray about everything; tell God your needs, and don't forget to thank him for his answers. If you do this, you will experience God's peace, which is far more wonderful than the human mind can understand. His peace will keep your thoughts and your hearts quiet and at rest as you trust in Christ Jesus."

Granny pointed to the passage and Fannie read it again. This Bible had no "thee' and "thou shalt not" words, but in plain English. She looked up at Granny. "Is this *The Message* Bible? The one Jeb had a problem with?"

"*Nee*, the *Living Bible*. And Jeb has *The Message* now. Jonas and Jeb read so much and so many versions of the Bible are referenced, I think Jeb has nine Bibles now. Some point out things more clearly." Granny took the Bible and fingered the verse again. "See here, *'Don't worry'* but *pray*, be *thankful* and God will keep your *heart* and *mind*. So, I'd say He keeps us in our right minds. Speak real honest to God. And if your *mamm* is a thorn in your side, tell God about it."

"What? He'd think I'm wicked!" Fannie croaked.

"*Nee*, He'd think you're human. Someone not perfect in need of a savior."

In need of a savior. Fannie let the thought rumble through her mind. Yes, she needed help, saved from a mind that was troubled. Was it that simple?

"And you told me about these thoughts," Granny added. "You asked for help. Things kept in secret can grow worse, but do you feel better since your thoughts are brought out into the light?"

Fannie did feel lifted. Not as guilty. "*Jah*, I feel better talking to you."

"And that's why we need each other. *Confess your faults to one another that ye may be healed.* That's another verse for you."

"Granny," Fannie sighed. "I have another confession. I'm so afraid you'll move to Montana. Who will I have to talk to like this?"

Again, Granny gripped her hands. "You're filled with anxiety, Fannie. You're pregnant and tired. I'm not going anywhere. I'm at home right here in Smicksburg." She smiled. "Now, you go off and have a quiet time." She pushed the donuts towards her. "And take all these. You're eating for two now."

~*~

Jeb sliced hot zucchini bread and slid it on to a dessert platter. "Deborah, I think this circle plum exhausts you. Why couldn't Fannie help you bake when here?"

"Jeb, she's pregnant again. I know you could hear, sitting in the living room."

"*Jah*, I heard, but what does that have to do with anything?"

Granny huffed. "She's exhausted and not thinking straight. Remember long ago when I was carrying the *kinner*?"

Jeb put up a hand. "I forgot it on purpose. No recollection."

"You walked out of the house many times." She put her hands on her hips. "Now that I think of it, you started fishing more when I got pregnant."

"*Jah*, I did. A man has to keep himself sane for nine months straight. Fish don't talk."

"Come again?"

"You were non-stop chatter when pregnant. Thought I'd go deaf or insane."

Granny nudged him with her hip and laughed. "Old man, you have your ways that make me go batty at times still."

He grinned. "And how do you stop from going batty?"

"I knit and bake, and I do it more and more the older we get."

He turned and grabbed her by the middle, lifting her off the ground. "You knit and bake all the time." Jeb twirled her around. "Am I that hard to live with?"

She kicked her legs. "Put me down, old man. I see a car. Someone's here for circle."

"Give me a kiss and a promise first."

"What?"

"Promise me that if this here circle continues, the womenfolk take turns baking dessert. It's too much for you."

"Jeb, I love to bake. Put me down!"

"You're not a spring chicken anymore."

"Jeb!"

"Deborah. Promise. Tell them no circle when we get back from Montana unless they all pitch in."

Granny knew Jeb would not release her if the whole circle were standing right there in her kitchen. "Okay. I'll mention it."

"Now give me a kiss," he said with his eyes mellow. "I love you Deborah Weaver."

She leaned into a kiss. "I love you Jebediah Weaver."

"Oh, this is the sweetest thing I've seen in my entire life!" Marge exclaimed as she stood in the door opening. "I knew love could last a life-time. How romantic."

~*~

"So, I found Jeb holding Granny in his arms, her feet dangling and they were kissing," Marge informed the circle that was cozily tucked into her living room, the air too chilly outside to knit in comfort.

"Marge, Jeb was teasing me is all," Granny huffed, cheeks growing red. "He made me promise him something."

"What's that?" asked Fannie. "No emotional visitors before knitting circle?"

Granny gave Fannie a smile. "You can visit anytime. *Nee*, Jeb thinks I'm too old to do circle like I've done it."

"I live for this circle," Ruth gasped, looking around the room. "You've all helped me so much. *Ach*, Granny, why not continue?"

"I didn't say we weren't continuing, but Jeb wants me to stop baking for it. I bake for Forget-Me-Not Manor and now Arbor Creek. Truth be told, Jeb's gained a few pounds around the middle. Maybe he can't take all the sweets in the house."

Laughter echoed around the room.

"Is having it here too much for you?" Lizzie asked. "We can always go over to my place."

"*Jah*, I suppose we could. My house too small?"

"*Nee*, not at all," Maryann said.

"I love your place, Granny," Becca chimed in. "It's cozy."

"My store's small, I know, but like you all convinced me, it's more intimate." Suzy put her knitting needles down. "How about we switch houses? The person who hosts the circle will bake the dessert."

"*Gut* idea," Mona said. "Would be like *Gmay*."

"*Gmay*?" Janice asked. "What's that?"

"Our word for church. It means community," Mona said rather smugly.

"Well, we could have it at the church," Janice continued. "I've missed this circle for six months and like they say, you don't know how much you love something until it's taken away."

A round of '*amens*' and '*jahs*' filled the tiny room.

"I loved when we read books," Marge said. "Could we have another knit-lit circle?"

"Well, I'm leaving for Montana this weekend." Warmth filled Granny's soul. "You all can meet without me and decide what you want to do."

"Decide without you?" Fannie blurted. "You started this circle. Granny, you lead this circle."

She shook her head. "I took the fearful step of sending out invitations to five women who were on my heart. I know half the town thought I was lonely, and maybe I was and didn't know it, but I think it all came from my need to nurture younger women, not having a daughter of my own."

Silence. Granny gazed around the circle. Had she said something wrong? And then a sniff was heard on her right. It was Lizzie. She turned to see tears running down her cheeks. "Lizzie, what on earth?"

Lizzie put an arm around her. "I may have not gotten married to Roman if it hadn't been for this circle forming. I'm thankful. Tears of joy."

"*Ach*," Granny said with relief. But then she heard someone blowing their nose. It was Marge. "Marge, are you all right?"

"*Ach*, Granny, we've had our differences, but you helped me when I came here trying to live off the grid." Tears slid down her cheeks and she smiled. "Remember when you called it 'living off the grind'?"

"*Jah*, I still stumble over the term."

"Well, you helped me see that living without electricity doesn't make life simple at all, it's all in here." She pat her heart.

Maryann's chin quivered. "Marge, you helped nurse me when I had cancer. And Granny, I'd never have gone and found that lump if you hadn't dragged me to the hospital."

Granny had no idea how one little invitation to a knitting circle could have had such a chain reaction. Like loops on a knitting needle made a garment, every little talk that seemed so insignificant to her meant so much to others.

"Granny," Janice said evenly. "You have to continue this circle."

Fannie stood up. "We need to continue this circle. We all need to do what Granny did, invite women on our hearts that need help."

"You can't have a good knitting circle with twenty people," Suzy said. "Should we be splitting up?"

Silence again. The women looked down, intent on their knitting, needlework or crocheting.

"We all need to think about this," Janice said. "The good thing is that we want to have a winter circle."

"*Jah*," Ruth said slowly. "I already know of someone to invite."

"Who?" Lizzie asked.

"Angelina. Her house hasn't sold."

Granny gasped. "She can't live there by herself with no family around."

"I know. Her son wants her to move to Toronto and rent out the house."

"If she came, she could teach us tatting," Suzy said.

"What's tatting?" a few women asked in unison.

"Making lace with little crochet hooks. I love knitting more than crocheting, as you all know, but lace is so delicate. I can picture a lace runner across my Jane Austen tea table."

"Well," Mona said grumpily, "she's old and that's all there is to it. She needs to live with her family. Ruth, you worry about her. Luke, too. It's too much."

Ruth rubbed the slight bump on her middle. "*Jah*, with another one on the way."

Fannie stood up again. "I have news. But I'm afraid."

"Is it bad news?" Granny asked.

"*Nee*, Granny, you know what it is."

Granny's brows knit together. "What?"

"You know," Fannie said. "My news. It may upset someone…"

"Me?" Mona asked. "Being your *mamm* and all, I guess it's me. Go on. I can handle it."

Fannie eyed Lizzie. "I'm pregnant. I hope you can all be happy."

Cheers and claps erupted, and Lizzie's eyes were aglow. "Lizzie, I'm so glad you're not upset."

"*Ach*, Fannie, I'm content with the girls and Roman and I may adopt in time. It's *wunderbar* news."

"Well," Mona moaned. "I'm upset. You told Granny before me?"

Fannie, shoulder's slumping, took her seat. "*Jah*, I did."

"Well, I'm your *mamm*, for Pete's sake. And I babysit Anna and should know about it first."

Anger rose in Granny. Jealousy was not love. It was selfish. She bit her lip and tried to drown out Mona as she continued to complain. *Lord, help my Fannie endure such a mamm. Such a bold woman!* And then she realized something. Mona was being open about her feelings, so she would, too. "Mona, you don't seem to see the rare

375

treasure you have in this *dochder* of yours. You were a dark cloud when you first came to circle and then turned into sunshine for while. Why are you like a storm cloud now?"

All eyes landed on Mona. She looked like a deer on the road ready to get hit by a car; dazed. "I'm not a storm cloud."

Maryann gently put a hand on Mona's shoulder. "*Jah*, you have been. I miss my kind friend."

Mona's round eyes slowly closed. "I'm tired."

"Tired?" Granny asked. "Then you need to go to the doctor's, *jah*?"

She shook her head and pensively looked over at Fannie. "I've been putting this off. I can't babysit Anna anymore while you work in your shop. Your *daed* agrees. I'm tuckered out. Not young anymore." Mona coward, looking fearful of Fannie's shock.

"*Mamm*, why didn't you say something?"

"I was trying to be a *gut mamm* and *oma…*"

Fannie sprang up and crossed the circle to embrace her mamm. Granny's heart soared. Danki, Lord. Something about getting together in a circle, knitting or doing any craft helps us open up somehow. It's a mystery. And it must go on.

Buggy wheels on gravel was heard and Granny peered out the window. It was Colleen and Lottie. Why so late? And why in such a hurry? Was there an accident?

Granny sprang to her feet to meet them as they entered the side door. Lottie's face was pink and glowing. "What is it, Lottie?"

Lottie ran into the circle, twirled around and then threw up her hands. "I'm going to miss you all, but I'm moving."

"Back to Ohio?" Ruth asked. "Excited to live near kin?"

"*Nee*, I'm moving to New York with Ezekiel Coblenz. We're engaged to be married."

The screams that erupted made Granny jump, but within a half second, she was shouting for joy herself. She was right all along. Lottie and Ezekiel were made for each other. *Ach*, she couldn't wait to tell Jeb she was right.

Jeb ran in from outside. "What's wrong? I heard screaming."

"Jeb, glad you came in. A big announcement. Lottie and Ezekiel are getting married," Granny said satisfied, a smirk lining her mouth.

Jeb chuckled. "*Gut* news. Congratulations, Lottie. And to think you two met here. My idea, you know."

Granny got up, hands planted on her hips. "It was my idea."

"I put it in your head. Don't you remember? I plant the idea and you run with it."

Granny glared at her husband. After all the *Emma* Jane Austen jokes, couldn't he admit she'd successfully matched two people? But Jeb's turquoise eyes were dancing with merriment and she soon knew he was teasing her. "Old man."

"*Jah*, I am old." He looked over at Maryann. "Did you tell Becca?"

"*Nee*, not yet."

"Do you want me to do it?"

"*Jah*. It was your idea," Maryann said, glancing at Becca.

Jeb took a spare chair and plunked himself down, looking mighty satisfied. "Becca, we see the way you tutored Denny over at Arbor Creek. Are you up for being the new teacher?"

Becca paled and dropped her embroidery hoop on her lap.

"Jeb, tell her the whole big news," Maryann prodded.

"*Ach*, I forgot. Your parents feel you need some adventure. You want to travel, *jah*?"

Becca slowly nodded, still not speaking.

"Well, we have a ticket for you to travel with us out to Montana."

Becca's brown eyes were round as chocolate whoopie pies. "*Danki*, Jeb. Granny." She ran across the circle and embraced Granny.

"Becca, your parents paid for the ticket. It was your *mamm's* idea."

Becca spun around. "*Ach*, Mamm. So *gut* of you. I want to see the mountains." She ran into Maryann's outstretched arms and hugged her, but then slowly went to her seat. "Wait. Are you saying I'd be a teacher in Montana? Move from Smicksburg?"

Jeb hit his knee. "I got it wrong. Let me back up. The school board met and we need a new teacher. Lizzie has a hankering to teach and will teach until you get back in a few weeks. Then you can have a go at it, and then you two can decide what you want to do. Maybe share the responsibility." He looked over at Lizzie fondly. "Roman's on the board and Lizzie was to keep mum about it, and I see she has."

Lizzie beamed. "It was hard, but I haven't told a soul."

Becca threw her arms up. "*Jah*, I'd love to do this. I miss tutoring."

Rounds of congratulations to Becca were made by the whole circle.

Jeb rose and went and stood behind Granny, hands on her shoulders. "This old woman will miss *yinz*. It's only a two week trip, I'm thinking. You'll all write to her, *jah*?"

"On rose embossed stationery," Ruth said, eyes brimming with tears.

Granny felt her mouth grow dry. "*Jah*, I'll miss my Little Women, but when I'm gone, pray and ask the *Gut* Lord who you can invite to our next circle. Write an invitation on your best stationary like I did, two years ago. I think the nicer, more expensive stationery lets someone know they're special."

"I felt that way when I got my letter," Fannie said, chin quivering. "This circle's changed my life. Don't be afraid to send a letter to someone who's a real mess."

Granny let her eyes rest on each of the women at the circle, giving thanks for them all. They'd all come together to overcome illnesses, wounded spirits and grief over the past or death of a loved one. And how full her life was with all these beautiful women. "Fannie, we're all messes by ourselves. Hopelessly flawed, like it says in Little Women. But being spun together like my yarn, we're strong. *Jah*, please make plans for a winter circle."

"And if you want to meet her in this house," Jeb said, a catch in his voice, "you're all welcome here."

Granny pat his hand. "*Jah*, even if I'm an old woman."

~*~

Granny took a seat on the Amtrak train, Jeb on one side, Becca on the other. She felt like a *kinner* waiting for a taffy pull, not able to sleep for all the anticipation. She'd see Nathan and Lottie and all her boys at the wedding. That Roman was staying home to tend to their little homestead was mighty big of him, never complaining. *Bless Roman, Lord.*

She closed her eyes and with a full heart prayed:

Lord, I don't know why I am such a blessed woman. I'm still amazed that the girls at the circle aren't tired of coming to my house. Lord, lead them as they meet to talk about the new circle. If it's at Suzy's or the Baptist Church, I don't care, it just needs to continue. We're all spun together and strong, like a three strand cord, and it seems like the circle's spinning out of control, having too many for one circle. Lord, give the girls wisdom.

I know our circle or circles are needed. Lord, to think that Lottie grew from a nervous chatter-box and is now making wedding plans for a wedding out in Millersburg makes my heart leap for joy. And Lord, it was you who put the idea in my mind about the two of them, not Jeb. We know that.

Bless Lizzie as she teaches a roomful of kinner. Guide and bless her, and prepare Becca's heart out in Montana for what you have in store for her. If it's to be my English son Denny's wife, Lord, let it be. I do think they're for each other and like Jeb said, Denny is an Amish man deep down.

Help Angelina's house sell. Show her how old she really is, even though she acts like a middle-aged woman. She needs to be around family. Until then, give Ruth and Luke the strength to help her and as the two of them give, they will be blessed. Ach, danki Lord that you helped Ruth out of her pit, losing her dear mamm. Luke's love was tested and he passed. Praise be.

Ach, and Lord, help MJ's health. What a delightful woman who's in such pain. I know Ruth and Luke learned from them and it goes to show that we Amish can learn from the English.

Ach, Lord, bless all my Little Women and bring us all back together in a few short weeks.

In Jesus name,
Amen.

Dear Readers,

We've come to the end of Granny's fourth circle! Thanks you all so much for your encouragement. I cannot write without reader involvement and knowing that women are encouraged and growing spiritually. Knitting circles are being formed, or just circles where women talk and do various activities together, bonding and helping each other through life's up and downs, joys and sorrows. A friend of mine started knitting crocheting....and coloring circle. No kids coloring though, but grown ups! I never knew there were intricate more complicated coloring books for grown-ups! (I like cutting out old-fashioned paper dolls, so I've ordered some from Dover Publications, since they have the best selection and prices.) It really doesn't matter what you do, but crafts sure have a way of relaxing us all and helping us chat and open up.

Again, thank you and blessing to you all! Granny's next circle will be set in the winter to spring and the women will crochet and read poetry, ponder great hymns and some start to write their own in *Amish Knit & Crochet Circle: Smicksburg Tales 5*

As usual, I leave you with a recipe. Enjoy!

Zucchini bread

3 eggs
1 c. oil
1 ½ c. sugar
2 tsp. vanilla
2 c. grated zucchini
3 c. flour
1 tsp. baking soda

1 tsp. salt

1 Tbs. cinnamon

¼ tsp. baking powder

Grease and flour 2 loaf pans. Beat eggs until fluffy. Add oil, sugar, vanilla and zucchini and mix well. Add dry ingredients and pour into pans, baking at 325 degrees 40-60 minutes. Insert toothpick and if clean, bread is done.

ABOUT THE AUTHOR

Karen Anna Vogel is a trusted English friend among many Amish in rural Western Pennsylvania, Karen wants to share about these wonderful people she admires. She writes full-length novels and short story serials and hopes readers will learn more about Amish culture and traditions, and realize you don't have to be Amish to live a simple life.

She's a graduate from Seton Hill University with a B.A. in psychology and elementary education, and a Masters from Andersonville Theological Seminary in Pastoral Counseling.

In her spare time she enjoys knitting, homesteading, & photograph. Karen also loves old houses, and has helped her husband of thirty-three years restore a century old farmhouse (with the help of Amish workers). They have four married adult children, and two grandchildren they've nicknamed *Precious* & *Prince*

Karen is represented by Joyce Hart of Hartline Literary Agency.

OHER BOOKS BY KAREN ANNA VOGEL

Continuing Serials:

  Amish Knitting Circle: Smicksburg Tales 1

  Amish Knitting Circle: Smicksburg Tales 2

  Amish Knit Lit Circle: Smicksburg Tales 3

  Amish Knit & Stitch Circle: Smicksburg Tales 4

  Amish Knit & Crochet Circle: Smicksburg Tales 5

Novels:

  Knit Together: Amish Knitting Novel

  The Amish Doll: Amish Knitting Novel

  The Herbalist's Daughter: Amish Herb Shop Series

Novellas:

  Amish Knitting Circle Christmas: Granny & Jeb's Love Story

  Amish Pen Pals: Rachael's Confession

  Christmas Union: Quaker Abolitionist of Chester County, PA

  Love Came Down at Christmas: A Fancy Amish Smicksburg Tale

  Coming in the fall of 2015

  The Herbalist's Son: Amish Herb Shop Series

"Author Karen Vogel has approached the often misunderstood beliefs or the Amish with tact and tenderness, and I highly recommend this heart-stirring story."

Kathi Macias award-winning author of Deliver Me from Evil, Red Ink and 30 other novels

"Karen writes with heart-touching insight and her characters are gripping. Highly recommended."

Jennifer Hudson Taylor, author of Highland Blessings

"Karen Anna Vogel writes from her heart and complete knowledge of the Amish. Her love of these beautiful people is so evident."'

*Karen Malena author **of** Reflections from my Mother's Kitchen*

Amish Knit & Stitch Circle

Made in the USA
Coppell, TX
27 June 2020

29451135R00223